Blood and Ashes

Also by Matt Hilton

Dead Men's Dust

Judgement and Wrath

Slash and Burn

Cut and Run

MATT HILTON

Blood and Ashes

First published in Great Britain in 2011 by Hodder & Stoughton
An Hachette UK company

1

A CIP catalogue record for this title is available from the British Library

ISBN Hardback 978 0 340 97833 7
ISBN Trade Paperback 978 0 340 97834 4

Typeset in Plantin Light by Hewer Text UK Ltd, Edinburgh
Printed and bound by Clays Ltd, St Ives plc

Hodder & Stoughton policy is to use papers that are natural, renewable and recyclable products and made from wood grown in sustainable forests. The logging and manufacturing processes are expected to conform to the environmental regulations of the country of origin.

Hodder & Stoughton Ltd
338 Euston Road
London NW1 3BH

www.hodder.co.uk

DEDICATED TO:
My little sister, Isabella 'Izzy' Hilton
and to
my brothers, David, John, Jim and Raymond
collectively known as Jacky's Boys
and to
my lad, Jordon

Battle not with monsters, lest ye become a monster, and if you gaze into the abyss, the abyss gazes also into you.

Friedrich Nietzsche

PROLOGUE

Brook Reynolds woke up screaming without knowing why. The last few minutes were a blur; she could recall thinking of her children but why would that make her scream? She only knew that it was the right thing to do.

Then, with a jolt, it all came back: how everything had changed so horribly in a matter of minutes.

She remembered the car behind hers, barely a distraction at first. Her thoughts were fully on her husband and children. Brook smiled as she pictured their faces. Soon she'd be home and there'd be hugs all round. She'd missed them all while away on business.

The mountain roads were familiar, if twisting, and her mind was preoccupied with the impending happy reunion, so the following vehicle didn't register with her too much. Not until it moved in close and her rear-view mirror reflected the harshness of its lights. Her pulse fluttered in her throat and her eyes stung at the glare.

'What in God's name are you playing at?'

The vehicle was a silhouette beyond the stark beam, and it loomed massively in her mirrors. Brook couldn't see the occupants, but they must be reckless idiots. Didn't they know the road took a series of sharp turns just ahead? As a gentle reminder she touched the brake pedal, hoping they'd back off. She watched the vehicle dwindle, but had to tug her eyes from the mirror when its lights were flicked up to full beam.

'Asshole!'

She didn't want to get into a sparring match, but she had to warn this lunatic to back off. Again she toed the brake, and her lamps turned the night red. The following vehicle speeded up, and the interior of her car was invaded by its lights. Its horn screeched.

'What the hell are you doing?' She shouted this time, touching the gas pedal to avoid a collision. She pushed the car into the first bend, snatching her attention from the curve ahead to the blazing lights behind, back to the road again. Then, coming out of the curve, she put her foot down. Unperturbed, the car shot by her, spitting up grit from the side of the road. Brook avoided looking at the driver: probably some crazy redneck high on something. This was the last thing she wanted. All she needed to do was get home.

The car roared on and into the next bend.

Thank God, it kept on going.

Brook didn't slow. She kept her foot steady on the gas.

Coming round the tight bend she saw the dark form of the other car in her path. It was parked across the narrow road, lights extinguished, someone standing by its rear. The figure stepped forward, raised his hand. Oh, my God! Was that a gun? Something flashed. She let out a cry of disbelief, yanking hard on the steering wheel. It was reflex, or panic, perhaps both.

The tyres bit into the soft verge at the edge of the road, then there was nothing beneath them and the car began to roll. The forest opened its arms to greet her. The next instant was filled with showering sparks and raining glass, the shriek of tortured metal and numbing collisions as her head was repeatedly slammed and jostled. Her mind was full of darkness.

And that's when Brook had come to, screaming.

Her body felt immensely heavy, and the pressure behind her eyes was overwhelming. She didn't understand that she was hanging upside down, or that the pain across her throat was the seat belt cinched garrotte-tight.

She wanted nothing more than to be home. She had no time for *this*!

There was a stench in her nostrils and her face and hair were slick with fluid. The liquid wasn't blood; it was more acidic than that. Like chemicals.

She stopped screaming to spit out the vile stuff, and turned her eyes to seek out the source of a new sound invading her mind. Voices, talking excitedly as they approached.

'Help me,' she croaked.

'Is she dead?'

'I don't know.'

'Help me,' she said again more loudly. And she suddenly understood what she was soaked with. 'I'm covered in gasoline. Please . . . somebody help me.'

'She's still alive,' the first voice said.

'Yeah,' said the other. 'We need to do something quick.'

Thank God, she thought, I'm going to see my children again.

Then the first one said, 'Yeah. Take these matches. You'd better finish her off.'

I

The clouds failed to conceal the moon. It scowled like a drunkard's bloodshot eye over the rim of an empty glass. The disc was low on the horizon, bloated and red, and I couldn't help aiming a derisive snort its way. A hunter's moon: how ironic was that?

Walking slowly, my hands stuffed in my coat pockets, I felt the same breeze that made ribbons of the clouds tug at my clothing. In a baseball cap, scuffed leather coat and denims, I wandered up the centre of the main street of Bedford Well, with no care for traffic. It was after three in the morning and the only things moving were the cats with which I shared the night.

There was no one around. I hadn't seen another soul since arriving in town and parking my Audi in the darkened lot of a Seven-Eleven. That suited me. I'd rather be here and gone before causing a blip on anyone's radar. Should any insomniac glance out of a window I'd appear unremarkable, just another guy down on his luck with no real destination in mind, passing through on his way to an undetermined destiny. That suited me as well.

Three nights ago I'd been on the Florida Gulf Coast and it had been warm enough for shorts and a bare chest as I'd reclined on the deck that overlooked the beach. Now the leather jacket was necessary for more than concealing the gun in my belt. The wind sweeping down off the Pennsylvanian hills held a lingering nip of winter and that didn't suit me at all.

My limp wasn't very pronounced, not after three months of hard exercise to get back up to speed, but the cold reminded me that not too long ago I'd been both shot and stabbed in the right leg. The pain was just a dull ache and I pushed it to the back of my mind. Pain is an ally; it confirms that you're still alive. I'd been fed bucket-loads of similar psychobabble when in the military; some of it helpful, most of it horseshit. Mostly pain hurts and it slows you down. How could that be a soldier's friend? Made me wonder if maybe I wasn't fit for this line of work any more, and that the accumulation of injuries picked up throughout the years was conspiring against me. Or, like my best friend Rink often joked, age was beginning to catch up with me.

Maybe there was something in that, but I wasn't ready for the scrap heap just yet.

The limp did serve some purpose. It added to the disguise I'd affected. Studying this stubble-chinned man, holding himself tightly against the chill, looking thoroughly miserable, who'd ever guess I was here for a deadly purpose?

On the drive up I'd questioned my motives for coming to this dead-end town and more than once had almost turned the car round and headed south again. It's a weakness, but I can't say no. I should've told Don Griffiths to take a hike, concentrated on getting healthy again in the sub-tropical sun. But here I was. Apparently it's true: you can't teach an old dog new tricks. I've never learned to roll on my back and wasn't about to now.

The main street of Bedford Well wasn't much more than a hundred yards of family-run stores and amenities, all shut up tight for the night. At its northern end it opened into a circle of dwellings around a central green, complete with a wishing well that explained the town's name. The well had a bucket, but no one would be able to draw water from it because a metal grille had been bolted over the top. A huge brass padlock fastened the grille to the stonework, but it was shiny and proclaimed that the well was regularly emptied of coins. The town council, it seemed, had claim on the nickels and dimes as well as people's aspirations.

I leaned my hips against the well, dug a couple of coins from my jeans pocket and dropped them through a slot in the centre of the grille. I heard them hit bottom. They hadn't fallen very far, making me wonder if this was just a folly designed to please the tourists. Regardless, I made a wish.

Waste of money, because my wish was already redundant.

I was already *here* and now there was no going back.

Testament to this was the presence of the black SUV that nosed out between two stores further along the street. Two shadows filled the front of the vehicle, topped by pale ovals that were turned my way. Under the peak of my cap, I returned their casual observation until the driver hit the gas and peeled out, heading back along the street. The brake lights flared, then the SUV took a turning to the right. The grumble of the engine carried on the air until the wind shifted and snatched it away.

What was that all about? I mentally shrugged: nothing good, I bet.

I headed across the green towards an imposing house that held sway over the smaller dwellings to either side. The house looked Victorian but for the satellite dishes in the garden and the cars on the drive, a Lexus and a Mercedes SUV. For all his claims to the contrary it looked like Don Griffiths was doing OK even in this cul-de-sac of a town.

I leaned on the doorbell.

The house remained very still. As if it held its breath.

I pressed the bell again.

Beyond the door there was a shift in the darkness and a light came on above my head. I fought the urge to glance up at the light, an old habit to protect my night vision. Waited while the person inside hooked a security chain in place, then opened the door a sliver.

Don is a heavy-built man in his early sixties. He has short steel-grey hair and a neatly trimmed beard to match. The person looking out at me didn't match any of those points. She was slim and dark and no more than thirty years old.

It was more than fifteen years since I'd laid eyes on her but I'd have recognised Millie anywhere. She had the vivid green eyes and raven tresses of her mother, but the strong nose and high cheekbones were every inch the image of her father.

Millie Griffiths studied me for a while. I raised my head so the peak of the cap was no longer casting such a long shadow on my face. Finally Millie closed the door and I heard the unhooking of the chain. She opened the door fully this time.

'Come in, Joe.' Her head dipped as I stepped by her into the darkness of the entrance hall. It looked like all the rooms on the lowest floor were unlit.

'Where's your father?'

Millie locked the door before turning to look at me.

It was weird standing there in the dark, staring at her silhouetted against the front-door glass, all that was evident being the soft sparkle of her eyes. When she moved past me her shoulder brushed my upper arm and it was brusque. I settled my heels as Millie walked away without comment. Then, sighing, I followed.

Without flicking on a light, Millie led the way along the hall to the back of the house. There she opened a door and a flight of stairs led down into the basement. Another door at the bottom was etched around its frame with a dim glow.

I paused before descending.

Didn't need to hear her sob to know.

'I'm too late,' I said. 'I heard what happened and I'm sorry.'

Millie nodded: a single hard slash of her jaw. 'My sister died because you *wouldn't* believe him.'

She turned away before I could reply, her tread heavy, then quickening as she fled up the stairs to a bedroom. Overhead a door slammed and I listened to the young woman sobbing uncontrollably.

'Shit . . .'

I pulled the cap off and jammed it into a coat pocket. Scrubbing a hand through my hair I took the stairs down to the basement, counting the steps. With each one it felt like I was descending into the abyss.

2

'I hear you're supposed to be some kind of knight errant, these days.'

I shook my head. 'That's not the way I'd describe myself.'

Don Griffiths was sitting in an old chair with sunken upholstery and faded patches on the arms. How many hours had he spent sitting in this selfsame place over the years? How many memories could that old chair recount if it was given a voice? Over Don's shoulder an archaic cine-camera projected some of those memories on to a makeshift screen. The flickering images were the only source of light in the otherwise dark room, two small girls playing in a paddling pool while first a younger Don and then his late wife, Sally, mugged and danced for the camera.

Don didn't look at me. His gaze was lost among the images on the screen. 'How would you describe yourself? I thought you were someone I could rely on. Where were you when I needed you?'

I exhaled, and turned to view the girls happily playing. Even back then, Millie was distinctive. Her slightly older sister, Brook, was pretty as well, but with the elfin qualities inherited from her mother. It was difficult coming to terms with the thought that the little girl – who was so full of life and wonder on the screen – was now dead and buried.

'I was injured.' Though no excuse, it was the only thing I had to offer.

'I noticed you were a bit lame when you came down the

stairs.' Don wasn't interested in any one else's pain, only his own. 'But you've been injured worse than that before. Wounds never stopped you then, Hunter.'

'I was younger.'

'Yeah,' Don agreed. 'We both were. But my daughter won't grow any older, will she? Her children will never know their mother's love again.'

There was no answer to that. I could only watch as Don shuddered, his chin dipping on his chest. The man wept silently. Laying a consoling hand on his heavy shoulder wouldn't help. Don wouldn't welcome my pity. Always pitiless to others, he saw emotion as weakness. Maybe it would do him good to experience some of the grief.

It was as if Don could hear what I was thinking. His head came up and he fixed his gaze on me. 'I know you don't owe me a damn thing. In fact, if you told me to go to hell, I guess I'd understand. But I didn't think Joe Hunter was the type to turn his back on a woman or her children.'

'I'm not.' Even as I said it I realised how ineffectual my words sounded. I turned back to the screen. Millie and Brook had moved on to chasing each other around the garden with buckets of water. There was no sound accompanying the home movie, but by the rapture of their faces both girls were squealing in glee. Closing my eyes didn't help.

The chair creaked, and there was a grunt as Don stood up. He turned off the projector and the room was plunged into darkness that was evident even behind my closed eyelids. Only at the click of a light did I turn and look at the older man. Don had both hands folded across his bulging stomach, his head dipped: he looked like a monk in prayer. But I recognised the stance for something else – it showed an old man shattered by the loss of his child.

'Tell me again what happened, Don.'

'What's the point?'

'Because I've travelled days to get here.' I stopped. I didn't care for Don one bit. Not after what had occurred between us all those years ago, but it was like the man had already said: I wasn't one to turn my back on women or children in need. 'Look, Don. Let's put our differences behind us for now. Tell me what happened . . . maybe there's still something I can do. If what you originally told me is true, then this may not be finished with.'

Don probably wasn't even conscious of chewing the end of his moustache. He was too busy studying my face for a sign of insincerity. He must have come to a favourable conclusion because he slow-blinked like an old bull frog. 'It *is* true. As crazy as it sounds.'

Three days on the road had left their residue on me. Perspiration had dried on my skin, my clothes were grimy and uncomfortable, but that wasn't the reason for the prickling sensation in my flesh. It was as though my nerve endings were charged with static. 'It just takes a little coming to terms with, Don. How could a dead man be threatening your family?'

'It's gone way beyond threats, Hunter. Didn't you hear what I told you? *Brook is dead.*'

The tingling in my skin was becoming painful, and a seething rush shot through my veins. I resisted the urge to scratch and bunched my fists in my pockets. 'Brook was killed in a car crash. The police ruled it an accident.'

Don grunted. Next to his battered chair was an equally worn cabinet. He pulled open the top drawer and drew out a folder which he opened and held out. I was still thinking about the gleeful faces that had only moments before flickered on the screen and didn't want to see what Don offered.

'Take it,' Don said. 'Have a good look and tell me if you still think my daughter died accidentally.'

I'm no stranger to death in any of its horrible forms. To some I've inured myself, but not all. Once, I bore witness to the aftermath of an attack by guerrilla fighters on a village of innocents. Some of the victims – mostly women and children – had been burned alive. The images of their bodies twisted into blackened husks still occasionally plagued my nightmares. I didn't want to see Brook like that.

But I looked.

The rushing heat in my veins went cold.

There were photographs from the accident scene. They showed a vehicle on its roof, so consumed by fire that even the tyres had been burned clean off their rims. The distance shots weren't so bad; only when the camera had zoomed into the interior did it became apparent that the bundled form lying amid the ashes and molten components had once been human. That was nasty. But nowhere near as horrific as the follow-up photographs from the morgue where Brook's remains had been taken. Under the stark glare of lights, surrounded by dull steel, the extreme charring of the woman's corpse was shocking. There was little left of her, just a blackened skull and the withered husk of a torso. The larger bones of the upper arms, the pelvic girdle and legs had survived, but all the lesser bones of her extremities had gone to ash. She had been twisted by the intensity of the heat into the classic pugilist pose, but it wasn't that evident with her hands gone.

My blink was slow, and I held my lids shut for a time afterwards.

'Well?'

Well, what?

I handed the file back to Don.

'It's a terrible thing,' I said. 'I can't begin to imagine the terror your daughter must have gone through. But, Don . . .'

'It was no accident.'

'The car rolled, the fuel tank erupted. A spark from the engine ignited the spilled fuel.'

'That's what it *looks* like.' Don opened the file; thrust the photographs under my nose. 'That's what it was *made* to look like.'

'The report is conclusive.' I gently closed the flap on the file, covering the images. 'Before you say anything, I've read it. I already had Rink get me a copy of both the police and ME files.'

'And you believe a couple of hick cops and a washed-up medical examiner over me?' Don snorted. 'They only saw what they wanted to see.'

'Nevertheless, they didn't find anything suspicious. No evidence that Brook's death was anything other than a tragic accident.'

'But now that you've seen the photographs?'

'It doesn't change a thing, Don. Your daughter died by the flames that also burned out the car she was trapped in.'

Don chewed his moustache again. After a few seconds he lifted a hand, pointed at the stairs. 'I want you to leave. If you don't want to hear my take on what happened, then just go. I'll find someone else who *does give a damn*.'

The old man's words were like a slap in the face. I squinted at him, anger riding on my tongue. But I let it go. I headed for the stairs. I ignored the tug of scar tissue in my thigh, in a hurry now to get away before I said something that I'd regret. There were enough regrets for me to contend with without hurting a gricving fathcr.

Don's next words halted my hand on the door handle.

'I got an email, Hunter. It said: "Who must you lose next?".'

Without turning, I pressed on the handle and tugged the door open and went up the stairs. 'He's dead, Don. How could he send you an email?'

'Whether it was him or not, I was still sent the goddamn thing.' Don walked to the base of the stairs but he didn't follow me up. 'It was a direct threat to *my* family.'

I slipped into the dark hallway, hearing the rage building in the old man like the rumble that precedes an earthquake.

I made it all the way to the front door, but for a second time in less than a minute my hand was halted by words.

'You're just going to walk away from this, Joe? Do you hate my father so much?'

Millie was standing in the hallway, her arms wrapped round her body as though she was freezing. Strands of her hair were plastered across her face and clinging to the tears on her cheeks.

Hate is such a strong word. I didn't hate Don, just what he'd once led me to do.

'He's hurting and confused, Millie. You both are.'

'Yes,' she said. 'We're all confused. But so are you. When will you open your eyes and see what's really happening here? He *is* back.'

I gnawed my bottom lip. It wasn't possible. The bastard's body was ravaged by flame, immolation of his corpse as complete as what had happened to Brook. Carswell Hicks had fallen over the precipice into his promised eternity in hell.

But then there were the emails. Someone must have sent them.

I opened the door.

'Tell your father I'm sorry for his loss.'

3

There was an ache in my right hand which was compounded by the cold, and more than the slight tugging in my leg, this concerned me the most. When adrenalin rushed through my system the wounds to my leg were no hindrance but I required the full range of movement and dexterity of my fingers. My hand had been shattered during the same battle where I'd picked up the other injuries, and I'd had to undergo micro-surgery to put it right. As I walked, my fists in my pockets once more, I periodically flexed the hand to promote movement.

I had the feeling that I was going to need it in fully functioning order.

For someone in my line of work, speed of hand is the difference between life and death.

I hear you're supposed to be some kind of knight errant these days.

Don Griffiths' words had been meant as sarcasm. Right now they elicited the required response: a wry smile. Knight errant? That was just onc fancy term that had been levelled at me. I suppose it was better than *vigilante*, which was more often the case. At least the term carried the honourable connotations that I hold dear. Without my sense of decency, I accept that I could very well be labelled alongside those other balaclava-clad hooligans who take the law into their own hands. But then – it's all a matter of perspective. To some I'd still be seen as a man of questionable morals. Perhaps I was the type of knight who wore tarnished armour.

As I walked a cat kept pace with me.

It was a gnarly old tomcat, and judging by the scars that criss-crossed its body it had fought a number of battles during its lifetime. We had a lot in common. It watched with luminous yellow eyes from the opposite sidewalk, perhaps recognising its human familiar.

Occasionally cats have questionable morals too. Some people judge them as cruel killers, but not all their kills are for fun. Sometimes they have to kill to survive, or to protect their young.

This took me right back to Millie, and to Brook's children. My friend, Rink, who runs a successful PI outfit down in Tampa, had brought me up to speed on Brook's death and the family she'd left behind: her husband, Adrian Reynolds, and nine and six year olds, Beth and Ryan. Don was an ex-cop, and, judging by the photograph I'd seen of his son-in-law, Adrian was no stranger to a gymnasium, so they could look after themselves. It was only Millie and the two kids I was worried about.

I was uncomfortable about walking away from them. But I couldn't believe that there was any truth in Don's concern. How could a dead man be a threat to him or his family?

Don was hurting; he was stricken with grief and grasping at anything that would make sense of Brook's seemingly pointless death. In the same circumstances, some people raged at the world, or at their cruel god, while others looked for excuses. Don was clutching at old hatreds in order to add reason to his pain.

But then he wasn't the only one allowing hatred to shadow his judgement, was he?

Someone must have sent that bloody email.

I stopped walking and looked across at the cat. The old tom mirrored my movement. We stared into each other's eyes. I was the first to blink. The cat sat down and began licking its old wounds. In my pocket, I again flexed my fist.

The cat stood up and slunk forward, and now I was the one who matched it step for step.

I got the message. The time for licking wounds was done, and I should get back to doing what I did best.

I was near to the Seven-Eleven where I'd left my car. On my right was an open lot full of weeds. Beyond it the forest that encircled Bedford Well swayed under the bitter wind, undulating like a pitch-black sea. Across the way, the cat was all that stood between me and the forest on that side. The cat had come to another standstill, but this time it was staring past the convenience store to where I'd parked the Audi. Its shoulders hunched and its ears flattened on its head; its mouth opened in silent challenge, baring teeth that glinted red under the moon.

Suddenly the cat bolted, heading away into the cover promised by the forest. But I wasn't going to run.

I continued forward, to meet the two men who were resting their weight on my car. Once again, I flexed my hand, pleased to find that the bubbling warmth flooding my body had anaesthetised the pain.

It was near to four in the morning: too late for revellers and too early even for dayshift workers to show up at the convenience store. Their black SUV was parked a dozen yards away, and yet they chose to sit on the bonnet of my car. They were waiting for me and there was no good reason for it. I didn't need the cat's reactions to tell me that these men were dangerous.

'You mind, guys? The car's a rental and I have to pay for any damages.'

Both men pushed off the Audi, one of them, stocky with a shaved head, leaning back as though inspecting the paintwork for scratches. The other, a tall man, who looked like he'd been constructed from too many bones and sun-dried leather, lifted his chin, his nostrils flaring.

'Fee-fi-fo-fum . . .' he said in a surprisingly melodious voice.

I smell the blood of an Englishman, I finished the thought. I'd heard plenty like it since my move to the States.

The second man finished his inspection of the paintwork, then used his sleeve to buff out an imaginary scratch. Then he turned his attention to me, holding an empty palm towards the car. His smile was wide but colder than the wind gusting round the parking lot. 'No harm done, buddy.'

'No harm, no foul,' the tall one echoed as he picked at a patch of dry skin on his bald head.

Taking the car keys from my pocket, I aimed them at the Audi and disengaged the locks. Nodded amiably at both men, then moved to go round them.

'A moment if you please.' The second man was shorter than me, but he was heavier built, and I noticed he had self-inflicted prison tats on his fingers. He stepped in the way, barring me from the car. He raised his ink-mottled hand and touched it to my chest. The contact was little firmer than a caress, but it sent a jolt through my body. Not because he held an electrical device – or any weapon – but because I'd allowed him to do it. The rule I'd always followed was that if an enemy could touch you, then they could kill you. This man was without a shadow of a doubt an enemy.

Subtly I stepped back, knowing that the next time he tried to lay hands on me would be the decisive moment. I watched the man's eyes and saw the same thought flashing through his mind.

'Ease up, buddy,' the man said. 'I'm only being friendly. You're not from around here, right? England is it? Just wanted to say hi and ask you a question or two.'

He was obviously lying, but I wasn't averse to playing that game. 'Look, fellas, I'd love to stay and chat but I've got to get on my way.'

'On your way already?' The stocky man shook his head. 'Why, you just got here. Surely you've a minute or two to spare? Especially when we've gone to the trouble of turnin' out to say hello.'

'Wasn't expecting a welcoming committee, I bet?' The tall man leaned close, and his breath, stinking of garlic and something sour, washed over me. 'Not at this time of night, huh? You shouldn't be surprised: I never sleep. I'm up before the roosters. Cock-a-doodle-doo!'

I didn't reply to either. One was a liar and the other was crazy. But both were very dangerous. Instead I held the stocky one's gaze as I manoeuvred the keys round in my grip.

The stocky man nodded in the direction I'd just come from. 'Who did you visit with in town?'

'Who says I visited anyone?'

'Can't see any other reason for you being in Bedford Well. Not like there's much to see in the dark.'

'There's a nice wishing well on the green.'

'Yeah, we noticed you at the well. We were going to say hi then, but we didn't want to spook you.'

'I saw you too,' I said. 'But then you left and I walked back here. Slowly.'

The man smiled at the tit-for-tat lies.

So did I.

Finally I said, 'Let's just get this over with, shall we? You're here to give me some sort of warning. Well, I'll save you the trouble. I'm leaving and I won't be back.'

I went to move past the man, and his tattooed hand came up. It wavered inches from my shoulder like he'd read my earlier thoughts. With his other hand he held open his jacket, showing the gun tucked into his belt. 'Not very satisfying if we just let you drive away, buddy.'

'No, but it'll be a lot less painful.'

'We don't have to hurt you,' the stocky man said. 'Just make sure you head outa here and know what it means if you come back.'

'Of course, I don't mind causing a little pain.' The tall one grinned, showing rotting teeth. 'If it comes to that.'

I dipped my head. 'I must have lost you in the translation there, guys. I didn't mean it was going to be painful for me.'

Both men exchanged glances just as the stocky man dropped his hand to pull the gun from his waistband.

It was what I'd been hoping for. When they both looked back at me with incredulous grins on their faces I was already moving.

I'd been twiddling the car keys for more than the exercise: I'd lined up one of them so that it was protruding from my clenched fist.

The sharp point rammed directly into the side of the stocky man's neck an inch below the lobe of his ear. On its own it wouldn't stop him immediately, but the force of my fist behind it also rocked his skull and the man went down in a heap on the ground.

Turning, I lifted my fist and a scattering of blood arched away from the key on the night breeze.

Seeing the leader of the duo dispatched so decisively should have given the tall one pause. But he was even crazier than he looked. Unfazed by the sudden violence he merely let out a laugh and launched himself at me. 'It looks like *it's come to that*!'

He appeared ungainly and loose-limbed: in fact he was anything but. He threw a series of punches, and I was hard put to avoid them all. One cracked against my cheek, another in my chest. As I stepped away from the clawing fingers that tried to rake my eyes, I missed the man's leg coming up and kicking at my groin. Only the angles saved me from a crippling blow, but it was still agony when the man's boot landed square on the point where I'd been knifed.

Chewing down on the pain, I pivoted and avoided the next kick. I dipped the keys into a pocket, then snaked my hand under the tail of my jacket to grab my gun.

Again the tall man surprised me by pivoting the other way and kicking out with his heel with a classic reverse roundhouse kick from tae kwon do. His foot slammed into my gut and pushed me back against the Audi.

I forgot about the gun. The crazy man was already coming at me, fingers tightened to spear into my exposed throat.

'Cock-a-doodle-do!'

He should have concentrated on fighting instead of crowing.

Sweeping the attacking hand aside, I drove my opposite elbow directly into his face. There was a wet sound from where the elbow hit and he staggered backwards, spitting out loose teeth. The sour smell washed over me again but this time it held a distinctly coppery tang.

Following him, I drove a kick into his groin. More fragments of rotting teeth were spat on the floor as the man bent over at the waist. I avoided the foul stuff. It wasn't easy while looping an arm over the man's skull and under his throat so that the blade of my forearm was jammed tight against his windpipe. Catching hold of my wrist with my opposite hand, I reared back, arching my spine. All the pressure was centred on the man's trachea, and I felt it collapse.

I kept the pressure on.

At first the man tried to claw at my arms. But when he couldn't get any oxygen into his lungs instinct took over and all he did then was scrabble at the ground with his feet and flap his elbows. Now he really was like a rooster.

It took him the best part of a minute to die.

Finally, I released him and he flopped down face first.

Looking down on him, I guess my gaze would be best described as dispassionate.

Cock-a-fucking-doodle-to-you, I thought.

The stocky man hadn't recovered from the stab to his carotid. In fact, judging by the widening pool of blood reflecting the disc of the moon, he never would.

Violence still surged through my veins. The same cold rush I'd experienced earlier in Don Griffiths' basement when I'd recognised that – however I looked at this – more people were going to die. Releasing a ragged breath, I attempted to calm the rage within me.

Then it was as if sense kicked in.

I'd just killed two men in the middle of a car park without concern for who might have witnessed the brutality. Sloppy work, Hunter, I admonished myself. I checked for anyone watching.

Across the way the cat was back.

It sat looking at me as though nonplussed by the violence. This time the cat blinked first. Then it lifted a back leg and began licking. Maybe that was as near to a nod of approval as I could expect.

4

The Seven-Eleven was three hours from opening, but it didn't mean that no one would happen along much sooner than that. A delivery truck loaded with fresh produce and other perishables could arrive prior to store hours and staff would likely be on hand to unload it. It wouldn't be a good idea to be near the place by then.

But I couldn't simply drive away and leave the two men lying out there for anyone to find. Someone had sent them and it wasn't a stretch to imagine they'd checked in with this person while waiting for my return. When they were found dead, the same person would suspect who was responsible for killing them. The men's mission had been to ensure that I wouldn't return to town: well, the police would do the job for them by locking me up. If the men were only missing, at least I could buy a little time before the cops came knocking.

I'd lied about the Audi being a rental: it was a verbal tactic to disarm them. I didn't want to chance moving the bodies in it because however careful I was there'd still be forensic traces that would tie me to their deaths. I'd grown fond of the import – a reminder of the car I'd driven back home in the UK – and wasn't ready to give it up just yet.

Leaning down, I checked the tall man's pockets for keys. There was nothing, apart from half of a Hershey Bar, a torn wrapper folded round it to preserve it for later. Evidently the guy had had a sweet tooth; maybe that was why they were so rotten.

Next I checked the stocky man, and this time was rewarded by a bunch of keys to the SUV. I left the gun tucked in the man's belt. Neither of them had a mobile phone, so maybe time was still on my side.

Watched by the cat, I loaded both men into the rear compartment of their vehicle and then used a blanket from the back seat to cover them. I checked around, paying attention to the Seven-Eleven, but it seemed as if surveillance cameras weren't deemed necessary out here in the sticks. Lastly, I brought a couple of handfuls of dirt from the weed-strewn boundary next to the forest, and scattered them over the pool of blood that had leaked from the stocky man's neck. It wouldn't fool a determined investigator, but that depended upon if anyone ever looked here and recognised it as a crime scene.

A single road led in and out of town, two lanes of blacktop that stretched arrow-straight back through the passes of the Allegheny Mountains. On the drive in, I'd noticed that the trails leading off from it had been disused in some years. Logging was a thing of the past here, and though the town got its share of tourists in the summer months, it wasn't on the hiking trail map. The chances of anyone wandering up any of them in winter were probably negligible.

A mile out of town, I pulled into a rutted track that led up into the deep forest. It would have been preferable to take the corpses even further out in the wilderness but I still had to return to the Audi before the early shift arrived at the store. It was a given that I wouldn't be bringing the SUV back.

Finding an offshoot from the trail, I turned down it, the branches of spruce and fir trees scraping on the paintwork. Two or three hundred yards in, I abandoned the vehicle and the dead men inside. With luck it would be weeks before they were discovered.

The trek back to town should have been a chore, but I welcomed the exercise. I jogged, and within minutes my blood was flowing freely and the ungainly limp – not to mention the residual pain from the kick I'd taken – were left somewhere in my wake. But I carried a new burden all the way.

I'd killed both those men with impunity.

I argued that given the opportunity they would have killed me, that my actions were pure self-defence. But now, with the heat of battle expunged, I couldn't help feeling that perhaps I'd overstepped the line that I'd always drawn in the sand before now. The men had been dangerous enough, particularly the crazy one who seemed to know a thing or two about unarmed combat, but on reflection they were mugs. Nobody but a rank amateur shows their gun like that if he intends to use it. The mad one hadn't even come with a gun. I got the nasty sense that the stocky man had been telling the truth. That they were there only to talk; to dissuade me from any further involvement and see me safely out of the way.

But the reason remained elusive: why did they want me out of the way?

They hadn't just turned up by chance. They'd been watching me and waiting for my return to the deserted lot. Was there any truth in Don's suspicions that Brook's death was anything but a tragic accident? Had these men been involved? It was beginning to look that way.

If they were responsible for burning Brook alive then I'd no reason to regret killing them so savagely. In fact, if there was any truth in that, I'd have been happy that they were now dead and gone.

But a small grain of doubt remained.

I was running full-tilt by the time the forest opened up and I saw the town limit sign. I began to slow. If anyone had arrived at the Seven-Eleven in the interim, I didn't want to turn up sweating and blowing and attract their attention. Better that I approach quietly, get in the Audi and drive away unobserved.

When I walked into the car park, only the car waited. I dug in my pocket and pulled out the keys, the largest still clotted with the stocky man's blood. I grimaced, but then used the inside of a coat pocket to clean the mess. The coat would have to go, but there was no rush. The auto-locking mechanism had rearmed itself and I bleeped the locks open and climbed inside the car. As I was about to close the door, movement caught my eye.

The tomcat was sitting next to where I'd scattered the dirt over the blood. It was watching me while it lowered its head and sniffed at the floor. It nuzzled the earth once, probing with its tongue.

'Hey!'

The cat jerked up its chin and scowled at me.

'Are you hungry, boy? C'mon and we'll see what we can find.'

The cat's eyes widened and it stood up languidly. It began to pad towards the car. I held open the door and the cat came inside, surprisingly at ease with its new friend. It sat in the passenger seat and stared back at me, purring like an idling engine. Maybe the cat shared some kind of affinity with me. Maybe it simply wasn't as feral as it looked. Or it was twice as hungry.

Holding out the back of my hand I allowed the cat to sniff it. Then it lowered its head and allowed me to rub the hair between its ears. At least there was someone in this godforsaken place who didn't greet me with enmity. I'm a dog man and have never owned a cat – they seem too aloof and uncaring of the ways of humanity, but I saw now that perhaps I'd misjudged them. A bit like I was often misjudged.

Starting the Audi, I pulled out of the parking lot, trusting the arrival of customers' vehicles to obliterate the proof of violence under their tyres.

The main strip was still deserted, as was the loop round the green. The wishing well, complete with peaked roof and ornamental bucket, stood proud at its centre, but hadn't yet attracted any visitors. Not that it mattered even if there was a group of tourists hanging around. My intention of being gone from town before anyone noticed was redundant now. Even if I personally had not been expected, the two men I'd fought were proof that Don Griffiths' house was under surveillance. Therefore it was pointless hiding; may as well drive up and park on Don's driveway.

The tomcat allowed me to tuck it under my left arm. Idly scratching the cat's chin I walked up the path to the front door. The cat purred louder as it enjoyed the unfamiliar contact, uncaring that I was actually scrubbing blood from its fur.

I leaned on the doorbell.

It took longer than the first time for the light to come on above me. While waiting, I peered back across the green towards the main road. No dark-coloured vehicles nosed out of alleyways this time. There was a heavy tread from within, and then the light above flicked to life. So did the one inside. The silhouette beyond the glass was too bulky to be Millie.

Don opened the door tentatively. When he recognised who was standing on the stoop, he jerked open the door and peered past me, checking all sides and then across the green. Finally he turned his attention to me. 'You came back? You actually believe me?'

'Something happened to make up my mind.'

'So you're going to help?'

'If I do this I want something from you in return.'

'I'll pay you. Just name your price.'

'I don't want your money.' I held up the tom. 'Feed the cat.'

Don looked down at the ragged old thing. 'You're kidding, right?'

'No,' I said. 'I want you to take him in. The old boy needs a home.'

Don shook his head in incredulity. But he reached out for the cat.

Immediately the tom hissed, and I felt its muscles bunching as it prepared to defend itself. I dropped the cat, expecting it to make a dash for freedom. To my surprise it swerved round Don and into the house. I smiled: the cat was evidently a good judge of character, but it also knew where it was well off.

'Probably flea-ridden and has feline AIDS,' Don muttered. He moved back allowing me to come inside. 'But if those are your terms, you've got a deal. The grandkids will love having it around.'

Glancing down I saw a gun lying on the stand next to the door. It hadn't been there earlier; Don had obviously brought it. Don caught me looking and coughed in embarrassment. He picked up the gun and tucked it into his trouser pocket.

'I take it you weren't expecting me to come back?'

Don shook his head. 'You said something happened to change your mind?'

My head went down, a shadow flitting across my features that had nothing to do with the cap's brim. 'I just killed two men who were watching your house.'

Don took a step back, a hand going to his throat. He tugged at his beard, pinching it between index finger and thumb. From the way he stared it was as if he was awaiting the punchline of a sick joke. When I didn't deliver, he asked, 'You're not serious, are you?'

'I don't take killing men lightly, despite what you might've heard.'

Don moved for the front door, as if checking that the corpses were piled on his front lawn.

'Relax, Don. I've got rid of them.'

'Where?'

'Out in the forest.'

'Jesus!' Don ran his hands through his hair. Sweat from his palms made his hair stand up. It didn't take long for the truth to sink in. 'So I was right all along? Hicks is after my family?'

I pulled off my cap and thrust it into a jacket pocket. 'I killed two men. I'm just not sure that they had anything to do with *whoever* is threatening you.'

Like the tugging on his beard, and the chewing of his moustache, the way Don's hand went inside his trouser pocket was an unconscious act. He folded his hand round the butt of the gun. Hopefully he'd had the presence of mind to lock the safety on. 'Who else could have sent them?'

'I don't know.'

'But you killed them anyway?'

'It was me or them.' There was no conviction in my voice. Don was no shrink, but he didn't have to be to recognise the doubt in my mind.

'Sometimes we all do things we regret, Hunter.'

I held the older man's gaze. He wasn't referring to the two men: he was trying to smooth over the act that had driven a wedge between us all those years ago. 'It's just a shame that people have to die for our mistakes.'

Don nodded slowly. No argument from him.

I touched the old man's wrist and then gently took his hand off the gun. 'Put that away before someone else gets injured.'

Don opened a drawer in the stand, slipped the gun inside. He locked the drawer and tucked the key into his back pocket, then searched my face as if it held all the answers. 'What are we going to do, Hunter?'

'Leave it to me, Don. You'vc a job of your own.'

Don had no idea what I was referring to. As a reminder there was a racket from the kitchen, a clatter of pans and dishes shifting as the cat rummaged for scraps.

'He's very hungry,' I said. 'Feed him. I'll try to find out who those two guys were.'

'And if they were sent by Hicks?'

'Then we get ready for the next ones to come.'

5

Daybreak came late to Bedford Well. The wooded slopes that surrounded the town blocked the sun's march over the horizon, throwing jagged shadows across the green and over the rooftops of the houses on the western side. Those on the eastern side remained in darkness and people inside had to turn on lamps so they could see to eat their breakfasts. The wind had picked up exponentially, casting detritus and litter across the otherwise deserted street, adding to the grim outlook of the day.

Looking out of a window on the ground floor, I had my thumbs tucked into the waistband of my jeans. I was wearing a denim shirt, the sleeves rolled up to my elbows and the tail out to cover the SIG SAUER P226 tucked in the small of my back. Earlier I'd stuffed my leather jacket into the furnace to get rid of any trace evidence from the two men I'd killed. I was pretty sure that I was clean, even if the same couldn't be said for my conscience.

Millie came into the room behind me. She'd dressed in navy trousers and a lilac blouse nipped in at the waist with a belt. Her dark hair had been pulled tight into a ponytail and she only wore the slightest dab of make-up – strategically placed to conceal the dark rings beneath her eyes. She looked exactly like someone who'd cried herself to sleep.

'Here.' She held up a large steaming mug of coffee.

Accepting it gratefully I inhaled the aroma and took a deep gulp. It hit the spot and I sighed. 'Thanks, Millie, I need this. It's about the only thing that keeps me going these days.'

She nodded at my words, but there was more to her gesture. 'I was surprised to find you here when I woke up. When you left last night, I thought that was it.'

She thought they'd been abandoned to their fate.

'I reconsidered.' Neither Don nor I had told her about the two men I'd killed.

'You don't look particularly happy with your decision.'

I sipped the coffee. Watched her over the top of the cup. 'I've a lot on my mind, that's all.'

'Want to tell me?' There was little conviction in her offer. 'A problem shared . . .'

Isn't always a problem halved. In fact, if I told her what was on my mind it would only cause more concern for the young woman. It was enough that she was grieving the loss of her sister, without worrying about what my actions might bring.

'It's nothing I can't deal with,' I said with equal lack of conviction.

When I'd been demobilised from the Special Forces I'd been recalled to the secret base on the north-western Scottish coastline: Arrowsake – a codename derived from a mispronunciation of Arisaig, the fabled home of the Special Operations Executive, the forerunner of the modern MI5. There I'd undergone debriefing and what I'd come to understand as *debugging*. It was necessary that the military shrinks did their best to reintegrate me into society without any of the baggage associated with killing men for over fourteen years. The last thing the military wanted was to let me loose unhinged and with the capacity for ongoing slaughter. I suspected that they'd only partially succeeded.

Proof of that theory was my overreaction to the threat posed by the two men in the Seven-Eleven parking lot. I possessed the skills to disarm both and to put them to sleep for a short spell while making myself scarce. But the old reactions had kicked in unchecked and I'd dealt with the men in the same way as when hunting terrorists and enemy soldiers.

Now in the cold afterwash of battle there was no excuse for my actions. I could lie; argue that I was merely defending my life; that if I hadn't acted that way then it would have been me who was dumped out in the forest for the wildlife to feed upon.

The truth of the matter was that I hadn't been fearful of the men. In fact it was the exact opposite: I'd relished the confrontation. For three months now I'd been healing from my previous encounter with a genuine challenge. Luke Rickard – a professional contract killer – had almost ended my life. He'd shot me, stabbed me in the leg, pulled me off the roof of a building in his last moments. I'd been broken and bleeding to death; the medics had fought to save my life. Surgical intervention had saved my physical being, but what of my mental state?

Doubt had set in. I was lame and my hand wasn't in full working order. What good was I to anyone in that frail condition?

Thinking on it now, it wasn't disbelief of Don's story, or even the old enmity that the two of us shared, that urged me turn the car round and flee back to Florida. It was the self-doubt; that I'd be unable to do anything to help. Subconsciously I'd killed those two mugs to prove something to myself. But at what price? Had it made a murderer of me? A bully? The very thing that I'd always despised?

I studied Millie, and decided. No. At the back of my mind I'd seen the men as a threat to her, and to her sister's children.

'Do you want more coffee?'

Millie reached out for the mug that I'd drained. I hadn't been conscious of finishing it, or that I now held the empty mug to my lips. I handed it over. 'I'd appreciate it.'

'Breakfast? I could cook something for you.'

'Coffee will be fine.'

'You should eat.'

I should, I might need the strength. But I wasn't sure that I could hold anything down for long. 'Just coffee . . . please.'

Millie swung round, heading out the room.

'Millie.'

She turned back. Her mouth was pinched and there were two red spots on her cheeks. I said, 'I'm sorry I didn't come when your father first asked. I truly am.'

'I'll get your coffee.'

Following her to the kitchen would serve no purpose. Millie's offer to cook breakfast was her way of breaking down the barrier her sister's death had placed between us. By my refusal I'd done nothing to help the matter. Going in there would only make things more awkward. When she came back with the second coffee there would be an opportunity to try again.

Turning back to the window, I peered across the green towards the main road into town. There was movement now, people finally bracing themselves against the elements to get on with their lives. Kids were hanging out by the green, waiting to be picked up for school. On my walk through town last night I'd noticed a school house, but it must cater only for the younger children. These older ones were probably bussed to a high school in the larger neighbouring town of Hertford. The college-age kids maybe only returned to town during holidays, if they returned at all. There didn't seem much here to hold them; other than the family businesses and occasional chain store I hadn't noted much else in the way of industry.

Kids were pretty much the same wherever I travelled. Fashions in clothing and hairstyles, the colour of their skin, might be different, but the group fooling around as they waited for the school bus could have been standing on any street corner in the western world. Pennsylvanian kids weren't so different from those I'd been familiar with back home in the UK.

The two standing by the wishing well were different though.

Not only in appearance but by the intensity with which they stared back at me through the window.

It was a boy who, when I studied his smooth features and gangly frame, didn't look like he'd made twenty years old yet. He was wearing jeans and boots and a black leather jacket emblazoned with patches and flags. He'd an archaic quiff hairstyle, greased and coiffed to Elvis perfection. The girl with him looked older. She had a retro look about her too. But she was more punk rocker than greaser. She had on a tartan mini that was strategically frayed around the hem, over bright yellow stockings and pink shoes. A white T-shirt daubed with splashes of colour was only partially hidden by the leather jacket she'd decorated with studs and chains. Another thin chain looped from her right nostril to her right earlobe, and her platinum hair was spiked high and then tipped with pink.

I stepped closer to the window, meeting their gaze. The boy and girl shared a glance. The girl said something and the boy sneered at me before they turned and walked unhurriedly across the green.

They look dangerous. Go after them, Hunter. Why not kill them as well?

I sighed and turned back to the room, putting the kids out of my mind. Don was walking in ahead of Millie and he was clutching a steaming mug similar to the two she carried. He also had the police file he'd shown me earlier tucked under his elbow.

'I thought you might want to take a look at this again.' As Don sat down he snapped the file against his thigh.

Taking the proffered mug from Millie, I said, 'I don't need to, Don.' What I really meant was, 'I don't *want* to.' 'I'd rather see your grandchildren. And there's something I want to show you on the way . . .'

Don caught the tone of delivery and had a good idea what the something was. 'I don't want to leave Millie here alone.'

'She can come with us,' I said. 'She can wait with the kids while we—'

Millie held up a hand. 'Hold on. Don't I have a say in this?'

Don and I shared a glance.

'I'm not a baby,' she said. 'I can look after myself. And I can certainly make up my own mind when it comes to where I'm going to wait. *She*'s going to wait right here.' She looked pointedly at me for my choice of words.

'It may not be safe here,' Don said.

'Dad!'

'I mean it, Millie.'

'What's going to happen here? Who's going to do something in *this* town?'

Once again we shared a glance. More could happen here than she could ever suspect, and we both knew it. Finally, I nodded. 'You're right, Millie. Nothing's going to happen to you.' I looked at Don. 'Leave the key for her, though.'

Don frowned, but then dug in his back pocket for the key to the drawer where he'd left the gun this morning. He placed it on the arm of his chair. 'It's just a precaution. You remember how to use it, don't you, Millie?'

'Your gun? Yes . . . but . . .'

'It's just a precaution,' I echoed. 'You won't need it, but it's there just in case.'

'Just in case I get frightened, you mean?' Millie shook her head and turned to walk out of the room without picking up the key. Before she reached the door, the old tomcat graced us with his presence. He swanked into the room, his tail held high. Millie crouched, opening her arms, and the cat immediately sprang up to be cuddled. She turned back to us, holding the cat. It stared at us without blinking. So did Millie. 'See. I'm not here all alone. *We'll* be fine while you're gone.'

We could only acquiesce. Don grabbed a jacket and a spare for me. I shrugged into the winter coat as Don gave his daughter a warning eye. 'Just keep everything locked and don't answer the door to any strangers.'

Millie walked away stiffly, the cat looking back over her shoulder at us. 'Like we see many strangers around here?'

6

From seats in the window of Benson's Drugstore Vince Everett and Sonya Madden watched the two men drive away in the dark-coloured Audi.

Sonya was slurping on a milkshake. She batted her mascara-laden eyelashes at the young man next to her.

'We gonna follow them, Vince?'

With a fingertip stained by nicotine he teased a drip of milkshake that trembled on her lip. 'No, we just stay cool.'

Sonya looked over her shoulder. The motion appeared languid but was practised. At the counter, the old man – a third-generation Benson – paid them no more attention than he did any other kid in the place. Sonya leaned towards Vince. 'We were told to keep an eye on them.'

'They'll spot a tail too easy.'

'What if we lose them?'

'They'll come back. Now drink your shake and shut up, will ya? I'm trying to think.'

Sonya caught links of her nose chain with the tip of her tongue and pulled it into the corner of her mouth. 'You're thinking about the woman.'

Vince tilted his chin her way. His hair flopped on his forehead and he rolled his head to flick it back in place. 'Only one woman I'm interested in, baby.'

Sonya let the chain pop loose as she concentrated on pouting. 'So you say, but I know what's on your mind. You're looking forward to paying her a visit, ain't ya?'

'A man's gotta do what a man's gotta do. Doesn't mean I have to take any pleasure from it.'

'I want to come with you.'

'No. You have to wait outside and keep watch.'

'I want to watch *you*.' Her eyes flared at the suggestion.

Vince touched her on the tip of her upturned nose. 'Don't worry, baby. When I do it, I'll be thinking about you.' He stood up, kicking back the chair with a heel of his silver-tipped boots. 'Wait until I'm outta here, then go on over to the well. You see those guys come back, you ring me right away.'

'Yeah, whatever.' She slurped her milkshake again, managing her pout around the straw this time. 'Knock yourself out, Vince.'

He stared down at her. Then he curled his lip and held her under his smouldering gaze. She smiled, but then she hunched her shoulders, ducking her head coyly like she couldn't bear his sexy look any longer.

All an act. But he liked it.

He hitched up his jeans and then pimp-walked out of the store looking back over his shoulder.

Sonya watched him go. He saw her head come up and the innocence vanish from her features. They loved playing their little game, but now Sonya was all business. And so was he.

Vince Everett was a fake name, but that was all he'd allow. Everything else about him was the real deal. In the movie *Jailhouse Rock* Elvis Presley played the character of Vince Everett, the ex-con who became a big singing star. It didn't matter that Vince couldn't sing a note, or that his hip-swinging was more akin to someone taking a fit, there was something this Louisiana Cat possessed that the man whose name he'd assumed couldn't claim. Elvis was famous for shooting at TV screens, but had he ever shot and killed a man?

Vince Everett had.

More than once.

He was also suspected of murdering a cop by beating him with the PR24 baton he'd taken off the cop's belt. Vince had reputedly laughed for joy as the cop's face went from stunned surprise to ground beef under the repeated whacks of the baton.

Unlike the Presley character, Everett had never been caught. He was no ex-con, and all being well things shouldn't change.

School kids were clambering to get the best seats on a yellow bus as he walked across the green. From the misted windows a couple of older girls watched his progress. He swaggered for their benefit; but their laughter was too harsh to be appreciated. What did they know about sex on legs, anyway?

The bus puttered away, sending clouds of smoke out of its tailpipe. Vince kept walking. At the gate on to Don Griffiths' property he paused. Back across the way he saw Sonya come out of the drugstore and walk towards the green. She was already clutching her cell phone, ready to warn him of the men's return.

She was a good catch, that one.

He'd met her out East at one of them burlesque clubs in Greenwich Village. Not a dancer but a punter just like he was; someone who liked the archaic fashion and musical styles of bygone eras. It only took a glance and they both knew it: there was something else they shared. That night they'd danced and drunk and fucked, and things had been pretty much like that in the three months since. And twice already they'd shared their lust for violence. Sonya liked to watch him. Afterwards they'd screwed their brains out; high on the agony of the ones they had hurt.

She was probably pissed that she was going to miss out on what he was about to do to Millie Griffiths, but he'd tell her all the gory details afterwards. Right now she had to watch from a distance, keep an eye out for Don and his visitor returning.

There'd be nothing to tell if Vince was disturbed on the job, nothing to spice things up when he ripped off her clothes.

Vince wondered who the newcomer was.

Looked nothing special to him, but who knew?

The guy was older than him, heavier built, and he looked a little tense when he walked. Old and slow. Vince was pretty sure that the man was no threat.

But then he thought of the way that the man had returned his stare out of the window earlier. Something about the guy made Vince wonder if maybe he should reconsider. The man had a similar look to the one he'd recognised in Sonya's eyes that first time in Greenwich Village. It was the same look he knew that he carried. They all had what Vince's grandpa called 'Cain's eyes' – the eyes of a killer.

Yeah, but what did Grandpa Everett know? Vince's grandfather hadn't recognised the killer eyes of the kid who shot him through the throat with a .22 revolver when he'd discovered him trying to boost the cash from the till in his store.

Or maybe he had, but the shock of seeing them in his own grandson's face had thrown him off.

Vince shrugged. Who gives a fuck anyway? If the guy comes back, Sonya will warn me. If he wants to get it on, then so be it. He'd kill the guy and see how *hot for it* that made Sonya.

Feeling the stirrings of an erection, Vince smiled to himself. Then he dipped a hand into the hip pocket of his jeans. He couldn't play guitar like the King, but he always carried a spare string.

The 'G' string – Sonya always laughed at that, usually lifting the hem of her skirt to show him hers – had never been on a guitar and likely never would be. He'd taken the two ends and fastened them to large steel washers. The weighted ends made it easy for snaring round a throat, then gave him good handles while he throttled his victim. The string was a medium gauge, with a nylon filament and sheathed in a wound brass coil: tough enough not to break and not too slim that it cut deeply. Vince wanted his victims aware while he strangled them to death.

7

A little under a year ago, I'd launched an assault with my friend Rink on a derelict building in Little Rock, Arkansas. We'd been searching for my brother, John, who'd been in the employ of the men inside. Though we'd both expected to be met with violence, I'd cautioned against the use of lethal force. The men inside were little more than low-end criminals and, without knowledge of John's fate, I couldn't reconcile myself to the thought of murder. Even when the guns started blasting, I'd reined in my instincts and hadn't aimed to kill.

So what's happened here?

I held back the blanket so that Don could look at the two dead men. I avoided looking at their purpling faces and their staring, accusatory eyes.

I concentrated instead on Don's reaction to their identity. Please tell me that you don't recognise them, I prayed.

My worst fear was that the two men were merely local punks, who, misreading my arrival in town, thought I was someone looking into their criminal activities. Maybe they were dealing dope or had an illegal cook shop hidden out in the hills and they thought I was there to upset their enterprise or even take their customers away from them.

'I don't know them.'

There was relief at Don's words but only for the space of a heartbeat.

'You're sure? Take another look.'

'I don't need another look. I've lived here in Bedford Well for years and know every deadbeat out there. They're not from round here, Hunter.'

This second wave of relief was tinged with the realisation that Don's original suspicion was probably right. Someone had sent these men to watch Don's house and to dissuade anyone from lingering there very long. It went some way to justifying my actions, but also it would be likely that more men were coming. And that could mean I might have to kill them too.

'How'd you do it, Hunter?'

I allowed the blanket to drop back in place. The smell coming off the corpses wafted out of the interior of the SUV, and we moved away hurriedly. When I didn't immediately reply, Don added, 'I didn't see any bullet holes. How'd you take them out?'

In the worst way imaginable.

'Does it matter?'

Don shook his head. Then he planted his fists on his hips and looked around. The forest encroached on all sides, and an outcropping of limestone jutted across the trail, hiding the SUV from anyone who might travel up the service road. But it wasn't exactly the middle of nowhere.

'They'll be found sooner or later,' he said.

'Let's hope that it's later then.' I closed the door and sealed the men in their tomb. It would stop the wildlife from getting at them but wouldn't deter the insects for long. 'You OK with that, Don?'

'Not really. I was a cop and I have to admit that this really goes against the grain.'

'I hear you. But now you're just a father looking out for his family.'

'Exactly.' Don rubbed his hands over his face, the bristles of his beard rasping against his palms. 'That's why I'll keep this secret. If they were here to hurt my family, well, I'm glad that you killed the bastards.'

But what if they weren't?

I mentally shook myself. Enough worrying about the identity of the two I'd killed; they were punk criminals and given the opportunity they would have killed me. They got what was coming to them. That was all I had to keep telling myself.

We'd left my Audi a short stroll away on the main service trail and we walked back to it in silence. It gave us the opportunity to clear the fetid breath of decomposition from our lungs. I started the engine and threw the car into reverse. Driving back down the trail until I found an area flat enough to turn on, I then directed the Audi down towards the road.

We had to wait until a yellow school bus had passed before nosing out on to the road and following in its wake, allowing enough space between the two vehicles that no one would recall anything about the car seen leaving the scene of the body dump. Sooner or later the corpses would be discovered and I didn't want a group of school kids carrying tales to the cops. Kids noticed much more than they were given credit for.

'I guess I'd best warn you,' Don said.

Concentrating on the road ahead, I merely flicked Don a glance.

'Adrian isn't happy that I've called you in.'

I'm not happy either, I thought. 'Why not?'

'He has just lost his wife. He has come to terms with the police findings and won't accept that her death was anything but a tragic accident. He might be a little . . . difficult.'

'Yeah.' Better and better. 'When all comes to all, he's the children's father. If he doesn't want me there I don't see what I can do about that.'

'*No*. Whatever he says, he's wrong. I won't have my grandchildren put at risk.'

'He's their father, Don. He decides what's best for them.'

Don shook his head adamantly. 'He doesn't realise the enormity of the threat.'

Maybe he does and has realised that you're just a paranoid old man. But I had to bite down on that thought. If Don was misguided, then what did that make me?

Don was chewing on the end of his moustache. His eyes were fixed on a spot only a couple of inches from the end of his nose. Suddenly he turned towards me, quivering in anger. 'Apart from when I was a policeman, Adrian knows little about my past, what I did or what I was involved in. He doesn't understand what kind of enemies I've made. And anyway, he does not have a final say on what happens to the children.'

'I think you'll find that he does.'

'No, he doesn't. I've asked you to look after my family and even he won't be able to do anything about that.'

'He's their father, Don. He has every right in the world to tell me to sling my hook.'

Don snorted. 'Adrian has no say where Beth or Ryan is concerned. He was married to my daughter, yes, but he isn't the kids' biological father. They're *my blood*, not his.'

I was surprised by this announcement but didn't let it show. If the truth were known, I'd already suspected that the children weren't Adrian's. Brook and Adrian were dark-haired, with green and brown eyes respectively. In the photographs dotting the living room of Don's house, both kids were blond with the palest blue eyes I'd ever seen. There were often anomalies in birth, but the difference was a bit too dramatic to be explained by ancient DNA reasserting itself.

Then there were the dates.

Beth and Ryan's births both pre-dated their parents' wedding. Not unusual in this day and age, but enough to have placed doubt about parentage in my mind.

'Who is their dad?'

Don shook his head, unprepared or unwilling to answer.

'It may be important, Don.'

'You think that this has something to do with *him*; a waste-of-time drunkard who left her with two small babies when the going got too tough for him? No, Hunter, you can forget that line of thinking. I'm telling you: this is all Hicks' doing.'

Up ahead the school bus was a yellow stain in the steamy haze rising from the road. Then it was gone and I realised that we were approaching the intersection where the mountain road joined the main highway.

'Take a left,' Don said.

Don had already informed me that Adrian and the children lived in a house in its own walled enclosure, but had been a little vague on its location, saying that he'd direct me when we were on the road. So it was a distance from the city of Hertford where the school bus was heading to? Good and bad. Cities made things difficult if I had to respond in kind to violence: the cops were too close by and that severely hindered my options. But out in the wilds a house was exposed and difficult to defend. It was beginning to look like I was going to have to call in back-up.

No, not yet, I decided, I still didn't know what I was up against. For all I knew I was just being sucked into Don's fantasy. It wasn't a nice thought, but perhaps it would be better if the two men I'd killed turned out to be nothing but local low-lifes who'd made the mistake of confronting me.

Something in me, though, also hoped that wasn't the case.

8

If he chose, Vince Everett could be a real charmer. Sometimes he put his raffish good looks to the test, giving the ladies the flick of his pompadour and the curl of a lip. Other times he just shot them a glance from his baby blues. In fact in his late twenties, he appeared much younger, and he could rely on his teen-idol face and chirpy demeanour to disarm even the most cynical. Usually he would use this approach to inveigle his way past a person's defences, but he had the sense that this time a more stealthy approach was in order. Don Griffiths was on edge and it stood to reason that his obsession with Carswell Hicks' imminent return might also have rubbed off on his daughter Millie.

Past experience told him that going in through the front door was never a good idea. Not when the potential for witnesses was too great. The back door would most likely be locked, but he'd find a window off the latch or some other form of ingress soon enough.

Don's vehicles, a Lexus and a chunky Merc SUV, were parked on the driveway but that wasn't surprising. The door to the carport was wide open, and there were kids' bikes and other toys taking up the area inside, relegating their grandfather's vehicles to the whim of the elements. The kids' belongings cost a fraction of what it would take to purchase a tyre for the Lexus, but wasn't that the way of those that loved their brats?

Vince glanced back and saw Sonya perching on the lip of the wishing well. She had her legs crossed, one ankle hooked under the other. She was waving her cell as if it was a microphone and she was conducting an interview with the invisible man. She caught him looking and flashed him a grin: loving playing the game.

Vince glanced at the front windows. He couldn't detect any movement. He then walked directly into the carport, negotiating his way around a spillage of *Star Wars* action figures. He had to step over a multicoloured tricycle. One of the kids had tried to make the bike even more colourful with juvenile slashes of a wax crayon. The child had outgrown the bike, but it still took precedence over Don's super-expensive vehicles. Good sign, Vince decided. It showed how much he doted on his grandchildren.

Vince didn't get that. When he was a brat, his lot was to be seen and not heard. Usually his parents didn't even want to see him and reminded him with a well-placed kick in the ass. He couldn't understand why Don felt such an attachment to Beth and Ryan, but decided that the psychology of it didn't matter. He loved them and that was good. That love could be used to control him.

He laid his ear to the back door. Beyond it he guessed he'd find a utility area or kitchen and wondered if the woman had gravitated to either since the men had left the house. They were always his mother's designated areas, but maybe not every woman's domain in these more liberated days.

He couldn't hear anything from inside. He tried the handle and was gratified to find his suspicion borne out. The door opened easily on well-oiled hinges. Apparently Don had been keeping busy in his retirement.

He found a large kitchen that doubled as a dining area. There was a cooking range, a work surface and a large breakfast bar along one wall with stools beneath. The kids probably ate snacks there, he surmised, while the adults dined at another table further inside the house. The sink held a trio of unwashed mugs, but otherwise the room was pristine and felt a little deserted. The only thing that told him the kitchen had been used recently was the faint fishy scent of tuna spooned on to a saucer on the floor. The saucer had been licked clean but little flakes of fish lay scattered around it.

The information supplied to him had revealed that the Griffithses didn't own any pets. Dogs in a home always made a stealthy approach difficult and he'd checked that some hound wasn't going to give him away. A cat was no concern though: they were self-centred critters that couldn't give a hoot about the comings and goings of humanity.

He walked towards the door to the hall. He paused there, glancing round the frame into the dimly lit space towards the front door where the weak daylight struggled to push through the patterned glass. He paused to check his cell phone. He had it on silent, but pressed buttons to check it would vibrate if Sonya called to warn him that someone was coming. Happy, he dipped the phone in his shirt pocket, making certain it was secure as he'd need it pretty soon. Then he spooled out the guitar string, wrapping the weighted ends round his fists so that there was approximately a foot and a half of wire dangling between them. With a flick of his wrists he snapped the string tight, smiling at the thrum that went up his forearms.

He heard murmuring from a room to his left. The woman speaking on a telephone?

Typical, he thought. It would mean waiting until she hung up otherwise the person on the other end of the line would be alerted to his presence. If it was Don or the other guy that might not bode well for him getting everything done before they came racing back.

Better that he remain silent in the hall, wait until she was finished and then go introduce himself. Except he couldn't contain himself and took a quick peek around the door frame. Millie wasn't on the phone; she had her back to him, arms folded loosely as she stared out of a window. Vince followed her gaze and saw that she was looking across the green towards where Sonya sat on the well. Millie was muttering distractedly to herself and he was worried that maybe she'd made Sonya. Any second now she could call for reinforcements, spoiling his plan.

He rolled his right wrist. The guitar string formed a loop and he allowed it to widen just far enough that it would encompass the circumference of the young woman's head.

Then he started forward.

The room was thickly carpeted and even his silver-tipped boots were silent as he approached. He held his breath, moved as slow as dripping honey. Little flutters of anticipation raced through his body, making him jerk spasmodically.

Three feet from the woman he stopped.

He'd noticed the sudden squaring of her shoulders.

Had she heard him?

Had his faint reflection in the glass warned her of his presence?

Maybe some sixth sense had kicked in and told her that she was about to die if she didn't goddamn *move* . . .

With the thought he took a half-step towards her and dropped his hands, the loop of wire trailing only a second behind.

But Millie was also in motion.

She dodged to the side, letting out a wordless cry, and she bounced off the window frame, spinning to face him.

The guitar string garrotte missed her by a mile and Vince snapped it taut between his fists even as he swung to face her.

'Son of a bitch!'

His curse came out high-pitched. Not because he'd missed her, but that he'd come to the wrong conclusion. Millie hadn't been talking to herself, she'd been cooing and comforting a goddamn cat she held to her chest. One look at the ragged old thing told Vince that it wasn't only humans who possessed Cain's eyes. The skanky old tom shot him a murderous look even as Millie's arms came up and tossed the cat at him.

In an attempt to ward it off he tried to snare the cat on the wire, but it came at him like a dervish, spitting furiously, its claws raking his face.

The cat fully intended blinding him by the way it tore at his face, but it was also a wild thing whose instinct was to flee danger. Its assault lasted only as long as it took to rake him into red stripes, then it was tearing over the top of his head seeking escape. It was just about the most ferocious few seconds of Vince's life – even worse than when he was kicked senseless by a group of liberals who took offence to the Confederate battle flag emblazoned across the shoulders of his leather jacket.

The cat was gone in a flash, streaking out of the room still yowling like a demented thing.

Then Vince was similarly yowling, in pain but also in a rage.

His fingers were dotted with blood from where he tested his face. His first instinct was to go after the cat and stamp it to death under the heels of his boots. Movement to his right refocused him on the task in hand. Millie, open-mouthed in a silent scream, rushed to follow the cat out of the room.

'Oh, no, you don't!'

Vince took a step after her, hands reaching. The guitar string was great for throttling a victim, but it was an encumbrance when wound round both fists. His outstretched hands missed Millie and he staggered after her as she twisted round the door jamb and out of his line of sight. His boots clumped from carpet on to hardwood as he charged into the hall. Millie was ten paces distant, heading for the front door. In seconds she was there, but he'd already covered half the distance. Sure that he could catch her before she could pull open the door, he lunged for her even as he allowed one end of the wire to slip from his grip.

Apart from the rapid tattoo of his boots on the floor there was very little noise. The scream still appeared to be caught in Millie's throat and Vince wasn't aware that he was holding his breath. Even the tom had stopped its caterwauling now that it'd found a dark place to hide.

Millie surprised him.

She didn't go for the door. There was a chain in a bracket, a couple of locks, no way that she could free them all before he was upon her. Instead she dived at a small table standing next to the door, grabbing at the handle of a drawer. She tugged at the drawer but it refused her until she practically lifted the table off the floor and slammed it down again. The warped lock mechanism popped open and she dragged the drawer out, the contents spilling on the floor.

There were papers, pens, an address book and a couple of business cards.

And a gun.

'Shee-it!' Vince's gaze went to the gun even as Millie was bending to snatch it up.

He was caught in a flux: carry on with the plan or run for it? His momentum decided the dilemma for him.

He skidded the last couple of feet, and his shoulder rammed into Millie, jamming her against the front door. Her body, bent over, missed the glass but she banged against the wooden bottom half and the sound was like an explosion in the confined space. Vince tumbled over her and his face whacked the window sharply. As he rebounded there were smears of his blood on the glass. He neither noticed nor cared. All he was interested in was wrenching the gun out of her grasp. First he softened her up with a smack of his forearm to the nape of her neck. Millie grunted and went all the way down to her knees. Vince felt like he was climbing on her back, his silver toecaps digging into her body as he fought for balance. Then he reached down, trying to snatch the gun away.

Millie suddenly found voice. She shrieked but it was paper-thin and wouldn't carry beyond the confines of the house.

Vince was cursing savagely, but not in words he'd remember later. He punched her twice on her shoulders, hoping to deaden the muscles to make the task of taking the gun from her numbed hand easier. But that forced Millie down further and she sprawled under him. Vince lost his balance, banged against the door glass again, then scrambled to his feet. One heel skidded away from him and he felt an explosion of pain in his knee, making him swear all the more.

'Enough!'

Vince thought the word, but it wasn't him that shouted it.

Millie had twisted under him and the gun was now aimed at his gut.

'I said *enough*. Now back away or I swear to God I'll shoot you.'

In a state of madness Vince – like anyone else – might ignore the fact that a bullet was faster than his ability to kick the gun out of her hand, but something clicked in his mind and he blinked down at the muzzle of the gun pointing directly at him. Millie angled it so that he got a good look down the barrel; a hole leading to an eternity of blackness.

He stepped away.

'Whoa! Easy there, Millie.'

'Further,' Millie snapped, the fact that he knew her name not lost on her. She jabbed the gun in cmphasis. 'Now. Do it!'

Vince lifted his palms in what was supposed to be a non-threatening gesture but the wire still dangling from one fist told the lie. He glanced at it, then shrugged. Time for the baby blues, he guessed.

'Hey! You've got me all wrong. I wasn't gonna harm you. I was just surprised by that devil of a cat. Why'd you throw the goddamn thing at me like that?'

Millie slowly came to her knees, then grabbed at the wall to steady herself as she came to her feet. The gun never wavered from its target. Vince's admiration of the woman's cool actually forced a smile to his lips. Small and slim but tough as a goddamn nut, she was. He didn't doubt that she'd have it in her to put a round through his brain if he went after her again.

Not that he believed she'd put a bullet in his spine if he turned away.

Which was what he did.

'Hold it right there,' Millie barked.

Vince ignored her, kept walking. He crunched his eyelids together, hoping that he'd read her properly.

'I said hold it!'

Vince kept going.

The fact that he made it to the kitchen with his wits intact meant that he'd been correct. She couldn't shoot him in the back. Not cold-bloodedly.

He glanced at the kitchenware; saw a wooden block with a range of knives slotted into it. Take a big-assed knife and go back? No way. He made it to the door to the carport, ensuring it slammed loudly behind him. No need for stealth this time, he just kicked the kiddie cycle out of his way, stamping through Chewbacca and Darth Vader as he hurried out on to the drive.

He snuck a glance towards the house and saw Millie staring at him out of a window next to the front door. Her features were as pale as the dead, her mouth pinched as she glared at him.

He kept going, picking up speed.

Peripherally he saw Sonya get up from her perch and swerve away from the wishing well. Best that he didn't go directly to her or Millie would see and know that Sonya was working with him. Vince angled around the green, heels clipping on the cobblestones that had been laid to give the old-world town an air of quaintness.

There were people out and about, but evidently none of them had been alerted to what had happened in Don Griffiths' house. He kept his head down, hiding the claw marks on his face as he surreptitiously shoved the guitar string into his jacket pocket. He cursed under his breath. Normally Vince Everett strutted, but this time he was forced to slink away like a kicked dog, limping slightly on his twisted knee.

They'd parked their car in an alleyway between two stores.

Vince saw a handwritten note tacked to the windscreen by the wipers, a polite notice asking that he didn't park there in future. He crumpled the note in his fist and dropped it on the ground just as Sonya caught up to him. Her mouth made a hollow 'O' as she stared at him.

'Don't start in on me,' he warned.

'Jesus, Vince, baby, your face is a mess.'

'Fucking tell me about it,' he groaned, testing the scratches with his fingertips. He winced, sucking in a breath. 'No. On second thoughts, never mind. Tell me what the fuck we're gonna tell the big man?'

9

Don's words about Adrian's lack of a claim on the children had been heavy, but tinged with disappointment rather than anger. As I pushed the Audi along the blacktop, I studied the old man. His moustache was flecked with spittle. There was some tough thinking going on. I cleared my throat to get his attention. 'So what's Adrian's problem?'

'There won't be a problem, Hunter . . . just expect him to be reticent in accepting your help.'

'My help or yours, Don?'

'That son of a bitch doesn't deserve *my* help . . .'

I had got it then. In Don's mind, Adrian had failed to keep Brook safe and it was highly likely that the recriminations had been flying back and forth between them. With Don bringing in outside assistance, it would only rub further salt in the rawest of wounds. What Don suggested was that Adrian might feel his manhood was being threatened. Well, this wasn't a pissing contest; it was all about Millie and the kids and neither of the men should be allowed to compromise that.

'I'll step carefully around him, OK?' I was no knight in shining armour, as Don had sarcastically put it, no paragon of virtue, but I still considered myself a man of morals and integrity. In my book that meant that Adrian had a huge say in his children's welfare.

'Treat him any way you please. He's a gold-digging son of a bitch and he'd have *nothing* if it weren't for marrying Brook,' he said.

My grunt told Don how pathetic I found his aversion to his son-in-law, but to be sure, I reminded him, 'Apart from two beautiful children, Don.'

'Not if I get my way . . .'

Before I could tell him how pitiful he sounded, a trilling phone interrupted my thoughts.

I looked down at my phone cradled in the hands-free holder on the dashboard, but by the way Don scratched through his pockets he was the one who had an incoming call.

Don pulled out a Samsung that looked tiny in his thick fingers. He flipped it open and juggled it to his ear.

'Millie? What's happened?'

The tone of Don's voice, the way his bottom lip hooked over his teeth, were enough for me to stop the car. I pulled in at the side of the road, in the shade of the fir trees towering over us. I tensed, ready to spin the car round if need be.

Don held out a hand, made waving motions. He quickly glanced across to make sure his instructions were clear: keep going.

I waited though. A bead of perspiration broke from Don's hairline and trickled down his forehead. It shivered on his thick eyebrows. I didn't need to hear Millie's words to understand that something terrible had happened.

'We're going back,' I said, thrusting the gearstick into reverse.

'No, no, wait,' Don said. 'It's over. Best that we get to the kids. *Right now.*'

Shifting gears, I gave the Audi throttle, the tyres spitting up a shower of gravel and pine needles as they bumped back on to the road. According to Don's vague directions we couldn't be far from Adrian's house now and I pushed the car to its limits as we raced the last few miles. Don got the space to speak to Millie while I concentrated on keeping the car on the uneven blacktop. The only time I snapped him a glance was when I heard Don say, 'No, Millie. Whatever you do, do *not* call the sheriff's office. Just keep the gun handy and keep all the doors locked. We'll be back for you in no time.'

Don shut the phone and pushed it into his shirt pocket with trembling fingers. 'Dear God . . .'

'What happened?'

Don closed his eyes, all his thoughts directed inward. He let out a long sigh laden with all the grief he'd felt at the loss of one daughter. His in-breath had to be relief that his other child had escaped a similar fate.

'Don! What the hell has happened?'

Don finally opened his eyes, but he was seeing nothing other than his inner thoughts. 'I was right, Hunter.'

'Someone tried to hurt Millie?' The question was redundant even before it left my mouth.

'She's OK. Thank God. But I was right. I told you, goddamnit! Hicks sent a man to kill my daughter. He went in *my* house after *my* daughter.'

'We should go back,' I said.

'No. Don't you get it, Hunter? That's three of the bastards; the two that you killed and now this son of a bitch. If there are three of them it could mean there's more. We have to get Beth and Ryan out of here now.'

There was no argument to that.

Don's phone trilled again, and he handled it like it was a hot coal as he juggled it up to his ear.

'No, no, no, Millie. You wait right there . . . aah, goddamnit!'

He snapped the phone shut, threw it on to the curve of the dashboard. The phone immediately slid off and into the footwell next to his feet, but he left it there as if the phone was the bearer of all his woes.

'What?' I demanded.

'Millie's following us up here. She's found the keys to my Lexus.'

'Maybe it's not such a bad idea,' I said. 'It's better if we get everyone together.'

Don shook his head. 'That'll only make us a sitting target. They'll be able to get us all in one go.'

'It's easier to defend one location.'

'But way out here? We'll be too vulnerable.'

'At least you won't have to worry about the cops turning up.'

Don squinted at me.

'You told Millie that she mustn't call the sheriff. It's obvious that you don't want them involved.'

'I don't, Hunter. You killed those men this morning. It's probably better for you that the cops don't come snooping around.'

'You're not concerned about me, Don. There's another reason you don't want the police involved.'

'My reputation . . .'

'Bollocks! Your reputation was shit all those years ago, why'd it bother you now?'

The old man folded his arms, resting his chin on his chest like a sullen child. 'Just forget it, will you? We call the cops, they'll split us up. There'll be no way to protect the kids then.'

'The police can protect them better than I can,' I said.

Don slowly lifted his head. All the anger and deceit had gone out of him. Now he just looked like a scared old man. 'I don't believe that, Hunter. You have the skills I need to get the job done.'

Down-gearing, I spun the Audi into a wide driveway between towering red-brick gateposts. The drive had been topped with crushed seashells that pattered on the undercarriage. I reasoned that the noise was what set my teeth on edge, but I was fooling myself.

The skills Don referred to were those I'd gleaned as a hunter of dangerous men. For fourteen years I'd honed those abilities while stalking terrorists and enemy combatants, shooting, knifing and even killing with my bare hands. Killing a man is easy. On the other hand, protecting someone is about the most difficult task in the world. I'd learned that lesson well, and it still cut a slice from my heart every time I thought about Kate Piers.

'I'm not *that* good.'

'That's not the way I see it.'

'It takes a team, Don. One man isn't capable of offering round-the-clock protection. However you see it.'

'I don't want you to wait around to take a bullet, Hunter. It makes more sense to be proactive and—'

'Hold it! Before I came here, I told you, Don. I'm not a killer for hire.'

'Aren't you?'

The Audi crunched to a stop in front of a large house that looked like it had been plucked from an estate in the English countryside and dumped here amid the Allegheny Mountains. We stared at each other, Don's gaze boring into mine. My glare was ice-hard. Like the feeling that had just dug into my soul.

'You killed for me before,' Don said, his voice barely above a whisper.

'I was a soldier following orders.' My voice was as cold as my anger.

'And taking a wage,' Don added. 'So what's the goddamn difference this time?'

My fingers gripped the steering wheel. Damaged hand or not, the leather covering creaked under them.

For the briefest of moments Don must have wondered if he'd gone too far. He visibly readied himself for a blow which he wouldn't even see coming. But I wasn't looking at him now. My gaze had zoned past him to the two children racing from the hastily opened front door. They came at a run, their little faces bright with excitement and love for their grandfather.

I blinked, sighed wearily. 'Take them inside, Don.'
'What about you?'
'I'll be right behind you.'
This time the children were the difference.

10

Bedford Well boasted only a part-time police resource, and right now the two constables were conspicuous by their absence. If Millie Griffiths had telephoned to report the intruder in her home it would be some time before a squad car responded from Hertford, which was a good fifteen-minute run even on blue lights and sirens all the way.

'Don't think we have to worry about the cops turning up.'

Vince was behind the wheel of a nondescript Ford Focus, dark blue but smeared with trail dirt so that it blended with the colourless drizzle. He'd have preferred a pink Cadillac with chrome trims and whitewalls – more befitting his retro image – but the Ford made more sense. Across from him, Sonya sat with one shoe propped on the dash, flashing him the smooth flesh of her inner thigh each time she rocked her knee along with the country music coming from the stereo. When she didn't respond, Vince explained, 'Looks like Millie's on her way out.'

Millie got into the Lexus and reversed on to the road round the green. She glanced about before setting off. Vince and Sonya both slid down in their seats until the Lexus went by the alleyway where they were parked. Millie didn't see them, too intent on her destination for that. Vince popped up again and twisted the ignition key. Sonya shuffled upright and again propped her foot on the dash. Her mini had crept higher and now the show was even more distracting.

'You mind?'

Sonya glanced at him.

'Gotta concentrate on the road, babe. Can't do that with my eyes straying to your stocking-tops every coupla seconds.'

Sonya slowly lowered her foot, nipped both knees together primly. She sucked her nose chain into the corner of her mouth. 'Like, you can't multitask?'

'It's one thing taking a leak while whistling "Dixie"; quite another keeping my eyes off something as beautiful as you.'

'Shut up!' She slapped him on the forearm playfully, her eyes large, lashes batting. Vince shook his pompadour and a curl flopped strategically across his forehead. Sonya feigned unimpressed. She arched her fingertips on her knees, jutted her chin, her gaze skyward. Vince grinned, but then he turned back to the road. He nosed the Ford out of the alley, looking for the Lexus. It was a good way down the main street, accelerating towards the town limit signs.

'Where's she going?'

'To her father, I'm guessing,' Vince said as he pulled into the road.

'You going to stop her, Vince?' Her eyes flashed with excitement.

'Would like to, babe, but not yet.' The plan was to see to Millie inside the house without Sonya bearing witness. He would have done it too if it hadn't been for that damn cat! He touched the scratches on his face and found that they were still oozing blood. He cursed under his breath. 'But the plan was always flexible.'

'It was?'

'Yeah.'

'No one told me.'

'Didn't want to worry you, babe.'

'What's to worry about? At least next time I get to watch . . .'

'Sure, babe,' Vince said. He gave the Ford an extra nudge so that he still had a view of the Lexus up ahead. Rain had begun to fall with more vigour now, splinters of ice mixed in with it, and visibility was little more than a few hundred yards.

'Maybe next time I can, like, help?'

Vince sniffed. 'Not a good idea, babe.'

'Why not? You know I've got what it takes.'

Vince recalled the way Sonya wielded a knife. A redneck trucker had tried his luck with her in the washroom of a roadside diner. Vince almost felt sorry for the punk. Yeah, she had what it took all right.

'Griffiths' visitor might be there.'

Sonya shrugged. 'You mean that lame guy?'

Vince nodded. The way the man had stared back at him had stuck like a thorn in his brain. It was a constant scratch. The more he thought about it, the more he felt uneasy. The killer's eyes might only have been a trick of the light, but Vince had to concede he'd need to take his presence seriously. It was no coincidence that he had turned up at the Griffithses' house at the most inopportune of moments. Vince got the feeling that Don Griffiths had called in the man as extra muscle.

Those damn emails, he thought. Now Griffiths was on high alert and readying himself.

'He could be more dangerous than he looks,' he said.

Sonya snorted, then reached into her jacket pocket. She pulled out a flick knife and snicked open the blade. 'An old gimp? What the hell is he going to do to stop us?'

Kill us.

Vince didn't say the words, but they went through him like a jag of electricity. He gripped the wheel, took a sharp glance over at the Seven-Eleven at the outskirts of town. The lot was busy with customers but there was no sign of who Vince expected.

'Now where the hell do you think Rooster and Cabe are? They were supposed to meet us here hours ago.'

'Probably got themselves in trouble on the drive over,' Sonya said. 'You know Rooster? He's, like, a complete nut, that boy!'

'Not like Cabe to let him get outa line, though,' Vince mused.

'Rooster brings trouble to him. It's his ugly face, I guess . . .' Sonya fiddled with the knife, closing and opening it again.

She had a point there but Vince didn't add to it. Rooster and Cabe were a pair of goons, sure enough, but usually they were reliable.

Vince didn't think that their absence would change anything. The rest of the gang had got in last night and had already set up. And even without Rooster and Cabe, they far outnumbered those who would be in the Reynolds house.

A fucking cat won't be enough to save you this time, Millie, he thought as he dabbed a finger to his oozing wounds.

Even the man with killer's eyes won't be enough.

11

Ordinarily direct action is the order of play. Throughout my military career and beyond I've always believed in taking the war directly to my enemies. Sitting around waiting to be attacked never plays well with me. Except this time I'd no option.

I looked across to where the two small children clung to their grandfather's legs, staring up at him with a mix of adulation and fear. Clearly they loved the old man, but they were astute enough to pick up on Don's disquiet. He had been careful to avoid mentioning anything in front of the children but his body language screamed his unease to all in the room.

Beth and Ryan were full of questions, most delivered by the whites of their huge eyes, and Don tried to reassure them with hugs and pats of his trembling fingers on their heads. The kids cast occasional glances my way and I smiled at them. That didn't help. On the contrary, the children grew more concerned; maybe my smile looked more like a grimace of pain.

Finally, Don ushered the children across the sitting room.

'Who wants ice cream?' he asked. Anything to distract them.

'They haven't had breakfast yet. They're not allowed treats until after they've eaten.'

Adrian Reynolds had met us at the door with enough disdain that it radiated from him like a chill wind. He hadn't spoken since, and now that he did it was with a continuation of his apparent disapproval. He scowled my way, then at Don.

'I think we can make an exception this time, Adrian,' Don said, his eyes steady on the younger man's face. 'What do you say, guys? Ice cream . . . or would you prefer pancakes?'

'Pancakes,' Ryan said.

'Ice cream,' Bethany corrected.

Ryan's face split into a grin. 'Pancakes *and* ice cream!'

Don chuckled, but the humour sounded forced. He snapped a final look at his son-in-law, before leading the children from the room. 'Pancakes and ice cream it is.'

Adrian snorted and folded his arms on his chest as small feet rushed towards the kitchen. It was like Don had said earlier; where the kids were concerned Adrian had no say.

Following Adrian's lead, I crossed my arms.

Body language again spoke volumes.

The tableau held for a half-minute while we both studied each other from across the room. Finally Adrian asked, 'So, are you going to tell me what the hell *you're* doing here, buddy?'

'I'm Joe Hunter.'

'I didn't ask your name. I asked what you're doing in my home.'

'I'm not your buddy. Call me Hunter. Then maybe we can start again.'

Adrian sneered. 'OK, *Hunter*, what the hell are you doing here?'

'Don asked me to come. You don't want me here . . . fair enough. But I'm not here for you.'

'Then get the fuck out of my house.'

'No.'

Adrian grunted. He took a step forward but then thought better of it and rocked back on his heels. He was a big guy, as tall and muscular as my friend Rink. The difference being Adrian's muscles looked the product of gymnasiums and personal trainers, not the type developed in the brutal arena of warfare. In the corded tendons of my crossed arms he probably recognised the futility of getting into a pissing competition he couldn't win.

'Don hired you? What are you, some sort of bodyguard?'

'I'm just an old friend.' The final word came out after the briefest of pauses, but Adrian picked up on it.

'Friend? Don doesn't have friends. All he has is people who owe him or people who hate him. Which are you, Hunter?'

'I don't owe him a damn thing.'

The big man gave a bark of laughter. 'Maybe we do have something in common after all.'

'If you're referring to keeping the kids safe, you're right.' I allowed the corners of my lips to turn up, but the smile had as much effect as it had on the children.

'Has Don suckered you into his bullshit paranoia?'

You're not paranoid if everyone is after you. The thought brought back the quack-wisdom of one of my combat instructors at Arrowsake. The arms instructor had been drilling his troop on the importance of being constantly aware of the potential for danger, using a traffic-light sequence to explain the heightened level a soldier must work on while in the field. 'Red always,' he'd bawled. 'Green's for cattle, orange is for civvies. You don't stay at red, boys, you're fuckin' dead!'

A freckle-faced Scot named Gregor Stewart fancied himself as the troop clown. He'd quipped, 'Don't worry, boys, you're no' really paranoid if everyone is after you.'

The instructor immediately swept Gregor's feet from under him and jammed the barrel of his SIG in the young trooper's ear. 'Out there *everyone is after you*, boy.'

After that Gregor stayed in the red zone; at least for as long as it took him to stop blushing.

Shaking my head, relegating the memory to a corner of my mind, I looked at Adrian. I nibbled at a lip in thought. 'Your wife was killed.'

'An accident. A tragic accident, that's all it was.'

'Maybe,' I conceded, 'but Millie was just attacked in her home.'

'She was *what*?' Adrian's arms finally unfurled, his hands spread as he grasped at handfuls of air. For the first time he looked anything but bitter. 'Is she . . . ?'

'She's OK. She's on her way here.'

'What happened?'

'I haven't had the full story from Don yet, but, reading between the lines, someone broke into the house and tried to attack her. Does that sound paranoid to you?'

Adrian's dark hair had been perfectly brushed until now. He jammed his sweating palms through it and left it standing at odd angles. 'Holy Jesus,' he moaned. 'Then Don was right? No, that can't be. Brook was killed in an accident. It couldn't possibly be connected.'

Horror spread across Adrian's features and for a second I felt sorry for the man. It was bad enough for me losing my wife Diane through divorce, but to have your wife burned to ash in a road accident was a hundred times worse. To then consider that such a shocking tragedy could have been murder must have been torture.

Adrian shook his head. 'No. It must be a mistake. Whoever attacked Millie . . . well, it must have been random. Some vagrant who thought the house was empty. Maybe he watched you and Don driving away and saw an opportunity and broke in looking for money or something to sell for drugs.'

He was babbling, his words running together as he tried to find a theory he was happy with. I thought about mentioning the two I'd killed in the early hours but decided against it. 'We'll find out when Millie gets here.'

'That's another thing!' Adrian's hands went through his hair again. 'Why is Millie coming here? She should wait for the cops at her place.'

'She didn't call the police.' To allay Adrian's response, I said, 'Don told her not to.'

'He did what? What the hell is he doing?'

I don't know, and I don't like it, I thought. There was more to Don's reticence than protecting me from a murder charge.

'Don told me you know nothing of his past,' I said. 'You know he was a cop, right? But what about before that?'

'Brook told me that he was in the military years ago.'

'He was a marine,' I agreed. 'When he demobbed he went back to university and graduated with honours, met his wife, raised his family. He took another job to make ends meet.'

Adrian was peering at me, mouth open, wondering no doubt what all of this had to do with anything and why it should affect the here and now.

I went on, 'He worked as an analyst and profiler, Adrian.'

'That sounds like something the FBI would do?'

I shook my head. 'Not FBI. Don was recruited by a private firm. It was the equivalent of the modern-day risk assessment companies you hear about; those "think tanks" that work on behalf of the government.'

'Are you telling me that Don was a spy?' Adrian laughed out a single syllable that sounded like the bark of a dog. 'You're serious?'

'Depends on your take on the word. He didn't work in the field, if that's what you mean. It was Don's job to collect and analyse information, to identify and then track possible domestic terrorist and extremist groups. Sounds like a modern phenomenon, but even back in the eighties and early nineties radical extremist groups were a substantial threat to the stability of the nation. As the Cold War was ending, more immediate enemies were being identified on a regular basis. White supremacists, right-wing paramilitary groups, religious cults – you name it. Don was tasked with finding these people before they acted out their demented plans.'

'And that's how you got to know him?'

Looking down at the carpet as though all the bad memories of those times were hidden in a secret weave of the pattern, I decided that confession might be good for the soul.

'I was on a team that brought these groups to task. Don was only one of many analysts who fed us the intelligence necessary to complete our missions.'

'You were with *our* government?'

'I was a soldier.'

'But . . . you're a Brit, aren't you?'

'My team was made up of specialists from a number of NATO countries.'

'Specialists?'

My eyes strayed to the carpet again.

Adrian blinked in dismay. 'Maybe I'm jumping to conclusions here, but are you telling me that you were an assassin?'

That snapped my chin up, my eyes going as cold as the underbelly of a glacier. 'I was a soldier.'

'Whose mission was to take down these extremists? Is there a difference?'

'We didn't kill them all.'

I watched as the man went through a range of emotions. Finally, Adrian nodded to himself as though he'd come to some conclusion.

'Carswell Hicks.'

'You've heard of Hicks?' That surprised me.

'Brook once mentioned that her father was involved in his capture. But I never gave it much thought. I assumed he was just one of many cops on the task force that brought him down.'

'Don wasn't a cop when Hicks was captured. But he was *the* person instrumental in capturing him. He compiled the file that was handed to the FBI and it was Don's evidence that guaranteed Hicks received a death sentence for his crimes.'

'Except Hicks never did get the lethal injection, did he?'

No, he never did. Human rights activists fought for Hicks and had his sentence commuted to life imprisonment in a high-security prison. I thought that of all the extremists Don identified Hicks was the most deserving of a bullet in the skull. Instead I said, 'Last I heard he died while attempting to break out of jail. Some of his supporters staged an attack on the hospital wing he'd been moved to following an injury. During the getaway, Hicks and his colleagues supposedly perished when they crashed the medi-vac chopper they'd hijacked. But Don believes that he's back and it's Hicks who's trying to destroy him by targeting his family.'

'But how could that be possible?'

'Don sent Hicks to prison. But there were others involved in his organisation. Maybe they're finally looking for payback.'

'Dear God . . .'

I nodded slowly.

'Now you know who I am, and what the fuck I'm doing here. Do you still want me to leave?'

12

Millie's arrival was announced by a spray of fragmented shells as she gunned the Lexus up the drive and then swung alongside my Audi with a screech of brakes. She clambered out of the car, ducked back inside and came out holding a bundle in her arms just as Adrian opened the door, with me at his shoulder.

Millie's face was rigid with fear. No, that wasn't quite right. Her face was set with anger, and it was directed only one way. Adrian stepped forward, but I pushed past him. As I moved quickly on to the drive my limp was forgotten, and my hand seemed in full working order from the way it dipped into my waistband and came out gripping the matt black SIG SAUER P226 that went everywhere with me. Holding the gun down by my thigh I stalked past Millie and partway along the drive, searching for anyone who might have followed her here. Behind me came the urgent words of Adrian and Millie, which sounded like both were casting bitter recriminations. They were joined seconds later by Don's baritone. I tried to shut out their voices as I listened to the forest. All that came back was the rattle and hiss of the trees swaying in the breeze, and the drip of rain pattering on the ground. Dissatisfied, I completed a full circle while attuning to the natural rhythm of my surroundings.

No vehicle was moving along the road beyond the gates. I couldn't discern the movement of bodies slinking through the woods. I caught no clink of metal or brush of a boot heel through the undergrowth, but still I wasn't happy. I felt that *they* were here.

I could almost feel eyes upon me and it wasn't a feeling I was about to dismiss. My biggest problem was that I couldn't vector in on where the unknown watcher crouched. My gaze went back in the direction of the house and the knot of family members all converging in the driveway. Even the children had joined them, and the little ones were fussing over the bundle in Millie's arms. Christ, I thought, she's even brought the cat with her.

'Everyone get inside.' I began to hurry back to them. They were all bunched around Millie, asking questions in a rapid-fire manner and not one of them even glanced my way. 'Now!' I shouted. 'Get inside the house!'

The family group all turned as one, gawping. Little Ryan even took a couple of hurried steps away, and it was only then that I realised I was gesturing with the barrel of my gun. I quickly lowered it so that it was hidden by my hip.

'What is it?' Don was moving in the wrong direction, towards me instead of the house.

They're here. I wanted to shout out loud, but knew to do so would panic the children. Keeping calm, I went to the old man and gripped him by his elbow. 'Get your family inside, Don.'

Don's tightening features said it all. He grabbed at the children and pulled them to him, at the same time ushering Adrian and Millie towards the front door. He glanced back at me but I gave him no mind, once more turning my attention to the woods. I was in a semi-crouch, unconsciously offering a smaller target. Little good it would do against a man with a scope on a rifle, but it was as much a natural reaction as it was a product of my training.

'What in God's name is going on?' Adrian was torn between pulling the children out of Don's grasp and racing for cover.

Neither won out, and he swerved round Don to demand answers.

'Get back inside,' I hissed at him.

Adrian had no idea of the danger he was in.

His first inkling would have been when the high-velocity round punched through his upper torso. His flesh and bones were no impediment to a steel-jacketed round, and the bullet only flattened when it hit a wheel of Don's Lexus.

Adrian barely staggered.

Then he looked down, mouth hanging open in shock as he saw the hole in his shirt that had opened up like a blooming rose.

Very, very slowly he blinked.

Around me time and motion had slowed.

A guttural moan arose from Adrian.

It felt like I was wading through a bog. Adrian's eyes widened perceptively as he registered the dismay on my face as I looked at the crater in his chest. His mouth moved but I could hear nothing but my own moan emanating from somewhere deep inside. Then I turned away and my hand came up as slowly as a feather in an up-draught.

Crack!

The sound imploded within my skull, pushing down the moan for the briefest of seconds.

Crack! Crack! Crack!

Flame – beautiful, blue, edged in yellow – shot from my gun in time with the jarring staccato rhythm.

My vision zeroed in on the glorious colours, which in the next instant were replaced by a seeping scarlet that clouded like ink in water. The red zone enfolded me.

Reality crashed to life around me.

Adrian fell face first on the driveway and didn't move.

I fired another volley of shots, but I was shooting blind. No way could I tell where the bullet that killed Adrian had come from. Then I turned and rushed towards the others. Seeing Adrian fall they'd all stopped. Shock dominated them.

'Get inside,' I yelled.

Wishing to draw fire towards me, I ran from the family as they clambered for the front door, went over to Adrian and clutched at the man. I'm no doctor, but I'd seen enough dead bodies to know that Adrian had joined their ranks. Still, I grasped Adrian's arm and began dragging him towards the cover offered by the parked cars. A round caromed off the roof of the Audi, the spent bullet spinning away into the woods on the far side. I pulled Adrian between the two vehicles. Judging by the direction from which the last bullet was fired, I was now out of the shooter's line of sight but that meant nothing. A round from a rifle could pass directly through the body of a vehicle with little problem. Ducking low, placing the front wheel between us and the unknown rifleman, I rolled Adrian over on to his back. Adrian's glassy eyes confirmed my initial prognosis, but I still pressed the tips of my fingers to the pulse point in his throat. There was only the putty-like feel of death.

'Fuck sake,' I sighed. Not very articulate, but it about summed up my feelings. I'd barely met Adrian Reynolds, and though I didn't necessarily care for the man the senselessness of his death weighed heavily on my shoulders. It was a growing burden.

I popped up from cover, fired a short group of three rounds. Ducked low again.

A bullet shattered the windscreen of the Audi. Another punctured the front right tyre, thankfully the one on the far side.

I'd been counting my bullets. Eleven of seventeen were gone already. Feeling for a spare magazine, I found one tucked into my hip pocket. All the others were locked in the boot of my car. No way could I reach them without giving the shooter a clear target.

Crabbing to the rear of the car, I bobbed up again and fired the remaining six rounds in the clip. I swept my arm in an arc that took in twenty yards of the treeline in a little under two seconds. Even as I was ducking, my thumb worked the release on the gun and dropped the depleted magazine, and I rammed the other one in place. Then I was up and running, only vaguely aware of the scar tissue tugging horrendously in my thigh.

Bullets followed my trajectory towards the house, streaking by a foot behind as the shooter tried to adjust his aim on my charging figure. Then I threw myself at the door that the family had slammed behind them in their haste. The door crashed open as I thrust my way through it. I spun and kicked it to. A bullet cut through the wood, tugged at my shirtsleeve.

Swearing again, more savagely than before, I realised that this bullet had come from another direction. Evidently we were up against more than one attacker.

The door wasn't solid enough to stop a bullet, but it would halt a man for a while. Risking another round, I twisted the locks and threw a bolt in place. Then I sprinted for the back of the house following the babble of voices and crying children.

'Get away from the windows,' I shouted, even before I reached the kitchen where they were gathered.

There was a splintering bang at the front door, someone ramming against it with a shoulder.

I twisted and fired a shot through the door and was rewarded by a shout of surprise. There was no pain in the words, which meant I'd missed, but at least the attacker fell back.

I'd still no idea how many were out there, or who they were. It didn't matter now. The time for pondering such nuances was over and all that mattered was doing everything in my power to stop them getting inside. Millie and the children were, and always would remain, my priority, though, and I wanted to check that they were safely tucked away. Last thing

I needed was for a stray shot to find its way to them. I headed for the kitchen.

What I found didn't bode well for getting them to follow instructions. Millie had the two children enfolded in her arms as she crouched low behind a granite-topped island in the centre of the room. Both children were hysterical, screaming for their dead daddy who they'd watched gunned down. Millie was crying too, but her tears were more for the children than their father. Don was grabbing at his shirt front with both hands as he paced back and forth, muttering to himself.

'Don,' I snapped. 'Get a hold of yourself, man. We have to . . .'

Have to what?

I wasn't sure.

If it was just me, I'd take the fight to my enemies and show them the folly of their attack. But my actions now had to be governed by the need to keep the children safe.

I asked, 'Where's your gun? Did Millie bring it with her?'

Don looked to Millie who glanced up from the crying children. She looked forlorn. Lost. 'I left it in the car,' she moaned. 'I'm sorry . . .'

I moved towards the back door. Threw the bolts in place. Turned back to Don. 'What about Adrian, did he have a weapon?'

Don shook his head. 'No, not that I know of.'

'Check,' I told him. 'He may have one hidden somewhere so that the children couldn't get their hands on it. A strongbox; possibly in his bedroom.'

'You want me to go upstairs? I'm not leaving my family!'

'OK. But at least grab a knife or something. If they get inside, we have to be ready to fight them.'

Even as I said those words they proved more than prophetic. It wasn't a case of *if* but *when* the attackers stormed the house. They'd be coming soon, that was for sure.

'Now, Don. You as well, Millie.'

'But the children,' she said.

'They'll be safer if you have some way of defending them.'

Don rushed across to a counter and opened drawers. He pulled at utensils, sorting through a clutter of silverware, and came out with a broad-bladed knife. He held it out to Millie who took it from him tentatively. Then he rattled through the drawer until he found a meat cleaver. Neither knife looked like they'd seen use in the past.

Taking my own advice, I dipped a hand to my left ankle to retrieve the military KA-BAR sheathed in my boot.

I glanced at the motley bunch of defenders. Knives wouldn't do much to halt the concerted attack of enemies coming with rifles and handguns but they were better than nothing. Hopefully my SIG would even up the score a little.

Fleetingly I wished I'd thought to call Rink sooner. My big friend would have been a welcome ally just then.

I looked for a telephone. There was one on the wall next to the cooking range.

Not that I had the time to call Rink but a rapid 911 emergency wouldn't go amiss. All I'd have to do was stab in the numbers and the emergency call would be picked up. Even if there wasn't an opportunity to speak to the operator, I could leave the line open and the situation would be overheard. The cops would be coming.

Probably too late to help us, but I had to try.

Don had forbidden Millie from calling the constables, but that was under different circumstances. Fuck him, I thought as I reached for the phone.

'We've already tried,' Don said. 'The line's dead. I think whoever's out there cut it.'

Ignoring him, I picked up the handset. Listened to empty sound. Slammed down the receiver.

'You must have your cell?' I said, but recalled Don throwing it on the dashboard of the Audi on the way here, and the phone clattering in the footwell. In his anger, the old man hadn't picked it up again. 'Millie? What about you?'

Millie shook her head slowly. 'I rang my dad from the house. I didn't remember to bring mine. I was in too much of a panic and I just grabbed the cat and the car keys and got out of there.'

'Shit,' I growled. And I could just bet that if Adrian had a cell phone it would be in his bloody trouser pocket and as inaccessible to us now as all the rest. Of course I couldn't complain about any of the others' short-sightedness, not when my own phone was mounted in the hands-free holder in the Audi.

The cops wouldn't be coming. It was solely down to me to save these people from a brutal death. It wasn't a job I'd envy any man.

And judging by the crashing at the front door, I'd be called to task very soon.

13

Samuel Gant strode back and forward just inside the treeline that bordered Adrian Reynolds' home, directing the attack over a radio he brandished like a flaming torch. None of the others disputed his position.

He wasn't the largest of men, but there was more to him than the assault rifle he carried that won him the respect of his followers. He was a proven killer, but again so were the others, so that wasn't why he commanded them without question. He looked quite sinister, with his pale, almost yellow eyes and skin like wrinkled parchment, an intricate pattern of tattoos beginning above his right eyebrow and extending down below the collar of his coat. Hidden amongst the Celtic symbolism was a repeated pattern of numbers: eight-eight inked in scarlet over a stylised swastika. Normally, strangers didn't get close enough to spot the hidden numbers. But he made no secret of them; anyone who met him knew that he was a white supremacist, and anyone who didn't get the message early on found out soon enough. Usually at their own expense and paid for in agony.

Gant was supremely vicious. He would kill for the most minor reason, and sometimes his fury was even inflicted on those who considered him an ally. But he was also shrewd and a born leader. That was why Carswell Hicks had elevated him to his right hand, and why Gant had commanded his army while Hicks had been otherwise detained.

He had ten men at his disposal. A further three, plus that punk rocker bitch joining them soon. Fifteen of them against

Don Griffiths and his family. Ordinarily that would be ample, but that was before the stranger had arrived with Griffiths. Gant had no idea who the man was, but he knew he was going to be trouble. It was almost as if the man had sensed the rifle Gant aimed at him. For some unknown reason Gant had pulled his aim away, swung it on Adrian Reynolds instead. Maybe he just wanted to find out what kind of man Don Griffiths had at his back.

When the stranger had responded, Gant had been forced down on his belly. One of the retaliatory bullets had come so close to his head that he'd felt the disturbance in the air beside him. By the time he'd made it back to a firing position, the man had dragged Reynolds to cover between the parked cars and he'd missed the opportunity to finish him.

Now he wondered if he'd made the wrong decision in killing Reynolds first. This man knew about guns. He also had the finely tuned senses of a warrior and though he'd initially moved as though in pain, he definitely looked like someone capable of holding his own in battle.

Gant cursed to himself. The hit on the Griffiths family should have been a sure thing, but now he wasn't so confident. It was going to be more difficult than anticipated. He glanced around at the crew he'd assembled. To hell with them, he thought, they're expendable. As long as I'm still standing, who gives a flying fuck?

Gant watched as one of his men, a tall skinhead called Howard, expended bullets through the closed front door of the house, then had to dive clear when the stranger fired back. Give the idiot his due, Howard went back at the door like he'd been ordered and started butting it with his shoulder.

Gant called to the others over his radio. He sent some round the back. Others were dispatched to deal with the Lexus and Audi, setting the cars aflame so that the family had no quick way out. Then he ordered a full-frontal assault on the house.

As he charged across the lawn towards the back of the house, he said: 'Let's see just how dangerous this asshole really is.'

14

I didn't know it at the time, but the Reynolds house was erected over one hundred years ago, built by an English gentleman who desired a reminder of his homeland deep in the Pennsylvanian mountains. He'd brought in master architects and craftsmen, and had used the best of materials to create a house that would stand firm against the elements. Over the intervening decades it had defied the storms and blizzards that occasionally shrieked through the northern Alleghenies, resisting with the stiff-upper-lip character of its creator. But extreme weather was one thing. The house didn't stand a chance against assault rifles and explosives.

Rounds blasted the hinges of the front door, and then someone threw their weight against it. The heavy door crashed back against the inner wall, the sound echoing through the house like the tolling announcement of Doomsday, which would prove apt if I didn't get my arse in gear.

'Don! Millie! Get round this side of the island.' I gestured to the granite-topped counter, indicating the side least exposed to the back door. 'Keep your heads down and only use those knives if you have to.'

'We'll be trapped here,' Millie croaked as she ushered the children to their hiding place.

I nodded sharply. She was right, but at least the granite would stop some of the bullets. Then I swung to the door jamb, pushing against it with a hip as I aimed my SIG at the men hurtling along the vestibule at us. I picked my target, calm and measured. Crack! Crack! Crack!

A tall skinhead led the charge, and it was he who took all three rounds. He crumpled, fell and the H&K assault rifle he dropped rattled along the hall towards me. Not quite far enough, but its position was noted for later. I fired another two rounds, and the two men following let out yelps of pain, both throwing themselves out of the line of fire. One of them was lucky to find an open doorway, but the other caromed off the vestibule wall, taking a family portrait down with him. He scrambled, tried to place himself behind a chest of drawers, but I shot him again, taking the heel off his left foot, and the man screamed in agony.

Another figure appeared at the front door, a quickly moving amorphous shape in my peripheral vision. I fired once, causing the attacker to fall back and I rushed out, scooping up the dead skinhead's H&K. Encumbered by the SIG in one hand and KA-BAR in the other I merely tucked the rifle under my armpit and kept walking.

The shrieking man cradling his blasted foot deserved barely a second's notice. I just swung sideways with the razor-sharp KA-BAR and the screaming stopped. In the next action I'd jammed the military knife into my belt and transferred the SIG to my left hand. The skinhead had thoughtfully primed the rifle. I moved into the room where I'd so recently spoken to Adrian Reynolds. The man I'd forced there brought up his gun but I ripped him to tatters with a controlled burst of the assault rifle. I went and plucked his rifle out of his grasp, swinging it over my shoulder by the carrying strap.

It sounds perfunctory, the way I slaughtered those men, but I was on autopilot, doing what was required. Emotion wasn't necessary. All the interlopers who'd made it thus far were now dead. But this was just the beginning and it could very well be me who was a steaming corpse in the next few seconds.

Like emotion, I couldn't allow that; not if I hoped to save the children.

Returning to the door, I propped the assault rifle round the jamb. Two more men were coming inside. I rattled a storm of rounds at them and saw one of them dance a jig before collapsing beneath a red mist. The other cried out and back-pedalled quickly. He fired as he went, and this time I was the one who had to jerk out of the line of fire. Beside me the door jamb was chewed to shreds. When next I poked my head out, the man was gone, seeking cover outside.

Beyond the open portal were flickering orange flames and gouts of black smoke; the cars were no means of escape now. Had to find another way out. I went into the vestibule and began backing up. 'Don. Millie. Bring the children. You have to get upstairs.'

Just as I said it, there was a detonation from outside. One of the cars exploding? No. That wasn't it. Someone had thrown an explosive device against the side of the house. The blast was followed by the tinkle of glass shattering, the rumble of falling masonry.

Diversionary tactic, I decided. Why would they bother blasting a way inside when there were so many windows and doors to come in by? Whatever the reason, it didn't bode well. My initial thought was to take the family to an upper floor where I'd have more chance of defending them. Little good the high ground would do, though, if grenades were thrown in through the windows at us.

Someone popped into the open front door, a bird-like figure with a hawk nose and large Adam's apple. He fired, and so did I. Neither bullet found its mark as both of us jerked away. Then I was back at the door to the kitchen. I met Don and Millie, each carrying a terrified bundle in their arms. 'Forget it,' I said. 'Get back behind the island.'

'We can't stay here!' Millie cried.

There was a thump at the back door, proving her right. I unslung the second rifle from my shoulder, while passing the first to Don. Encumbered by Beth hanging tightly to his neck, and the meat cleaver in his hand, Don almost dropped the rifle. He allowed the cleaver to fall instead and brought up the gun.

'Don't know how many rounds are left,' I told him, 'so use them wisely.'

There was another splintering thud on the door, and I snapped my gaze that way. Why were they using an axe when they had grenades that would blast the door into fragments?

The thought was fleeting. What did it matter? An axe would get them inside soon enough. Lifting the rifle, I flicked it to semi-auto and fired a short burst directly through the door. It was gratifying to hear another thud, this time as a dead weight fell to the ground.

Glass tinkled, someone lifting a gun through the hole he'd just smashed in the kitchen window. The gun rattled and pots and pans lifted off a counter next to Don. The old man returned fire, but his aim was panicked and wide and drilled holes in the ceiling. Bethany squealed at the rapid chatter of gunfire so close to her face.

'Get out! Get out!' I yelled as I swung to offer covering fire.

I shot at the window, blasting it to smithereens, but also forcing the attacker to throw himself down to avoid being cut to ribbons. Don, Millie and the kids all scrambled past me to get into the vestibule. I swung after them: the hallway was a shooting gallery if another attacker had made it inside.

Luckily the front door remained open and no shadow lurked there. Perhaps the bird-like man who'd ducked outside moments before had gone off in search of a safer route of ingress. I wasn't familiar with the layout of the house, but it was an easy guess that the door opposite led into a utility room. I didn't bother with the handle, just booted the door open and shoved the others inside. I followed, slamming the door and putting my back to the wood. If nothing else I'd stop the bullets before they reached the children.

Shouts filtered into the room. Men were climbing into the kitchen via the shattered window. If I'd urged the family into a dead end . . . well, we were supremely fucked. However, I found that my assumption held some logic. We were in a room furnished with a washing machine, dryer and a dishwasher. From a water heater on the wall pipes led away to the ceiling and floor. I gestured at a small hatch in the wall. 'Through there, quick.'

Millie glanced down at the SIG in my hand. 'Give me a gun.'

'Forget it; just get everyone through the hatch while we have time.'

'But I can help.'

'You can help by doing what I ask. Go, Millie. We've only got seconds before they come through that door.'

Millie opened her mouth to argue, then thought better of it. She turned, hitching Ryan in her arms, even as Don placed Beth down. The little girl was crying, her face as pale as virgin snow. She looked down at the tomcat huddled by her ankles. She stooped and picked it up, and the old tom allowed her to cradle him without complaint. It blinked slowly at me, and I spared a moment to frown back. I'd idly thought that the cat and I had much in common. Well, nine lives would come in very handy.

Don lifted the assault rifle and used the butt to slam open the plyboard hatch. A draught washed over us; smelling the tang of petroleum I sighed with relief. The hatch had once opened into an anteroom that had since been converted to a garage connected to the side of the house. Brook's vehicle had been reduced to a tangled burnt-out wreck, so I could only hope that the Reynoldses had been a two-car family.

Don lifted Beth and her charge through the hatch, followed by Ryan, then there was a moment of pushing and shoving until Don finally went first. He squeezed through the gap, his big body defying the dimensions. Millie turned back to me. Her eyes flashed before she swung round and went through the gap more easily.

The door shuddered behind me. The lock was already burst from my injudicious entry. My weight held the attacker back, but that would only last for so long. Hearing muffled voices, I knew that I didn't have much time left on earth if I didn't get out now.

I ducked across the room expecting to be cut apart by bullets, or ripped into chunks by a frag grenade. Instead I made it to the hatch, just as the door burst inward. I caught the flash of a face – a crazy pattern of tattoos up one side, framing a pinched yellow eye. Then I was through the hatch, thighs bumping painfully on the edge as I flung myself bodily into the garage beyond. Ignoring the pain, I lurched back to throw the hatch closed again. Once more I saw the tattooed face, and caught the glare of hatred its bearer shot at me; but my own return look was equally ferocious. To the right was an old cabinet, like the Welsh dresser that had been in my parents' house when I was a boy. Adrian had reclaimed the old item of furniture to hold the tools he used when he tinkered with his vehicles.

Without urging, Don joined me and together we muscled the dresser in front of the hatch, just as the pounding began on the other side.

I would have cheered if I'd had time, but Millie was already helping the two children and the cat into the back seat of Adrian's vehicle: a minivan that he'd undoubtedly used to transport the kids to and from school. Please, I prayed, let the keys be in the ignition.

They were, and I started the minivan even as Don scrambled into the passenger seat. I revved the engine, looked at the closed door. It was a tin-sheet roller shutter. No time to open it. 'Everyone . . . get your heads down,' I said through gritted teeth. Then I released the brake and the minivan bolted forward.

The door resisted the onslaught, but couldn't withstand it for long. The minivan burst through, the buckling door gouging stripes in the paintwork. The wheels sent up plumes of gravel and shells, and the vehicle slewed to the side before I got it under control. Ahead of us were the flaming carcasses of the Audi and Lexus, and I had to yank on the steering to avoid them. I caught a glimpse of Adrian's body burning like a flare between them and hoped that the kids weren't looking. 'Keep down,' I yelled again. Not to ensure that the children didn't have nightmares – it was already too late for that – but because the bird-like man was rushing towards the minivan lifting a rifle. I'd jammed my guns inside with me, but had no way to shoot the man, not without letting go of the steering wheel, and I saw that Don was equally hindered. Our only chance was to keep going, trust to speed and hope that the man was a lousy shot.

The engine was roaring too hard for me to hear the shouted command, but I saw the man respond. The gun dipped away, and the man just watched in futile fury as we drove past.

I couldn't decide why the man had been denied his shot unless the tattooed leader wanted our deaths to be more personal – or permanent.

I gave the minivan throttle and raced it along the drive, twin fans of seashells marking its progress like spume on waves. Then we'd got as far as the gate on to the mountain road.

'Holy God,' Don muttered under his breath. 'I think we're going to make it!'

'Not yet.' I swung the wheel to the left, away from the relative safety of Bedford Well or the city of Hertford.

On the road, I accelerated away.

Still the minivan wasn't moving fast enough to avoid the Ford Focus rear-ending it.

The collision forced the minivan to fishtail and I had to fight the wheel to keep us going straight. I won the battle, glancing in the rear-view mirror.

Fuck, I thought, as I recognised the pompadour of the Ford's driver, the spiky hair of his passenger. I also recalled my dark humour when first I'd noticed the oddball couple outside Don's house. *Maybe I should have killed you after all.*

15

Having had a good idea where Millie was headed, Vince had thought it best to fall back and allow plenty of distance between them. On the mountain roads, there was very little traffic and the car would stand out, anonymous as it was. No hurry, he'd told Sonya. But there was. He knew that Gant and the others were already in place around Adrian Reynolds' house, and it was imperative he got there before things kicked off.

Sonya had suggested pulling over, having a little fun before joining the others. Chances were that once things got underway they'd be too busy for fooling around. Except Vince wasn't up for it. To keep her happy he'd reached across to her but she'd slapped his hands away.

'Offer's gone, lover boy. We don't want to, like, miss anything, do we?' she said.

'Suppose not,' Vince replied gloomily. He sighed dramatically to cover his relief, and caught a pout from Sonya.

Thinking to appease him, she laid a hand in his crotch as he drove.

'As much as I like that, babe, maybe you'd better fill your hand with something else.'

'I've small hands, isn't it full enough?' she asked with a gleam in her eye.

'I hear you, babe, but I'm serious . . .' He nodded towards the back seat and Sonya twisted round so she could haul the knapsack on to her lap. She unzipped it and tugged out the first of two Glock 19s. Inside the bag were extra magazines and she expertly inserted one into the butt of the gun, racked the slide to arm it, then flicked on the safety. She repeated the process and dropped a gun between Vince's thighs. He whistled.

'Easy, babe, you could have shot off my dick.'

'I'd have to be a better shot than I am to hit that teeny-weeny thing,' she smiled.

'Think you could hit a car?' he asked.

Sonya followed his gaze, watching open-mouthed as a pale blue minivan roared out of a driveway ahead. It was like the vehicles that soccer moms drive, loads of seats in the back to cart around a horde of children. She recognised Don Griffiths in the front passenger seat before the minivan spun away from them.

'Shee-it,' Vince yelled. 'Looks like Gant's blown it, big time.'

He pressed the gas pedal, and raced after the minivan. With momentum on his side, he caught up with it in seconds, rear-ending the heavier vehicle. Coloured glass bounced up the windscreen of the Ford as the van's rear lights shattered, but the van absorbed the collision, then powered away.

Sonya looked left, saw the flames and the smoke around the Reynolds household. 'Can't believe they started without us . . .'

'You know Gant,' Vince snorted. 'Never was the patient type.'

'Do you think he'd want us to stop them?'

Vince raised his eyebrows, puffed out air.

He rammed the pedal to the floor, pushing the Ford on. 'That's why we're here, babe.'

Sonya bounced up and down in her seat in her eagerness to get started. She pressed buttons, lowering her window and leaning out. Wind battered her making her spiky hair dance like Medusa's snakes. She squinted, but that only helped her aim the Glock. She'd been joking a moment ago: she was actually a damn fine shot.

Twice she fired at the back of the minivan. Both bullets struck metal. She heard corresponding screams even over the roaring engines.

'Easy, gal, we just want to stop them.'

Sonya glanced inside the Ford. Stop them? She wanted to kill them all.

'Not much fun if they're all chewed up in a wreck,' Vince explained.

'Dead's dead, whatever way you look at it,' Sonya said, firing again. This time she aimed so that she blasted a mirror off the side of the car. Basically she was showing off.

'Yeah, and Gant will kill us if he doesn't get a chance to—'

Vince stepped on the brakes.

From a side track, concealed until the very last moment by the trees, came a black van. It roared out of hiding, bouncing up on to the road directly in front of the minivan. At this speed the two vehicles would be smashed to pieces, and then the Ford would join them. Vince spun the wheel. Better that they hit side-on than plough right into the wreckage. Sonya was caught by the centrifugal force and almost plucked out of the window, but Vince grabbed at her with one hand, snaring an ankle. With his other hand he wrestled with the steering. If they hit, Sonya would be squashed like a bug. If he let go, she'd tumble out of the Ford, go under the wheels and be squashed all the same. It was way too soon in the proceedings for that.

It was almost a blessing when he saw the minivan swerve off the road and on to the verge. Its tyres dug into the rain-drenched earth, throwing up clumps of dirt and grass. Branches from the overhanging trees scored new lines in the paintwork. Then it was past the front of the black van and had swerved back on to the road. Vince kept his hand down on the wheel and the Ford pirouetted in the road, forces almost beyond his control trying to yank Sonya to her death. Finally, a full one-eighty from where he'd been headed, the Ford screeched to a halt. Its back bumper nudged the idling van.

Sonya clambered back inside, her eyes like twin moons. She was shivering with the excitement of the last few seconds. 'Like, Holy Jesus, Vince! What a ride that was!'

'You OK, babe?' Vince was trembling almost as hard as the girl.

'Freakin'-A, baby! Let's do it again.'

Vince leaned out of his window, craning round to see. A face at the passenger side of the black van blinked back at him in surprise. Goddamn skinhead assholes, Vince thought. The idiots that Gant had brought in were even stupider than Rooster. Repeatedly he slapped a hand on the door of the car. 'Move that goddamn piece of shit, you moron. They're getting away!'

The passenger conveyed the message to the driver – another of Gant's boot boys. When he looked back, he repeated the driver's reply: 'Who ya calling morons, Vince?'

'Just get the fuck outa my way,' Vince snapped. He jammed the car into gear, spinning it in the road and on to the verge that the minivan had churned up. As he powered past the front of the black van Sonya leaned out the window, giving the two skinheads the middle finger.

When she slipped back inside, she bounced a few times on the seat. 'Why are we working with these clowns anyway?'

' 'Cause Gant said we should.'

Sonya frowned. 'Gant can barely lick his lips without drooling, let alone say anything sensible.'

Vince shrugged his shoulders. Then he glanced at his girl. 'Trust me, babe, it's just the way it's gotta be.'

'Fair enough, but if any of those, like, *wieners with ears* gets in our way again, they're going to be sorry.'

'I'm with you, honey cakes. But right now, we'd better catch the family. If they get away Gant won't be pleased.'

'To hell with him. Why's he the boss? You're, like, ten times the man he'll ever be.'

Vince didn't reply. Let Sonya say what she wanted, but he wasn't going to mention anything that might get back to Gant before he was ready. He knew what that would bring him: his head handed to him on a plate.

He concentrated on catching the minivan. Whoever was driving – Vince guessed it was the stranger with the killer's eyes – was doing an expert job of it and it wouldn't be easy. He looked in his mirrors, saw that the black van was following, and from concealment further down the road, other vehicles were joining the pursuit. Gant and the others were coming fast.

The minivan was a hundred yards ahead but the gap was closing. Sonya leaned out of the window, fired a volley at the tyres. Vince didn't comment, but the likelihood of puncturing a tyre at this range and this angle was next to zero; if they were alongside with a shotgun maybe, but not from behind with a handgun. Vince looked for his own gun. Miraculously after the spin the Ford had completed, the gun was still between his thighs. He picked it up and wedged it out his window. Left-handed he'd hit nothing viable, but at least he could lay down enough firepower to keep them moving in the right direction. He fired a half-dozen rounds, saw that, despite the jouncing of the car and the distance, most of them did strike the metalwork.

The minivan swerved, then straightened. Its forward momentum was disrupted and the Ford gained another twenty yards.

'Get ready, babe, I'm gonna try and get alongside them.'

Sonya slapped in a fresh magazine. 'Do that and I'll take the driver out.'

'No,' Vince said. 'Do that and they'll roll. We don't want 'em all to die.'

'Yeah, we do. What's wrong with you, Vince? Lost your sense of fun?'

'Just do as I ask, babe. We want to stop the van. Shoot by all means, but don't shoot—'

'The brats? Gant said that they *all* have to die. Are you calling the shots after all, Vince?'

Vince frowned. He wasn't going to mention the kids. After a second or so, he said, 'I was gonna say "the driver". Don't shoot the driver.'

Sonya looked at him. Her face had gone very still. 'No, you weren't.'

Vince flicked a self-conscious smile. Busted, he thought.

Sonya snorted. 'You don't want me to shoot Millie. You want that bitch all to yourself.'

Vince touched the claw marks on his face, said, 'Can you blame me?'

She shrugged, sucked her nose chain between her teeth. All coy again, she grinned. 'As long as I get to do the children, Vince, I don't care. I've never killed a brat before.'

16

Trees flashed by, twin walls of greens and browns and everything in between. The road surface was asphalt, but the further we progressed it became ill maintained and was warped and rutted. Compounding the difficulty of controlling the vehicle on the damaged road surface was that the rain was growing heavier, forming pools and deep channels that sucked at the tyres and almost threw them out of line. Heavy droplets battered the windscreen, and it was a fight the wipers could barely win. The bullets fired at us added to the effort of keeping the minivan on track and at a steady speed.

I didn't complain, just tried to stay focused on the road ahead. Even a momentary distraction would be enough to send the vehicle into a roll that would do the job for those trying to kill Don Griffiths and his family. If anything the bad road and the rain were allies: they meant those following couldn't be too reckless either.

After almost ramming into the black van, and being forced to take diversionary tactics, I'd just kept going. I'd no idea where we were or where the road would lead to. Both Don and Millie had been unhelpful with directions, concentrating instead on calming and consoling the children. It wasn't an easy task with bullets ricocheting off the vehicle. At least the shooting had slowed over the last few minutes, and the only thing coming our way now was an occasional round fired in frustration.

It felt a little compromising, sitting in the driver's position. Normally I used a car with the steering wheel on the right, but this being an American car it was on the opposite side. I could shoot with my left hand, but nowhere near as well as with the right. Along the way I'd juggled the assault rifle over my shoulder, passing it back to Millie so that I'd have room to use the SIG if it became necessary. For now I concentrated on driving.

Beside me, Don finally settled back into his seat. Millie had the children under control, and she'd got them to crouch down between the seats to afford them a little more protection. She lay across the back seat, keeping her head down, but also so that she could touch both children to help comfort them.

I checked the mirrors – the ones that hadn't been shot off – and saw that four vehicles were doggedly on our tail. The black van had been left behind somewhere along the way. Either that or it had cut down one of the forest trails to try to intercept us further on. That hardly seemed possible, seeing as the road we were on had stretched arrow-straight for the last couple miles. Even as I thought it, though, I saw warning signs showing a series of bends ahead. Also, we were beginning to climb.

'Where does this road lead to?'

Don shook his head. 'No idea. I've never come this way before. I've never had a reason to.'

From the back, Millie said, 'I've been out this way. Me and Brook used to come up here hiking.'

'So what can we expect?' I asked.

'The road climbs up into the mountains. There used to be logging camps up there, but they've all shut down. There's a hydro-electricity plant further on, but the road ends there.'

'Is the plant manned?'

'I don't know. I imagine it is, but we never got that far, I've only seen it from a distance.'

The plant sounded like our best hope of help. At the very least I might be able to force an office door and get to a telephone. 'How far?'

'Twenty miles, maybe more.'

Forget that plan then. At this rate it would take us twenty minutes to get there. Those pursuing us wouldn't wait so long to make their next move.

'We'll have to chance one of the logging camps.'

'They're closed,' Millie reminded me.

'There could still be a telephone hooked up, or a radio or *something*.' In truth I wasn't thinking about phones; I was looking for somewhere that I could mount a defence. Maybe a logging camp would offer hiding places for the children while I could take the fight back to the pack hunting us. I decided that giving the family hope of rescue would stop them from further panic. I met Don's eye. The old man knew what I was thinking. He busied himself with the assault rifle, getting ready to help if a last stand was unavoidable.

'Long time since you've held one of those, I bet,' I said.

'I'd be happier if I never had to handle one ever again. But now that things are looking inevitable . . . well, I'll do the best I can.'

I touched the old man on the forearm. 'I know you will.'

There'd been bad blood between the two of us, but just like me, Don had no real control over the decisions of our superiors. Don's intelligence had caused the deaths of innocents, but he couldn't be held responsible for the bullets spewed from ill-guided weapons. I saw that now and knew that my enmity shouldn't be directed at him, but at our controllers at Arrowsake. It was time to put our differences aside.

Don nodded solemnly at my words. He got their meaning. He opened his mouth to speak, to maybe explain how things had gone so wrong.

'Just leave it be, Don. It's enough that it's behind us now, OK?' What I really wanted to understand was who our pursuers were, and why they were so determined to kill Don's entire family. But now wasn't the time for that either.

Up ahead, the forest had been felled back all the way up the slopes, the hills bare of cover. Rain sheeted across the valley like billowing smoke. The road looked like it had been widened here, possibly to accommodate large machinery, and there was a broad area of hard-packed dirt on one side. A portable cabin once used as a control hub for the worksite had been abandoned. It listed severely to one side where the elements had done their best to wipe it from the landscape, and weeds and brush had sprung up around its base. It was poor cover, and the chances of a working phone or radio inside were nil.

Behind us the vehicles were revving into action, seeing the opening as their best chance for corralling the minivan between them. They were more powerful vehicles than ours and we'd no hope of outrunning them now. From the Ford the spiky-haired woman leaned out the window so that she could get a clear shot. The Ford veered right, swinging on to the hard-pack so that she could fire at Don.

'Everyone get down,' I said stiffly.

Don didn't have much hope for concealment; he was way too bulky to scrunch down in the front seat. Instead, he swung the assault rifle out of the window. It was an awkward angle, and he had to hold the gun wedged under his opposite armpit. He fired off a short burst, but he had more chance of hitting the moon than he did the Ford.

From the back seat the children's cries were plaintive and I felt a pang in my heart.

This is not right, I thought, it's just not right.

Let these bastards come after me and Don, fair enough. I could accept that. But to endanger the children was supremely wrong. It was both cruel and cowardly.

Rage flooded through me like an icy tide.

'Millie,' I said. 'Get the children to cover their ears and close their eyes. Things are about to get scary.'

No sooner had I said it than I slammed on the brakes.

Taken by surprise, the driver of the Ford was slow to react and the car flew past, the woman missing the opportunity to shoot Don. Don twisted the gun, propping it against the door frame and rattled off another short burst. Silver-edged craters appeared in the metal body of the Ford and the car skidded away as the driver took evasive action.

The cabin was now dead in line with the Ford, and I watched as the driver tore at the steering. The Ford clipped the back corner of the cabin, blasting through rotting boards and finishing the job started by the elements. The cabin twisted with the impact and came apart. Wood and dust flew everywhere. The Ford spun out, and it hadn't survived the impact undamaged. Bits of plastic and metal joined the flying detritus. Steam erupted from the engine and blocked any view of its occupants.

Then we were past the wreck, and I floored the throttle as the other vehicles roared after us.

'How far is it to the logging camp?' I called back to Millie.

'Not far now, take the next road to the left.' Millie's voice was as high-pitched as the children's screams.

Next road? Where? Where?

I saw it a hundred yards ahead: a narrow track that was little more than a beaten path winding up the hillside.

You've got to be kidding me, I thought. We'd need a 4×4 to negotiate that trail.

But there was nothing else for it.

Bullets *spanged* off the minivan.

A black SUV roared up on our right, trying to cut us off, and I saw the face of the tattooed man snarling at us as he raised a shotgun. Don struggled to bring the rifle round on him, but he had it wedged, the carrying strap impeding him.

The shotgun flared, the load holing the front fender.

Thankfully he hadn't fired at Don, but at the tyre in an attempt at stopping the van.

'Get back.' I leaned past the old man, my elbow against Don's chest. I wasn't fucking around with trying to disable their vehicle. I aimed the SIG directly at the tattooed man's face.

Fired.

But already the man was reacting, throwing himself backwards as far as his seat would allow.

My bullet missed him, but it didn't matter. It hit an even more viable target.

The driver of the SUV couldn't do his job with most of his forehead missing.

Easing down on the brakes, I watched as the SUV streaked across in front of us at too sharp an angle, and I turned into the trail even as the SUV flipped and rolled in a shower of dirt and mud and shattered metal.

The trail was slick and muddy, but the minivan was sturdier than I'd first assumed. It hauled itself up the hillside, the engine moaning but not ready to give up.

Looking down the hill, I saw the last two pursuing vehicles veer off to check on their fallen comrades. Three men clambered out, rushing to the SUV, dancing around futilely as they searched for their leader among the steaming wreckage.

I'd bought us some breathing space, but they'd be coming again. At least there'd be fewer of them to contend with next time.

17

'Well . . . we made it.'

'Just.' Don added, looking at the ramshackle collection of buildings, 'But was it worth it?'

My nod was more confident than any of us felt. 'We've a better chance here than we do on the open road.'

'We didn't do too badly. We stopped two of them.'

'We were incredibly lucky, that's all,' I said.

'Is your glass always half-empty?'

'My glass got shattered a long time ago.'

It was a hell of a climb up the slope but we had made it without bursting the suspension on the people carrier. Once we were off the barren hillside, the forest encroached again, but at least it offered some respite from the driving rain. I had flicked on the headlights to negotiate the gloom, and then put my foot down. The earlier opinion was still strong in my mind: the bad guys would be coming again. We had to find shelter for Millie and the children, then set Don up to cover me while I took the fight to our enemies. We wouldn't be able to do that while dawdling on the mountain trails. We had found the abandoned logging camp ten minutes later.

Parking the van near to a decrepit cabin, I said, 'Millie, I want you to go and check inside. See if there's a telephone or radio. Then come and join us.'

'Where are you going?'

'In there.' My nod indicated a series of huts and industrial sheds beyond a chain-link fence. The fence had drooped in places and was no real security.

'Why not just check those huts?' Millie asked.

'This one is outside the compound. I'm guessing it was once a security checkpoint. If there's a comms area, that's the logical place to find it.'

'I'll go,' Don said, shifting to open his door.

'No.' I gripped his wrist. 'I need you to look after the children.'

'I can look after the children,' Millie said.

'Don can handle an assault rifle – can you?'

Millie just stared for a long three seconds. Then she opened the door and slid out. Hunkered against the rain, she headed for the abandoned cabin. I drove away and through the open gate, all the while watching Millie in the mirror.

'What was that all about?' Don asked.

'What do you mean?'

'It's pretty obvious that you wanted Millie out of the way. What's on your mind, Hunter?'

I chewed my bottom lip for the briefest of time. 'Not in front of the children, Don.'

There were cabins on both sides of the trail, some faring better than others in the fight against the elements. None of them had successfully held back the forest from reclaiming its territory. Undergrowth grew all the way to the walls and sometimes even inside the buildings. Further back were the large sheds, the abandoned homes of saws and winches and all the equipment necessary for a lumber operation. Ignoring the structures, I drove to the furthest corner of the sprawling encampment. There I reversed the van under a lean-to. It was concealed from anyone coming along the trail until they were adjacent with it, and I elected to leave it nose out in case we had to trust to speed and manoeuvrability to get us out of a fix a second time.

'Grab the gun for me, will you.' I climbed out the van. 'And bring the children.'

'What about Fluffy?'

Beth was cradling the tom in her arms. The tatty old cat returned my stare as though defying me to leave it behind. Maybe if I didn't give the correct answer to the little girl, it would show me how it had earned its scars. Fluffy? Jesus, if there was ever a misnomer that was it!

The tom was a good distraction for the children, but if the time came when it became an encumbrance then I'd have to leave it behind. Except my ethos was that you never left a friend behind.

'OK, you can bring the cat. Just make sure he stays quiet.'

'He's always quiet,' Ryan said.

The little boy was right. I'd never heard the cat as much as miaow in the time it had been in the van with us. 'Do you think that the two of you can be as quiet as Fluffy?'

Beth and Ryan smiled up at me, nodding and blinking down on tears. It made my heart ache and I turned away quickly.

Don slung me a rifle.

I turned to make a reconnaissance of the area, but Don grabbed my wrist this time.

'What did you mean? Not in front of the children?'

'Not now, Don. We'll talk about this once we've secured the place.'

Don turned and searched for Millie. When he turned back, his face was like stone. 'You never had children, did you, Hunter?'

That was one of the reasons why Diane and I had split. There was nothing left to bind us together. As much as we'd loved each other, it hadn't been enough to span the gulf that grew between us after I left my unit. I'd tried to turn my back on the past, but inexorably I'd been pulled back into a world of violence where Diane didn't want to follow. Hector and Paris, our beloved German Shepherds, had been as close to children as we'd had. Diane and her new husband, Simon, kept them. I missed my dogs, and if the truth be known, I missed the children we'd never had.

'I'll do *anything* to protect my family,' Don went on. 'I'll take down *any* man who tries to harm them.'

We locked gazes for a long breath. Finally I nodded curtly. Point taken. 'Take the little ones inside and try to get them settled. I'm going to need you out here.' I paused again, thinking hard. 'Just forget what I said, OK?'

'Might not be that easy.'

Shit, and after we'd just buried the hatchet.

'Get the kids settled. Make sure that no one can see them, then get back out here.' I lowered my voice conspiratorially. '*Then* we can talk about how we intend killing these bastards who want to murder your family.' I walked away before the old man could argue.

I headed down the centre of the road, holding the assault rifle across my body. If the bad guys were here already, better that they zeroed in on me rather than the others. As I walked, I thought about the short discourse I'd just had with Don Griffiths. To say that Don had overreacted was the least of it. I'd only intended planning our strategy for taking out our pursuers without the kids overhearing. Christ, they were traumatised enough without listening to their grandfather plotting the deaths of others.

Don had thrown a curve ball that I hadn't been ready for. What the hell had he thought I'd meant? More questions to add to those I already wanted answering. I needed to sit down for a real heart-to-heart with Don. But now wasn't the time. Our window of opportunity was very limited and none of it must be wasted. It was enough that I knew the men after us were determined, and reckless enough, to try anything. For now, I didn't have to worry about the *why*, only about the *how* I was going to stop them.

I scanned the layout of the buildings, the high mountains surrounding them, the only vehicle access in and out of the compound. Next time they came the bad guys would have to do it on foot, whether they liked it or not. There was a ridge up on the hill to the west. If my friend Rink was positioned up there with a rifle, then he could stop a full military convoy from making its way into the camp. The attackers would be forced to decamp from their vehicles, and I would be waiting for them in the woods. I smiled grimly at the thought. But the smile was short-lived. Rink was back in Florida, oblivious of our plight. For how long, though? Would Rink recognise my failure to check in as a sign that I was in trouble? Of course he would, but not yet. Shit, despite everything that had happened so far, I'd barely been in Pennsylvania for twelve hours.

Rink wouldn't be coming yet. Don would have to do. I just wasn't certain that the old man had the skills to take out the leading vehicle.

Up ahead a figure moved through the drifting rain. Millie had hunched over and kept close to the buildings, having the sense not to walk out in the open as I did. Quickly I moved to intercept her.

'Anything?'

Millie blinked rain from her lashes.

'Nothing. You want me to keep checking?'

'No.' Taking Millie by her arm, I led her into the lee of one of the cabins. Maybe now wasn't the time for this, but I was afraid I wouldn't get another opportunity. Millie shivered against the cold, her clothing not much defence against the mountain winter. 'What's wrong?' she asked.

'I want to speak to you where the kids can't overhear us.'

She tilted her head away, and through the conduit of her arm I felt her shiver even more. 'What about?'

I didn't want to say as such, but I wasn't going to lie to her.

'There's a possibility that none of us will make it out of here alive.'

'I know,' she said, and it was a struggle for her to hold the tears back.

I pulled her in close and held her. 'Believe me,' I said, 'I'm going to do everything I can to make sure that you and the little ones stay safe. Only there are no guarantees.'

Millie closed her eyes, then surprisingly she leaned against my chest. 'I know you'll try your best.'

I held my breath. I thought about Brook and how maybe if I had come sooner then this could have been stopped before it escalated into this nightmare scenario. Deep inside though, I knew that wasn't the case. This had always been out of my hands. All that was left to me now was to try to end it without any further innocents perishing. It seemed like Millie had just realised that too. 'I'm sorry about the way I've treated you, Joe. You were never to blame for what happened to Brook. I see that now . . .'

'Don't worry about that,' I said. 'I didn't take it personally.'

She raised her head, and her eyes twinkled up at me. She was smiling, the first time I'd seen her do so, and she looked so damn pretty like that. I bent and planted a kiss on her forehead. Chaste, like she was my little sister.

'What was that for?' she asked.

'Just felt like the right thing to do,' I said, 'now that we're friends again.'

Her smile never slipped, but her eyes began to soften. The difference this time was that her tears were born of something other than grief or anger. There was hope, so at least I'd achieved what I had set out to do. Before her mind could be changed again, I patted her on the shoulder and set her on her way. She only made it a few steps.

'Wait, Millie!'

She turned to look back at me.

'Here,' I said, shrugging out of the coat loaned from Don. 'I don't want you freezing to death.'

She accepted the coat and slipped into its warmth. The sleeves trailed and the hem came to her knees. She looked like a little girl playing dress-up, except her next question was anything but childlike: 'Do you really think any of us will live long enough to worry about the cold?'

'Maybe not,' I admitted. I smiled at the irony and she returned the gesture. Then she headed off to the far end of the camp.

I looked towards the front gate. My glass got broken a long time ago. Under my breath, I muttered, 'There are no guarantees . . . but I'll be damned if I'm going to make it easy for the bastards.'

18

Gant was pulled bleeding from the wreckage of the SUV. He was hurt, but alive. His breathing was steady enough, and there was nothing to indicate that beyond the cuts and bruises there was anything life-threatening. He just wasn't ready to wake up yet.

The three able-bodied men carried him away from the smouldering crash scene and lay him across the back seat of one of the undamaged cars. One of them, a small, wiry man who moved with the jerkiness of a bird or someone high on amphetamine, left Gant in the care of his friends and went to check on Vince. He could see the young hillbilly standing alongside the Ford, his hands scrubbing at his hair. Messing with his goddamn pompadour, the man thought, like it mattered a fuck what he looked like.

'What're you doin' fuckin' about over here, Vinnie?'

Vince turned to him, a dazed expression on his face, still sculpting his hair. No, that wasn't it, the bird-like man saw; Vinnie was picking bits of broken glass and splinters of wood out of his scalp. He'd also been looking down on the still form of his girlfriend who was twisted in a way that wasn't normal.

'Is she dead, Vinnie?'

Vince blinked again at the jumble of clothing and oddly angled limbs. 'I sure as hell hope so, Darley. Would you want to live, lookin' all screwed up like that?'

Vince bent down and extended a finger to touch Sonya's face. It felt like putty, the rain wiping any trace of warmth from her skin. Absurdly, Vince hooked her chain with his finger, tried unsuccessfully to insert it back into the ruin of her nose. The silver links immediately slid away and pooled alongside her ear, along with a slow trickle of blood.

Vince gave a dull groan as he stood up. But that was as far as his show of grief could go. Maybe he should have been more vocal; Sonya had meant an awful lot to him – as far as any one ever could to someone with Vince Everett's twisted sense of attachment to other human beings. But the single moan was all he had. This was, after all, the response expected of a man who'd blasted his grandfather's head off when the old man caught him with his hands in the cash register. Vince hadn't missed the old fart after he was gone, and certainly hadn't cried for him as Gramps had been lowered into the ground.

'You OK, Vinnie?'

'But for one thing,' Vince said. 'Wish I'd pulled over on the road like she wanted.'

Darley didn't get it. He searched for wounds on the young man's frame. Apart from some scratches on his face Vince looked unhurt. The scratches weren't even bleeding, and Darley wondered when Vince had picked them up. The bird-like head jerked, staring back at the Ford. The front right fender was bashed in, but that was about all. He looked back at the torn body of the woman like things just didn't correlate.

Vince said, 'She was hanging out the window trying to shoot Griffiths when we hit. Goddamn fool's trick, but there was no tellin' her.'

'Ain't women all the same?' Darley said.

'Nah,' Vince said. 'Not many like Sonya. She was a free spirit, that one. I'll miss her.'

There was no emotion in his voice, like he was just going through the motions, saying what was expected, so it surprised Darley when the young man bent down and rearranged the woman's limbs. It took him a moment to realise that Vince wasn't ceremoniously laying her out; he was searching for something beneath her corpse. Vince finally stood up, clutching the Glock that had been wedged under her hip. The gun was smeared with dirt and also some of the woman's blood. Vince wiped it clean on her tartan miniskirt.

Even Darley, who didn't care for anyone who wasn't in their immediate clique – and he counted both Vince and Sonya outside of that description – frowned at Vince's coldness.

'Might need this piece before we're finished,' Vince told him. 'In fact, this was Sonya's gun. I intend using it when I put a hole in Don Griffiths' skull.'

'You think we're still going through with it? I mean, it's been a goddamn shambles up till now. Gant's hurt an'—'

'Gant's a goddamn fool. He shoulda handled this differently than the fuckin' ridiculous way he has.'

Darley's head jerked, almost like he expected their unconscious boss-man to hear them from all the way across here. 'Vinnie, man, you shouldn't be talkin' like that. If he hears you . . .'

'I don't give a motherfucking hoot what that Nazi hears.'

'He's the one that's paying you,' Darley reminded him.

Vince looked down on Sonya. 'This ain't about the money no more. It's about the freakin' waste of a good gal. That won't sit too well with *Adolf* over there, but that's the way it's gonna be.'

'Gant's the boss, man. You know he's the voice of Carswell Hicks out here.'

Vince brought up the Glock sharply, but it was a command for silence, not a threat. 'Don't give me any of that fuckin' *Hicks is God* bullshit, Darley. Gant's a goddamn maniac an' you know it. Only reason he's in charge is that none of you pricks had the good sense to grab the reins when you had the opportunity.'

'What you sayin', Vinnie?'

'I'm sayin' there's gonna be a few changes round here, Darley. You with me or against me?'

The relative closeness of the Glock to Darley's groin had a lot to do with his reply. 'Right now Gant's not in the best frame of mind for decision-making.'

'The way I see it,' Vince added, 'Gant's had his shot at handling things, and now it's time someone with a little sense put things right. Right?'

'Right.'

'You don't sound convinced. Hicks has promised a big pay day for us all, an' I sure as hell ain't letting Gant fuck that up for me.'

'You know the money doesn't mean anything to Gant or the rest of us.' Darley squinted at Sonya. 'And you said it wasn't about the money for you.'

'I'm gonna kill the ones who did this to her, but I don't mind gettin' paid good cash for my time. What about you, Darley? Do you want to go home scratching your ass, or holding a thick wad of Ben Franklins? Won't Hicks' mission be all the sweeter if you're a rich man at the end of it?'

Darley, like the other neo-Nazis he'd gathered to his side, was a staunch supporter of Carswell Hicks' hate doctrine. By that very token he was a loyal follower of his right-hand man, Gant, but it seemed wealth was a greater motivator to him than any creed. 'What about the others?'

Vince looked over at Tom Sweeney and Mike Dillman, the two bootboys fussing over their leader. He was certain that he could sway them to his way of thinking. Rick Wilkes and Duane Holland, the two assholes sent back with the black van to see to the disposal of the bodies at the Reynolds house, would join them soon, but once the balance of power had shifted to Vince, they wouldn't be in a position to argue. Rooster and Cabe wouldn't be a problem. He'd guessed that their no-show meant one of two things: they'd gotten themselves in trouble with the law like he'd first thought, or in some other trouble that they'd been unable to handle. They'd been tasked with advance recon on Griffiths' house. Maybe they'd made it there after all but they hadn't recognised the stranger's killer eyes when they looked into them. Whatever the reason for their absence, Vince didn't think that Rooster or Cabe would be joining them soon.

Vince hiked his jeans over his lean hips, tucking Sonya's Glock in his waistband alongside his own. He checked his pockets, feeling the makeshift garrotte, but not what he was looking for. If he was going to be the leader, he supposed he'd better look the part. 'Hey, Darley, do you have a comb I can use?'

Darley just stared at him, the rain pattering off his bald pate.

'Nah, didn't think so.' Vince grinned. Then his face smoothed out. 'But there's one thing I will ask from you if you're gonna be my second. Don't call me Vinnie again, or I'm gonna have to kill you.'

'Uh, yeah, sure thing, Vince.'

Vince winked at him. 'I'm just foolin' with you, Darley. Don't you skinheads have a sense of humour?'

Darley grunted out a laugh, but it was as empty as Vince's words. Vince smiled coldly, because he sure as hell hadn't been joking.

Vince headed for Gant's impromptu ambulance. There, waiting for him, was another skinhead who wouldn't be laughing any time soon.

19

After stationing Millie to guard Beth and Ryan, I instructed Don to make his way to the ridge I'd picked out on the western slope. Up there, as the day waned to late afternoon, the meagre light that the rainclouds allowed through would cast the man into deep shadow, making it unlikely he would be spotted by anyone approaching. I made my way to the front of the camp, intending to set up beyond Don's position in the woods. First, though, I detoured to the cabin.

Entering, I was assailed by the stench of must and cobwebs clung to my face and shoulders. The rest of the cabin was as decrepit as the entrance. Worn desks and chairs had been abandoned to the elements when the logging company went bust and pulled out fast. Sheaves of papers lay scattered on the floor and on every available surface. Immediately I saw a phone attached to the far wall. Moist, muddy tracks led directly to the phone and I could tell by their size and shape that they were the footprints of a woman: Millie's, as she'd inspected the telephone. I followed them and bent to study the phone. It was an old black plastic type with a dial, now defunct in this press-button age. The power cord had been snatched from the guts of the phone, possibly the action of a disgruntled worker intent on vandalism on his way to the Welfare line.

Millie hadn't mentioned the phone, probably because it was broken. It could possibly be fixed with the right tools, but the thought had never occurred to her. To be frank, I didn't have the tools or the inclination. But I couldn't ignore it. I headed round the back of the cabin and checked the junction box. It was intact, as was the cable that connected it to the telegraph pole. Further on I saw that the trees had ensnared the cable, ripping it from the next pole and dumping it on the ground. The telephone wouldn't have worked even with the rights tools and all the time in the world to mess with it. I should have taken Millie's word for it.

I shook my head, urging myself to forget about it. Get your mind back on the job, Hunter. Distraction kills, remember? More words of wisdom from the arms instructor at Arrowsake. *Stay in the red zone, Hunter, or you may as well give up now. Anything else and you're a dead man. Got it?*

I checked my weapons, my SIG SAUER P226 and KA-BAR. I'd left the H&K assault rifles with Don. The old man would require both to lay down enough firepower to force our attackers from their vehicles. When our hunters were out in the woods, then I'd rely on the military knife to even the score. The SIG would remain as back-up for extreme circumstances, because stealth was everything now.

Returning to the busted gate, I pulled it to, then used a discarded log to bolster it by jamming it between the frame and the loops of wire. It wouldn't stop a vehicle from getting through, but it would slow men on foot.

For a second I wished that I hadn't been so quick in handing over the borrowed jacket to Millie. She was inside now, protected from the elements, but I was ever the chivalrous one. Sometimes to my detriment, I realised. I had on my boots, but my denim shirt and jeans weren't the most suitable garments for a stroll in the woods, especially not in the depths of a northern winter. At least it wasn't snowing. The rain kept the temperature above freezing, but people still succumbed to hypothermia in moderate climates. The core temperature's the thing. Soaked to the bones, I could grow lethargic and confused before I knew I was dying. First task on the agenda was to get warm.

My healing leg was still a hindrance, but it would take more than a quick jog to raise my core temperature anyway. Clothing that was waterproof and warm was an immediate requirement. I ducked back into the security cabin, hoping to find a discarded rain-slicker. No such luck. But in a supply cupboard there was a roll of garbage sacks. Quickly stripping out of the wet shirt, I made head- and armholes in one of the sacks and pulled it on close to my skin. I wasn't concerned that the rattling plastic would give away my position because it immediately clamped to my flesh like a second layer. I jammed the trailing edges down inside my jeans and then pulled the wet shirt back on. It was an uncomfortable feeling but it would soon pass.

The garbage bag trick was something learned from less-than-wealthy boxers who couldn't afford a sweat suit for when they needed to make weight. It promoted perspiration, but the plastic held the sweat in and heated it. I'd be nice and toasty in no time.

The blue denims were poor camouflage, but I wasn't going to find any DPM's around here. Not that I needed them when the best disruptive pattern material going could be found in nature. Returning outside I scooped handfuls of mud and rubbed them liberally over my shirt and jeans. Didn't bother streaking it over my face, because the rain would soon obliterate it and I didn't fancy a mouthful of muck. I washed my hands clean in a puddle, drying my fingers as best I could on the tail of my shirt. The last thing I wanted was to transfer grit to the firing mechanism of the SIG.

There was nothing I could do about my wet hair. Most heat was lost from the head, but with my body now heating up like a boil-in-the-bag snack, I thought I'd be OK. I scrubbed the rain from my scalp, and off my face, feeling two days of stubble rasping against my palms. Normally I was fastidious about keeping well shaven and clean – a habit instilled by military indoctrination – but in the circumstances the rules went out the window. As long as the gun was pristine, I could do my job.

Loping away from the compound, I entered the treeline on the east side so that I was opposite Don's position. Men are inclined to run away from an assault rifle not towards it, so I was better positioned on this side of the road. Then I made my way through the woods, towards the crest in the road where I'd see my enemies coming.

A little way inside the treeline was a group of boulders, and between them a natural hollow where the lower boughs of a spruce afforded respite from the rain. The hiding place was gloomy, but by contrast the trail ahead glowed silver, a trick of the light refracting from the moisture. I settled in to wait.

I waited.

And waited.

In the end I wondered if the men who'd chased us had had second thoughts about following people into the mountains who'd already decimated their ranks by two-thirds. I was in the act of getting up to return to the camp and gather up the family when I heard the high-pitched whine of an engine negotiating the steep trail.

After the inactivity it was almost pleasing that the men had the stones to follow through with the attack. I was in that place where my sense of justice demanded retribution. I hunkered back down, peering beneath the branches, feeling the adrenalin seeping through my core and pushing away the vestigial chill from my bones. Unconsciously my fingers flexed on the hilt of the KA-BAR, and it didn't occur to me that the pain I'd been experiencing in my hand had fled. Action was the best medicine for a fighting man's pain.

A sedan crested the mountain trail, followed closely by an SUV. The two vehicles were those that had survived the earlier encounter. There were only four figures in the cars. That was all? I doubted it; there had also been two men in the black van that had almost collided with us. Where were they? And where was that crazy girl who'd tried so hard to shoot Don?

What about the girl? I didn't make war on women. If I could help it I wouldn't hurt her, but if the choice between stopping her and saving the children came up, then my decision could go only one way. Hopefully she'd had enough after her boyfriend crashed the car, and she'd taken off somewhere to lick her wounded pride. Maybe Fonzarelli had taken off with her, because all the heads I could make out in the vehicles were shaved to the skin.

Had to plan for six men at least. Not an insurmountable figure if Don did his job right.

The sedan crept by, followed moments later by the SUV. I studied the faces inside. No sign of Tattoo. If the guy had died when his car rolled, then so be it, but I was a little pissed that I wouldn't get to look the bastard in the eye when I killed him. I wanted to comment about the tattoo, the significance of the eight-eight pattern. Unlike many people, I was familiar with the number. Not eighty-eight as some might think, but two separate figures. Eight and eight. The eighth letter of the alphabet repeated twice, standing for Heil Hitler. Tattoo wouldn't be the first neo-Nazi that I'd killed, and I wasn't averse to teaching any other the error of his ways.

I waited until the cars were past me then rose up, gripping the KA-BAR tightly.

On cue, Don let loose with the H&K.

20

So what the hell just happened?

Vince lifted his head to see if anyone would respond to his question, before realising that he hadn't actually spoken out loud. There was another problem, too: no one was around to answer him even if he'd screamed the question.

He asked himself the question again.

When things became no clearer, he blinked into the surrounding darkness. He had no idea where he was, let alone what had just gone on. All he knew was that he was belly down like a pretty-boy on a prison cot.

He tried to get up, but found that it wasn't so easy a task. What the hell? His arms were twisted behind his back, something digging painfully into his wrists. His ankles were bound too.

He jackknifed on to his side, his head swimming with the effort.

From this position he had a better view of his surroundings, but it took a moment for him to make sense of them. The smell of damp carpet wafted round him, followed by the heady tang of motor oil. He swung his boot heels and heard the dull chime of struck metal.

He was in the back of the black van, the one that Holland and Wilkes had ridden earlier. There was only one reason for being trussed in the back of the van that he could think of . . . that weasel Darley had cold-cocked him from behind. Proof of that was the throbbing lump the size of a hen's egg that pushed out through his ducktails.

A flash of pain from the back of his skull brought it all back.

Darley had followed him to the car where Gant lay and as Vince greeted the other two skinheads, Sweeney and Dillman, the little shit had shuffled behind him. Vince thought his warning to the man had been enough to cow him, but it looked like Darley had his own ideas about who should still be their boss. And obviously his creed was a greater motivator than money. Vince felt the first smack of the man's gun barrel come down on the nape of his neck. As he turned, trying to grab one of the Glocks from his belt, Sweeney and Dillman had grappled him. He got a headbutt into Dillman's face, but then Darley had slashed the gun across his skull and that was that.

Till now.

He was surprised to be alive, but not really happy about what that might mean. Gant had probably survived the car wreck, and he wasn't going to be pleased when he heard that Vince had planned a coup. If what he'd heard about Gant's viciousness was even partly true then he was going to be put through a world of hurt before he died.

He had to get out of here.

When Gant finished up with the Griffithses, he'd be back. And with nothing more pressing to contend with, he'd take his own good goddamn time making Vince sorry that he ever contemplated betrayal.

Vince kicked and rolled.

His exertions were repaid by a hand slamming the partition that separated the rear compartment from the van's cab.

'Keep the fuckin' racket down, Vinnie, or I'm gonna come in there and break *your* fuckin' nose.'

Vince stopped kicking. He wasn't alone after all. Was Mike Dillman the only one left behind, though?

'I broke your nose, did I, Mike?' Vince hollered back. 'Pity I didn't get Sweeney as well. You there, Sweeney? Why don't you come in here an' I'll do the same to you?'

'Shut the fuck up, Vinnie. I mean it . . .'

Dillman again. So the prick was the only one left behind to guard him?

Now that he'd learned what he wanted, he'd no reason to goad Dillman any further. First he had to get free from his bonds. He took it easy, shifting round so that he could pull his knees up to his chest. Vince had a gangly frame, but he'd always been flexible. He shuffled his wrists down under his butt, then behind one knee while he slipped the other toes between his arms. The bindings made things awkward, but he managed to wriggle free. Once he had one boot through, the other followed easily enough and he straightened out, bringing his wrists up to his chin. His night vision had begun to kick in and he could make out his bindings. Insult added to injury, he thought, when he saw that his wrists had been strung together with his guitar string.

He chewed at the metal coil, hooking an eye-tooth round a loop and pulling. The medium-gauge string was good for throttling a victim, but wasn't the best for securing wrists. The copper-coiled wire spooled away from his flesh and he slipped one hand free. Then it was only a few seconds' work to loosen the other. He made a check of the wire, feeling a couple of kinks in the metal, but otherwise it was undamaged. He wound it loosely and jammed it into his jacket pocket. Then he set to the bindings round his ankles. Gaffer tape this time. It peeled off easily enough, but he had to take it slow so that Dillman didn't hear him.

Vince flexed his hands, rolled his ankles, to promote blood flow into his extremities. His fingers and toes tingled, and he decided to wait until they settled down before making his break for freedom. The last thing he wanted was to leap from the back of the van only to find his numb feet giving way under him. The tingle became pain, but it was endurable, even welcome.

He felt for his guns, his cell phone. All gone, though that was to be expected. He searched the compartment for anything he could use as a weapon. Nothing. That was expected as well. He still had his garrotte but that was a tool used for stealth work and not much good against a pissed-off skinhead with a gun, especially one holding a grudge over a broken nose.

His Glock would come in handy, more than that, though, he needed his phone.

He came slowly to his feet, carefully negotiating the van so that he didn't rock it and alert Dillman. He found the back doors, but the inside handle had been removed. It was pointless cursing, but he did anyway, making sure he held the swear words deep in his chest. Then he had a thought.

The metal doors were sheathed in panels with little more substance than thick cardboard coated with vinyl. He inserted his fingertips along one edge and slowly tore the panel down the middle, checking all the time for movement from the front. When the hole was big enough, he inserted a hand through the gap and felt for the wires that controlled the levers that locked the doors. He slowly exerted pressure and the wire dug into his skin but he felt the locks disengage.

Bang, bang, bang on the partition. 'The fuck you doing in there, asshole?'

'Just gettin' comfortable, Dillman. That OK with you?'

'Lie still, or I swear to God I'm gonna come in there and put a round through each of your knees. I gotta keep you alive for Gant, but he said nothin' about you having to be in one piece.'

Vince smiled at Dillman's bravado. The bullshitter's words helped cover the faint squeak as he pushed open one of the doors. He slipped out of the van, then gently closed the door. Dillman wouldn't even know that he'd escaped until he finally came out of the warm cab to check why Vince was so quiet. He guessed that could be a while.

Ensuring he stayed in a direct line with the van and out of Dillman's view in the mirrors, he hurried away. He kept going until he was a good hundred yards distant and hidden by the drizzle before he ducked to his right and sped off at a tangent. The lack of a corresponding shout or bullet whizzing after him confirmed that Dillman was blissfully unaware of his escape.

Vince found that they hadn't moved far from where Sonya had been killed. He followed the verge at the side of the road to where it widened out, then ran for the demolished cabin. His Ford had been shifted, sent down the embankment on the far side, and it was lying in a stream bed, on its side. Gant's men had made it look like the Ford had been in a tragic accident, and had gone to the trouble of placing Sonya and Gant's driver inside before they set the vehicle on fire.

Vince eyed the smouldering corpses inside and for the first time felt a genuine twinge of regret for Sonya. She was a crazy bitch, but he had to admit that there was a lot he liked about her. In a different world, maybe they could have been . . . No. That could never happen. He turned away, retraced his steps back to the demolished cabin.

Then he began sifting through the wreckage. When he couldn't find what he was looking for, he followed the trail to where Sonya had ended up on the floor, and began kicking over splinters of wood. That failed to turn up what he was after, so he stood in the spot where he'd rolled the woman's body over to retrieve her gun. Then he walked in a spiral away from her. Not as good as conducting a grid-pattern search, but it was faster. Ten yards out he saw it, and he stooped down and picked up Sonya's cell phone. Debris on top of it had kept it dry. At first he feared that the phone was broken, but the cover and battery had merely slipped when the collision had knocked the phone out of her pocket. He clicked them back in place and was rewarded with a glowing screen as the phone rebooted. The screen saver was a picture of Vince. He was giving her the Elvis lip when she'd snapped the image, his quiff flopping over one eye.

'You jerk,' he said.

Then he made the call.

21

Nostalgia made me smile, but it would be a death's-head image at best. I had on my game face and knew that even my closest friends found the sight perturbing. Rink, who'd shared many search-destroy missions with me, had found it scary, and he was a man who was normally frightened of nothing. When wearing this face I went way beyond even the red zone extolled by my combat instructor, straddling that plane lorded over by the Grim Reaper. It was my killing face.

I welcomed the rictus smile.

As well as the challenge ahead.

The fight with the two men back in Bedford Well had been driven by insecurity, and I realised now that I'd been allowing feelings of fallibility to control me for too long. The injured hand, the wounds in my leg, they'd all been excuses, and those negative concerns had made me feel – maybe even fear – for my mortality. Now there was no room for worrying about my well-being. Killing these men to save the children gave me purpose again.

The months spent recuperating had been a waste of time; all that was really needed was to jump right back on the bucking horse.

It felt good.

I moved smoothly through the woods, a mud-smeared wraith closing in on those who would harm Millie, Beth and Ryan.

Don Griffiths fired a second volley.

One engine died and the sound of doors flying open was followed by shouts of panic. Their return fire filled the woods with a staccato rap.

I hurdled over a fallen tree, kept running.

The second engine revved wildly, tyres spinning on mud, and then there was a loud screech and the impact of metal on metal.

Don's H&K rattled again.

More shouts, and another assault rifle responding in kind.

The bullet-ridden sedan was abandoned in the trail, its front doors wide. Its two occupants had retreated across the road and had taken up hiding places among the trees. They fired blindly at the crest where Don was invisible to them, their rounds churning up leaves and chunks of tree-bark but little else. Don, as instructed, fired and moved, fired and moved, never giving them a location to concentrate upon.

The SUV was still trying to force its way inside the compound, the front wheels bucking and bouncing on the slick log that I'd jammed in the wire, getting nowhere fast. Those inside were too busy to shoot at Don. They could wait, I decided, and moved for the men in the trees.

I was ten feet from the first when Don laid down another volley. I dropped and the rounds cut through the foliage above me. Then, with the cessation, the man returned fire, screaming wordlessly at Don. Mind engaged, he had no idea that death was swooping in on him from behind.

My left hand clasped the man's jaw, tugged up and back so the bald skull wedged tightly against my shoulder. I didn't slice the throat. The man could live for too long afterwards. Granted his life would be counted in seconds, but that was enough to fight back. A stray round could kill as easily as a well-aimed one. I jammed the tip of the KA-BAR into the soft flesh under the man's chin and drove it upwards, brutally sawing the handle back and forth. Making soup of his brain.

There wasn't even vestigial movement in the man's limbs as he fell at my feet.

Briefly, I thought about picking up the dropped assault rifle, but discarded the idea. Here in the woods, manoeuvrability was king. The rifle would be an encumbrance.

I dashed away, going almost to my belly as the second skinhead popped up from behind a boulder and fired towards the ridge where Don was hiding. The lack of a response from Don told me that the old man was possibly out of ammunition. Didn't matter; once this second man was dead, the rules would change. Don would already be moving through the woods to where Millie and the kids were.

Thinking about the children listening to the distant crack of gunfire, I wondered if they were again picturing the bullet that had torn out their stepfather's chest. For a second a bubble of my own insecurities threatened to pop in my chest. It tasted like bile in my throat and I swallowed it down. I wasn't going there again. The way to stop the children experiencing further nightmares was to stop these men.

I crept in on the second skinhead. The smell of fear wafted off him in waves: sweat and passed wind. I could almost pity the man.

On the man's jacket there was a stitched patch, a double lightning-bolt, like those worn by the original *Schutzstaffel* – Hitler's Praetorian Guard. He deserved the same lack of mercy as his forebears had shown the thousands murdered in their extermination camps.

Perhaps it was the man's supercharged nerves that warned him, because as I stepped close the skinhead jerked round, his rifle swinging with him. He pulled on the trigger as he moved and rounds made an arch of destruction through the woods.

At that moment, though, I was finer tuned. I lunged sideways even as I barrelled in, staying just beyond the angle of fire. The skinhead tried to track me, but my KA-BAR cut down and to the side, knocking the muzzle of the gun aside. The back stroke cut clean through his windpipe. Then I reversed the blade and jammed it down behind his left clavicle. Not as clean a kill as the first but equally final.

I kicked the corpse over on to its back, and reached this time for his gun.

Things had moved on.

The SUV had forced through the flimsy barricade and hurtled into the camp. I tracked it with the assault rifle, loosing a short burst. Rounds pockmarked the rear door in an oblique pattern but failed to stop the vehicle. I pulled the trigger again, but the magazine was empty. A quick glance at the dead body showed no sign of extra ammunition, so I simply dropped the useless weapon and raced after the SUV. As I ran the KA-BAR was exchanged for my SIG.

I vaulted through the hole in the gate, kept on running. Two hundred yards ahead the SUV came to a screeching halt and the front doors flew open. Men sprinted in opposite directions, seeking cover in the cabins on both sides of the encampment.

Preserve your bullets, I told myself. No way that I could hit them from here.

Swerving to the right, I jogged along a wooden walkway in front of a semi-collapsed storage shed, mentally figuring my chances and happy to note that I was still confident of taking out both these amateurs.

Overconfidence could kill me as quickly as the past feelings of insecurity, I reminded myself when someone lurched up in the back seat of the SUV. The first bullet shattered the rear window, but the follow-ups were aimed at me.

Bullets whizzed past, blasting holes in the storage shed and tugging at my clothing. Something so hot that it felt like the scorch of a brand laid a line across my left triceps. I knew what it was like to get shot. It was never hot like that; on the contrary it was like the poke of an icy finger. Some primal point in my brain acknowledged how close the round had come to cutting my arm in half, but just shelved it for processing later. My conscious brain screamed at me to move.

I tumbled ungracefully against the wall of the shed as more bullets churned the planks next to my feet. Splinters flew like a shower of needles. I skipped sideways, then threw myself backwards through a void only vaguely recognisable as a window. Glass tinkled around me as I fell on my back inside the shed. Above me rounds stitched a pattern of holes in the wall, causing laser-like strobes of dim light to cut through the shed.

The wooden wall, sick with mould and damp, was no barrier to the high-impact rounds of an assault rifle and it would be seconds before my attacker adjusted trajectory and fired where I'd gone through the window. I rolled away just as new shafts of light jabbed the space I'd vacated.

Coming to my feet, I raced back the way I'd come, doing the opposite to what my attacker expected. The wall behind me was split into flying chunks, and I was relieved that I'd read the man right.

Hunkering in the far corner, listening, I didn't attempt to fire back. I was rewarded a moment later by the clunk of the SUV's door being thrown open. I held my breath, so that my exhalations didn't compete with the stealthy sounds of approach.

Playing possum wasn't my usual way of dealing with armed men, but in the circumstances it served me well. Let the man think his bullets had cut me to pieces, then when he came and peered inside the window to check on his handiwork I would put a well-placed bullet in his skull.

There was the steady approach of boots in mud and I creased my finger on the trigger of the SIG.

Shadows shifted beyond the broken window.

Any second now.

I slowly exhaled even as I lifted the gun and aimed it at head height.

Then a strangled yell spoiled everything.

Don roaring in rage.

Apparently he wasn't fully out of bullets after all, because suddenly more strobes flashed through the shed. Boots pounded along the walkway outside as the man I was a second away from killing made for cover further away.

Son of a bitch, I cursed under my breath, the tattooed man had escaped death a second time.

22

Vince ran.

Not away from Samuel Gant as would be expected from anyone with the least bit of sense or a will to protect his own ass, but directly towards him.

There was no option left to him if he hoped to achieve what he'd been working so hard for.

Everything depended on him being there.

If he missed it, then, well, he'd be righteously fucked.

He wished he'd sneaked back to the black van, surprised Dillman by dragging that piece of shit out and stomping him stupid under his heels. At least then he'd have a van to climb the mountain in, instead of having to run the entire way in a pair of boots designed for shit-kicking rather than a goddamn marathon.

He stopped to catch his breath.

Damned if I ain't gonna have to get back to the gym.

Of late his lifestyle hadn't allowed him the opportunity and he was feeling the effects of too many beers, too many smokes, and too much time between the sheets with Sonya. No regrets, he warned, it had to be done. Damned if he hadn't enjoyed himself, too. But now, leaning with his hands on his knees while he sucked in great gusts of damp air, he knew he was going to have to do something to get his form back.

He heard the rattle of machine-gun fire.

'Jesus H. Christ, it's started!'

He began running again, his burning lungs begging him to stop, but his brain screaming like a drill-instructor to keep on going.

The mud made the going even more difficult, huge clods of it sticking to and building up under his heels and insteps. His jacket stank of overheated leather and perspiration. His hair, usually elegantly coiffed, whipped his face. Adding to his discomfort was the throbbing lump on the back of his skull, and the cat scratches on his face that stung like a sumbitch.

Forget it all, he told himself.

Keep going, Vince, just keep going. You want to come outa this on the right side, you just gotta keep going.

He exhorted himself all the way up and over the crest of the hill, all the while wincing at the sounds of a raging gun battle.

Ahead of him was a logging camp that hadn't known the presence of lumberjacks for the best part of a decade. It reminded him of a ghost town from a horror movie. The drifting rain added to the image, phantom mists crawling out of the forest and floating across the deserted streets. Or maybe it was clouds of cordite.

A little way ahead was an abandoned sedan car, peppered with bullet holes. As he approached it he scanned left and right, hoping he wasn't in the crosshairs of any of the skinheads who'd disembarked in a hurry.

Gunfire sounded again.

This time it was from inside the camp and he saw a man rush across the street and throw himself backwards through a window. He saw the flash of a rifle from the back of a dark-coloured SUV. Vince ducked down by the door of the sedan, watched as a figure clambered from the SUV and walked towards where the other had disappeared. The figure held his assault rifle low down near his hip, firing through the walls of the shed. When there was no return fire, the figure continued creeping forward. He was almost at the window when a cry rang out.

Vince swung to the new sound and saw Don Griffiths come out from between the buildings on the opposite side, firing wildly at the figure. As the figure turned to run, Vince recognised the tattoo like a dark stain down his face.

Gant, the motherfucker, ran off.

Further along, more rifles cracked and Don Griffiths was forced to retreat back towards the cabins. By the way he dragged his leg he'd taken a hit from one of the rounds.

Vince had to get inside the camp, but unarmed as he was, he'd be wandering into a shooting gallery where he'd be dropped as easily as a tin duck.

Maybe he could cut round back and take Don Griffiths' rifle away from him?

No way, he decided. The old guy looked like he knew his way round a machine-gun and would probably plug him before he got near. The way to win this was to go directly for Millie and the children; if only he had the faintest idea where they were hiding.

Back to square one, Vince. You still have to get by Gant and his bootboys. And don't forget the guy with the killer's eyes. Unlike Gant, he didn't think the silence since he went through that window meant that he was dead.

Need a weapon.

He looked inside the sedan hoping a gun had been dropped when those inside scarpered. Glass littered the interior, but that was it.

'Fuck, fuck, fuck,' he whispered as the gunfire started again.

There were just too many of them for him to take his chances.

My gang's bigger than yours, Gant, but where the hell are they?

He tried to figure out how much time had passed since he'd made the rushed call. How long until his buddies arrived.

Not soon enough for his liking.

He clambered inside the sedan, pulling out Sonya's phone, stabbing buttons. The phone clicked off and he read the message on the screen. Call disconnected. He checked the strength of service and saw that there was no coverage up here.

'Shit!'

An engine roared behind him.

Hopefully he peered around, looking for his friends.

But it was the black van. Dillman, his nose a red smear on his top lip, summoned here by radio by one of *his* friends. Vince ducked low as Dillman avoided the sedan and blasted through the remains of a gate and into the compound.

Damned if his chances weren't getting slimmer.

Still, he couldn't stay here.

He jumped out the car and followed the van through the gate, heading in an ungainly sprint for the nearest shed on the left. If Millie and the kids were anywhere, he might as well start his search there, at the furthest point away from the shooting. As he ran, he pulled out his garrotte and looped it round his right fist.

23

The plastic garbage bag sucked at my torso as I rushed towards the back of the shed. As I ran I tugged at the plastic through my shirt, loosening it so that it didn't impede movement. A trail of moisture dotted the hard dirt of the floor, but at least it wasn't blood.

Small consolation.

Despite my best efforts I'd failed to stop the gang from entering the compound, and, worse than that, the gunfight had forced the skinheads deep into the camp and close to where Millie and the children were hiding.

Have to lead them away. Use myself as bait.

At the back of the shed there was a door, swollen with damp and jammed in its frame. Noise would give away my location, and I wasn't ready to play my hand just yet, but there was nothing for it. Luckily, just as I pulled at the groaning door a vehicle sped into the camp, the engine screeching. The unexpected cover allowed me to pull the door open and exit into an area full of junk, discarded plastic drums and tendrils of undergrowth.

I picked my way through the rubbish, carefully avoiding roots that would trip me. As I went I flicked the catch to release the magazine in the SIG, made a quick count of the bullets. Not many left, but if I picked my targets I'd only require one for each man. I counted how many of the killers I'd seen alive: two from the SUV who'd run farther into the camp; that bastard with the tattoo; and however many had just arrived in this latest vehicle. There could be five of them – or more – so I'd have to be very selective when choosing my shots. Best-case scenario would be to liberate a gun from one of the others, or maybe find ammunition that would fit my SIG. Worst case was if one of the bastards got me first.

That was always a possibility. I wasn't bulletproof.

There was a twinge in my leg.

Stop it, Hunter. Forget your pain. Concentrate on your job, you arsehole!

I slapped the magazine back into the gun, raked the slide back and forth. Went on.

At the end of the shed I paused, took a quick glance around the structure to check in the narrow space between it and the next building. The alley was choked with abandoned machinery that was red with corrosion. No sign of movement. I lunged across the gap and into the cover of the next cabin.

The sound of the vehicle receded, up towards where the family hid. If the minivan was discovered, they'd begin their search there, and they'd come across the family's hiding place in moments. I began running, mindful of the possibility that the tattooed man was still nearby. Don would be paralleling my dash on the far side, but I was fleeter of foot than the old man.

A lean-to presented itself, and I swerved inside it, using a stack of logs for cover. I paused, peering through a gap in the logs to where the SUV sat in the middle of the road. It was doubtful that any of the skinheads would have had the presence of mind to take the ignition key when they decamped; maybe if I commandeered the vehicle I could use it as a weapon.

Starting towards the SUV, I caught a flash of movement from the far side of it. I dodged back behind the stack of wood even as a figure raced away towards a cabin on the other side. The floppy quiff hairstyle was instantly recognisable. That bloody kid who looked like a fugitive from a 1980s retro-Rockabilly band. Lifting the SIG, I tracked the running figure, easing pressure into the trigger. The opportunity to bring him down was there, but I didn't take it. Not that I had any qualms about killing the young punk, because he was anything but the kid that I'd first assumed when spotting him outside Don Griffiths' house. This was the same son of a bitch who'd attacked Millie, who'd then led the convoy that chased us into the hills. My reason for allowing the arsehole to live was a personal thing: I wanted to look him in the eyes when I dropped him, not shoot him in the back as he was running away.

Letting him go, I moved through the lean-to and then dodged right going to the rear of the next cabin.

Almost ran full-tilt into the tattooed man.

He was so close that the numbers on his face were discernible.

I skidded in the mud, trash catching me across the shins. Had to fight to stay upright, and bring the SIG to bear.

Tattoo leaped aside, also bringing up his gun.

Both of us fired, even as we both tried to save our lives.

My round took part of Tattoo's left ear, but I didn't come away uninjured. Not from the other's bullets, but from caroming into the corner of the shed and almost dislocating my shoulder.

Tattoo yelled in fury, his hand slapping at his disfigured ear, even as he brought round his assault rifle in his other hand. He fired.

Three things saved my life.

The assault rifle was ill aimed.

The man had flicked it to fire only a controlled burst of three bullets.

And my desperate dive round the corner of the shed.

All of which meant that I made it back to the stack of wood in the lean-to with only a shower of wood particles plastering my wet hair and shoulders.

I immediately spun round, gun aiming for where Tattoo would come charging after me.

Waited for a long count of ten.

It seemed that Tattoo wasn't the rash type who'd come hurtling round a blind corner, either that or he'd realised how close to death he'd come and had made a hasty retreat.

Doesn't make him a coward, just sensible.

Tattoo would be moving, trying to get a better line on me.

Move, Hunter, now!

I bobbed up and ran back towards the corner of the shed from which I'd fled moments before.

As I made it to the corner, there was rifle fire from the front. Tattoo was blasting my recent hiding place, the woodpile, to force me out.

I dipped out from the corner, SIG held steady.

Didn't have a shot.

The sounds of boots clumping away said that Tattoo believed retreat was the better part of valour. Muffled shouts followed as Tattoo directed his friends to cut me off.

I raced along the back of the cabin before I could be cornered.

A man emerged from the shadows of the next building.

'Gant! Gant! He's here!' The man was yelling into a handheld radio.

He should have been shooting.

Lifting the SIG, I continued forward and double-tapped the man, both times in the chest.

He went down, his legs swinging up like a clown doing a pratfall.

Skidding to a halt over him, I aimed my gun at the man's face. It was already bashed up, his nose having been recently broken judging by the dry blood smeared over his top lip, and the beginnings of bruising under his eyes. Maybe this was a result of the crashing vehicles earlier. Didn't matter.

He was dead, and he had certain items that would prove useful.

The radio and the gun.

Unlike the others he was armed with a shotgun, a sawn-off with a shortened stock and two barrels. I broke the stock and nodded. Two shells of 12-gauge shot were enough to kill anyone. A quick check of the man's body showed he hadn't brought extra ammo. I jammed the shotgun down the back of my jeans. It was uncomfortable, yes, but also a comforting weight.

Racing on, I thumbed down the volume on the radio so it didn't give away my position. I pushed the radio into a front pocket of my shirt, listening to the jumble of voices as the surviving skinheads called out to each other.

The radio traffic was largely indecipherable, but more than once the name 'Gant' was mentioned. The man who I just killed had called out the same name. Gant, I concluded, was the name of the tattooed man, their leader.

Good, because it's always preferable to know the name of an enemy.

Goading Gant was something to be considered, a way to force the battle towards me and away from Millie and the children. Except the likelihood was that Gant would order his men to turn off their radios, and then I'd have lost an advantage.

Something struck me: there were only three voices chattering over the channel. I had counted four still living and wondered why one of them wasn't involved in the plan to ambush me. I considered the hillbilly kid and how different he looked from the others, if in fact he was part of this group or if he had his own agenda. If that was the case then it meant I had two distinct enemies to contend with. That confused the issue and added to the danger stakes. Maybe I should have dropped him when the opportunity was there.

Racists and radical extremists come in all shapes and forms, some with hair and some without, so maybe it wasn't that unusual for Nazis to band with KKK wannabes when they had a common cause. However, I still had no idea what that cause was, other than they all wanted Don Griffiths and his family dead.

Well, my entire military career had been based upon fighting people who were governed by hatred and a desire to see anyone dead who didn't sit with their ideals. Stopping this bunch would have been an enjoyable nostalgia trip if not for the fact that the consequences of failure were more dire than usual.

An H&K rattled.

Don was still alive.

Two against four, the odds were piling in our favour every second.

OK. So let's get this done while things are swinging our way.

Rushing to the right, I gained the slope and the cover of the trees. The going would be a little slower, but there was less chance of running into any of my enemies while out in the woods. I thumbed the volume on the radio, listening as men reported the negative result of their search. If I could circle round behind them, gain entry to the structure where the children were, I could wait there for them and take them out one at a time.

If, I cautioned, wasn't a word allowed in my vocabulary. More psychobabble from my Arrowsake days, but I had to abide by the rule. You didn't plan on *if*, you made it so.

24

Gant was seething.

What should have been a simple forced entry to an unguarded house, a quick in-and-out mission, had turned to shit. Things didn't look like they were going to get any better, either.

He'd thought about the men accompanying him as being disposable, but now that wasn't the case. He wished that they were all back, hale and hearty and ready to lay down their lives all over again.

'Who the fuck is out there?' he yelled into his radio as he tried to staunch the flow of blood from his damaged ear.

'Fuckin' Rambo, you ask me,' came back Darley's whining tone.

'I don't mean *him*. I'm talking about our people. Sound off . . . one at a time.'

'Won't take much doing,' Darley said. 'There's only me and Holland still kicking.'

'Jesus . . .'

Gant pushed into the front of a cabin, shutting the door behind him with his foot. There he toyed with the oozing wound in his ear. 'You sure that's all there is, Dar?'

'I ain't heard much from Dillman since we last heard him shout out. I'm taking it that the bad-ass took him out.'

'Yeah,' Gant said touching his ear again. The bad-ass had come close to finishing him, too. Chances were that a hopeless cretin like Dillman wouldn't have fared better. He felt little regret. Dillman wouldn't be too much of a miss; the useless idiot had allowed Vince to get away. 'Holland, you still out there?'

'I'm here,' Holland said.

'Where?'

'Ass-end of the camp. Just spotted the minivan, but I can't get to it. Don Griffiths has me pinned down with a machine-gun.'

'You've found their vehicle? Tell me where.'

'Like I said, I'm at the ass-end of the camp.'

'That's a real help, Holland. This whole place is the fuckin' ass-end of the world.'

Darley cut into the conversation. 'Boss, I see the minivan. It's under a lean-to next to the last cabin on the right.'

'Can you get to it, Dar?' Gant asked.

'Will do.'

Holland said, 'I'd rather you gave me cover, Darley. Griffiths is getting too close for my liking.'

'So kill the bastard,' Gant snapped.

'You sure, boss? I thought you wanted to be the one to—'

'Things have changed, Holland. Or haven't you noticed? Just kill the bastard so we can get the fuck outa here.'

'With you, boss,' Holland said.

A machine-gun rattled in the distance.

'What about the other guy?' Darley asked.

'We see him, we kill him. Otherwise he's not our priority just now. Get to the minivan, Dar, and tell me what you find.'

Gant pinched his ear, trying to stop the flow of blood. Waste of time that was. He flicked scarlet drops on the walls, thinking about what he'd just said. Not a priority, my ass! If I see that piece of shit I'm gonna make it my life's work to put him in a grave.

Two machine-guns competed further up the camp. Gant opened the door of the cabin and peered out. A small figure sprinted through the haze of drizzle and gunsmoke, Darley heading for the lean-to. There was muzzle flash from where Holland was hunkered down behind an old flat-bed trailer abandoned when the last logging company truck rolled out. Gant added up his chances of getting round behind Griffiths and blasting the man, but discarded the idea. A far better plan was finding the kids and using them as a shield. He could then force Griffiths and whoever the fuck the other guy was into the open, where he could riddle them full of bullets with little fear of them shooting back.

'Van's empty, boss!'

Gant thumbed his radio up to his good ear.

'Say again, Dar.'

'The minivan's empty. What now?'

'Start checking the buildings next to it, I'm gonna make my way to you.'

He checked his assault rifle and it was almost empty. He dumped the depleted magazine then fished a fresh one out of his jacket pocket and slammed it in place.

As an afterthought, he called Holland.

'You get him yet?'

'Don't know, Gant. He's gone quiet all of a sudden.'

'So maybe you killed him, you fool.'

'Maybe that's what he wants me to think and he's waiting for me to come outa hiding.'

Holland had a point, but that meant nothing to Gant.

'Get your pussy ass in gear, Holland. Go check, now.'

'I'm going, OK?'

Gant waited, listening.

There was a single burp of an assault rifle.

'You get him, Holland? Holland?' Gant frowned at the radio, then sighed, 'Aah, shit.'

'Looks like it's down to me an' you, boss man,' Darley said a few seconds later.

Gant didn't bother answering. If he reckoned things had gone to shit before, now was much worse.

So it's time to turn things in our favour again, he thought, as he rushed out of the cabin and towards the next one in line.

25

A hollow in the lee of an ancient fir tree offered concealment. The boughs hung so low they were like widows' fingers digging at the soil as if trying to reclaim their lost husbands. Shadows cloaked me. The words coming from my pocket had a stereo effect now that I was so near to one of those talking, but the little bird-like man had no idea of how close to death he was.

I'd caught the gist of the radio-chatter. Discounting the young greaser, there were only two of the bastards left alive: Gant and this man called Darley. A well-placed shot, and then Gant would be seriously outnumbered if not outgunned, yet I was loath to pull the trigger. There were still so many questions unanswered that I thought about sparing the little skinhead for a minute or two while I beat some of the answers out of him.

Take the shot.

Do not underestimate this man. He may be small, but he's armed and intent on harming the kids. Slip up and you'll be one sorry bastard.

I raised my SIG, aiming through the branches, zeroing in on the man's chest. A head shot would be better, but the way it jerked about like a hen scratching for worms made for a poor target. I caressed the trigger, the progression on it smooth and easy. I was a hair's-breadth away from punching a cavity all the way through Darley when there was a flicker of movement which caused me to relax the pressure on the trigger, and watch as Don Griffiths came out from behind a cabin on the far side of the camp. The old man loped across the clearing, favouring one leg. But it wasn't my friend's appearance that caused me to spare Darley an immediate death, it was the fact that another man followed close on Don's heels.

Not Gant as I first feared, but the young man whose floppy quiff bounced with each jolting step.

Don glanced back at the young man, but he didn't stop. He didn't even flinch, just said something that I'd no way of hearing. The young man nodded, and they both headed directly for the cabin where Millie and the kids were hiding.

Shit, they've caught Don, was my immediate thought. The next was, *Don's got a gun but the greaser's unarmed. What the hell is going on here?*

When I glanced back at Darley, the little man had moved, squatting down behind the minivan so that neither Don nor his new companion could see him. I'd lost my shot.

'I bloody knew it,' I grunted.

From my pocket a voice hissed. I slipped the radio out so that I could hear clearly.

'Gant, you ain't gonna believe what I'm looking at . . .'

'I see them, Dar,' Gant replied in a voice close to a whisper. 'So that turncoat bastard's consorting with the enemy now?'

'How do you want to play things? I've got them both in my sights.'

'Hold it, Dar. I want Vince-fucking-Everett all to myself.'

'I can still pop Griffiths,' Darley said. In line with his words, the man leaned his rifle over the roof of the minivan. I half rose, lifting my SIG: it looked like I was going to have to go for a head shot after all.

'No, you could hit Vince.' Gant's warning made Darley dip back down again. 'I'm closer, I'll get Griffiths first.'

The tattooed man's words made me jerk upright.

Over seven years ago my failure to take a shot had caused repercussions to crash like a wave of destruction down through time. Many had died as a consequence and I'd almost perished before taking out the professional contract killer named Luke Rickard. Now, by missing the opportunity to take out Darley it looked like Don was going to die.

Don and the young man were out of my line of sight now, but they weren't deaf.

'Don! Get down!' I roared at the top of my voice.

Then I crashed out from below the fir tree, drawing Darley's attention. Little good it would do to throw off Gant's aim, and I could only hope that my warning was heard and acted upon.

There was the staccato rattle of a machine-gun, and I added a backbeat, firing as I ran at Darley.

The bullets struck the roof of the minivan, smashed a window, cut grooves out of the metalwork, but not one of them found flesh.

So much for conserving rounds, but that wasn't a consideration now. It was all about causing enough confusion to draw Gant away from Don. I fired again, swerving round the back of the minivan. If Darley was standing his ground, the move would be both reckless and suicidal, but the little man was still ducking and diving to escape the barrage of bullets. I was on him before he could swing the rifle round.

I don't like bullies, and felt a bit like the jock beating down on the nerd in the playground, but in the circumstances it was justified. I slammed a kick into Darley's chest and the man went down on his back. My next kick was aimed at the gun and knocked it out of his hands.

'You bastard,' Darley hissed between clenched teeth. His eyes were rolling in his skull as he sought to grapple with my legs. I sidestepped and jabbed his ribs with the toe of my boot.

Just finish the little shit, I thought, you haven't got time for this.

Ordinarily I would do so, but I was still experiencing a twinge of guilt, not liking the thought of killing the small man when he was already overwhelmed.

Remember the two in the parking lot, Hunter: did you give them a second chance?

I was still trying to put those two to the back of my mind, and now this?

Darley grabbed at his belt and came out with a knife.

That had an immediate and devastating result for Darley.

I avoided the slash of the knife, and Darley took the opportunity to swing up on to one knee. That put him directly in line with the knee that I rammed under his jaw. Darley's head snapped back, flecks of blood marking the saliva that flew from his mouth. His eyes were already rolling up into his skull, so he didn't feel the whack of the SIG's barrel as it slammed the side of his head.

Darley flopped to the floor, and a rattling exhalation spattered more blood on his chin.

I was already moving away, shoving the SIG in my belt as I stopped to snatch up Darley's rifle.

There was another rattle of gunfire.

Gant's first volley had missed Don, then? Either that or the tattooed man had now turned his anger on the young man. Worse than that was if he'd got both first time and this new sound was of Gant murdering Millie and the children.

Letting out a wordless shout I dashed from behind the minivan, heedless of the fact I might be in Gant's crosshairs. The cabin where the woman and kids were secreted was only two over. There was a new addition on the front boardwalk that hadn't been there when I'd last left them. The bundle proved to be the form of a man, and by the white hair and beard it could only be one person.

Dear God! No!

Gant had brought down Don Griffiths and he wasn't moving.

I spurred myself on, senses fighting to stay focused against the rush of self-loathing that assailed me like a suffocating cloak. It was bad enough that Don had been hit, but now the screams of the terrified children rang clear. The door to the cabin had been kicked in. Gant was already inside and terrorising the kids.

Stay in the red zone.

The thought struck at the same time as bullets singed the air around me. Caught off-guard, I stumbled and fell, rolling to avoid another volley of rounds churning the mud next to my body. A bullet struck the rifle and knocked it out of my hands. I let it lie and scrambled away, then came to my feet again and threw myself across the boardwalk and against the wall of the cabin, looking for targets as I snatched out my SIG. Movement flickered across the way and Gant rushed out from his hiding place in the cabin opposite. Gant fired as he ran causing me to jump for my life away from the bullets cutting into the wall beside me.

I fired in return.

One bullet was all I had left and it had to count.

Too many variables affected my aim, primarily the fact that Gant was moving while I was flinching from the bullets scoring the cabin wall next to my body. The bullet went wide and didn't even slow Gant's charge.

Well, this is it, Hunter. The thought echoed through my mind. This was thc placc I was going to dic, a muddy, stinking hole in the middle of nowhere, just like I'd always imagined it would be.

My next thought: you're not dead yet.

With my left hand I tugged out the 12-gauge and swung it on the advancing man, giving him both barrels.

The shotgun boomed like a canon.

Gant's legs were thrown from under him and he went spread-eagled in the mud, his gun sliding away from him in the filth. In the mist above him I could see a distinct red haze.

Go to him. Finish the bastard once and for all.

I heard Beth howl.

Then another voice, feeble but close by.

Glancing at Don Griffiths, I saw him roll over on to his back. There was a large red stain on the front of his coat, another near his left hip. Don craned up so that he could see me, and his face was white.

'The little ones, Hunter, check that my grandchildren are OK.'

Without further debate I raced to the cabin door and into the gloomy interior. Across the way Millie was shielding the two children, their eyes and mouths wide ovals. That was all I'd time to take in before something looped over my head, encircled my throat and was drawn tight. Blackness edged my vision immediately, followed a second later by the agony of savagely twisting flesh. A knee jammed into the small of my back.

Absurdly I thought: at least I'm not going to die in the mud.

Both my guns clattered on the floorboards. Empty, they were a hindrance, but that wasn't why I dropped them; I simply lacked the strength to hold on to them any longer. I lifted my fingers to the loop around my throat, tried to dig my fingers under the constricting coil, but had no hope of that. My killer knew exactly what he was doing.

I sagged, strength failing completely as pressure built within my skull. This was how the rooster-crowing man must have felt as I throttled him to death in the Seven-Eleven car park.

My mind was a scarlet sea now, waves crashing against the insides of my skull. The scarlet darkened to black.

Suddenly I was face down on the floor with no memory of drifting from one place to the other. No transition occurred between space and time, just as if my body had been jumped to this new position by the click of a magician's fingers. Gagging and retching, I sucked in life-giving oxygen. My throat was a circle of fire. I coughed and spluttered then heaved in a great gust of air.

Instinct made me grope for the KA-BAR, my only remaining weapon, but my fingers were crushed to the boards by the sole of a boot. I still didn't have the strength, let alone the presence of mind, to fight back, and could only growl out in pain as the bones of my recently broken hand were ground under the pressure. A hand groped at my clothing and snatched the KA-BAR out of my grasp. Thankfully the pressure on my hand was relieved and finally I rolled over on to my back to blink up at my captor.

My eyes were streaming with tears, but even so I recognised the pompadour sticking out from the top of the young man's head.

He gave me a lopsided grin. Then he said, 'You, my friend, are under arrest.'

26

'You're fucking kidding me! You're a cop?'

The young greaser shook his head as he kicked away the shotgun and lifted my SIG from the ground. He waved it loosely in my direction. 'Nope, I'm FBI. Special Agent Vincent at your service.'

Taking in the black leather, the jeans, the pompadour and his spare features, I snorted at the young man. 'Tell me your first name is Gene if you dare.'

Vince's lip turned up. '"Be-Bop-A-Lula"? Ha, you made the connection, right? None of those skinhead assholes would have had a clue. They think I'm called Vince Everett, but, no, my real name's Stephen Vincent.'

'Vince Everett? You were taking a risk calling yourself that. Any Elvis fan knows his movie characters.'

'Sounds like you know your music history,' Vince said. 'Gant and those other idiots had other things on their mind.'

'So have I,' I said, nodding over at the Griffiths children staring back at us.

Vince nodded in confirmation. 'I'm with you, buddy.'

'Hunter.'

'Hunter?'

'That's my name. Joe Hunter. You said I was under arrest. That's generally a cop's next question, isn't it?' I massaged my throat, worked my aching fingers. Vince's heels had taken skin off the knuckles. The garrotte still hung limp in his hands. 'Strange equipment you carry, Special Agent.'

'Just part of the cover, man.' He stuffed the garrotte out of sight.

Gave me the opportunity to roll up on to my haunches.

'Stay right there, Hunter. I don't want to shoot you after all this.'

I shrugged. 'Mind showing me some identification?'

'Left it in my other jeans, I'm afraid.' Vince looked over at Millie and the kids. 'Everything is OK now. Relax. You're going to be safe.'

'You attacked me,' Millie said in a small voice.

Vince straightened up a little, inhaling. 'You didn't give me a chance to explain, Millie. I was going to introduce myself when you threw that goddamn cat in my face. Well, after that, things just went a little haywire, didn't they?'

'You had that noose with you. You were about to strangle me.'

'I was just keeping up the act. One of Gant's people was outside watching. I was going to pull you away from the window with it. Get you out of the way.'

'The girl with the spiky hair . . .'

'Sonya Madden,' Vince confirmed. His eyes pinched as he said the name.

'Speaking of whom, what happened to her?'

Vince turned and saw that I'd come silently to my feet. He flinched, and lifted the gun. My hands were raised, a sign for Vince to relax.

Vince said, 'She died. Or more rightly, you killed her when you made me swerve into that goddamn cabin down on the road.'

I lifted my eyebrows, pursed my lips. 'I would've preferred it if that hadn't happened. But she was shooting at us at the time.'

'You're pleading self-defence?'

I nodded at the children. 'I was trying to save their lives. Seeing as the FBI was conspicuous by their absence.'

'First opportunity I had I called for back-up. They're on their way here now.'

'So in the meantime it was down to me to do *everything* I could to save these children.'

'Hell, you went through them like a one-man army.'

I just looked at the young man.

Vince stared back into my eyes, and said, 'The thing that concerns me is that you don't look like you give a good goddamn about any of them. Jesus, Hunter, how many of them have you taken down?'

'I lost count,' I admitted. 'Not that I'll put that on record.'

Vince scowled. 'Don't suppose I can use that against you seeing as I haven't Mirandised you yet.'

'Does that mean I'm still under arrest?'

'You're still under arrest, make no mistake about it.'

My shoulders lifted in a shrug. 'Does that stop me from helping a wounded man?'

Right on cue, Millie shrieked. 'Dad?'

Nodded over my shoulder. 'Out there. He's been shot.'

Millie scrambled up, hushing the kids, then sprinted across the room and bumped by Vince like he wasn't there. As she made to go round me, I grabbed hold of her and pulled her close. 'Let me check, first,' I said.

Before Millie or Vince could object, I went out on to the boardwalk. I had a horrible feeling what I would find. Don stared with the glazed-over eyes of someone who now looked on different vistas. I contained the groan rising in my chest, and was steeling myself to give Millie the terrible news when something else caught my eye. Stooping down, I pulled Don's rifle from limp fingers.

'The hell you doing?' Vince demanded from the doorway. 'You're still under arrest, you can't just . . .'

I indicated the place where Gant had fallen. The mud was churned up, mixed in with copious amounts of blood, but of the tattooed man there was no sign. Drag marks along the road surface showed where he'd been hauled away.

'Son of a bitch!' Vince breathed as he heard the black van burst to life.

His curse was echoed by mine as I took a couple of steps out into the road. I lifted the assault rifle and fired, but already the van was being reversed at speed through the camp and the bullets failed to slow it. After a couple hundred yards the driver hit a one-eighty skid then gunned the van away.

'I hope your back-up's coming up that mountainside or they're going to escape,' I said. Vince was too busy staring at the gun in my hands as though it was about to be turned on him. I grunted, and held out the assault rifle. 'Relax, Agent Vincent. We're both on the same side here.' I pointed at the SIG in Vince's hand. 'Trade you? My gun's no good to you anyway, not with no bullets in it.'

'Son of a bitch,' Vince said again.

The assault rifle was slipped on to the young FBI agent's arm, at the same time as I plucked the SIG away and shoved it down the small of my back. 'I'd like the knife, too, if you don't mind?'

'You're my prisoner,' Vince said, quite stupidly even to his own ears.

'Am I?'

'Aah, for God sakes!' Vince handed over the KA-BAR.

Behind us, Millie hugged Don. The children had come to the door and Beth was cradling her sobbing brother in an echo of her older relatives' pose. We shared a humiliated glance, and went to help them.

All of us were stunned to hear Don ask, 'Is it over?'

Don's eyelids fluttered and some lucidity came back into his face. Millie and the kids let out squeals of delight as they all threw themselves at the old man. I stepped back to give them clearance, smiling at them in turn when they glanced up at me in wonder. Between their hugs and questions and the general confusion Don's gaze fell on me. 'Is it over?' he demanded again.

'Over,' I said with a curt nod. But I kept my next words to myself. *Not by a long shot.*

Vince was watching me. The young man had lost the cocky persona he'd carried as Vince Everett and I guessed that the agent was thinking the exact same thing. Both of us turned and scanned the area where the black van had disappeared moments before.

We were still watching twenty minutes later when the first FBI vehicles began entering the compound.

Two minutes later and I was again face down while men held me under guard. From this prone position, I heard Vince say, 'Let him up, will you. He's one of the good guys.'

27

'There's a guy behind the third cabin along, another two out in the trees,' I offered to the group of FBI agents tasked with making sense of the war zone. 'Some others are down at the base of the hill where you turned off the road, and there's more back at the Reynoldses' house.'

'Is that it?' an agent asked, his face showing that he was actually serious.

'Isn't that enough to be getting on with?' They didn't know about the men from the Seven-Eleven yet, but it was best to let those two lie for a while. Everyone else I could put down to reaction under duress and argue self-defence. Some might see the first two as murder, albeit I was now thinking of them in terms of a pre-emptive strike. It eased my conscience that way.

'It's about twenty too many,' the agent said.

'I think you'll find that's an exaggeration.'

'Is it?' The agent looked me up and down, taking in the scraped knuckles. 'You seem to have come out of this relatively unharmed. You sure you were the only one responsible for killing them all?'

'Can't claim them all,' I admitted, rubbing at the red mark on my neck. 'Don Griffiths bagged one of the arseholes. You'll find him over by that flat-bed.'

The agent was scribbling on a clipboard, mapping the area and making notations with a black cross for where the bodies lay. He handed off the notes to one of his colleagues who ushered the others away to begin a more detailed search. The first agent looked at me again. 'You said two of them got away.'

'Sadly, yes. Two pricks who went by the name of Gant and Darley.'

The agent recognised the names, repeating them back to himself. 'That would be Samuel Gant and Darley Adams.'

I filed both names away for later. 'Are you going to tell me about them?'

'No.' The agent walked away. 'You haven't got clearance.'

Shaking my head, I sat on a stoop outside one of the abandoned cabins, away from the buzz of activity. I looked around, taking in the scene, reminded of when I took down the serial killer, Tubal Cain. On that occasion it was as if most of the available government agents in the South-West had turned up at the killer's hidey-hole in the Mojave. Then, they were there to recover bones, whereas here in the Alleghenies the corpses were much fresher. The number of agents was on a par, though, as was the proliferation of vehicles turning up. A medi-vac chopper had arrived earlier, but with nowhere to land in the hills it had diverted to the wide space on the road below. Don had been rushed away in the rear compartment of a government SUV to meet the chopper, medics working furiously to keep him alive. Millie, Beth and Ryan kept him company down the mountainside. The others required medical assistance too, chilled to the core as they were and were suffering from shock.

I hadn't been offered the same consideration.

Goes with the territory, I suppose. Some of the FBI personnel still weren't sure that I should even be at liberty. My weapons had been taken from me, bagged and sealed, but I still caught the occasional suspicious glance as though I was about to go off on another killing spree. Thankfully Special Agent Vincent – or just plain *Vince* as he'd told me to call him – had a lot of clout and had won me my freedom. Maybe

Vince was making up for almost taking my head off with that bloody garrotte.

Could've done with getting to a telephone. My first call would be to Rink, the next to Walter Hayes Conrad. On second thoughts, maybe I should call Walter first.

When I worked for Arrowsake I was part of an experimental coalition of Special Forces operatives. Due to their world-ranging scope, Arrowsake had controllers in each Allied country and on this side of the Atlantic Walter Conrad, a sub-division director of the CIA, was my handler. More importantly than that, he was my friend and confidant, sometimes a mentor and father figure. My real father died when I was a child, and though my stepdad, Bob Telfer, was a decent enough man, he just never seemed to gel with me the way he did with his own child, John. As a young soldier, fresh to Arrowsake, I had found the paternal replacement I'd been looking for in Walter.

In the time I'd been in the USA, Walter's influence had meant that my violent retribution wreaked on a gamut of killers had been looked on favourably by *certain high-powered government officials*. In layman's terms, Walter had kept me out of prison by calling in favours. He'd even wangled it so that I, along with Rink and our mutual friend, Harvey Lucas, was back on the government payroll when tracking and taking out Luke Rickard, the contract killer engaged in assassinating past members of Walter's unit.

Perhaps it would be a good idea to earn special dispensation from Walter this time.

I looked for Vince, my only ally in the entire compound.

Last time I'd seen him, Vince was deep in conversation with the SAC who'd arrived to take charge of the investigation. By the way that SAC Birnbaum – who should have been Vince's superior – deferred to the young agent, Vince had a little more clout than your average feebie behind him.

An FBI storm trooper strode by, dressed in tactical kit as though Gant and Darley might return for a second show. I waved the man over and he adjusted his Heckler and Koch MP5/10 as though readying to strafe me should I make any unwarranted move. I did my best to ignore the weapon pointing at me. 'Have you seen Special Agent Vincent lately?'

The trooper sniffed. He regarded me with eyes that rolled like marbles in a storm drain. 'I'll tell him you were asking after him.'

'If you just point out where he is, I'll go tell him myself.'

'No, buddy, you get to stay right there.'

The feebie strode away, leaving me with the impression that he'd no intention of finding Vince.

If you want something doing . . .

I stood up. My leg ached, my hand ached, my entire body ached, but that was what came from sitting on your backside after a burst of sustained activity. Got to get back in training, I promised, as I arched my lower back to loosen the kinks. I stretched and yawned, not even considering the fact that this was my second full day without sleep. As I went through the motions, I scanned the camp for any sign of Vince's give-away pompadour hairstyle.

I spotted the young agent striding away from a hastily erected white tent near to the back of the camp. Already, now that his cover was no longer an issue, Vince had shed the trappings of his Southern racist persona. Instead of his leather jacket with its Confederate battle flag, he now wore a black windcheater emblazoned with the FBI motif. His hair was under a cap similarly marked.

I took a step in the agent's direction. Something bumped softly against my shins. Glancing down I saw the old tomcat twining itself about my ankles. The cat's purr was like an idling bulldozer.

'So you stuck around, huh?'

The cat blinked at me, sat down and began licking its nether regions.

'My sentiments exactly,' I laughed. I reached down and the cat allowed me to pick it up. It sat in the crook of an elbow, eyeing me with its amber stare. I walked quickly to cut off Vince's route through the compound.

Vince glanced up from under the brim of his cap.

'Gonna get an executive order passed so I can shoot that damn thing,' Vince growled.

The cat tensed, hissed at Vince.

'Easy now, Vince, you're hurting his feelings.'

'Good. You've seen what that crazy animal did to my face?' He pulled off the cap so that his scratches were even more vivid. When he felt the drizzle, he quickly jammed the cap back on.

'He was just reacting to what he perceived as a threat. You aren't going to hold that against him are you?' I scrubbed behind the cat's ears, thinking I'd found a viable metaphor for my own reaction to the two at the Seven-Eleven. Vince continued to scowl at the cat, but it was as much an act as Vince Everett had been. I laughed. 'He's not a bad old sort when you get to know him better. The kids named him Fluffy.'

'Go figure,' Vince said.

I indicated the white tent. 'Anyone in there got a flask of coffee? I think we both could do with warming up a little.'

'This way,' Vince said, but he headed away from the tent.

We approached a large wagon parked outside the camp. A container on the back bristled with antennae. Mobile command unit, I guessed. What were the chances of the FBI having one of these on hand all the way out here? I shook the thought loose: what did it matter for now?

Vince led the way inside the container through a door at the back. It was a cramped space of desks and computer monitors, alive with electrical static and a background hum of fans. There was also the welcome aroma of strong coffee. Two support staff looked up at us, both unconcerned by my appearance or by the cat in my arms. Vince greeted them, then asked them for a few minutes' privacy. They took Styrofoam cups with them as they clumped down outside.

Vince poured cups of steaming coffee from a silver thermos. I sat down on one of the vacated office chairs and began pulling at the plastic bag beneath my shirt, releasing a trickle of moisture that darkened the floor. Then I scrubbed rain from my hair. I allowed the cat to slink away and it snuffled at a paper bag on a work desk. It must have found a juicy morsel inside, because it hunkered down and started chewing appreciatively. Hunger pangs dug at my insides, but the coffee was a more welcome prospect. I accepted it gratefully as Vince handed over a cup. I left the cream and sugar on the desk top: it was pure caffeine I was after.

'Probably tastes like dirty water,' Vince said.

Under the circumstances, it was just about the best cup of coffee I'd tasted in a long time. The steaming brew went down in two gulps. 'I wouldn't say no to another.'

Vince set about pouring again.

While he busied himself I studied the command unit. There was nothing in the makeshift office that gave a clue about what the bigger picture was, and the support staff had had the presence of mind to turn off their monitors before leaving. I caught my reflection in one of the darkened screens. Jesus, what a mess. My two-day-old beard was dark on my chin, hair plastered to my head from where I'd wiped the rain away. Streaks of mud and a spray of blood marked my shirt. No wonder I was getting suspicious looks from the FBI agents.

Vince delivered a second coffee and I savoured this one, cupping it between both palms and allowing the steam to trickle over my face. In the warmth of the command unit my clothing began to steam as well.

'I thought all you Brits drank tea?'

'I've been Americanised,' I said, smiling whimsically. 'I'm thinking of buying shares in Starbucks, I spend so much time there.'

It was small talk as a way into the weightier issues. I took a sip of the hot brew, then launched directly into what was bothering me. 'There are a couple of things I don't quite understand about you, Vince. I was wondering if you were going to enlighten me.'

'Could say the same about you.'

'You've already had me checked out,' I said.

Vince shrugged. 'Standard operating procedure. The problem is we kept on hitting brick walls. Most of your files are sealed.'

'You needn't worry. Like you said to your buddies, I'm one of the good guys.'

'The way you went through Samuel Gant and his goons, I'm inclined to challenge you on that.'

'I just did what anyone in the same position would've done.'

Vince laughed without humour. 'No, Hunter. Most people would have bent down, put their heads between their legs and kissed their butts goodbye.'

'I'm not the type to lie down and die, Vince.'

'SAC Birnbaum did a little checking of his own. His opposite number over in Maine speaks highly of you.'

'Hubbard,' I confirmed. It surprised me, because SAC Hubbard hadn't been my biggest fan when first we met. It didn't help that I was a suspected cop killer at the time, but clearing up the Luke Rickard mess must have endeared me to the FBI man.

'He told Birnbaum to give you his best regards . . . and to cut you some slack.'

'Nice of him.'

'He said you've proven helpful to the FBI on more than one occasion.'

Could have told him about Tubal Cain, but my involvement there was buried even from the FBI, courtesy of Walter Conrad. I guessed that Vince was referring to Jean-Paul St Pierre, the contract killer who went by the name of a fallen angel. Dantalion had murdered a handful of FBI agents including Kaufman, an SAC from the Miami field office, before I finally stopped him. 'I'm not a FBI groupie, if that's what you're thinking?'

'So what exactly are you?'

'I'm just someone who cares. I'm not going to stand around while children are being terrorised.'

'Donovan Griffiths hired you?'

'I didn't come for the money. I just wanted to help. Nobody else seemed to be doing much.'

'I was on the case.'

'I couldn't sit around waiting for the cavalry to come to their rescue, Vince. What do you think I should've done?'

'The FBI doesn't look favourably on vigilantes.'

'Vigilantes take the law into their own hands, Vince. Off the record? There aren't too many laws that govern what I sometimes have to do.'

'Sounds like you've practised that speech, Hunter.'

I grinned. 'It's good guy one-o-one.'

Vince regarded me over the top of his coffee, while I stared right back. 'I suppose you have a point; what I sometimes have to do isn't FBI procedure either.'

'The old quid pro quo game, huh?'

'I guess I owe you an explanation, seeing as I almost strangled you to death.'

I touched my throat. It was still hot from where Vince's garrotte had sunk into the flesh. 'Explain away.'

28

'Did you ever catch that TV series on the Fox network? *Twenty-one Jump Street*?'

Couldn't help but smile at the reference. It was almost as if I'd been expecting it. 'You know, Vince, from certain angles you remind me a little of Johnny Depp.'

The agent attempted to conceal the smugness, but some of Vince Everett's swagger returned. 'So I've been told.'

'Ever seen *Edward Scissorhands*?'

Vince made a noise in the back of his throat but my smile helped show I was only joking. I had in fact been thinking of another movie Depp featured in where he played a 1950s juvenile delinquent, the one with Ricki Lake and Iggy Pop.

'If,' Vince went on, 'you're familiar with the concept of Jump Street, you'll know that it followed a group of undercover cops who infiltrated youth gangs. Well, I'm part of a similar FBI operation. Only we target home-grown militant groups.'

'So you posed as a racist to get inside Gant's mob? Odd that neo-Nazis would welcome someone with so much hair.'

'It was a conscious decision to use the Vince Everett cover. It would have been too difficult carrying off an act that I was a Nazi. Sooner or later, my cover would have been blown. But you know what they say about birds of a feather?'

'They accepted you through your common hatred of everyone who wasn't a WASP?'

'Yeah, but it wasn't easy. The only way I got in was through Sonya Madden.'

'The punk rocker girl?'

'Yeah.' For a second Vince's eyes clouded over.

'You regret that she came to harm. I hope you don't hold her death against me?'

'I can't really do that, Hunter.' He flicked a glance around, checking for the electronic ears that were more than likely in existence in the command unit. He lowered his voice to a whisper and mimed a nudge of his elbow. 'Not when I helped her out the window as we crashed. Couldn't really allow her to harm anyone else, and it was the first opportunity I got.'

Accepting what he said without comment was difficult; the thought of murdering a woman was abhorrent to me . . . *usually*. Having the woman's death on my conscience would have been terrible if she wasn't trying to kill those under my protection. Instead I said, 'Vince Everett had to have been a real person. Gant would have checked.'

'Yeah, Everett was real. He was a young junkie who murdered his grandfather during a bungled robbery. He was also suspected of beating a cop to death with a PR24 baton, not to mention a number of rapes where he first throttled his victims within an inch of their lives with a guitar string. He was as heavy a white supremacist as any in Gant's outfit. Shame he turned up dead after overdosing: he should have gone to prison for a long time, maybe in a cell alongside some brothers.'

Yes, that would have been justice, rather than the relatively easy way that Everett went. 'The FBI kept his demise a secret, I'm assuming, and you slipped right into the role.'

'The name helped. I've been called Vince by all my friends since kindergarten, so I was never going to mess up and forget to answer someone calling my name.'

'There was more to it than that.'

'Of course there was. I had to get into his mind, become Vince Everett in every way. I had to think like him, act like him, do what he would do. It wasn't nice being in his head like that, but I had to show those assholes that I was a worthy ally. Plus there was the fact that Everett was just the kind of guy Sonya Madden found irresistible.' Again the agent's eyes clouded. 'Madden by name but mad by nature. It's a shame she was such a psychopath, 'cause underneath it all she was quite a girl.'

'Forgetting that she was part of a radical extremist network, as well?'

'Yeah, there was that.' Vince straightened his cap, winning a few seconds to compose himself. While he ordered his next words, Fluffy sauntered across the desk beside him. The cat glowered at him like he was something to be utterly and contemptuously destroyed. Vince broke open a carton of cream and offered it to the tom. 'Peace offering?'

Fluffy sniffed and sashayed, but then settled down to lap the cream from the tub. Its occasional glance my way demanded to know what I was worrying about, now that Vince was his new best friend.

'Traitor,' I called the cat. It turned its back on me.

Vince grinned at the cat. 'He has a lot in common with me, I guess.'

I squinted at him, not quite getting the reference. Vince said, 'To Gant and Carswell Hicks I'm a traitor to their cause.'

'Little notice Hicks will take. Last I heard he was dead.'

'You and millions of others . . .'

I didn't like the undertone of Vince's delivery.

'What exactly are you saying, Vince?'

'Carswell Hicks is as alive as you or me. The death story is just that.'

'You're kidding, right?'

'Why would I lie to you?'

'You're a feebie. You're undercover. You have your own agenda. Take your pick.'

'Christ, you're a cynic, Hunter.'

'It tends to keep me alive.'

'And you're full of pithy sayings.'

'Good guy one-o-one, I told you.'

Vince sipped coffee. I mirrored him. The cat nudged the empty cream carton along the desk, unaware of or indifferent to the silence between the two men in its presence.

Finally I placed the empty Styrofoam cup down. 'Carswell Hicks. Where is he?'

'Sure wish that we knew. As you probably heard, an attempt was made to break Hicks out of prison when he was transferred to a less-secure hospital wing. The hospital's medi-vac chopper was hijacked but later went down off the coast with no apparent survivors. Hicks' body was never found, although the general public wasn't informed of that in case it caused a furore. It was while Obama was running for president, and his supporters wouldn't take kindly to someone possibly back in the public arena who'd make it his mission to destroy a black presidential candidate. You could say Hicks earned a modicum of protection from the same government he'd tried to disrupt all those years. Go figure, man!'

'Sounds ridiculous, but not unheard of,' I said, as disgusted as Vince was. 'The British government released IRA murderers, and actually settled them on the mainland, under the Good Friday Agreement, gave them new identities so that no one would know who was living in their midst. Talk about pandering to your enemies.'

'As far as everyone's concerned, Hicks is dead and no threat to the president or the stability of our country. The reality is that the corpse they displayed was that of a homeless John Doe who bore a passing resemblance to Hicks. The guy had fallen into a river and drowned, so he fit the part. But to further disguise him, the JD was liberally doused in aviation fuel and burned.'

'Jesus, that's brutal.'

'Had to make it look real, Hunter.'

'OK. So what happened? Hicks took his freedom but that wasn't enough for him? He has reinitiated his old hate campaign?'

'Yes. He laid low for a while, but then . . . Bam!' Vince waved his arms like the flourish of a magician. 'Suddenly he's back and people are beginning to die. We're concerned that he's planning something big.'

'But you've no idea where he's currently hiding, so it's difficult to check?'

'It's why I infiltrated his group, to try to get a lead on his location.'

'And when you find him he's going to be taken right back to prison?'

Shaking his head, Vince smiled, and it was like a reflection of the smile I often view in mirrors. 'Don't forget, Hunter, he's already dead. Can't suddenly dump him back in the system, can we?'

'Your job is to take him out?'

'What I sometimes have to do isn't FBI procedure.'

'Assassination isn't even CIA procedure these days,' I said, though I knew differently. Another thought struck me. 'The attacks on Don Griffiths and his family have nothing to do with revenge, have they? Don found him first time, and now Hicks is making sure that history doesn't repeat itself.'

'It's worse than that, Hunter. I wasn't party to everything that was said – unfortunately all our orders came via Gant – but what I understand is that Hicks wants *something* from Griffiths. And if Griffiths doesn't hand it over then his family will pay.'

I went very still.

Vince studied me, noting the coldness slip into my face. 'Your killer eyes are back,' he said.

'Yes.' My voice seeped across to him like a freezing fog. 'You knew that Gant was going to attack the family, yet you allowed it to happen.'

'I didn't have an opportunity to call it in, not with Sonya at my side every second,' Vince said. But he knew his excuse sounded lame.

'No. You wanted them to get what they wanted from Griffiths. You fully intended helping them. That way, Gant would trust you and then lead you back to Hicks. It's why this FBI task force was on hand and in such numbers.' Fisting my hands, it was a struggle to keep them on the desktop.

To his credit, Vince didn't attempt to lie. Instead he said, 'Sometimes small sacrifices have to be made. The needs of the many outweigh the needs of the few.'

'And you call me pithy.'

Vince threw up his arms. The sudden movement startled Fluffy, who instantly reverted to his former self. The tom arched his back and spat and then retreated to crouch between the protective walls made by my forearms. Wary of both the cat and the man, Vince said, 'Well it's all fucked, isn't it? My cover's blown, there's no way I can get close to Hicks now.' He waited a beat before saying, 'I guess we move to Plan B and send a new man after him.' Vince grinned. 'We have, of course, got someone in mind. In fact, Walter Hayes Conrad endorsed the idea and says he knows the ideal person for the job.'

29

The following morning found me sitting in a plastic chair, again sipping coffee, this time from a waxed-paper cup. The room was as utilitarian as the interior of the command unit vehicle, except this time the smell wasn't of perspiration mingling with ozone, but the antiseptic odour characteristic of all hospitals. From beyond the closed door came the soft clinks, the hurried footsteps, the low conversations familiar to a medical facility.

I was in a small antechamber off the main waiting area of Hertford City Medical Center, twiddling my thumbs and upping my caffeine quota. I didn't like sitting around like this.

Earlier, I'd visited Don Griffiths' sickroom, but the old man was heavily sedated and had given away nothing save for the one answer I'd been seeking.

I've never appreciated the term *assassin* spoken alongside my name, but I wasn't so blinkered that I'd lost sight of what my military designation had meant. I could dress it up in fancy metaphors, argue that I was simply a soldier doing his duty, but when all came to all I was charged with killing those deemed enemies of the countries under Arrowsake's protection. However, that was then. Now I was no longer under the Arrowsake sanction, and would argue vehemently against the notion that I'd ever again become the guided missile of the past. Not that it was a serious argument: twice in the past year I'd become just that. Dantalion had been a personal kill, as had those who'd died as a result of hunting

Kate Piers and Imogen Ballard, but when taking down Luke Rickard and Tubal Cain, I'd been working to some extent on behalf of the shadowy agency. Arrowsake was no more, but it seemed that its influence resonated to this day.

In previous circumstances where Walter Conrad had shown his hand, I'd convinced myself that my quest was personal, that I'd have taken on the mission without official approval, and that Walter's help was only a means to achieve my end. Pushed into this latest situation, the same terms could apply.

Looking at the problem objectively, I'd come to Pennsylvania to help an old friend whose family was being terrorised by bad men, and though the dynamics had altered, the problem persisted. The only way that the Griffithses would ever be safe was if their enemies were stopped. Gant and Darley were the patsies of Carswell Hicks, which made Hicks the major factor in the problem. As ever, I preferred going directly for the largest bully in the gang. Without its fountainhead, Hicks' organisation would rapidly dry up, and any remnants would blow away on the wind or be mopped up as necessary. If the FBI, CIA or any other acronym-headed organisation chose to give me the weapons necessary to get the job done, then so be it.

I'm no killer for hire, and never will be, but I'll do it for free where need dictates: I often laughed at the absurdity of that.

But now, having looked at the old man, who – even through a heady cloud of anaesthesia – still moaned in agony, I wasn't laughing.

I'd decided I was going to accept Special Agent Vincent's offer: help him to take out Carswell Hicks and my slate would be wiped clean.

Under congressional ruling, the CIA was no longer allowed to conduct their activities within the United States, and torture and assassination were strictly forbidden. I knew otherwise. Walter was like a surrogate father to me, but sometimes even the most loving father uses his children for his own selfish ends. I was under no illusion. This was a case of *plausible denial*: in other words, if I fucked up it would be on my own back. The government would deny all knowledge of or involvement with my actions.

In one sense this was good. It meant that they'd keep the hell out of the way. Red tape and bureaucracy were always a stumbling block to the fulfilment of a mission. I'd use their resources to find Hicks, but once I'd found him, it would be down to me.

Not that I was above accepting help, especially when the offer came from my friend, Jared Rington, who had answered the call to arms without question. The questions would come later, after Rink verbally kicked my butt for getting us into another mess. My big friend liked to think himself the voice of reason, but he was as much up for action as I was. The kick in the backside would be followed by Rink's toothy grin and the query, 'So when do we start, brother?'

There was a knock at the door, bringing me back to the present. I stood up, subconsciously putting my back to the wall and facing the entrance, as though meeting the advance of an enemy. It was too soon for Rink to have arrived, and for a moment I didn't recognise the man standing on the threshold.

He was clean-cut, with short hair in a side parting, a pristine white shirt and steel-grey tie under a flawlessly tailored dark suit. His shoes were polished to a mirror-perfect sheen, as black and glossy as the attaché case he carried. The only thing that spoiled the preppy good looks was the stripes down his cheek where Fluffy the cat had marked him.

'You going for the DiCaprio look this time?'

'This is the *real* me,' Vince said, stepping inside the room. 'You don't think I'm really into that old-time stuff? Jesus, Hunter? Elvis is dead, haven't you heard?'

'Not true,' I said, straight-faced. 'His death was a cover-up; didn't you know he was an undercover DEA agent? He had to go into hiding after making some nasty enemies in the Colombian cartels. I know . . . I've met the man.'

Vince stared and I shook my head ruefully.

Vince surprised me by shrugging. 'Maybe you have a point. The world thinks Carswell Hicks is dead, but really he's still running around. Those stories about the King flipping burgers at a joint in Seattle might not be as crazy as they sound.'

I'd been suckered by the old double-bluff. The kid was as sharp as his new look. I made a point of keeping that in mind.

Vince was still grinning when he placed the attaché case on one of the plastic chairs. He flipped open the lid, pulled out a blue zip-lock bag, and then held it out like an offering.

I wasn't surprised to find my SIG SAUER P226 and KA-BAR inside. I'd demanded their return as part of my side in sealing the bargain. The stack of money and credit cards raised an eyebrow though.

'I know that morally you won't accept payment, but don't look on the cash that way. Call it expenses if you want, Hunter, because you're going to need money to see you through.'

No complaint from me. I had military pensions, savings I'd stashed away over the years, my wage from the periodic work I conducted for Rington Investigations, but I didn't have an infinite pot of disposable cash to fall back on. I jammed the wad of notes into my jeans pocket, before looking over the credit cards. 'Who the hell comes up with these names?'

'Sounds English at least,' Vince said.

I flicked the cards. 'Danny Fisher was Elvis's name in *King Creole.* You aren't concerned that people won't put two and two together and get the connection with Vince Everett?'

'It's not a problem. You aren't going to be using the name anywhere near Hicks or the others. They're just for further expenses when you need them.'

I shoved the cards into the pocket alongside the cash.

Vince looked me up and down.

'Maybe your first purchase should be some new clothes. You look like a bum.'

I'd long ago got rid of the garbage bag body-warmer, but still wore the denim shirt and jeans I'd been dressed in while fighting in the forest. The use of a sponge in one of the hospital bathrooms had removed a lot of the mud, but my clothing was still stained, and blood-spattered. A few eyebrows had been raised by the hospital staff, plus the civilians who were there, but worse sights were commonplace in an A&E waiting room. To all intents and purposes, I could have come directly from the scene of an accident, so nobody commented. When I was offered the use of the antechamber, it wasn't the look of me that was disturbing the others in the room.

'I smell like one, too,' I admitted.

Vince dug a plastic key card from his pocket. 'Once you've got yourself kitted out, I've booked you an overnighter in that motel. You can take a shower there.'

I read the hotel's address off the card. 'Walking distance?'

'Got you a car sorted out.' Vince held up some keys. 'You'll find it in the parking lot outside. I know you prefer a stick shift, but . . .'

The military had taught me to adapt, so an automatic gearbox wasn't going to be a problem. It was the FBI adaptations I wasn't too keen on. Doubtless Vince's words of 'a car sorted out' held more meaning. At the very least it would have a transponder fitted so that they could trace my every move. Chances were there'd be hidden microphones and wireless CCTV, so they'd see and hear everything, too.

Playing dumb, I accepted the keys.

'One more thing,' Vince said. He tossed a cell phone over. 'My number's pre-programmed. Check in with me every four hours.'

'Night time as well, Vince? Won't that cramp your style?'

Vince grunted. 'Night time, I'll call you.'

'Not a good idea.'

Vince grimaced at my scruffy appearance. 'Well, I don't think I'll be cramping *your* style any time soon.'

'No, but you could compromise the mission.'

Packing the SIG and knife back into the zip-lock bag, I stuffed them under my left arm. Vince shuffled from one foot to the other, waiting while I drained the vending-machine coffee. Ready, I nodded affirmative.

'Four hours, remember,' Vince said. 'I'll give you a location to meet. Bring you up to speed on what we know.'

'I'll bring a friend.' Before Vince could object I stepped past him and reached for the door handle.

'Danny!'

I turned with a smile.

'Just checking,' Vince grinned.

'Vince, I was doing this when you were still chasing cheerleaders for your first kiss.'

The agent spread his hands, gave the raffish curl of his lip. 'What do you mean? I still chase cheerleaders every chance I get.'

I left the hospital, found the car, a plain, three-year-old Ford, and drove away, still smiling about Vince's parting shot. Despite having got off to a strange start, I had to admit to liking the young agent. There was much in common with the young Joe Hunter who'd joined the Parachute Regiment over twenty years ago. Back then, I was also the devil-may-care type who laughed a lot. It came from the sense of immortality that went with acceptance into one of the toughest military regiments in the world. I learned a valuable lesson when shot by a Provo sniper while touring Northern Ireland. Didn't laugh so often after that. Being devil-may-care and staying in the red zone were at opposite ends of the spectrum. Thinking of when Special Agent Vincent would learn this life-changing lesson brought a scowl to my face.

I found a strip mall, with a men's outfitters wedged between a bail bondsman's office and an estate agency. After surreptitiously signing them, I used the Danny Fisher credit cards to purchase T-shirts, over-shirts, underwear and socks, each in multiple packs. I also selected a couple of pairs of jeans and two jackets, one lightweight, the other more suitable for the northern Pennsylvanian weather, which I pulled on. I dumped the purchases in the car, then wandered along the mall to an AT&T store where I purchased a pre-paid mobile phone.

Inside a thrift store I used the pre-paid to call Rink and tell him where to meet.

When I came back out of the store the same white panel van, marked with a local plumber's merchant motif, which had followed me from the hospital was parked in a lot across the way.

I pulled out the phone given to me by Vince. Pressed the call button.

'Vince?'

'I wasn't expecting your first call for another three hours.'

Ignoring the young agent, I said, 'Call your bloodhounds off. If Gant or any of his boys are around, they'll spot the FBI tail as easily as I have.'

I shut the phone down and dropped it in a pocket, giving the men in the white van a little goodbye wave.

Less than a minute later the van peeled out of the parking lot and drove away. If a white van could look abashed, then this one did.

As soon as they were gone, I pulled out the FBI phone and opened the battery compartment. True to form there was a tracking device under the battery. I slipped it into the grocery bag of an elderly woman walking past. The phone I switched off. I knew that the phone could still be traced by virtue of its internal programming, but that would require time to organise, and maybe they wouldn't realise that I'd dumped the transponder until they figured out that Joe Hunter wasn't the type to attend a cribbage league at the local community centre.

I was being obstructive simply for the hell of it, but I didn't like the feeling that my every movement was being observed, even if it was by a supposed ally. And that was where the problem lay: *supposed.* I liked Vince, but I didn't trust him. Even when hunting the most dangerous terrorists in the world, I would never have slept with a woman, then nudged her out of a window to her death, whether or not she was a psycho-killer. I had to keep Vince in mind at all times.

30

At face value Jared Rington was an anomaly. He was built like a pro-fighter, but he was no brain-damaged pug. His features had more in common with those of his Japanese mother than his Scottish-Canadian father, and yet he spoke with the drawling twang of a country and western singer. He was an imposing man whichever way you looked at him, but he was also quick to smile and carried gentleness within him that was belied by his capability for extreme violence which smouldered beneath his surface like a lit fuse. Like me, he was an Arrowsake alumnus, a graduate of that school of hard knocks, but following his demobilisation he'd managed to integrate himself back into society without carrying the same baggage that weighed me down.

I was damaged. I'm well aware of that fact. On leaving the military, I also had tried to settle back into the mundane life of a civilian, but the impulse to atone for what I perceived as a black mark on my soul ensured that I'd never know peace. Diane left me, though we loved each other, because she didn't want to see her husband die. Diane knew I wouldn't – couldn't – change, and I was the first to admit that she was right. Often I'd reasoned that morality made me a good person, but my knack for embroiling myself in trouble argued against that. The saving grace was that I was helping decent people, and by that virtue it made me decent, too. That was my lot in life. My creed was simple: I didn't like bullies and I'd go down kicking and screaming before I'd let them have their way. The only problem with my creed was that those loyal to me were dragged into my personal quest, and there was no one more loyal to me than Rink.

Rink would probably love to shake some sense into me, but at the same time whenever I stepped into the fray I didn't have to look over my shoulder to know that my friend was standing right there. That was a given.

I'd just done showering, shaving and pulling on fresh clothing when the big man proved the point. He grabbed me in a spine-cracking bear hug, told me how happy he was to see me, then set me down. His face was like a thunderhead growing on the horizon.

'Hunter, most guys take off to Vegas, play the slot machines, maybe hook up with a gal for some no-strings fun, but not you. They come back with empty pockets and a shit-eating grin on their faces. When you told me you were taking a couple days out, I thought, great, go an' do some fishing or hiking or whatever. 'Specially when you headed off to the ass-end of the Alleghenies, I thought, surely he can't get himself in trouble up there . . .'

Rink gave me the eyeball.

'What do you want me to say?'

'For a start, you can tell me why you didn't even mention *why* you were coming up here. I shoulda known when you asked me for a copy of Brook's file, but I thought you were just planning to make peace with her old man. If I'd've known you were gonna get in this kinda shit, I'd've come along with you from the start.'

'I didn't tell you because I wasn't sure if I'd even make it here. I almost turned back, Rink, more than once.'

'Goddamnit, Joe! I know you, there was nothing gonna hold you back.'

I touched my thigh unconsciously, but the gesture wasn't lost on Rink.

'Hunter, you've nothing left to prove. 'Specially not to yourself. You can spout all that bullshit you want about feelin' whole again, but you're not feared of the wound in your leg, it's the hole in your heart you're trying to fill. The things you've done to atone! Shit, man, you've done more good than anyone I ever knew.'

'I've also done more bad than anyone.'

'Bullshit!'

'Rink, you weren't there.'

'You're talking about that goddamn cult thing, ain't ya? You didn't kill those children; it was their own parents that stood them in the way of the bullets to cover their own cowardly asses. If anyone's to blame it was those clap-happy sonsabitches.'

'I still pulled the trigger, Rink.'

'You weren't to know the children were there. You were given bad intelligence, but you were working in good faith. You shouldn't hold yourself responsible for other people's mistakes.' Rink went stock-still. 'Oh, wait. I get it now. That's why you're here . . .'

I nodded solemnly. 'Don Griffiths was the one who supplied the intelligence. It's why I almost turned back, Rink. I set off thinking that I could help him. By the time I'd made it halfway here I'd changed my mind. All I wanted to do was put a bullet in his heart.'

Rink sat down on the motel bed, the springs creaking ominously under him. 'So why didn't you?'

'As soon as I saw him, I knew I couldn't. Took me a little longer to realise he was no more responsible than I was, but I got there. I was still going to walk away at first, but something happened to change my mind.'

I told Rink about the men at the Seven-Eleven and how I'd killed them with impunity. It took until then, but the truth struck me as hard as if Rink had karate-kicked the side of my head. Killing the two men had been an excuse, my way of burying my hatred of Don Griffiths. By doling out violent frustration on the two men, I'd exorcised the ghosts of those children who'd died.

'You're sure that the two men were with Gant and his crew?' Rink asked after I finished.

'I'm sure. In fact, Agent Vincent confirmed it. He asked me if I'd come across them in Bedford Well, called them Rooster and Cabe, described them to a tee.'

'And you told him?'

'Rules of the game were that I came clean,' I said. 'I think Vince already had a good idea that their disappearance was down to me. I didn't want a lie to come back and trip me up later. A team was being dispatched to recover them this morning.'

'They're cleaning up behind them as they go,' Rink observed.

'As far as anyone around here knows, *nothing* has happened.'

'You told me on the phone that Don's son-in-law was killed, that his house was burned to the ground. They cover that as well?'

'The way they're spinning the story it was just another tragic but unrelated accident to hit the Reynoldses. What's the chance of both the husband and wife being burned to death in such a short space of time? Far as I know, the locals are buying it, though.'

'How'd they cover Don Griffiths gettin' himself shot?'

'That hasn't been mentioned, yet. A story has been put around that Don has taken Millie and his grandkids away for a while, to protect them from the terrible tragedy.'

'They'll have to show sooner or later. You said Don was shot in the legs, how's he gonna explain when he turns up on sticks?'

I didn't know, and didn't really care. Hopefully the Carswell Hicks problem would no longer be an issue by then.

'I'm surprised the feebies even brought him here, so close to his home town,' Rink said.

'Nearest trauma hospital they could find, I suppose. Don was near death when they medi-vacced him out.'

'So where are Millie and the little ones?'

'Don't know,' I admitted. I'd thought about asking, but it was better that I didn't know. If I was captured alive, Hicks' crew might think they could force their location out of me, and it didn't matter how well trained, sooner or later any man will break.

Rink didn't press the issue, he understood.

'So tell me about Special Agent Vincent.'

I had already told Rink about the agent, how he was an undercover operative working to infiltrate Carswell Hicks' organisation. But now I told my buddy about how Vince had been teamed up with Sonya Madden, and how he'd tried to warn Millie about the impending attack on her brother-in-law's home, but been scuppered by the intervention of a cat. I also related how Vince had pushed Sonya to her death, and attempted to usurp power from Samuel Gant in order to delay the assault on the logging camp until his FBI friends arrived, but how that plan had also gone to pot. Finally I admitted that Vince had got the drop on me with that damn garrotte, but had spared my life when it became apparent that I was a worthy stooge.

I waited for Rink to absorb it all. He wasn't long in offering his summation. 'So he's a sneaky little weasel?'

'That about sums him up,' I agreed. 'But I have to admit, there's something about the kid that I like.'

'I'd step carefully, Hunter. He sounds like the type who'd crap on you from a great height first chance he got.'

'Like we haven't worked under bosses like that before?'

'Speaking of bosses,' Rink said. 'Walter's got his fingers in this pie, too?'

'I don't know how that came about, but you know Walter. I can't really complain, Rink. Without Walt's intervention I'd probably be looking at a fifteen stretch for manslaughter.'

On Rink's chin was a livid scar, courtesy of Tubal Cain, and he rubbed at it now. He often did so when he was thinking deeply. Coming to a conclusion, he stood up, stretching his tall frame. He yawned – a natural bodily reaction to relieve stress – then grinned. 'So when do we start?'

'In an hour I phone Vince. Then we take it from there.'

Rink huffed. 'Damn, I'm ready to go now.'

'You and me both.'

31

Carswell Hicks believed he had a God-given right to walk the streets of his home town, and no number of FBI and Homeland Security agents scouring the nation for him would put him off. As far as he was concerned, this great country had been fought for and won by good white stock just like him, so he shouldn't have to scurry in the dark like a rodent. All these Chinese with their garish clothing and shop fronts full of tat, their garbage piled high on the kerbsides, were the ones the government needed to persecute. Lord almighty, he thought, isn't China big enough for all them to get the hell back where they belonged?

Last time he was in Manhattan, this part of town was lorded over by the Italians, now just look at it. Now it seemed like they'd been pushed up and over Canal Street to give way to a profusion of red and yellow banners offering to buy scrap gold, paper lanterns strung everywhere and the smell of five spice pervading the air. There were little saffron-skinned men and women everywhere, so many of them that the sidewalks couldn't contain them all and they spilled around the mounds of garbage on to Mott Street. The traffic moved noisily around them, exhausts fuming in the cold air.

Hicks walked like he had an impenetrable bubble around him. The older people moved out of his way, but now and again he got some hard-edged looks from the younger men, who stood like sentries in doorways, their slicked black hair reflecting the blue of the sky. They quickly looked away when the two hulking men at Hicks' shoulders returned their stares.

Hicks turned off Mott and on to Pell, stepping out along the narrow sidewalk so that people had to scatter before him or be walked over. Just the way he liked it. An old lady, leaning from the front of her store to offer freshly squeezed orange juice for five bucks a pop, quickly withdrew her hand as Hicks shot her a look to curdle milk. She ranted something in her own language, but her unresponsive husband stacking rice on shelves didn't even bother to glance at her.

Hicks found the entrance to Doyers Street. There he paused, jamming his hands on his hips like he was surveying his domain. He snorted, striding into the alley and heading for where it bent sharply to the left. When he was a college student he'd often leave Greenwich to come here to purchase cheap noodles and rice, and to play pinball in an arcade famous for having a fortune-telling chicken. But that wasn't all that Doyers Street was famous for: back in the old gang days, the Tongs fought street battles here, using the tunnels connecting the buildings to launch surprise attacks on their enemies. Doyers would forever be called the Bloody Angle, and it had little to do with the sharp bend in the road and everything to do with the gore that once slicked this place.

Wedged between a shop offering spit-roasted ducks with their heads, necks and feet still intact, and a wholesale distributor whose mode of transportation seemed to be a rickety bicycle chained to a railing outside, was a fairly innocuous door. The door was painted in the predominant red and yellow, but was scuffed and peeling. There was no identifying sign or number, just the evidence that the door had been in use as far back as the days of the Tong wars. A single bullet hole pocked the surface near the upper left corner, and though the door had been painted in the interim, no one had bothered to fill the hole. Hicks heard that it was a historical mark of honour; apparently the bullet missed a prominent Tong leader by a hair and hit the door instead, a moment before the leader struck down his would-be assassin with a meat cleaver. Bullet Proof Tzu carried quite a rep after that poorly-skilled assassin missed his shot.

These days the Tongs held little sway over Manhattan's Chinatown, the local criminals now being those young toughs hanging about the doorways, but Hicks didn't care about any of that. He wasn't here to see anyone even half Chinese. He banged on the door.

The door clicked open and Hicks stepped into a narrow hallway, shadowed by one of his minders. The second man stayed on the street, scowling at the rotating ducks in the window next door. Hicks' minder had barely made it inside when a hidden piston closed the door tight. Locks engaged. Hicks had been here before, so already knew that the door that looked so brittle from outside was sheathed in steel and armed with sturdy locks on the inside. Like many who'd experienced war, the man who lived here was paranoid enough to live in a fortress.

The corridor smelled faintly of dog pee and something else with an acid undertone that nipped at Hicks' nostrils. He ignored it, walking along the dimly lit hall to the flight of stairs at the far end. The door at the bottom was openly steel this time, smudged with palm prints and streaks of rubber where it had been kicked in the past. Locks disengaged and the door nudged open. Hicks pushed through it and went up the stairs sprightlier than many men approaching sixty years old. His minder puffed along behind him, twenty years younger, but also twenty pounds heavier.

A third line of defence stood in their way, but clicked open as they approached. Hicks couldn't see the CCTV cameras monitoring their progress, although they were obviously there. As he stepped through the third door a waft of Tiger

Balm washed over him. That was the source of the aroma he'd detected in the hall, only ten times more potent. Hicks' grey eyes began to water.

The second floor apartment was as stark as any monk's cell, with a cot pushed up against one wall and a metal footlocker the only furnishings at this end. A door opened into another room further along, where things were a little more ramshackle. Hicks recognised the worn office chair and desk, the computer monitor, the battered sofa in one corner, the throw rug with the beer stains. The stack of boxes teetering in a far corner was a new addition, as were the heavy drapes pulled over the window to thwart spying from the opposite building. Making up for the lack of natural light, a lamp threw a slant of yellow across the workstation and the man sitting in the chair observing the video images on the screen.

The chair swung round and the man peered up at Hicks from under a tangle of long salt and pepper curls. In the man's lap was a small dog. Chihuahua, Hicks thought.

'It's been a while, Carswell. Wasn't even sure it was you when you knocked on my door. I had to look twice.'

Hicks didn't tell the man he'd undergone a series of cosmetic procedures in the past few months, because Jim Lloyd could already see the end result. Hicks' predominant feature had always been his hawk-like nose, but that had been reduced, his thin lips thickened, his hairline adjusted so that he now wore a widow's peak where he used to be bald. His hair was white, as was his newly acquired goatee beard and strap moustache. For someone allegedly dead, he looked strong and healthy.

On the other hand Lloyd looked like he had ten years before. He was still a shaggy bear of a man, stiff with arthritis and old wounds, and Hicks was certain that the combat trousers and plaid shirt were the same he always wore. A patchwork of wrinkles making a spider web pattern around his eyes counted off the years since last they'd met. At sixty-three years old,

Lloyd's face looked every second his age, but the shoulders swelling his shirt, his thick arms, looked like those of a much younger man.

'Wasn't sure I was going to open the door, even after a second look. You don't look a thing like the Carswell Hicks I used to know.'

It was the first time that the two men had shared space in the last decade, but they'd been in regular communication via email and telephone. Hicks had never found it necessary to send an updated photograph. 'I'm the same man I always was, Jim, just better looking.'

Lloyd eyed him quizzically. 'You gotta give me the number for your surgeon, Hicks. What they say ain't true: you *can* make a silk purse out of a pig's ear!'

Hicks smiled, but wasn't really enamoured of Lloyd's wit; he was neither silk nor a fucking pig, never had been. He let the slight go, because that was just Lloyd's way. Any other man would be doing a header into the Hudson, trying to find where Hicks had thrown his balls into the river.

Hicks turned to his minder. 'Wait in the other room.'

The man didn't raise an objection, just did what he was told. Hicks pulled the door to. Lloyd stood up from his chair and walked like a tin man across the room to where a bottle of cheap whiskey waited. He placed the chihuahua down and took up the whiskey. He held up the bottle, saw Hicks jerk his head, then chugged a shot from the neck of the bottle. He wiped his mouth with his shirtsleeve. He waggled the bottle at Hicks. 'Where the muscle-rub fails, this always works.'

Without preamble Hicks asked, 'You heard about your daughter?'

Lloyd's jaw firmed a little, but that was all the sign he gave. 'I always knew the crazy little bitch would get herself in trouble, just not on this trip. I thought that Gant would look after her better'n that.'

'Gant isn't responsible, Jim, it's the prick that she hooked up with that's to blame.'

'Vince Everett.' The way Lloyd breathed the name it was like a curse.

'Right,' Hicks said. 'Except it turns out that isn't his name at all.'

Lloyd took another shot of whiskey. This time he let the drips fall on his chest. 'Undercover cop?'

'FBI,' Hicks corrected. 'Special Agent Stephen Vincent was a plant assigned to find me.'

'You kill that bastard for me, Cars?'

'Not yet, but I will.'

'I'd do it myself, but . . .'

As potent and disabling as his arthritis, agoraphobia had made a prisoner of Jim Lloyd years ago.

'Leave it to me, Jim. I'll make sure that Agent Vincent gets paid back *everything* he's due.'

Lloyd nodded and then went back at the whiskey again. He finished it this time, but cradled the bottle in his arms like a baby, maybe thinking about what a poor father he'd turned out to be. Sonya Madden had been his only child, and Lloyd hadn't even had the decency to marry her mother.

Lloyd moved back to his computer but he didn't relinquish the bottle. He propped his hips against his desk, rocking back and forward, his curls swinging. 'What about Don Griffiths?'

'He's momentarily out of our reach.'

'Gant fucked that up too?'

'You sound like you've got a hard-on for Gant.'

Lloyd sneered. 'He's an asshole. Always was, always will be. Thinks he's some kind of tough guy; he wouldn't have lasted two minutes in the jungle.'

Lloyd was full of stories about his days hunting the Viet Cong. In his estimation, anyone who was anything had shared the adventure with him. It was why he respected Hicks but hated his younger lieutenant, whose only experience of war was firing tank shells at pussy rag-heads a mile out in the desert. Hicks happened to know otherwise, but didn't deem it necessary to put Lloyd straight on Gant's military record.

Hicks studied his old comrade. Lloyd was a paradox. On the one hand he was a staunch patriot, but on the other he was as keen to disrupt his nation as Hicks was, primarily because he believed that the heroes returning from Vietnam had been fucked over by their own country. Lloyd's argument: men just like the two of them had been reviled by the liberal fuck-wits who then abandoned them to some corner of history they'd prefer to forget. He pointed out that today's fighting men were being held up as paragons of virtue, while their old buddies were sitting on street corners begging change for food. He had a point, Hicks agreed, but he didn't give a damn. Hicks' hatred of the government went much deeper than that.

'Where is the goose-stepping little shit anyway?' Lloyd went on. 'I thought he'd have come with you.'

'He's busy,' Hicks said.

'I bet he is. What's he doing, touching up those ridiculous tats he's so fond of? Beats me why you let him hang around, Cars. You've gone to all this trouble to change your face and he'll give you away in an instant.'

Hicks ignored the comment. Instead he said, 'Don Griffiths had help. Gant's trying to find out who it was.'

'Probably another feebie,' Lloyd said.

Shaking his head, Hicks said, 'From what I hear the guy sounds more like one of our old team. Took out almost everyone Gant sent against him. He even wounded Gant.'

'Shit, that wouldn't take much. An eight-year-old girl would be trouble to the kind of assholes that Gant's pulled around him.' Lloyd went very quiet very quickly. He moved on. 'Anyway, it's probably best he stays out in Pennsylvania. I don't think our contacts would appreciate him turning up at the meeting.'

'It's set up?'

'Of course. All they need is paying and it's a done deal.'

'They've come through?' Hicks couldn't help glancing at the boxes stacked in the room.

Lloyd laughed. 'Sure they've come through. But you don't think I'm going to be as crazy as to store the goods here, do you? Are you insane, Cars? I've enough Agent Orange bubbling through my veins without exposing myself to any of *that* crap!'

Hicks shared the laugh, again unimpressed by Lloyd's offhand insult.

'When and where?'

Lloyd turned to his computer, placing down the empty whiskey bottle so he could jab at keys. He brought up an email account for which he and Hicks shared administration tasks. He opened a draft document and typed in the details. He didn't send the message. Hicks could enter it from any console and read the draft, before deleting it. That way there was no record of the message and no chance of them being traced by it. It was the same method used to communicate by many terror cells, the way in which 9/11 and the London bombings were allegedly planned.

When Lloyd turned round again, he was surprised to find that Hicks had opened the door and that the minder was standing in the doorway. In his hand was a gun, a tubular suppressor screwed on to the barrel. Lloyd, a veteran of combat, couldn't even get his feet to move, let alone reach for a weapon. 'Cars? What the hell is this?'

Hicks smiled coldly. 'Thanks for setting up the meeting with the Koreans, Jim. I couldn't have done it without you.'

Lloyd eyed the gun pointing directly at his face. 'This is some way to show your gratitude.'

'Oh, no,' Hicks said. 'This is payback. I think you set us up, Jim. You were the one who introduced Vince Everett to your daughter, knowing full well he was FBI, and you're the one who warned Don Griffiths that we were coming. And you know something, Jim, I think you were the one who tipped off Griffiths the first time round and had me jailed for more than nine years.'

Lloyd's groan told Hicks that everything he'd just charged his old friend with was the truth. He jerked his chin and his minder fired in response. The bullet struck Lloyd's forehead and he dropped to the floor with a flexibility that gallons of Tiger Balm would never give him. The little dog yelped in response, cowering in a corner of the room.

Hicks pulled on a pair of leather gloves, then accepted the gun from his minder's hand. He went and stood over his old comrade. Looked down on him. Fired twice into his chest. This time the dog stayed quiet.

'And just in case I was totally wrong about you, Jim, I'm sorry. But I had to kill you anyway. Seeing as you aren't capable of leaving this dump, I wouldn't want you to suffer through what I've planned for the Big Apple.'

When he'd read what Lloyd had written on the screen Hicks deleted the message. Then for good measure he shot Lloyd in the head a second time.

'By the way, that's for calling me a pig's ear, Jim.'

32

SAC Birnbaum's helicopter transported me, Rink, and Agent Vincent to a clearing alongside a tumultuous river in the Adirondacks in New York State. On the opposite bank of the river the trees grew thick on the sloping hills, but on this side the ground had been cleared and made way for a two-storey wooden cabin and outbuildings. Cars parked at the rear of the buildings had been visible as the chopper descended. They were town cars, black with tinted widows, sitting low on their chassis due to the concealed armour plating. Hard-looking men in heavy overcoats stood ready by the cars. They weren't an unusual addition, considering who we'd come here to meet, but the numbers didn't seem to add up.

'What kinda party are we gatecrashing here?' Rink asked.

'Beats me, but there's only one way to find out,' I said.

Vince didn't offer an explanation. He'd been unforthcoming about many things since we met him the day before. All he'd allowed was that we had to make the trip to the Adirondacks due to an urgent change in plans. He'd left the meeting telling us to eat and to get some rest. His parting shot, 'You're going to need all the strength you have.'

We'd dined, but neither of us had got much rest.

On the flight from Pennsylvania, Vince had conducted business over a satellite telephone, often shouting to make himself heard over the thrum of the rotors. Despite the racket Rink snored but I was too wired to doze, even though I could count on one hand the hours of sleep I'd caught in the last few days. I felt mildly nauseated, telling myself it was due to the turbulence as rain-laden wind assaulted the chopper from all angles, and it was a good feeling when I finally set my feet on sturdy ground. But that wasn't why I'd felt queasy; it was the horrible sense of foreboding clawing at my insides that was responsible.

I was wearing the winter coat purchased in Hertford, and was glad of it. It was even colder here than it had been in the Alleghenies and the rain had built from a steady drizzle to a deluge. It was like the winters I'd left back home in northern England, but I didn't feel even slightly nostalgic. I joined Rink and Vince in jogging towards the beckoning warmth of the log cabin a hundred yards away.

Before we'd made it halfway there the door of the cabin swung open and a man stepped out, an unlit cigar jammed between his teeth. Maybe it wasn't that warm inside the cabin because the rotund man was sheathed from knees to throat in a quilted parka and had a flat cap pulled low on his round head.

The rain conspired to soak us before we reached sanctuary, driving from the heavens. The sound was like the thunder of hooves, and a sheet of teeming water obscured Walter Conrad from sight.

'I'm missing Florida already,' Rink muttered into my ear.

'Tell me about it.'

We ducked under the canopy at the front of the cabin, but the pounding rain made greetings pointless. Rink shook himself like a dog. I stamped. Vince tried to put his hair in some order. Walter directed us all inside, using his cigar like a band leader's baton. I was last through the door, and as I entered it wasn't the plushness of the interior that gave me pause for thought: it was the three men reclining on easy chairs.

Each was as old as the next, probably in their mid- to late seventies. Like Walter they all had the grey pallor of men who spent their days in places hidden from the light of day. They reminded me of a cabal of ghouls who'd risen from their crypts in the dead of night to feed on the corpses of humanity. It wasn't the disquieting affect these men exuded that made me pause, but the fact that I knew all three faces. Here, in Walter's bolt-hole in the Adirondacks, sat the men behind Arrowsake. Without exception I'd believed each one of them dead. Rink cast me an indiscreet frown, equally perplexed by the reanimation of these supposedly dead men.

All three of them smiled at me, but with expressions reserved for prodigal children. A worm of unease crept up my spine: if we'd been manipulated by Arrowsake in the past, then this was positive proof that they weren't finished with us yet.

I never pretended to understand the politics behind the shadowy organisation, of which even those in the top echelons of government had little or no genuine knowledge. Arrowsake had fielded search-destroy teams in total contradiction of political convention and international treaty, under the aegis of total deniability. As such, the men at the head of the organisation were neither politicians nor military leaders, therefore member states could not be held culpable for their actions. In effect, Arrowsake was a ghost organisation that didn't *officially* exist, and it was headed by men who had no tangible presence upon the earth. When Arrowsake fell foul of the modern war on terror, its members had been disbanded, and those at the head of the organisation had been struck from the annals. In effect, the three men here had been metaphorically killed, if not physically so. They had disappeared without trace.

But now they were back.

My next and more important thought was, had they ever been gone?

Conspiracy theorists argue about a hidden world government, giving it a fanciful title like the New World Order, but as absurd as it sounded, I feared there was some validity in it. The men sitting opposite me were living proof.

More worrying than their re-emergence was why they had chosen now to rear their heads. The men from Arrowsake wouldn't emerge from obscurity because of a low priority threat like Carswell Hicks. These men were concerned about the overall stability of nations, primarily anything threatening the security of international finance, infrastructure and commerce, with the loss of life being tacked to their list almost as an afterthought. From what I'd learned about Hicks, he was a vicious son of a bitch suspected of a number of racially motivated murders, who'd also executed a series of bombings against financial institutions before Don Griffiths had thwarted him. If he was planning something similar now he would be palmed off on to the FBI to deal with, which explained the presence of Vince, but wouldn't raise as much as a blip on these men's radar. Therefore it was obvious that Hicks had stepped up dramatically and the reason for my being drafted in wasn't to cover up a government blunder as I'd been led to believe, but to end a threat capable of rocking the entire Western world.

All I'd wanted to do was save an old friend and his family. What the hell had I got myself into this time? I looked at Rink, trying to impart my most sincere apology. My friend had followed me here through blind loyalty, and I had more than likely dragged him into more crap than either of us could possibly imagine.

My next glance was for Walter, but the man who was famous for twisting the truth to fit his own ends could only study the drips marking his floor. This *was* something big when even Walter was ashamed of himself for pulling us into it.

Under the gaze of the Arrowsake men I pulled to attention, not quite as formally as I once would have, but the old indoctrination was still there. Alongside me, Rink shoved his hands in his pockets in a show of nonchalance but I felt his impulse to straighten up like it was a static charge.

'Sirs,' was all that I could think to say to the men. At least I didn't salute.

They nodded like sages but didn't offer a reply. I considered their silence and recalled that though this wasn't my first time in their presence I'd never heard any of them speak before. It looked like nothing would change now. They each stood, nodded at Walter and then filed out of a door at the back of the cabin. Engines started and then receded as the vehicles were driven away, bearing their silent occupants back to their hidden holes in the ground.

'Why don't you all sit down?' Walter pulled off his cap.

'What the hell was that all about?' I demanded.

'Sure wasn't like any show and tell I've ever been a part of,' Rink said. 'If I didn't know otherwise, I'd say we just met the three wise monkeys.'

I couldn't find a smile for Rink's joke; those three had seen, heard and talked more about evil than any other people on the planet.

Walter busied himself with shedding his parka and cap, now that he had no reason for going out in the rain again. He must have had to bow and scrape to the Arrowsake men when first they arrived, greeting them at their vehicles, and he hadn't had the opportunity to get comfortable before now. The CIA controller did a good impression of Edward G. Robinson by jamming the cigar in the corner of his mouth. As ever, the cigar was unlit, but by the sheen of cold sweat on Walter's brow he sure as hell was battling the urge to set it ablaze.

'You got any coffee on the go, Walt?' I asked. There was much for the old man to tell, and something strong that didn't come from a liquor bottle wouldn't go amiss.

'I'll have some made.' Walter looked grateful for the opportunity to step out, no doubt his first opportunity to order his thoughts before we launched ourselves at him like rabid pit bulls. I couldn't recall the last time I'd seen the black-ops man flustered by anything.

As soon as Walter was out of the way, I turned on Vince. 'So when do you come clean, Vince? You're no more an FBI agent than we are.'

'Why would you come to that conclusion?'

'First off, SAC Birnbaum didn't get to where he is by being the whipping boy of a lowly special agent,' I said. 'Then there's the fact that you're here. You wouldn't get to see those men's faces without special clearance. What are you? CIA? Homeland Security? What?'

Vince thought for a second. 'Let me throw a question back at you. Back when you were active, did you ever admit to being with Arrowsake? No, I just bet that you were Sergeant Hunter of One-Para, and Jared there was just plain old Private Rington of the Seventy-Fifth Ranger Regiment. Well, for that reason I *am* Special Agent Stephen Vincent of the FBI.'

'Nothing plain about the Seventy-Fifth,' Rink stated.

I had caught the weight of what Vince was trying to say. I stared at the young man, waiting for him to confirm the truth, and finally knew the reason for my unease on the flight here.

Vince threw up his hands. 'OK, you've got me. I'm an Arrowsake alumnus, just like the two of you. Just don't tell Walter that you got the confession from me so easily, eh?'

'Arrowsake was demobilised.' Even as I spoke I realised that my words held no meaning. Both Rink and I had been lied to. Following 9/11 and the change in methods employed by Western governments, the counterterrorism services had come under close scrutiny. Objections to Guantanamo Bay and then the furore following the alleged torture of prisoners in Iraq had forced rules which made the old style tactics intolerable, leading Arrowsake to be rapidly dismantled before an even greater scandal could be discovered. Rink and I, and all our colleagues, had been seen as virtual dinosaurs who had no place in the modern war on terror. Our demobilisation, I understood now, was nothing but a smokescreen, a lie.

'*Your* Arrowsake was,' Vince confirmed. He gave a flourish like a Shakespearean actor. 'Meet the new wave.'

Incredulous, I could only grunt. The truth had been staring me in the face for a long time now. When I thought about it, Walter seemed to have more sway than even a CIA subdivision controller should have. He had the ear of presidents and prime ministers, and had manipulated even the decisions of the US Secretary of State before now. Arrowsake hadn't died; it had simply been buried even deeper than before – at the expense of the men who'd fought loyally for it in the past. Rink and I had been kicked loose to give way to younger hotshots like Stephen Vincent.

'This is bullshit!' Rink looked ready to go on a rampage.

I couldn't have agreed more. For almost five years since we'd been cut loose I'd drifted, feeling like there was a huge hole in my life. The rift had destroyed my marriage, destroyed some of my humanity when considering what I'd become, and for no other reason than that we'd been treated like garbage to be disposed of before we became an embarrassment.

Rink jabbed a finger at Vince. 'You ain't part of us, boy. Never will be.'

Vince shrugged. 'Don't want to be, Rink. You're old timers now. No insult intended.'

'No fucking insult . . .'

I grabbed Rink, told him to take it easy. Rink snarled at Vince over my shoulder. 'That little punk thinks he's a better man than we are, Joe! Just give me a couple seconds an' I'll show him the truth.'

Vince straightened up. 'Maybe you won't find me so easy, Rink. I did all right with your buddy. Right, Hunter?'

I thought about Vince's sneak attack with the garrotte. OK, he'd got the drop on me then, but a tactic like that wouldn't help Vince if Rink wanted to kick his butt. Or if I decided a little payback was in order.

A door snicked open and all three of us swung round to see Walter standing in the threshold. He seemed to have got a grip on himself, because he wore the featureless expression he reserved for moments just like this. 'I thought I'd better interject before this turns into a pissing competition. Jesus, it's so bad that you can smell the testosterone in here!'

'What you smell is the crap you've been feeding us all these years,' Rink snapped at him. 'I can't believe you'd do this to us, Walter.'

'You're upset, and rightly so,' Walter said.

'Fucking upset? This little punk as much as says he's a fuckin' blue ray disc and I'm *just* a Beta-Max. Dead right, I'm fucking upset!' Rink wasn't one for going off like this and his fury was a surprise; normally it was Rink who had to caution me.

I turned a hurt look on my adopted father. 'This doesn't come as a surprise to me. Arrowsake was outmoded, but it was obvious that something else would take its place. What I am shocked at is the way we've been lied to.'

Walter waved me down. 'I've never lied to you. I've just been selective with the truth.' He looked me in the eye, before switching his scrutiny to Rink. 'You know that I've protected you both, but it never occurred to you just how that could be?'

'Friendship?' Rink said sarcastically.

'Yes, friendship. But also because you were important to me in another way.'

'We were trained dogs to bark at your command,' Rink snapped.

'I wouldn't put it that way.'

'How would you put it?' I asked. 'You've been using us, Walter. You weren't thinking of us as friends, you thought of us only in terms of personal assets.'

Walter shook his head. 'No, Hunter, that isn't the way it was.'

'The Harvestman? Luke Rickard? Weren't they hits designated by Arrowsake?'

'Do you truly believe either of those assholes would be any concern of Arrowsake? I helped you with those problems, as well as the colossal fuck-ups you got yourselves involved in down in Florida and in Texas, because I wanted to. Like I said, you were important to me.'

I laughed mirthlessly. 'You were saving us for a greater cause. Well, fuck you, Walter.'

Vince placed himself directly in front of me. 'You can't step away from this, Hunter. Have you forgotten the problem of a dozen dead people over in Pennsylvania? Maybe you should think about that.'

'Is that right, Vince?' I palm-heeled Vince under the chin and knocked the young man sprawling on his back. Only the fact that I'd tempered the blow meant that he was conscious enough to hear my next words. 'There's also the small matter of a dead girl who was shoved out of a car window, or have you forgotten about *that*, you son of a bitch?'

'Sonya Madden was a potential murderer,' Vince spluttered from a bleeding mouth.

On hearing the rumble of laughter from Rink, I couldn't help shaking my head at the irony of it all. We looked at each other, and that was it. We both broke into loud laughter.

I pointed at the young upstart. 'With people like him it's no wonder that you've had to keep us on retainer, Walt.'

'Then . . . you're happy to be back?' Walter asked.

Speaking for us both, Rink said, 'We were never happy to be gone.'

A smile flickered over Walter's mouth. The only one who didn't look so pleased with the turn of events was Vince who scowled up at us as he checked for loose teeth. Around his fingertips, he muttered, 'You took me by surprise, old man. Won't happen again.'

'Not unless you give me a good reason.' I held a hand out to Vince. 'That's us square now, Vince. I owed you that for almost taking my head off with your garrotte.'

Vince thought about it, and again I noted that he was much sharper than he seemed. He stretched up and took my hand and I hauled him to his feet.

Vince gave Rink a steady look. 'What about us? We OK, Rink?'

'Call me Jared. You ain't earned the right to call me Rink yet. That's just for my friends.' But then Rink clapped Vince on the shoulder and gave him a wink.

The door opened again and one of Walter's ever-present bodyguards appeared carrying a tray laden with a jug of coffee and all the makings. Walter pushed his cigar between his teeth, using the excuse of playing host to move things on. 'Excellent. Now we can get down to the real business.'

'Yeah,' Rink agreed. 'It's about time we got some answers.'

'So what is the deal, Walter?'

A few minutes later I wished I'd never asked.

33

'We've been recalled to Manhattan?' asked Darley.

'Yes, and it's about time. I'm growing sick of hiding in the boonies like a runaway slave.'

'You think you're well enough to travel?' The little man's head dipped and bobbed as he ran a quick diagnostic check of his friend's well-being. Gant had been in a car wreck and then shot, but he did look relatively well considering the alternative.

'Get in the van, Dar. I'm fine.'

'Fine, huh, boss?' Even when he smiled, Darley looked like a bird weighing up a juicy worm.

'Just get in the goddamn van.'

Samuel Gant was hurting like he'd been kicked by a mule and stung by a swarm of yellow-jackets, and he wasn't in an easy-going frame of mind. The only saving grace was that the flak jacket he was wearing had saved him from the full force of the buckshot when Griffiths' hired gunman shot him. The jacket had taken the brunt of both barrels, but some of the spreading shot had peppered his thighs and arms. Checking himself after Darley had dragged him clear, he'd discovered a massive haematoma on his ribs and all four limbs looked like they'd been drilled by weevils. And his mangled ear stung like a sonofabitch. For two days he'd been laid up by fever, and he still wasn't certain that the doctor Hicks supplied had removed all of the shot from his system. Maybe somewhere along the way he'd die from lead poisoning, but he wasn't going to let that stop him now. He wanted to be around when Hicks' plan came to fruition; at least he'd know that the future was brighter than he was feeling just now.

'I'm surprised that we haven't been told to go and finish off the job,' Darley said. He started the black van while Gant climbed in, the tattooed man taking his time and moving very gingerly. He knew how his boss felt; his head was still pounding from where he'd been struck unconscious and he didn't think that all the Tylenol in the world would be enough to shift the pain. That fucker who'd smacked him around was going to hurt bad before Darley was happy again. 'Why don't we just walk into the hospital, shoot his guards and then kill Griffiths once an' for all?'

'We've talked about this before, Dar. It's enough that we've confirmed where Griffiths was taken and that he's fully sedated. In his present state he's no threat to the operation. Hicks has capitalised on that and has moved the timescale forward. You should be happy he still wants us there for the big day after our righteous fuck-up!'

'I suppose we can always come back later and finish what we started with Griffiths.'

'If everything goes to plan, we won't have to come back,' Gant said. 'Anything that Griffiths has on Hicks will be old news by then. Now get a move on, I want to be back in New York before nightfall.'

Pulling out of the lot behind the motel where they'd been holed up, Darley sent the van east, picking up Route 80 towards New Jersey, lost in his own thoughts for a few seconds. Drizzle streaked the windscreen like a greasy film that the wipers struggled to contend with. Finally he looked across at Gant. The tattooed man had rested his skull on the headrest and had closed his eyes, his lids flickering in time with his ongoing pain. Darley didn't want to disturb him, but there was something that had just come to mind. 'When you say Hicks has moved the timing forward, how soon are we talking about?'

'Very soon. Days, I'm not sure,' Gant muttered without opening his eyes.

'Won't Hicks' statement lose a little meaning?'

'How'd you come to that conclusion?'

'We're months away from November ninth, I thought Hicks wanted to mark the anniversary.'

Gant shrugged, turning his head away from Darley in a none too subtle attempt to shut him up. 'Maybe he'd prefer to have his own date on the calendar. Anyway, I'm beginning to think that Kristallnacht Two is a poor name for what we're planning. There'll be more for the Jews to worry about than broken glass, Dar, much more.'

Darley nodded glumly, letting out a sigh that roused Gant. The tattooed man looked over at him. His yellow eyes were the proverbial piss holes in snow. 'By the sound of things you're worried about that.'

'Just concerned that the statement we're making is a little too big. One-Four, brother, all the way. But that shit's poison to everyone, Gant.'

One-Four. Code for the fourteen words in the racist skinhead pledge: *we must secure the existence of our people and a future for white children.*

Gant grunted. 'Yeah, it's poison, and that's the whole point. No Jew-boy will ever tread there again.'

'Neither will any of us whites.'

'Darley, the white race is on the verge of extinction, and if we don't strike now we're doomed. Unless we do this thing there won't be a white man setting his foot any place, because we'll all be gone. So don't go quoting the One-Four to me without remembering exactly what it means. We have to tear down US society and rebuild it as a segregated nation with us whites back in control. That ain't going to happen while the Jews are at the head of the wave of colour that's engulfing us. Other people don't care, and that won't change until we show them what's really happening here. When we make this statement, when we make our stand, then every white man will rise up at our sides and finally do what needs doing.'

Darley had heard similar anti-Semitic propaganda for years, and he didn't need reminding. He hated what was happening in his country, how whites were being bred out of existence, all of them becoming grey men. He knew that the Jews were behind the conspiracy to infect the nation, using feminism and liberalism to take away the white man's masculinity. Hell, the Jews were behind the immigration laws that took away all the manufacturing jobs that were the mainstay of the white-skinned, blue-collar classes, and he was certain, too, that they were guiding the blacks, the poisoners of the white race with all their drugs and genetically inferior blood. He hated the Jews with as much passion as Gant or Hicks or any of them, but still, what Hicks had in mind was extreme even for a *radical* extremist like him.

'I grew up there, Gant . . .' he whined.

Gant slammed his hands on the dashboard. 'Are you turning into a fucking race-mixing left-winger, Dar? Don't you see that's exactly what I'm talking about? You can't even walk through your own neighbourhood without feeling like you're the fucking foreigner. You want to just hand over the place you grew up to those bastards? White people built this country, and we can sure as hell tear it down overnight.' Gant blinked slowly, sitting back in his chair. When he continued his voice was steadier, and held more promise.

'Marches and demonstrations are old school. They didn't work. Burning niggers on crosses didn't work. We have to do something much bigger if we ever hope to get the mongrel races out of here. There's only one solution: kill every one of them that're here, and make sure they can never return. That's the only way we can start over.'

The little man still wasn't sure. A bomb he was OK with, but this?

It was as if Gant could read his mind. 'McVeigh tried with a bomb in Oklahoma and achieved nothing. We have to do something with more impact than that. That's why Hicks has declared war against the destructive forces that are taking over our country. We all know that the Big Brother central state is destroying us. We have to see our government, and the Jews controlling it, for what it is . . . our mortal enemy. We have to strike against them where it really hurts. Ultimately nothing changes in this world without violence, you have to see that.'

'Course I do, Gant. I'm with you all the way, but it's one thing kerb-stomping a nigger, another doing something as . . . as *brutal* as this.'

Gant laughed. 'Darley, the white man is the most brutal, the most vicious creature on the face of the earth. And this is the white man's way of showing that when we get our backs up, then we won't stop at nothing to reclaim what's rightfully ours.'

Darley concentrated on the road, pretending that the hammering rain demanded his silence. He reflected again on his pledge, the One-Four, and was as staunch a follower as ever. The only problem: Manhattan was a part of this white nation, but he couldn't see how it could figure in any future, let alone that of his people or their children. There'd be no reclaiming it when Manhattan became a no-go area for everyone.

34

'Ever feel like we're being poked and prodded like a bug in a Petri dish? That we've been cultivated all this time, till we're a more virulent strain than the disease itself?'

That caused me to blink at the morose face of my friend. 'Christ, Rink, that's heavy thinking for an ignoramus brute like you.'

Rink nudged my ribs with an elbow, taking the gibe for what it was. 'You know exactly where I'm coming from, Joe.'

'That I do, Rink. That I do.'

We were back in the FBI chopper, swooping low over the wooded hills of northern Pennsylvania, en route for Hertford. Vince had sat up front this time, alongside the pilot. It was as much an excuse to nurse his painful jaw without looking a wimp as it was an opportunity to conduct business in private. I was glad that the FBI-cum-Arrowsake stooge was out of the way. It gave us the opportunity to talk about Walter's denouement without having to worry about our words reaching the wrong ears.

'I'm even surprised that Arrowsake chose to show its face in this,' Rink said.

'They didn't have to show up; I already had no option but follow instructions,' I said.

'You coulda chose to go to prison.'

'Yeah, right, like I was going to do that? Seriously, the FBI offered me a deal. Stop Carswell Hicks and my involvement would be buried. Now you and I both know that the FBI doesn't have the power to offer a deal like that, so it was obvious that someone else was behind it. Soon as I heard Walter's name mentioned I knew. Still, I have to admit it's strange that the commanders made things official by giving their personal nod of approval.'

'Maybe they don't trust that frog-gigger, Vince, to get the job done.'

'There's more than Vince dealing with this. Rest assured. Homeland Security, NSC, FBI, CIA; everyone will have their own team on it. Plus, there'll be others from Arrowsake.'

'It's not a good feeling knowing that there are others from our unit out there.'

'Not from our unit, Rink. These are a new breed.'

'Yeah, I get that, but you know where I'm coming from. And what that might mean.'

'You think they're using us as scapegoats and they're prepared to sacrifice us?'

'Like I said, germs in a Petri dish. If we're their superbugs, you can bet your sweet cheeks they've designed an antidote.'

'If that was the case, Walter would have warned us.'

'Walter would sell us down the line as quick as that!' Rink snapped his fingers. 'Don't know how you can trust him after the way he's used us all these years.'

'We've used him, too.'

Rink didn't make comment, he knew that without Walter's intervention we'd both be doing hard time, or dead.

'I suppose you're right. Walter has helped us, but it was always for his own reasons. Maybe he was even *ordered* to help us, I don't know. Perhaps that's why Arrowsake have chosen now to show their faces, so that we realise who it is we're really obligated to.'

'I don't feel like we owe them a thing. They made monsters outa us, then they kicked us loose like we were dog shit on their shoes, remember?'

Dreams still tormented me: the screams of accusation, the faces of the countless dead, all those sent howling into my nightmares because Arrowsake pointed at them and ordered me to kill. In those dreams I was under a bruised sky where the clouds were the shifting faces of the damned, striding across the blood-soaked earth, the arms of my victims reaching for me, tearing at my clothing and flesh, the ground sucking at my boots, trying to draw me into its embrace. Sometimes I'd give in to the inevitable, and wake varnished in sweat, but other times I'd fight my accusers, blasting their faces apart with my fists and my gun that seemed to have a never-ending supply of ammunition. While doing so I'd laugh hysterically, like it was the greatest enjoyment imaginable. Yes, Rink was right when he said that Arrowsake had made a monster of me.

'Walter's still our friend.' There was finality to my statement.

'I know that you love the old fart, Hunter, but you've gotta see him for what he really is. Where his loyalties lie.'

'I just don't see him standing by and doing nothing to warn us. Not if you're right and we're not coming back from this.'

'If what he says is true, then there's little hope of that happening anyway.'

'There's no need for you to come along, Rink. I'm the one who has the threat of prison hanging over me.'

The suggestion didn't merit an answer. Rink shook his head. 'I vote we tell Arrowsake to go fuck themselves, then we disappear. We could do that, you know.'

Rink was as serious as an April Fool prank. He grinned, shook his head again, resigned to the fact that we were buried in Arrowsake's plan as deeply as an Arkansas tick in a bull's ass. It didn't matter that we were being manipulated into becoming assassins again; I had a personal reason for wanting Carswell Hicks and his followers dead. I'd sworn to end the threat to the Griffiths family and to get that done even Rink could see that it was better we worked with Arrowsake than against them.

The weather front coming down over the Great Lakes had finally spent itself over the Alleghenies, and Hertford was spread out below us, twinkling wetly under the winter sun. Hertford City Medical Center was a series of whitewashed buildings on the northern side of town, and the chopper banked that way, heading directly for the hospital's helipad. I adjusted my coat. Covering my weapons was a necessity, but I also suspected that the sun didn't hold much warmth yet.

Disembarking from the helicopter, we attracted a crowd of onlookers who were familiar with the local air-ambulance but not this sleek airship. Maybe they were expecting the *men in black*, because they seemed singularly nonplussed when Rink and I stepped out. Vince followed, and he did look more like the popular image of an undercover agent. It helped when he thumbed on some obligatory dark shades and strode purposefully for the hospital, his mouth set in a tight line. We shared an amused glance at his expense.

Don Griffiths was no longer ensconced in the Intensive Care Unit, but had been shifted to a private room. It was as much for the privacy of other patients as for Don, due to the number of FBI personnel who'd come and gone over the last few days. There was a guard on his door, who moved away when Vince gave him the signal. Don was lying in his bed, eyes closed, with the soft beep of machines marking his progress back to recovery. Don looked twenty years older than the last time I'd seen him. I turned to Vince. 'Give me a few minutes, will you?'

'I want to know everything he says.'

'Fair enough, but he won't say anything with you standing there.'

Vince scowled at the old man in the bed. 'It doesn't look like he's going to say anything whether I'm here or not.'

Rink took Vince by the elbow. 'C'mon. You can go get a coffee with your old pal, Rink.'

'Oh, so we're friends now?'

'So long as you're buying.'

Vince pointed a finger at me. '*Everything* he says. OK?'

'As long as you get me a coffee, too. Strong as it comes, extra shot of espresso.'

Rink ushered the FBI agent away, closing the door behind him. When I was sure that Vince was out of earshot, I said, 'You can stop pretending now, Don, the feebie's gone.'

Don slowly opened his eyes, as though checking the coast was clear. He shifted himself on the bed, groaning as much as the springs. 'How did you know I was awake?'

I nodded at the cardiac monitor, how closely together the spikes and corresponding beeps had become. 'Bit of a giveaway. Luckily Vince was too busy listening to his own voice to notice.'

'There's no fooling you, Hunter.'

Don's words held more meaning than even he'd intended. His cheeks flushed, a stark contrast to his white hair and beard.

'I need to know it all, Don. Everything. You ready to talk?' The question held room for only one reply. Don closed his eyes. He was ordering his words, and I gave him the time. There was a jug of water on a bedside table and I poured a glass, held it out to the old man. 'Here, take a drink.'

Don sipped, holding the glass in both hands like a chalice. The glass was something he could concentrate on, to help steady himself.

'When I first came to see you, you mentioned that you'd received an email,' I began. 'I didn't attach too much importance to it at the time, but it's been there niggling away at the back of my mind. I assumed that you had received a message – perhaps intended for someone else – and had read into it something that wasn't even there. But when events overtook us, I never bothered asking who it was from or how many times you'd got mail prior to that because by then, well, it was a given that the mail had come from Hicks or someone close to him. I was wrong, wasn't I?'

Don's mouth made a tight gash and he dipped towards the glass again. He licked his lips, trying to get his mouth to work in time with his thoughts. 'You're partly right, Hunter. The messages did come from someone close to Hicks, only they were without his knowledge.'

'Someone betraying Hicks from the inside? Not Vince?'

'No, not Vince. I had no idea . . . *what* Vince really was until he came across me at the logging camp and told me.'

'Who, then?'

'Better that you understand what than who. Back when I was an analyst for the think-tank, I discovered this man. He was deemed a low threat, no one of any consequence. He had a deep-seated hatred of the government for what he saw as a betrayal of the Vietnam veterans, but he was more hot air than anything and was never going to progress further than nasty words or propaganda. Under the first amendment, he had a right to shout and scream all he wanted, and he was happy to do that. Posing as a sympathetic ear, I got close to him and he began telling me about this other bunch, an offshoot disowned even by the National Alliance, white supremacists who were planning a major event. Are you familiar with *The Turner Diaries*, Hunter?'

As someone who had been tasked with taking down paramilitary killers I was all too familiar with the book. Written under the pseudonym of Andrew MacDonald, it was actually penned by Dr William Pierce, the founder of the National Alliance, and was about a race war with a group of militant whites successfully overthrowing the US government. Many racists saw it as a prophetic tale of future events and some had used it as a blueprint for their actions. Timothy McVeigh, the man convicted of the Oklahoma bombing, had confessed to attacking the Federal Building after reading the book. Back in the 1980s, Robert Matthews and his group had gone on a spree of robberies and murder before he was killed in a stand-off with the FBI. Matthews was also an advocate of the book.

'Hicks was planning a coup?'

'That's what my contact told me. Except it turned out that Hicks was more interested in attacking the banking system than the government.'

Hit them where it really hurts, I thought. 'Which was when you supplied the information and Hicks was arrested.'

'That's right,' Don said. 'My *friend* was pissed at me of course; he suspected that I was the one behind Hicks' capture. But he was a forgiving soul, so as long as I paid him a few grand he promised to go away.'

'And you gave in to his demand.'

'It suited me,' Don admitted. 'Cracking that case was the making of me, gave me everything I needed. I was grateful and paid him.'

'When Hicks escaped from prison, this man found out that he wasn't dead. He didn't come back to warn you as an old friend, he was after more money?'

'I didn't believe him. As far as I was concerned Hicks was dead and gone; what threat was he to me or my family?'

'Then Brook died.'

Don's eyes grew teary. 'Then Brook was *murdered*.'

The words of the email made sense now. How many more must die or who will you lose next? Something along those lines. The message was really asking, 'How many are you prepared to lose before you pay me?'

I said, 'You sent for me, even after you paid him. You didn't trust this man.'

Don shook his head wearily. 'I sent for you, I only got back in touch with him after you turned me down. Remember how you walked away from me? Well, I transferred the cash to him then – fifty thousand dollars. I wasn't to know that you were going to change your mind, was I? Maybe if Hicks' men hadn't approached you at the Seven-Eleven then you'd have got in your car and headed back to Tampa.'

I couldn't deny that Don had a point. 'So what was this man offering in return? He obviously didn't give a damn about you or your family. What was the money for this time?'

'Information on Hicks' latest plot.'

'Did he send it to you?'

'Yes.'

'So where is it, your computer?' The FBI had already trawled through Don's computer and had come up with nothing of significance. There wasn't even a history of the alleged emails.

Don tapped his head. 'It's all up here, Hunter. We used the draft email facility between our computers and deleted as we went. There's nothing but what I've retained up here.'

'This man—'

'Jim Lloyd,' Don interjected. 'You know what he is now, so you may as well know his name.'

'OK. This Lloyd, do you trust his information?'

'I've no reason to doubt him. He wants Hicks stopped as much as I do. He's frightened that Hicks has figured out who supplied the info that originally betrayed him, and that harm will come to his family as a result. He told me his daughter is part of Gant's crew and he was terrified of what Hicks would do to her.'

Sonya Madden. I thought of what Vince had done to the girl and that Lloyd's fears had come true, albeit in a roundabout manner.

'Yet he was more interested in extorting money from you than getting his daughter out of harm's way.'

'I think he was planning on using the cash to take his daughter somewhere safe. He wanted out of Manhattan, that was for sure. That was another reason he wanted Hicks stopped. He says that Hicks forced him into bartering a deal with some old contacts of Lloyd's out in the Far East. He said that if Hicks' plan works out there's no way he wants to stay in New York.'

'Tell me Hicks' plan.'

Don told me.

Holy shit, Walter wasn't that far away from the truth, only it was much worse than he or Arrowsake had even anticipated.

I was running when I met Rink and Vince returning from the cafeteria. The extra shot of caffeine would have been good, but I just snatched it from Vince's hand and slung it in a waste bin. They followed me, pounding towards the waiting helicopter, Vince asking what the hell was going on. Over my shoulder I said, 'The deal's still on, Vince. You bought the coffee, so I'll tell you everything Don said. But I'll tell you on the way to New York because we haven't a single second to spare.'

35

Port Authority officials were as numerous as fleas on a junkyard dog here. They could arrive at any second to check out the men standing on the dock overlooking Newark Bay towards Staten Island. Carswell Hicks wasn't worried, though, because many meetings were conducted here on the waterfront. This was the principal facility for container ships serving New York City and Jersey was a buzz of activity at all times of the day or night. The port was a boiling pot for races from all over the globe, so it wasn't unusual for whites to be mixing with Asians, and their meeting would raise no more suspicion than any other mongrel grouping of men would. Looking closely a Port Authority cop might notice the tenseness between the men, but when deals were being struck, sometimes for billions of dollars, a little uneasiness could be forgiven.

Nevertheless, Hicks didn't have time for any distractions, the worst of which would be a nosy cop. He wanted to get this done and over with but it was necessary to ensure their privacy first. He'd set some of his people at strategic points around the port, on the lookout for anyone who might disturb them. Those he was meeting doubtless had similar men keeping watch.

Keeping things low-key he had brought only his two minders with him. Both hulking men had the look of boxers gone to seed, but their conservative suits and hairstyles weren't as obvious as the tattoos and bald skulls of the others that Hicks had at hand. They served their purpose well: they were intimidating, but didn't look like they hated anyone for any specific reason, and wouldn't offend their North Korean friends with a racist slip of the tongue that Samuel Gant, for example, couldn't rein in.

'Which of you is Kwon?'

As was agreed the Koreans had come in a similar small number. Hicks didn't know their names beyond the codename supplied in Jim Lloyd's introduction message, and couldn't care less. All he was interested in was doing the deal and then getting back to Manhattan. Things were moving along and he didn't want to stall the momentum by making small talk among the rankness of rusting containers and diesel oil.

The man who came forward had the high forehead and long chin, the epicanthic fold that turned down the outer edges of his eyes, that defined the Korean racial trait. His suit was well cut and his shoes glossed to a high sheen and judging by his easy grace he was no stranger to a martial arts studio. He was handsome enough that he'd pass for a chop-socky movie star, Hicks decided, but so what? He was still a gook whichever way you looked at him.

'I am Kwon.'

Jesus, Hicks thought, he even sounds like a chop-socky flick. The only thing that spoiled the image was how Kwon's lips worked in sync with his words: that never happened in the kung fu movies he'd seen. At least the Korean's codename was fitting for an action star, Kwon being a catch-all translation of 'hand' or 'fist'. In any other circumstance it would be laughable, but, other than that he was a delivery boy, Hicks decided that Kwon was inconsequential and didn't deserve the consideration he'd already given him.

He nodded at the men behind Kwon. 'I don't see any sign of the product you promised.'

Kwon raised his chin, staring down his nose. He was an inch or so taller than Hicks. 'I don't see the money.'

Money was an intangible commodity when it only existed in cyberspace; the days of suitcases stuffed with cash transferred between couriers were a thing of the past. Who wanted the trouble when a press of a button was so much easier? Hicks held up a mobile phone. 'I have a man poised to deposit the agreed amount into an account of your choice. Once I see the product, I give him the go-ahead. You have the facility to check that we have made good on the deal, I take it?'

Kwon indicated one of his colleagues who took out a BlackBerry and jabbed buttons. That done, Kwon made a swooping gesture with his arm asking that Hicks follow. The two groups didn't converge, but moved along the dock alongside each other. Conversation was unnecessary as well as unwelcome.

Metal containers, stacked three or four high in places, formed a series of corridors that stretched into the hazy distance. Company names and loading directions stencilled on the cargo containers were in more languages than could be counted and further proof to Hicks to what extent his nation was turning into a sink-hole for the world. Distractedly he wondered how many of those containers had brought aliens into the country, smuggled past the immigration authorities in the same manner as his product had arrived here. Out of the hundreds of containers, Kwon led them unerringly to a particular one. As they approached, the door swung open slowly and a fourth Korean emerged carting with him a large silver box with snap-locks. The box looked extremely heavy, even for the muscular man who carried it.

Hicks peered both ways along the corridor they stood in. He could hear the dull roar of machinery from a distance, and somewhere a man shouted to another, but there was no one nearby. He looked up, checking that a helicopter wasn't hanging in the sky with a camera trained on them. The low clouds billowing overhead made that almost impossible.

'I'd care to check the product before we do the deal. I'd hate to hand over two million dollars for an empty box.'

'You Americans are so untrusting.' Kwon's sneer should have been enough to seal the deal, but he was right: Hicks didn't trust the Korean one bit.

'Show me.' Hicks held up the cell phone, his thumb poised over the send button.

Kwon rattled off something in his native tongue and while Hicks had spent time in the Far East, he was only familiar with Vietnamese and that was unlike the language Kwon spoke. The man lugging the box set it on the ground. He unsnapped the locks and opened the lid. Sweat broke along the Korean's hairline, all the proof that Hicks needed. Still, he leaned close enough to see the padded interior of the box and the product it protected.

'Would you like to open one of the packages?'

Kwon was standing smugly, with his arms crossed on his chest.

'No. I'll take your word for it that they're good.'

'Excellent decision,' Kwon said. 'Then we have a deal?'

Hicks thumbed his phone. 'Do the transfer.' He looked back at Kwon. 'The account number?'

Kwon told him and Hicks relayed the details through the phone. The Korean with the BlackBerry watched the screen then nodded almost imperceptibly to his boss. Kwon turned his gaze back on Hicks. 'It's all yours.'

The fourth Korean shut the lid and snapped the locks in place. He stepped back, appearing glad to be rid of the box. Hicks stood aside for his minders who between them hauled it off the ground like an overladen picnic hamper. Both men frowned at the weight, but said nothing.

Deal done, Hicks had no more time to waste. He walked away, following his minders, Kwon and his men as insignificant to him now as any other insignificant race.

'Hey, Yankee!'

Kwon was wearing a supercilious sneer when Hicks turned back. It seemed that racism was a two-way street. Hicks thought about shooting Kwon and his entourage, shutting them in their container and shipping them back home. But who knew? He might want to do business with them again.

Kwon said, 'Where is your famed hospitality? We are in town for a few days. Won't you show us the sights, my friend?'

'I'm afraid that I wouldn't be very good company, Kwon, so you boys are better off on your own.' Hicks turned away, adding, 'But if you want to see the sights, I've some advice for you: get it done today.'

36

'The Bloody Angle continues to live up to its name,' said Special Agent Vincent as he took the Lincoln town car out through Bowery and on to Chatham Square, then eased it into the meagre traffic heading down Park Row.

Sitting in the back of the government car, I wasn't surprised by the revelation that Carswell Hicks had beaten us to Jim Lloyd, but I could have done with a look around the Vietnam vet's apartment without having to take Vince's word that it was a dead end. That had proved nigh-on impossible. When we'd turned up at Doyers Street, the NYP was already there in force, and the street had been taped off to keep back the ghoulish onlookers. Vince had flashed his badge and got through, but we had been left to twiddle our thumbs in the Lincoln. Rink, who could normally sit still enough for birds to alight on him, was fidgeting so much that he'd finally clambered out of the car and gone off in search of nourishment. He arrived back with barbecued spare ribs and spicy General Tzu's chicken wings, plus a couple waxed cups of Java. I took the coffee but declined the food. My appetite was a non-starter. Now that Vince had brought us up to speed on the mess they'd found Jim Lloyd in I was glad there was nothing substantial in my stomach. It wasn't the bullet holes that disturbed me, it was the fact that Lloyd's pet chihuahua had abandoned all loyalty to its master when it grew hungry. Greyfriars Bobby, it wasn't.

Park Row was a restricted area, the road running down behind the civic centre and court houses on Federal Plaza, and we were hailed over by a private security guard. Vince flashed his badge at the guard, who glanced suspiciously in the back at us. Perhaps the guard thought that we were prisoners of the fed, but for the fact Rink was mid-chew on a BBQ rib. He just shook his head, then waved Vince through. Rink waved back with the pork bone.

'Christ, Rink, those things stink,' Vince said. He cracked a window, and also thumbed up the A/C unit.

'Wait'll my guts start working on them and you'll know what really stinks. Sushi I can take, but Chinese food always has the same effect on me.'

'Too much information,' said Vince, and opened the window fully. 'Just promise me that you'll behave when we meet with Walter.'

'Walter cracks them off like any man. I'm sure he'll understand.'

Vince made a sound of disgust. 'Jesus! Hunter, can't you do anything with your buddy?'

I opened a window.

'Thanks, that's a great help . . .'

I swore under my breath. 'Don't you think you've more to worry about than Rink letting one slip, like the *whole of fucking Manhattan going to hell in the next few hours*?'

The fury of my words drove an uneasy silence through the car. Even Rink was surprised at my anger. 'Hey, take it easy, buddy.'

I scrubbed my hands through my hair. 'Yeah. OK. Sorry.'

I felt ashamed at the outburst. Vince and Rink were merely venting their fear through banter; I'd done the same a thousand times in the past. It was just that I'd fouler things in mind, and they demanded full attention. All we knew was that Hicks was planning a major attack somewhere in the metropolitan area of New York, which in all likelihood would be as devastating as the events that occurred on 9/11. The problem was that we had no idea about where, when or how the strike would take place, only that it would be soon and with catastrophic consequences. I wished we'd managed to speak to Jim Lloyd before his dog snacked on him: up-to-date details would have helped.

I was still mulling things over when we entered a private chamber in a nondescript office across Broadway from the Woolworth Building. Ironically, we were less than a stone's throw from Ground Zero.

Walter was waiting for us, his Adirondacks costume replaced by a Western-style suit, pale blue with contrasting black stitching: the Boss Hogg look. He was chewing furiously on the end of a cigar like it was one of the ribs Rink had so recently polished off. Three laptop computers were glowing on the desk in front of him, their muted light turning Walter's face the same colour as his suit. From this angle, I couldn't make out what was on the screens but guessed that Walter had a direct line to his Arrowsake commanders, and maybe others. I wondered if the President had been filled in with the details yet.

Walter came out from behind the desk, shaking each of our hands in turn like a politician on the campaign trail. 'Sit down, sit down,' he said, indicating leather chairs arranged along the wall.

Neither Rink nor I took him up on the offer, but Vince followed the order without comment. A few seconds later he must have felt a bit hemmed in because he shifted uncomfortably. He sat side-on, perched on the edge of the chair so he could see between our shoulders.

'Anything to report?' Walter's expression said that he didn't expect so.

'Jim Lloyd was a dead end,' I said. The corresponding grimace was for my choice of words. 'If he was using the same draft facility as he did with Don Griffiths, then his computer will be clean, no way of tracing anything back to Hicks. We don't have any other leads.'

Walter waved his cigar while he propped himself against the edge of his desk. 'Then we have to concentrate on what we do know. We know what Hicks is planning and that it is going to happen very soon, the main difficulty is that we have no idea where.'

'Don said it would be here. Manhattan.'

'Manhattan is a big island,' said Walter. 'With a population of more than one and a half million people spread over twenty-three square miles, it would be almost impossible to find him in time to stop him.'

'Sounds defeatist,' I said.

'Just being realistic, son.'

I snorted at Walter's use of the term of endearment, hearing for the first time how empty it sounded. Walter didn't catch the reason for my cynicism, maybe assuming that he hadn't made himself clear. 'Hicks won't be acting alone. He'll have his team working with him. Our emphasis is on finding them, and they'll lead us to their boss.'

'Vince tried that already,' I said.

Vince got up from his chair, muscling between us to stand alongside Walter. 'I have inside knowledge on their hangouts, it's worth a try.'

'What's the likelihood of any of them being there, seeing as Hicks now realises you were a plant? They'll have abandoned all the places that you were familiar with. Moved on.'

'Not so many places a gang of skinheads can congregate without someone noticing,' Rink offered.

'I already thought of that and have the NYPD keeping a lookout.' Walter glanced over his shoulder as one of his computers chimed the signal for an incoming message. He ignored it. 'We've also coordinated with the Anti-Defamation League to see if they can give us any up-to-date information on the racist skinhead movement. SHARP is helping us too.'

'Sharp?'

Vince offered an explanation. 'Skinheads Against Racial Prejudice. Anti-racist skins, if you can believe such a thing exists?'

'I can believe it,' I said. The skinhead movement began back in the UK. Originally it had nothing at all to do with racism and hatred; it was a working-class social commentary, all about pride and respect. As a youth, I'd even dabbled in the scene before the National Front and BNP subverted the movement to their blinkered way of thinking. Here in the US, the neo-Nazi organisations had taken on the uniform of shaven head and braces, the Doc Marten boots, and had twisted it until anyone with less than flowing locks was now looked on as a thug. As a Para, there had been times when I was on the wrong end of abuse, simply because I had a military haircut. I didn't react to the baiting, because my accusers spoke from ignorance. Even now, most people didn't know that there were skins out there who held to the original values: decent, law-abiding people who hated their bonehead contemporaries.

'What about Homeland Security?'

'They're concentrating on the other angle,' Walter said.

'Any proof in it yet?'

'They tracked an incoming Russian freighter. Preliminary tests on board the ship have proved negative, but they can't be sure. The captain swore ignorance but did admit to having brought a small group of passengers from Vladivostok. They jumped ship to a private vessel thirty miles offshore at Montauk, Long Island. Homeland and the CIA are currently studying satellite imagery to validate and track the trajectory of this phantom boat. We should have the results through soon.' Walter studied the tip of his cigar like it was a divining tool that would offer up all the answers. 'They're treating this as serious, Hunter. The passengers were all North Korean and they made no secret of their hatred of the USA. They were carrying a "very heavy" box between them when they disembarked at Montauk.'

'It's a lead-lined box?' I asked. 'Then the probability is that they have supplied Hicks just as Lloyd warned.'

Walter nodded glumly. 'That's the problem with allowing the Koreans to continue running their nuclear programme. We can never be sure that their due diligence process will be as stringent as ours. If Lloyd was right and there is a black market trade in by-products, well, I hate to think what that means.'

'Lloyd was more specific than that. He said that Hicks wanted a plutonium isotope. If they've got their hands on the makings of an atomic bomb . . . Jesus.'

Walter's eyes clouded as though searching distant memories and finding nothing he liked. 'You ask me, Hicks doesn't have the technology or expertise for that. But it doesn't really matter.'

'Not when they have the makings of a dirty bomb,' I finished for him. 'Can you imagine the devastation that could cause on this island?'

'If we don't find him soon, we won't have to *imagine* anything.'

Back in my days with Arrowsake I'd been put through an ABC warfare survival training programme. It comprised a number of technical sessions, interminable hours of videotaped instructions delivered by a morose voice-over. By the time it was finished I'd gained a multitude of injections jabbed into my veins and the knowledge that without the full protection of a hazmat suit I'd be fucked whether in the blast zone or not. If Hicks' plan came to fruition, Manhattan wasn't going to be the place to be for decades to come.

A few days ago, running through the woods and cutting down my enemies, now that was my idea of combat, not being torn apart from within by a creeping isotope infecting my cells with cancer. I stole a glance at Rink. My friend shouldn't have been here, he should've been back in the relative safety of Florida, but I wouldn't say as much; Rink would be offended, and stick around out of sheer stubbornness.

'We'd best get looking,' I said.

'There's a place on Forty-Third Street I'd like to check, where some of Sam Gant's buddies used to hang out,' Vince said. 'Maybe we can squeeze a location out of them that we aren't already aware of.'

'I'm all for squeezing,' Rink said. 'Lead the way, Special Agent.'

I was all for getting moving. The longer we dallied here the easier it was for Hicks to put his plan into motion. But bashing in the door of a skinhead clubhouse wasn't the way. Anyone who was important to Hicks' plan would be working from a strict set of instructions, primarily one that demanded total secrecy. Smacking heads would alleviate some of our frustration, but that would be all. Time was too short for that. Maybe even too short for me to make a phone call.

My relationship with Imogen Ballard was one we both recognised as being a shared convenience of comfort and friendship. When we first made love, I had wondered if she thought of her lost lover the way I did of her sister, Kate. But had her memory faded, and when we were together, did she now lose herself totally in me the way I'd reciprocated of late? I knew that I loved her, not with the full-on passion I'd found with Kate, or the lifetime devotion I felt for my ex-wife, Diane, but I loved her nonetheless. The least she deserved was a goodbye.

Rink was already moving for the door, Vince wavering because Walter hadn't yet given the go-ahead. I took the moment of indecision to feel for the mobile phone in my pocket. Both the phones were there – the one Vince supplied and the pre-paid I'd purchased, and I rolled them between my fingers. If I phoned Imogen then what was I going to say? Hi, babe, sorry but I won't be coming to Maine next week like we planned, cause I'll probably be dead by then! Did I just tell her something had come up, a matter of life and death . . . probably mine and about a million others? But then where did the farewells end? I also wanted to speak with Diane, ask her about Hector and Paris, my dogs. Tell her to give them a hug for me, tell her I still loved her despite what had happened between us. My mother, Anita, and stepdad, Bob, they deserved a goodbye too, as did my brother, John, if I could even find him. Harvey Lucas, Don Griffiths, Millie, Beth and Ryan, the list went on. For such a solitary person I had a lot of people who turned out to mean a great deal to me.

Too many and too little time. The phones fell back into my jacket pocket. The only way I would see any of them again was if I stopped Hicks and his monstrous plan.

I moved to follow Rink. One of Walter's computers chimed another incoming message, and in the sudden silence it sounded more insistent than the one before. Walter grunted, stepping round the back of his desk, and I watched his face, sensing that the message just might be the lead we all needed.

A shadow of a smile flickered at the corner of Walter's mouth.

'They've found him?'

'No,' Walter said. 'But we've got a location on those who may have supplied him the plutonium. The FBI has them under observation in a titty bar on the Lower East Side.' Walter tapped keys furiously, replying to the message. 'I've told the team to hold back till you're finished with them. If we want to know exactly what it is we're up against we have to find out what they've supplied to Hicks. The way I see it: we haven't time for the normal mode of lawful interrogation.' Walter allowed his last words to hang between us.

The message rang loud and clear.

37

In the packed streets, men and women hailed each other, shaking hands, exchanging hugs, laughing and dancing jigs to their own music. Some held Graggers – noise sticks not unlike soccer rattles – which they shook in time with their laughter, adding to the general air of festivity. Many wore fancy dress, while others were happier with their everyday garb, predominantly black, but joining in the celebratory joy just the same.

It made sense.

The Purim Feast is an important public holiday in the Jewish calendar, marked by the exchange of gifts, feasting and general wine-induced merriment, a time for people to let their hair down and enjoy themselves. Traditionally celebrated in the Hebrew month of Adar, it was a feast to mark the liberation of the Jews from their Persian overlords, when Esther outwitted the wicked Haman and led the Jews to victory over their persecutors.

It was the ideal time for Hicks to cause havoc and add validity to his statement to the government, more so when this year the fifteenth of Adar corresponded with today. Added to that he had found the ideal location. Lincoln Square between West Sixty-Sixth and Seventy-Seventh Streets on Amsterdam Avenue gave him everything he required. Here were the West End and Lincoln Square Synagogues, the Chabad of the West Sixties, all destinations of the Jewish community during this festive time. Nearby were schools, both Juilliard and

La Guardia, which could only cause even more terror and confusion.

He thought of Kristallnacht, and how he'd planned his own night of broken glass, and decided that his original plan of detonating a bomb in Times Square would have held nowhere near the significance it would here in the heart of the Jewish community. Here and now was more befitting his character and his message. Forget Crystal Night, this would be his Day of Broken Spirits.

Feeling that there was no time like the present, he thumbed the button on his cell phone. A corresponding cell began to ring in a parked vehicle at the intersection of Sixty-Eighth and Amsterdam, but no one could hear it over the simultaneous percussive roar of flame and debris blossoming between the buildings. Carried on the super-heated wind was Hicks' statement to the world.

38

'Let's hope that it's nothing more serious than a car smash.'

Squinting over Vince's shoulder, I saw the traffic coming to a shuddering halt and I didn't think a collision was the reason for this sudden hiccup to the flow of yellow cabs and limousines that normally hurtled along here. 'Unless there's an accident on the other carriageway as well, I wouldn't bank on it, Vince.'

The cars on our left were also coming to a stop, and their drivers were fiddling with the buttons on their car radios, dawning shock and disbelief on their features.

'Holy crap,' Rink moaned. 'You think we're too late? It's happened already?'

We were passengers in the back of Vince's government car, Vince driving. We were on FDR Drive between the twin spans that arched over the East River towards Brooklyn Heights. On Manhattan Bridge the traffic heading on to the island was coming to a standstill and if I bothered to turn my head, I was sure that Brooklyn Bridge would paint a like picture. The only discernible movement was on those lanes of the bridge heading out of the city, and if anything they were speeding up as people realised they should make themselves scarce as rapidly as possible. As with any traffic jam, the air was filled with honking horns and racing engines. People were shouting wordlessly, some in frustration but others in anger or dismay.

I dropped a window and smelled the tang of exhaust fumes, wondered if that was all the poison that the air held. From a distance came the wail of multiple sirens, first responders heading to a scene of catastrophe. 'Turn the radio on.'

Vince did and the voice of an announcer cut into the middle of an R&B track to confirm out worst fears. A bomb had exploded in the Jewish quarter at Lincoln Square. Details were sketchy, but preliminary reports said an improvised explosive device in the trunk of a stationary vehicle had detonated causing chaos and destruction. Casualties were in their dozens, but as of that time fatalities were unconfirmed by the police. The announcer suggested what everyone else must have been considering: that this was a second wave of attack launched by al-Qaeda or another radical-fundamentalist Muslim cell. The police were coordinating an immediate evacuation of the surrounding area, the announcer said in a grave voice, for fear that further devices were timed to explode.

'That's the lie they're telling people? More bombs? They're evacuating 'cause of the goddamn fallout.' Rink shifted in his seat as if he wanted to climb out of the car. It wasn't through fear of being irradiated, but from a need to put an end to this inaction. I knew exactly how he felt.

Cars were jammed to the front and back of us, and to all sides. 'We're going to have to find another way up town.'

Vince shook his head, as he started to lay his hand on the horn. 'You honestly want to be anywhere near Lincoln Square? You're crazy, Hunter.'

'I'm not talking about going to Lincoln Square. We still have to get to the Koreans.'

'Don't you think that's pointless now? Considering how Hicks has already detonated the bomb?'

'Those bastards brought their poison here. They're as responsible for this as Hicks is.'

'We can leave them to the FBI,' Vince said. By the look of him his plans didn't include staying on the island for much longer.

Rink touched my wrist. He held my gaze like we were children making a lifelong pact. 'Brother, if that bomb was laced with radiation we're already fucked. We might as well get a little payback before we start rotting.'

'I'm with you,' I said.

'We should concentrate on Hicks!' Vince twisted round so that he could look at us, his face stricken with anger. My take on it was that the young man was panicking as the truth of the situation began to dawn on him. If we stayed on the island, we were probably committing ourselves to a slow and painful death.

'You heard what Walter said. We have to find out how much isotope he had with him. That's our mission Vince, now suck it up.'

Rink rumbled, 'We'll still get our chance at Hicks. You don't think he was standing near to where the bomb went off, do you? He's positioned himself upwind of the explosion, but my guess is he's close enough to see the consequences.'

'That's quite a goddamned supposition,' Vince said.

'Would you want to be standing in the way of a dust cloud laced with plutonium?' I demanded. 'The wind's blowing towards the north-east. If Hicks doesn't want to get irradiated along with everyone else, my guess is he's not a million miles away from where we're going now.'

'Have you seen the road?' Vince indicated the jam of cars all around us. 'We won't be going anywhere soon.'

'Jesus,' Rink said. 'What kinda lame-asses are Arrowsake employing these days?' He stabbed a finger into Vince's forehead, none too gently. 'Don't you have the capacity to improvise? Use your head, boy, cause there's always more ways to get to where you're going than swanning around in limo-fuckin-sines.'

Stretching over the seat, I dug in the young agent's pocket. 'Give me your badge, Vince.'

'Hey! What do you think you're doing?'

Snatching the FBI ID badge from his pocket, I threw open the door. 'I'm improvising.'

I approached two men on motorcycles who had been weaving through the stalled traffic, stepped in their way, forcing them to stop, and held up Vince's badge. Rink clambered out of the limousine, Vince calling after him. 'Hey, I can't just abandon a government vehicle like this. They'll have my ass if it doesn't go back in one piece.'

Rink leaned back inside. 'So stay here. Leave what needs doin' to someone who gives a shit.'

Cowed, Vince came out of the car, jabbing numbers into his phone. I didn't know who Vince was calling – and I didn't really care. Vince swore as he listened to what was most likely a recorded announcement stating his call couldn't be connected. All over Manhattan other callers would be getting the same message as telecommunication systems overloaded. Vince returned to the car and used the satellite phone instead.

When he came out, we were straddling the two motorcycles while their owners stood kicking at the road surface in bewilderment.

'What about me?' Vince asked.

'Get on the back,' Rink said. 'Or stay with the car, the choice is yours.'

Vince took one last forlorn glance at the Lincoln, then he climbed on the motorbike and wrapped his arms round Rink's middle. 'Y'know,' Rink grinned, 'I always wanted to commandeer a vehicle like you see the cops do in the TV shows.'

We set off, weaving our way through the stalled traffic. Some drivers had left their vehicles and were standing in the road, hands on hips or shadowing their eyes as they sought some sign of the catastrophe a couple miles away. We shouted at them to move. A few cars picked up scratches as we squeezed through. There was a bottleneck where the jam had bunched up at the intersection for the Williamsburg Bridge, but then we found a clear stretch and hit the throttle, making up ground. At a turn-off I went right, swooping back under FDR Drive with Rink and Vince hurtling along behind. We skipped through service alleys, dodging parked vehicles and dumpsters, and came out on to surface streets that would take us back to Delancey where the Red Moon Club awaited.

As we sped along, I thought about how this entire thing had started with a red moon over Bedford Well; now I was approaching another. I considered how symbolic that might be: would this be where the trail ended for me? Only one way to find out, I decided.

The news of the bombing in Lincoln Square had apparently reached the interior of the go-go bar, bringing a halt to the proceedings as even the scantily clad dancers had jumped down off bar-tops to stare at TV sets or to try phoning home. Some had tried leaving the bar, to find that they had been blocked by a cordon of FBI agents and NYPD cruisers. The customers and staff were in a mild panic, which had grown ten times worse when the small group of Koreans realised who the real prisoners here were. By the time we arrived, the scene had descended into chaos.

In fear of injuring any of the innocents inside the bar, the law enforcement officers had refrained from returning fire, but the Koreans had no such scruples. The front windows were smashed, glass glittering on the pavements, and gunfire rang out, forcing the cops and FBI to take cover. Already it looked like the Koreans had tried to make a break for it via a side entrance, but a cop car had been driven directly up to block the door. The door was pocked with bullet holes, as was the cruiser.

Vince was first off the motorbike, running to the officers in charge who were squatting low behind a NYPD cruiser across Delancey. I let him go, because, unlike the cops, I had no intention of trying to end this in a peaceable fashion. I pulled out my SIG and angled for the corner of the Red Moon, hearing boots slapping the pavement behind as Rink hurried to cover me. The Koreans weren't the only ones without scruples.

Slamming my shoulders to the red-brick wall, I saw Rink come up close to my side, raising his Glock. There were shouts coming from the cops, but they'd recognised us as allies, so I wasn't fearful of being gunned down. Vince snapped off orders at the scene commanders, and that was all the notice we gave them.

I was one for direct action. Always had been. Forget intricate plans, because anything more than getting in there fast and hard wasn't worth its weight in horse crap.

Inside the bar someone was shouting, the sing-song strains of an eastern language made discordant by anger and fear. I zoned in on the voice, which located one of the Koreans no more than ten feet away on the right. I measured my breathing with the man's screeching, then stepped forward, leaned in the window and fired a short burst of tightly grouped rounds. The man went silent.

There was a moment of shocked awareness that the tide had suddenly turned, and into this space I threw myself. The Devil himself could be waiting inside, but I didn't care; I was going to assault him in his lair if it meant saving Manhattan from a further descent into hell.

39

At the time it never entered my mind that I was engaged upon anything other than a righteous track. As perpetrators of the terrorist attack on Lincoln Square, the Koreans were as guilty of the atrocity as Carswell Hicks was, and all the proof I required was that they had reacted to the police's arrival with deadly force in their attempt to escape. Beyond that I had no idea who they were or why they'd chosen to come to a go-go bar when a dirty bomb had targeted the very city they were in. None of that meant anything as I vaulted inside the Red Moon. It was enough that they were murderers of innocent people and I had a duty to make them repay that crime with their blood.

Inside the main bar area it was dark, but coloured strobes bounced off the metal poles where girls had recently been dancing. A large plasma screen flicked through images of devastation streamed directly from Lincoln Square by circling media helicopters. I saw movement, the staff and punters caught in the middle of the gunfight seeking cover or escape. On my left lay a dead man, the muscular Korean that I had already killed. I moved to the right, placing the thick wooden bar between myself and where I guessed the other Koreans were. Aiming high, I fired twice, smashing a retro-style disco ball to smithereens. Glass tinkled and a kaleidoscope of colour exploded throughout the room as the strobes refracted wildly in all directions. People yelled and screamed which provided the ideal cover for Rink to come inside.

Rink scrambled over. 'This would be so much easier if we didn't have to keep one of the frog-giggers alive,' he said.

'Yeah, that's always the hard bit.' We scanned the area at the back of the bar room. Now that everyone had had the good sense to dive for cover no one remained in sight. There was a doorway on one side, behind a beaded curtain. It corresponded to the position where the NYPD cruiser had jammed the door shut. 'You think there's another way out?'

'I'm guessing the cops already have that covered.'

Standing up was a calculated risk but no bullets came our way.

Dropping down again, just in case I was wrong, I said, 'I'm thinking that our Korean friends have headed upstairs.' The Red Moon Bar was in a converted walk-up residential building. On arrival, I'd noted that it was an old structure with only two levels and a flat roof, dwarfed on either side by more modern constructions. 'Hopefully Vince has positioned snipers to watch the roof, which means they'll be on the upper floor.'

Rink glanced at his Glock, no doubt wishing he'd brought a Mossberg 500. The assault shotgun was always his weapon of choice for this kind of work. Heavier firepower came in handy when clearing a building while going room to room. He chewed a corner of his mouth, then waved the Glock. 'Suppose this'll have to do. You want me to go first?'

'Go for it, I'll be right behind you.'

Rink set off, using the bar for cover as he rushed to the far end. I scanned the room for any sign of danger. Rink positioned himself at the far end, his Glock levelled, and now I sprinted forward and past my friend. I made it to the back of the bar room where I rested with my back to the wall, the TV playing over my shoulder. A brawny man lay on his back, staring through sightless eyes at the ceiling. Doorman, I guessed, who'd tried his best to stop the Koreans;

unfortunately his best hadn't been good enough. Another man, a small ferret in comparison to the dead bouncer, was crouching in a nook beneath the dance stage. He pointed up, confirming my assumption that the Koreans had sought higher ground. I aimed the SIG at the stairwell. A sign tacked to the wall pointed to restrooms upstairs. A toilet was as good a place as any to find crap.

A scantily clad woman jumped up from under a nearby table, running screaming for the front door. I let her go, making my way instead into the stairwell. Rink moved to the position I'd just vacated. Then I entered a space that was one of the most dangerous for anyone tasked with clearing a building. On the stairs there was the twin disadvantage of being on the lower ground and confined in a narrow place. I went up the stairs with my left shoulder tight to the wall. Anyone above would have to exit fully from the door on the left before they would see me ascending.

Three steps down from the landing, I twisted across to the opposite wall and covered the open door while Rink came up the stairs. Down in the bar there was a rush of bodies as the staff and clientele made a break for freedom. They would be replaced within minutes by the police storming inside.

'Where are you, you chickenshit muthas?' Rink whispered to himself.

Normal practice would see Rink move on while I covered him, but before he could do so, I went up the remaining stairs and into the hallway. It was bad enough that Rink had followed me to his possible doom, let alone allowing him to go first. I searched the dim space ahead. Someone, probably the Koreans, had flicked off the lights. At the far end the doors to the restrooms were edged in a pale glow. They wouldn't be cornered in there; too constricting. There was another door on the left. As I crept along I noted that there was no light on in the room beyond and surmised this was where the Koreans were waiting. Still, we couldn't ignore the toilets. I'd have felt stupid if someone burst out from behind one of those doors and cut me down, though not for long, I thought grimly.

Using hand speak, I motioned Rink on, directing him to check the restrooms. Rink went without comment, padding silently along the hall. How such a large man could move as quietly as an errant breeze through tall grass always impressed me. I stepped out, raising the SIG to offer cover. Rink opened each restroom in turn, nodded the all-clear. I went down on one knee, crouching over to make the smallest target possible. Nudged open the final door.

Gunfire rang out, tearing up the wall above and behind me. Plaster particles drifted down. I ignored the sure death whizzing inches above my head, noting and zoning in on the muzzle flash of a semi-automatic handgun. Returning fire, I used the flashes as a gauge, and heard a high-pitched scream that was immediately curtailed when I fired another round at the source of the noise. Something thundered down, shifting stacked furniture by the sound of the resulting crash and rumble.

Rink sped to replace me at the door frame and I went inside. I got a snapshot image of the room, analysing it in the same moment I checked both sides were clear of danger. I dashed to where I'd brought down one of the Koreans, placing the ill-stacked pile of tables and chairs between me and the length of the room. The dead man had knocked over a table, which gave ample cover, and I peered round one side of it. The windows had been painted over in an attempt at sparing less-open-minded individuals getting an eyeful of what happened inside the Red Moon's upper level. Still, the years had conspired against the coating of paint, flaking it away in places so that bars of light cut through the dim interior. Motes of dust and a trail of cordite drifted through the laser-cuts of light, giving the room the look of a haunted space. The room had been partitioned off with rails from which drapes made private enclaves. In each booth was a mattress. It seemed that some of the dancers sidelined in further acrobatics for those willing to pay for a private show.

Before we'd left Walter, the CIA man had told us there were four Koreans, though this hadn't been confirmed. Any more than that and resistance would have been much more concerted than it had. In all likelihood therefore we had an equal number to contend with. The difficulty being, while we intended taking at least one man alive, the Koreans wouldn't be working under such constraints.

From below came the rumble of feet as the NYPD or FBI entered the Red Moon. Time now was the issue, because they'd be coming up and maybe they wouldn't be as indiscriminate about collateral damage this time.

Rink hollered a command in Korean. I understood enough of the language to get the gist: put down your weapons. Do that, you live, refuse, you die. The answer was much easier to comprehend. 'Fuck you!'

'You speak English?' I demanded.

'Better than your friend speaks Korean, Yankee.'

'So you know that when I tell you you're fucked, I'm telling the truth?'

'If that was true, then you wouldn't be waiting for me to throw down my gun, and come out with my hands up. Go ahead, Yankee. You think I'm finished, go ahead and see what happens.'

'OK. But you know how this is going to end, right?'

'Yes. I will kill you and every Yankee who comes into this room.'

'You sound pretty sure of yourself.'

'I am Korean.'

Rink grunted something that was a curse in any language. 'Goddamn pussies, you're all wannabe Japanese, but *very* poor copies. C'mon asshole, put down your gun, let me show you the real deal.'

'Ha!' said the Korean. 'I am *Kwon*. I will destroy you.'

'The Hand, huh? C'mon out here and I'll shove it up your ass like you're a glove puppet.'

'I would crush you in seconds.'

'So let's do it. I'm guessing your Korean style is as inferior to karate as everything else.'

It would have been laughable if the situation wasn't so dire. Listening to the loathing between two Eastern nations was no different to arguments that raged the world over. Allowing Rink and Kwon to exchange insults, I crept round the stack of furniture. Directly ahead was one of the booths and I slowly slipped the curtain aside and stepped over a futon-style mattress lying on the floor. Kwon evidently couldn't see me, because he continued to trade insults with Rink. I was no idiot, though, and credited Kwon with as much sense. The Korean was trying to play us as much as we were playing him. Rink was keeping Kwon busy, and Kwon was happy to oblige while the fourth Korean moved to a better position. I readied myself.

Had only seconds to wait.

As Kwon screeched something in his own language, the hidden Korean came out from the next booth, levelling his pistol at Rink. I didn't bother with a warning shout; bullets were much faster. I merely caressed the trigger of the SIG, fired a single round that punched into the would-be assassin's neck. The man fell to the side, becoming entangled in a curtain that wrapped round his body as he fell. Following the movement, I saw that the man was dying but still able to pull a trigger. Shot him again, once in the heart, once in the head.

Kwon fired, forcing me to skip away to avoid joining the man on the mattress. Rink's Glock made a rattle like a firecracker, bullets firing as rapidly as he pressed the trigger. The sounds of Kwon running for cover came to me, even as I tore a way past a curtain and through another booth. Footsteps sounded loud on the stairs as law enforcement officers hastened up.

If the cops came in the room we'd never get the chance we needed. Terrorist or not, Kwon would be arrested and afforded the treatment laid down by law. Torture wouldn't be permissible.

'Rink! Get the door,' I shouted, trusting that he would hold back the stampede while I got the job done.

At the same time I moved, and that was good because Kwon fired at the sound of my voice. Bullets tugged at the drapes, continued on and smashed one of the painted windows. Mid-afternoon light flooded into the room, the moving curtains causing a ripple and sway of shadows. I moved with them, dodging through the room like a living silhouette. Saw a figure ten feet ahead.

Again I wondered about how fate played games, how I'd travelled from one red moon to another. I remembered the cockerel-crowing man I'd strangled to death under that first moon and how he'd fancied himself as a tae kwon do expert. Kwon had the build of a fighter, and listening to his bravado, I guessed that the Korean was a true tae kwon do exponent, probably from military service since all soldiers in the North Korean army had to train to black-belt level. I was no black belt, had never felt the need to test my abilities when every day my work had done that for me. But the notion was there of how I wouldn't mind testing Kwon in combat. The pain from my injuries had miraculously fled now that I was fighting for the lives of countless others, and the challenge of taking down Kwon could do my self-worth nothing but good.

But this was no place for egotism.

I shot Kwon clean and simple. That put paid to any number of black belts the man might hold.

Kwon howled, rolled on the floor, holding his damaged knee to his chest.

'Drop the gun or I'll shoot you again.'

Kwon howled even louder, interspersing his scream with a rapid-fire curse. This time I didn't catch a single word.

My gun spat again.

Now Kwon didn't know which knee to cradle, so dragged both of them to his chest. 'You dog, you shot me!'

'And I'll shoot you again if you don't drop the gun! Believe me . . . I'm not fucking around with you.'

Moving close, I pointed the SIG directly at Kwon's head. The Korean's face was pinched tight with agony, tears streaming from his eyes. If hatred was flame it would have seared me to the core.

'Now!'

Kwon threw the gun from him. 'I surrender, I surrender, OK, Yankee? You have me. Now you must arrest me and get me a lawyer.'

'Yeah, right.' I kicked him in his shoulder, knocking him over on to his back. 'See, we've got a problem . . . I'm not a cop.'

Rink came up to my side, covering Kwon with the threat of his Glock. 'And you're not such a big guy now, *Kwon*.'

'*You are dogs with no honour!*'

Rink and I shared a glance.

'How'd you like that? Coming from a prick who wants to poison New York?' Rink asked.

I crouched down and jammed the SIG in the Korean's right eye. The barrel was hot from discharging rounds and I fancied I could smell the man's flesh sizzling. 'The cops *are* coming, Kwon. You *will be* arrested and given your rights. Chances are that diplomatic arrangements will be made for you to be released into the hands of your own government. You'll return home just like that arsehole al-Megrahi did to

Libya. Just think, you'll be hailed a fucking hero when you get back. That's if I don't happen to slip and put a round into your brain first. Now the only way to stop that from happening is if you give me what I want. Are you ready to deal?'

Kwon tried to pull away from the barrel of the gun, but only to nod. 'I will deal with you.'

'Good. Now, I already know that you supplied some sort of radioactive isotope to Carswell Hicks, so you needn't try and deny that. What I want to know is how much and in what form it was delivered to him.'

'You do not understand—'

'I understand enough. You supplied shit to an even bigger piece of shit. Now, tell me, or I swear to you, you will be going back to Korea but it'll be in a lead-lined box with a nuke strapped to your arse.'

'I demand to speak to your CIA,' Kwon said through gritted teeth.

'I'm afraid they're not here right now. It's me or a bullet, Kwon, take your pick.'

Pain made the man gag, perspiration running down his cheeks. He looked like he was going to throw up. The moment passed, and it was as though some new resolve stiffened his spine. He peered at us with calm eyes, like the deep dark pools found in hidden glades. Kwon described glass flasks sealed in lead containers, and the size and dimensions of each. He said there were two in total. I was no physicist, but in my estimation that'd be enough to contaminate the entire metropolitan areas of New York and New Jersey combined.

'Tell me about Carswell Hicks,' I said.

Kwon described how he'd met a man at a cargo-shipping compound near to the Elizabeth Town Marina, and how the transfer was completed. Then he cursed Carswell Hicks, whose name he hadn't known up until that point. 'You kill that bastard for me,' he spat. 'He told me to see the sights today!

He knew full well he intended detonating the bomb and he meant to kill me along with everyone else.'

Sneering down at him, I said, 'Sorry, Kwon, but I owe you nothing. I'm going to kill Hicks for all the people he has condemned to death. The same people *you* condemned when you handed over the isotope.'

'I told you before, you do not fully understand.'

'I understand enough to know a murdering son of a bitch when I look at him.' I lifted the SIG again, my face flat as sheet-steel.

Kwon squirmed away. 'No, wait! Remember that you owe me my life, Yankee. We made a deal.'

'There you go again with the misconceptions. I'm not a cop and I'm not a Yankee,' I said, face going lax. 'But you're right. I made a deal to hand you to the police.'

'Good,' said Kwon, smiling.

'Not that good. I didn't promise you a goddamn thing,' said Rink, and shot Kwon in the skull.

40

'Maybe that wasn't such a good idea.' Special Agent Vincent fiddled with his damp hair, as though he still wore the Everett pompadour. His conservative feebie cut just didn't have the same effect.

'He deserved exactly what he got,' I said. 'He's as responsible for the bombing as anyone, and do you think Hicks will be treated any differently when we find him?'

Vince jammed his hands in his suit pockets, staring down at the dead Korean. Kwon's features had relaxed in death, his eyes rolling up as though trying to see the bullet hole in his forehead. 'We could have learned much more from him. We could have traced the consignment of plutonium back to its source, found who was behind this.'

'And then what? Declare war on North Korea? Seems to me like Rink just did the world a real service.'

Vince wasn't swayed, he just shook his head. 'From what I gather, we won't let this rest. Walter will have a team on this already, plotting the Koreans' movements. We'll get to the bottom of it sooner or later.'

'It'll be a dark day if you do.'

'Maybe, maybe not. Those freaking Koreans have been given too much slack. Diplomacy isn't going to make them disarm; maybe it's time we showed them they can't fuck with the US any longer.' The agent turned and walked away, indicating to a couple of his FBI colleagues to take over. Feeling redundant now, I followed, going back down the stairs to the ground floor.

The Red Moon Bar looked like an NYPD convention. Interspersed among the officers were plain-clothed FBI agents, as well as others in black windcheaters and ball caps. The semi-naked dancers and the bar staff were all sitting along one wall while officers took their details and statements. The FBI people followed along debriefing them, maybe with warnings of what might happen if any of them blabbed about this to the press. The girls were the real victims here, not the terrorist scum that we had put down. A crew from the Medical Examiner's office had arrived and it was annoying to see that the Koreans were afforded the same respect as the dead doorman as they were bagged and transported away.

Vince wandered away to confer with some of his government pals, and I scanned the bar area for Rink. The big guy was sitting on a stool, sipping water from a tall glass, as morose as hell.

'You OK, Rink?'

Rink wore a dazed expression. He was a veteran of as many battles as I was, but where we differed was in our capacity for compartmentalising the delivery of cold-blooded death. In the heat of battle, Rink was as frighteningly effective as any warrior, but never at the expense of his morals or sense of honour. He was suffering from his split-second decision to shoot Kwon. I kneaded Rink's muscular shoulder.

'I'm OK, brother,' he said.

He wasn't, he was sickened that he'd fallen below the line he'd always set for himself.

'Desperate times, Rink . . .'

Rink shook his head. He couldn't help thinking that the measures he'd employed were anything but desperate: they'd been delivered with cool and deliberate calculation.

Rink lifted his chin like it was a dowsing tool, and pointed it across the room at nothing in particular. 'You haven't heard the good news, yet?'

From his deadpan delivery, I guessed there was nothing good about it. I looked at him, then over at the plasma screen. Someone had turned it off. 'What do you mean?'

'The bombing at Lincoln Square.' Rink studied his glass as though seeking out impurities. 'It was just that: an ordinary, everyday bomb. There's no trace of any radioactive particles.'

I felt weightless, like a giant hand had lifted me off the floor and suspended me bodily in mid-air, the burden of millions of dead bodies plucked from my shoulders.

'Thank God for that.'

Rink swirled the water in the glass, and continued to stare at it. 'Don't you see, Hunter? I executed that man upstairs because I thought he'd been pivotal in murdering thousands of people. I was wrong.'

'Whether Hicks' bomb failed to discharge the plutonium or not, Kwon was still responsible for supplying it. He deserved to die.'

'Did he?' Rink asked. 'Go get Vince over here, get him to explain to you how the flasks of *plutonium* held nothing more dangerous than this water.'

Inhaling deeply, I looked for Vince, but the agent had moved elsewhere. 'What are you saying, Rink?'

'Don't know. There are only two things I can come up with, and I don't like either of them.' Rink stood up, took my elbow and led me towards the exit door. 'C'mon, I gotta get outa this place.'

There was no argument from me. The stink of death was in the Red Moon, more pungent than the spilled liquor and sweat that permeated the place. Outside, we stood on Delancey out of earshot of any of the gathered law-enforcement officers. The rain that had pounded Pennsylvania had found its way to New York, and the streets glittered under the downpour. Neither of us gave it any mind. I, for one, felt that some of the associated dirt of our actions was being washed away.

Rink rubbed his chin, his fingertips playing distractedly with the scar he'd picked up while we'd fought for our lives with Tubal Cain, the Harvestman. The scar was a reminder of his mortality. My take on the scar was something different: it was a mark of how I'd torn Rink from a happy retirement and dragged him into the nightmare that dogged me everywhere. A little over a year ago Rink had been our voice of reason, reminding us that we no longer had a licence to kill: now Rink had committed the ultimate sin, reverting to the level of the executioner he'd striven so hard to leave behind.

'Two things,' Rink said, resuming his train of thought from inside the Red Moon. 'Two things, and I don't like the way my mind's working.'

I could guess where Rink was going with this, but allowed him to continue.

'I overheard a couple of those FBI guys talking. They were saying that the bomb that went off was more flash than substance. A number of people were hurt, but it was mainly minor burns or scrapes. When the car exploded it was rigged so that the trunk blew off and most of the flames went into the sky. To me it sounds like the blast was channelled to cause as little damage as possible.'

I hadn't taken much notice of the images on the TV screen at the time but when I thought back there had been very little structural damage. Plenty of paper and trash lay scattered around the site, some shattered windows, but none of the usual smoking debris and tumbled masonry. Now Rink was telling me that the supposed plutonium flasks contained nothing more dangerous than water. What did that mean: that Hicks had been bluffed into buying the bogus isotope or had been party to the sham? The fact that Hicks' bomb had gone off like nothing but a large firework gave credence to the latter scenario.

'What are you thinking, Rink?'

'I'm thinking I may have murdered the one man who could have given us all the answers we need.'

'Wasn't murder, Rink. Way I see it, it was justified.'

Rink snorted. He pushed back his hair, and droplets of rain spattered all around his shoulders. 'OK. There are two ways of looking at this, like I said. Either Kwon supplied the real thing, or he set Hicks up. Either way it doesn't make him a good man. But I still have a problem with that. Why would he set Hicks up? Makes me think he had no intention of hurting anyone, like maybe he wanted to save lives?'

'I doubt that. Maybe Kwon didn't know that the flasks were fakes.'

'Maybe not.'

'For someone who didn't want anyone hurt, he put up quite a fight,' I reminded him. 'If he was a good guy, why didn't he just put up his hands and surrender when the first cops got there? Why'd he let his friends die?'

'Maybe he had to put on a good show. He said we didn't understand. Understand what, Hunter? And why'd he say he wanted to speak to the CIA? Plea bargain? I don't think so.'

'He was just looking for a way out of his predicament. He knew that if he didn't talk, I was going to kill him.'

Rink didn't have an answer for that. Instead he said, 'There's always the chance that Hicks still has the original flasks. Maybe he's planning on using them for something else and Lincoln Square was just a warning of worse to come.'

I didn't credit that; why would Hicks go to the effort of fabricating an explosion? But I went along with my friend. Rink was trying to find justification for killing Kwon, and this was a feasible way out of his funk. It wasn't in me to deny him the peace of mind. 'I think we need to speak to Walter without Vince being in the same room. What do you reckon?'

The two commandeered motorcycles were still parked where we'd left them. 'I'm up for it,' Rink said.

Less than a minute later we were kicking the bikes into life, pulling out through the cordon of police vehicles. There was a shout and Vince came dodging through gaps in the parked cars, but I resolutely ignored him. Rink was correct: too many contradictory elements were at play. It was time we had a private conversation with Walter without the young agent eavesdropping on our every word.

On our way to FDR Drive, we discovered that the traffic had resumed its normal flow. Once they heard the news that the explosion at Lincoln Square had been nowhere near as disastrous as the first accounts had it, the people of Manhattan had returned to a semblance of normality. Finding a way back to the office opposite the Woolworth Building wasn't a simple task, but that was due to our unfamiliarity with this section of the city rather than the hold-up in traffic. Worried that Walter had already moved on, now that events had proven less serious than feared, we pushed the bikes to their limit. When we arrived at the building I was glad to see the CIA man's personal bodyguards flanking the door. I'd conversed with both these men on occasion, had done them a kindness in a hotel in Miami when they'd otherwise been ignored by their boss, but that didn't mean a thing. Both men reached for their handguns as we headed for the door.

Once the guards had checked with Walter that all was fine, they allowed us to enter. A wink their way was reciprocated by a nod of respect from both.

'I thought you might head back here,' Walter said, getting up from behind his desk. Then he craned his neck to see past us. 'No Vince this time?'

'We gave him the slip,' I said.

Walter touched a finger to his lips, then said loudly, 'Come with me. I just bet you're ready for a coffee?'

That the room was bristling with listening devices was a given, and we went with him extolling the virtues of a strong

Americano. Once out of the room, Walter told his guards to stop anyone entering his office. 'You don't let a soul in there. Not Stephen Vincent, not even the President if he turns up. Got it?'

He led us along a corridor and up a short flight of stairs. We went out through the main foyer of the building and found an espresso bar a short walk away. Walter ordered drinks, then patted his pockets. 'Ah, my wallet's back in my office.'

'Cheapskate,' I grunted, and handed dollars over to the barista.

The coffee shop was not the ideal location for talking over state secrets, so we walked, finding a bench in City Hall Park that was protected from the rain by the thick canopy of branches above. The leaves were long fallen, but the branches were thickly woven so the trees also served to conceal us from sight and directional microphones. The tinkle of a fountain made the only happy sound; everything else was the dull groan of traffic on Broadway, the hushed tones of pedestrians stunned by the recent events. Walter sat in the middle, like he was a tome wedged in place by sturdy bookends.

'What I'm about to tell you must never be repeated,' Walter began. 'I need your word on the subject, boys. No exceptions.'

Rink cursed. I felt as though someone had just drilled a white-hot spear into my guts and was twisting it with malicious glee.

'You'vc licd to us, Waltcr. Now you want us to swear a solemn oath to you?'

'You are honourable men, Hunter. Your word binds you. Without it our conversation ends here. You can go back to Florida and forget all about Carswell Hicks and everything else you've heard here.'

I sipped coffee, mindless of the steam burning my lips. I couldn't taste a thing. I leaned forward past Walter and met my friend's eyes. 'I gotta know,' Rink said.

I nodded for us both. 'OK, Walt. You have our word.'

Walter placed his cup on the floor between his feet while he searched for his cigar in his jacket pocket. The cigar was proof of Walter's concentration over the past few hours, having been chewed down to a short stogie. He jammed it between his teeth, a necessary emotional crutch as he gathered himself to tell all. As soon as he started to speak, I felt dirtier than when I had been muddy and blood-spattered back in the Alleghenies.

41

'The Senate Judiciary Committee has made life very difficult for the entire intelligence community, and as you know they absolutely despise the CIA. If it were up to them the Agency would've been disbanded a long time ago.' Walter shifted on the park bench, holding out his cigar and studying it: a habit he was no longer aware of, a conditioned response to something he found distasteful. 'Their lawyers scrutinise everything we do, enforce their liberal ideas of the way in which we should treat enemies of the state. You can blame Guantanamo Bay or Abu Ghraib if you wish. It was the furore over the *perceived* mistreatment of enemy combatants that has led to this.'

'You're talking about the reactivation of Arrowsake?' I asked.

'I am. Because we can't move without the full scrutiny of the Judiciary Committee, we had to come up with a new way to combat the threat to our country. You know the facts, and I don't have to reiterate them. We are allowing our enemies to defeat us through our blasé attitude to our impending destruction.'

Rink downed a mouthful of coffee. He turned and the wash of heat from his breath reached all the way to me. 'I get the feeling that we ain't talking about greenhouse gases or melting icecaps. You're talking about how the move for tolerance and indulgence is weakening us in the eyes of the world.'

'When the Nazis were defeated at the end of the Second World War, they laughed. They said there would be no need of a third war when they could dominate Europe through control of the financial institutions and by the subtle manipulation of peoples' beliefs. Well, you just have to look around you to see that they were right.'

'Carswell Hicks doesn't seem to think so,' I said.

Walter licked his cigar and placed it carefully in the corner of his mouth. 'I'll come to Hicks in a moment. And I'm not necessarily talking Nazis here. I'm talking about any nation which has a hard-on for the US, or the West in particular.'

Shifting uncomfortably, I took a look around the park. Nearby was a young mother pushing her twin babies in a buggy. She was hurrying and it had nothing to do with getting out of the rain. Where she was going I'd no idea, but the look on her face said she wasn't too concerned about that, only with actually taking her children there safely. I swished the dregs of my drink, hardly conscious of having downed it. 'Walter, this is taking too long. I get what you're saying. The West is perceived as weak, and Arrowsake has been reactivated to show the world how they've got it wrong.'

'Yes,' said Walter. 'That's pretty much it. Because of the magnifying glass the intelligence community has been placed under, Arrowsake has been tasked with conducting a series of incidents that will remind everyone how ineffective a softly-softly approach to policing the world is. Hunter, you were in the UK when the London subway system was attacked, yet, a few years on, the British people are tiptoeing around their enemies for fear they make a politically incorrect slip of the tongue. The Islamic community is growing so large that within twenty years there'll be no need for terrorists planting bombs on buses, they'll have a large enough population to vote in a Muslim as Prime Minister. Two decades from now, Britain could be looking at a government under Sharia law and thinking, How the fuck did this happen?'

'You're beginning to sound like one of them bonehead skins that rally around Hicks,' Rink growled.

Walter shrugged. It was an odd movement for a man whose neck was lost in his shoulders already, as if his head was slipping directly into his jacket collar. 'Just telling it like it is, Rink. All these imams are out there preaching that every Muslim should kill an infidel to assure their place in Heaven. And here we are extending the hand of friendship to people whose only desire is to murder us.'

'Don't recall reading anything in the Koran where Allah advocates murder,' Rink said.

'He doesn't, but those radical preachers don't care about that, they've twisted the words of the Koran to fit their jihad. Just the thought of seventy-two virgins is a great motivator to some of these nutjobs.'

'Except we aren't talking about Muslims here.' I was annoyed with my mentor's reluctance to get to the story at hand. 'Just tell us what the hell's going on, Walter. You said that Arrowsake were "tasked with conducting a series of incidents". I don't like the sound of that.'

'Me neither,' Rink said.

Walter closed his eyes. 'Boys, you know how I love you, right?' He got scornful grunts from us both, but he was resigned to it now. 'That'll never change. But I fear that I just might've placed you directly in the centre of something that'll ensure you'll hate me for the rest of your lives.'

Maybe he was expecting reassurance, but if Walter was leading to what I suspected then my adopted father would deserve our enmity. Rink had leaned back, allowing his head to loll, his eyes closed and I guessed my friend was thinking the same. 'This has been engineered by Arrowsake?'

Walter shook his head, and for a moment I did feel sorry for the utter look of devastation that flashed across his features. 'Not *engineered* exactly. But they have allowed things to progress further than anyone could have anticipated. They could have taken down Carswell Hicks at any time, but instead they've allowed him free rein to organise an attack on a major US city.' While we absorbed this, he went on quickly, 'Hicks was never meant to get his hands on the makings of a dirty bomb. They only expected him to plan something along the lines of the bombings he conducted before he was imprisoned.'

'They didn't know about Kwon bringing the plutonium into the country?'

'No.'

'I find that a little hard to believe,' I said.

'Tell me that Kwon wasn't on Arrowsake's payroll.' Now it was Rink who looked the picture of desolation. Walter patted him on the knee, but Rink shoved his hand away. 'If you sent us to kill one of our own . . .'

'He wasn't one of ours. Believe me. Do you think we'd have allowed anyone to bring radioactive material into our country? Remember, I sent you to extract information from him,' Walter said.

'You knew how that would end.' I flexed my hands, crushed the paper cup. I struggled to contain the urge to grab hold of Walter and shake him to pieces. Turning very slowly, I looked at the old man. 'Do you realise what Arrowsake has done to us? They've twisted and corrupted everything that we ever stood for. We fought against the terrorists of the world . . .'

'Only to become terrorists ourselves.' Walter's eyes sparkled with unshed tears, something alien to the man in all the years I'd known him. He tried to take hold of my hand, but was pushed away as roughly as before. 'Please hear me out,' he pleaded.

Fit to burst I stood up sharply. About to walk away, I stopped, recalling the woman and her children from minutes ago. How could she or her babies ever be safe when she was living amongst men capable of hurting them? I sat down again, roughly.

'OK, for old times' sake I'll listen, Walter. I'll even stay and do what you want me to do. But not for Arrowsake. I'm doing this because I believe that you disagree with it all. That you want to stop this before it gets even further out of control.'

'Yes,' Walter agreed. 'Yes, that's it. I hate what has happened, and what we've been forced to do. I want to put things right again. Right for you two boys, as well.'

'Forget about it,' Rink snorted. 'You didn't have to bring us in; you should have left us good and well alone.'

Walter sighed. 'Rink, I brought you in because you're the only ones I can trust. Don't you see? Arrowsake have their people who I am forced to deal with. They aren't singing from the same hymn sheet as we do. Stephen Vincent? If they'd told him to plant the bomb himself, I believe he'd have done it.'

'Always thought he was a fucking weasel,' Rink said.

Impatiently I said, 'Get back to Hicks. Tell us what the hell happened, what we're up against.'

'OK. Hicks was never supposed to meet with Kwon, or do the deal for the plutonium isotope. Arrowsake never anticipated he'd be capable of causing lasting damage to the city. But he'd have been seen as a viable enough threat to the state that it would make people sit up and take notice. Allowing a single bombing would be enough to cause panic, and only immediate and positive action would be enough to quell the public's feelings of vulnerability.' Walter stopped to gather himself. He was panting as though he'd just jogged up a hill. 'The intention was to create so much outrage that the public would demand a tougher stance against our enemies. Arrowsake were poised to take out Hicks and his followers as soon as that happened. And with their victory, the CIA, MI6, all the intelligence agencies, would shake off the constraints of the Judiciary Committees, with the full backing of the public again. Things would have gone to plan, except that Hicks grew more ambitious than anyone could have imagined. You've probably heard by now that the bomb at Lincoln Square didn't contain any radioactive substances, and we can only thank God for that.'

'Yeah. It's a goddamn crying shame, isn't it?' said Rink.

'Makes me wonder about all those crazy conspiracy theories,' I said. 'They're maybe not as stupid as they sound.' Some people argued that the Western governments had engineered the situation to validate a war in the Middle East. Proof was, there were no WMDs found, just plenty of oil. Now, hearing what had gone down here – that Arrowsake might be guilty of state-sponsored terrorism – it didn't seem that far-fetched. 'Tell me that Arrowsake aren't planning to let Hicks use the plutonium.'

'Of course not . . .' There was a slight tremor in the old man's voice. Maybe Walter wasn't as sure about Arrowsake's motives as once he'd been. 'They want him stopped for real now.'

'And they want us to do it for them.'

'Typical,' Rink said. 'They fuck up, then they look for a coupla scapegoats to clean up their crap for them.'

'So what happens now?' Walter asked. 'You can walk away with my blessing, but I'd rather you didn't. *Everyone* here needs your help.'

I thought back to another conversation I'd had with Walter. Having returned from a particularly violent mission where I'd lost a couple of colleagues, I'd questioned the need for men like us in the modern age. Walter had touched me gently over my heart as he said, 'George Orwell said something along the lines of, "We sleep safely at night because rough men stand ready to visit violence on those who would harm us." '

'I think you'll find that Churchill said it first,' I'd said.

'Does it matter? The words hold validity . . . whatever their origin. Hunter, son, don't you see? You are our rough men.'

Rough men, I couldn't deny that. And rougher now than ever before.

Back in the present I glanced at Rink, and got a nod of approval from him.

'The way I see it, Hicks still has his hands on two flasks of plutonium. Only thing that matters now is that he's stopped from using them.'

'I'm relying on you boys,' Walter added.

'So point us at him,' Rink said.

'I would if we had any idea where he was at.'

I said, 'Don Griffiths.'

Walter squinted, and I went on, 'Hicks was determined to stop Don from ruining his plans. Don must know something that can help lead us to him.'

Walter stood up quickly. 'We can go back to my office and make a call from there.'

With the space suddenly vacated between us, Rink and I were left blinking at each other. Finally, I asked, 'You with me, Rink?'

'I'm with *you*, brother. Sure as hell ain't with Arrowsake no more.'

I looked at Walter, my eyes gritty like they contained chips of dirty ice. 'Those are my terms, too. We don't do this for Arrowsake; we do it for those two small children and their mother.'

Walter had no idea who I was talking about, but he could only nod in agreement. Then, his eyebrows knitting, he said, 'Just be wary, boys. You're either with Arrowsake or you're against them.'

'Fine by me.' I touched the faint red ring round my throat.

42

Day had turned to evening.

The Staten Island ferry still shuttled back and forth, but the ubiquitous sightseers who normally hitched a free ride past the Statue of Liberty were absent. A feeling of unease hung in the atmosphere as the people of Manhattan internalised their bewilderment at what had occurred earlier in the day. Initial fears were that al-Qaeda had struck another blow, but it was now common knowledge that the bomb that exploded during the Purim celebrations in Lincoln Square had claimed neither lives nor buildings of religious significance. Some believed this wasn't all they had to fear, and their fears would be borne out, but most had gone back to their normal routines with little more than a shake of their heads. News had spread that a group of men had been killed during a stand-off with the FBI and NYPD – what was there to worry about now that those responsible for the failed attack were dead?

There was a hush over the city that never sleeps. The Big Apple was just resting in silent contemplation.

Out on the Hudson the sound of a motorboat reverberated between the wooden pilings along the riverside, sounding like the wheeze of an asthmatic forging uphill. The outboard motor died, went quiet and the boat drifted the last few yards to the much larger moored yacht. Deep blue in colour, its running lights extinguished, the yacht was like a solid wedge of night. Two figures clambered from the motorboat, up the ladder and on to the deck. One was taller than the other, the smaller man holding something in his hands.

They went unchallenged on the deck and approached the galley. This was no leisure craft, no glass doors or plush living quarters awaited them inside. The upper deck was utilitarian at best, an open space beyond double doors painted the same dark blue as everything else.

Samuel Gant slammed the doors with both palms, pushing into the room regardless of whether he was invited. The doors flew all the way open, crashing loudly against the walls, startling the two big men who were standing with their backs to him.

'Get outa my goddamn way, you freaks,' he snapped as the men turned to block his way. Gant was in such a rage that his features were as dark as his tattoo.

One of Carswell Hicks' bodyguards stepped in front of Gant, and Gant didn't pause to consider the consequences. He kicked the man in the groin, the full swing of his leg behind the blow. Back when he'd earned the red laces in his boots, Gant had kicked a man similarly, guaranteeing that at least one black man wouldn't spread his seed to further dilute the population.

As the bodyguard clutched at his mashed testicles, Gant snatched out his handgun and aimed it at the face of the second bodyguard. 'Back up, asshole, or you'll get worse than a set of crushed nuts.'

Sitting behind his desk, Carswell Hicks appeared nonplussed by the drama at the far end of the room. He was dressed in a grey suit, grey shirt, blood-red tie, a matching handkerchief tucked in his breast pocket.

'Let Samuel in,' he called, sounding almost jovial. 'We're all brothers here, aren't we?' He stood up, beckoning Gant deeper into the room.

The second bodyguard rolled his shoulders, like he was unfazed by the gun a couple inches from his face. He raised his eyebrows, jerked his head, giving Gant the all-clear. The tattooed man sneered at him as he pushed him out of the way with the flat of his hand. Behind Gant, Darley entered the room. He was wielding a shotgun, which he aimed at the bodyguards. 'Get him over against the wall,' he told the uninjured man. He covered them while the guard with the damaged testicles was helped over to the corner of the room. Darley bobbed his head. 'I know you're both armed. Lose the guns. Kick them over to me.'

While Darley collected the weapons, Gant continued to walk towards Carswell Hicks. His air-wear soles sucked at the planking.

'You seem awfully upset about something,' Hicks said, a smile half formed on his lips.

'I kind of get that way when someone I trust craps on me.'

'I've crapped on you?' The feigned expression of bewilderment belied the coldness in Hicks' voice. 'How so, Samuel?'

Gant threw his arms out expansively. 'That bullshit in the Jew-boy quarter! I thought we were supposed to kill thousands of them. I thought we were gonna bring down their temples and poison the rest of them that the explosion didn't get!'

'I had a change of heart.'

Hicks sat down, steepling his hands on his chest. With his close-cropped silver hair and beard he looked like a college professor preparing to lecture a dim-witted student. Gant slapped the handgun down on the desktop and leaned on his knuckles so he could look his leader directly in the eye. 'A change of heart? You pitied our enemies?'

'Not at all. I despise the Jews as much as I ever did.'

'So what was it all about?'

Hicks stood up sharply, taking Gant by surprise. The tattooed man snatched up his handgun, but when he saw Hicks walk away from him, he merely watched, befuddled. Hicks went to open a door that Gant knew led into an antechamber of sorts. Inside the small room the box that he'd purchased from the Koreans reflected the dull overhead light. 'That,' said Hicks, pointing at the box, 'cost me millions of dollars. If I'd blown it up, then I'd have been seriously out of pocket.'

'We're fighting the *Rahowa*!' Gant screwed his mouth around the shout, causing a hallucinatory twist to his tattoo. 'Money? You're more concerned about money than our *racial holy war*?'

'Of course. We cannot fight a war with empty coffers.'

The handgun was a dull matt grey: the same colour that threatened the white race. Gant swung it towards the man whom he'd once happily have given his life for. 'You have lost your way, Carswell.'

Unperturbed by the gun pointing at him, Hicks leaned down to unlatch the lid of the box. He swung it open and indicated the large vials inside. 'No, Samuel, I have seen *our* future.' He became animated. Light shone behind his eyes as though his inner being was lit by an epiphany. 'Don't you see? With the threat of using this weapon whenever, *wherever*, we choose to, we can hold the government to ransom. We can demand billions in compensation for the injustices served upon the white race; we can take it from the Jews and the niggers and hand it back to all the God-fearing white folk who have lost their homes, their jobs and their dignity. With this,' he shook a hand at the box, 'we can do anything we want. We can force the President to step down from office, if we desire. *We can take back our country*.'

'Genius.' Gant eyed his leader, allowing his gun to trail away.

'Yes. You see it now, don't you? The possibilities . . . no, *the reality*, we can achieve.' Hicks grinned and he no longer looked like a learned professor, more like a manic fool. 'Lincoln Square was only the start, Samuel, The Day of Broken Spirits.

With that one statement we showed them how vulnerable they really are, and we make them fear what we are further capable of.'

'Genius,' Gant repeated. Hicks' grin began to flicker as he noted the tone in the tattooed man's voice. Gant spat on the floor. 'I used to think that you were a genius. Now I see you for what you really are.'

Fingers trembling, he raised the gun again.

Hicks swayed, looked at the contents of the box, back at Gant.

There were tears in the eyes of the tattooed man. 'I followed you all these years, Carswell. I did everything you commanded because I believed in you. I believed in your vision because it was also my vision. Now I see how blind I was. This was never about establishing a segregated country for white men; it was always about greed, about money. That's all you're interested in. All that you ever were.'

'Samuel, I see that you're still hurting from your wounds. You're not thinking straight. Once you're well again, we will talk and you'll see that I am right. It's the pain that is making you act this way: don't worry, I understand. There are no hard feelings. I promise you that . . .'

Gant blinked at the crack of the pistol, mild surprise on his face as he watched Hicks grab at his gut and drop to his knees. There was another sound in the room, a deep-throated roar that swelled inside his skull. He couldn't tell if it was the shouts of Hicks' bodyguards or the pounding of blood through his veins. Probably it was both. He heard a double crash, but didn't look round. He didn't need to as he'd already told Darley what he intended doing and that as soon as he fired, Darley should kill both of the minders.

Staring at Hicks, he saw his fingers steeple on his chest again, the man reacting to the second bullet wound before Gant was aware of having pulled the trigger.

Gant took a step forward and placed the .22 calibre handgun to the top of Hicks' head. 'It was never about money for me, Carswell. It was always about our pledge: we must secure the existence of our people and a future for white children. Your plan would serve only to destroy us all. You are tainted, Carswell. You have joined them, the grey men.'

He heard the third bullet, felt the tug of the barrel across the top of Hicks' skull as the recoiling of Hicks' body tore the man away from him. He smelled the cordite, the coppery tang of blood, but for once the smell didn't offer him any satisfaction.

He stood there for some time, for how long he had no idea. Finally it was Darley's hand on his shoulder that roused him, and he withdrew his gaze from the middle distance and looked down at Carswell Hicks. Hicks' corpse had collapsed so that he sat against the silver-coloured box, his legs splayed, blood on his gut and chest, head bowed as though shamed.

'You OK, Gant?'

In a daze, Gant nodded. The bird-like man offered him a hand, but he shook his head. He saw that the two minders were as dead as their mark, their chests open cavities where Darley had blasted them. 'We did the right thing,' he said. His words were only partly directed at Darley, because he was still shocked that he'd gone through with it. Carswell Hicks had been everything to him, and now he'd murdered him. Gant regretted that it had come to this; he'd always thought that it would be him and Carswell standing side by side, looking out over a totally white nation. Side by side as it should be.

Darley scrubbed a palm over his shaved head, looking down on Hicks. 'Man, what a shame Hicks lost it. Must have been all those years he spent inside, alongside all those criminals. They must have turned him, Gant, so don't you go blaming him now.'

'What about you, Dar?'

'I don't blame him,' Darley said defensively.

'I'm talking about you turning. Way I remember it from our talk back in Pennsylvania, you thought that Hicks' plan was too extreme. Well, I've got another plan. Are you still with me?'

Darley made a pecking motion with his nose, indicating the dead man at their feet. 'I just helped you kill our leader, Gant. I can't believe you'd doubt me to follow you anywhere.'

'Good,' Gant said, and he laid a consoling hand on Darley's shoulder. ''Cause if you thought that was extreme, you ain't seen nothin' yet.'

43

I needed the time to think.

I'd made my apologies, headed off to find a restroom. My bodily functions weren't a major concern, but a necessity. Finished, I flushed, straightened my clothing, but stayed in the cubicle. Sitting on the lid of the WC wasn't the place I'd like to be found if Armageddon struck. The idea was mildly humorous; who'd still be around to discover my inglorious end?

There was something slightly sordid about sitting in the locked cubicle, but it was one of the few places where I was guaranteed a few moments for solitude and reflection.

Random images flickered through my mind, events of days ago mixed in with the past few hours, so I got a disjointed replay like scenes from a Guy Ritchie movie. I saw the flicker of 35 mm film, two small girls happily playing; then Kwon lying dead with a hole between his eyes; mean-tempered Fluffy the cat screeching and heading for the trees; my knife in the chest of a man; Rooster cock-crowing and flapping his elbows up and down; Millie, soaked and freezing, gratefully accepting the coat, her eyes full of hope. But then I saw Don Griffiths lying in his hospital bed, and then running across the logging camp with Vince Everett at his heels. I saw the tattooed face of Samuel Gant, the eight-eight pattern growing and swelling in my vision.

Groaning, I jammed the heels of my thumbs in my eye sockets. This wasn't thinking, this was not what I wanted. I scrubbed hard; saw black and red spots floating in my vision while searching for the lock on the door. I left the cubicle, went across to a sink and jammed down hard on the tap. The icy water helped; I splashed some over my face. I shuddered out a breath, leaned both palms on the sink and stared at the reflection in the vanity mirror. Now there was a misnomer if ever I'd heard one. There was nothing vain in the image staring back at me. I looked like I'd lost a few pounds, my cheekbones like vertical slashes, dark rings under my eyes, skin sallow. Maybe that was only an effect of the stark overhead lighting. I pushed fingers through my hair, making strands stick up like thorns on my head. The look didn't suit and I smoothed them out again.

'You aren't getting any younger, Joe,' I whispered at the reflection.

I thought of the younger man I once was, Sergeant Hunter, One-Para. How back then I'd been full to the brim of life and expectation. Back before Arrowsake had tainted me. I hadn't seen it coming, the descent into the dark place they formed for me. Only those who loved me noticed. Diane had stuck by me at first, but even her love wasn't strong enough to quell the need for violent retribution that Arrowsake had instilled in me. Maybe by leaving me she thought I'd see the light. For a while I had, but always the tug was there, and it had finally reeled me in. In Kate Piers I thought I'd found salvation, but the compulsion bred within me had spoiled everything. When I should have run away with her, found somewhere safe for us both to hide, I'd sent her away while I indulged a selfish desire for violence against her tormentors. Kate died and I'd felt the bitter stab of failure ever since. Imogen, Kate's sister, was a lifeline, but how many times had I even thought about her over the past few days? Once, and only when I considered saying goodbye. I was stuck firmly on their hooks again: Arrowsake still owned me.

No! I slammed a palm into the mirror reflection, cracking the glass into a spider's web. The refracted image of the Arrowsake assassin glared back at me. That was what it signified to me, a broken man. *That's not who I am.*

I threw water in my face again, spat a nasty taste into the sink.

When I was younger I understood that Arrowsake manipulated me, but I obeyed their orders to the letter, I'd been loyal and idealistic and believed that what I was doing was for the greater good. They said kill and I killed. But it was always to save the lives of countless others, or to release them from the yoke of a tyrant. Arrowsake back then had been the figurehead of a just and noble cause. But what about now? Now, they were becoming the antithesis of everything I stood for.

They had allowed a terrorist free rein on their own soil, using the tactics of their enemies to instil fear in their own people. Those three nodding men, the cabal hidden behind the government, played with the lives of innocents to serve their own ends. They desired empowerment again, they wanted to establish a world rule based upon their own despotic view that was no less horrifying than that of Carswell Hicks or any other extremist. What kind of monsters were they? *What kind of monster have they made of me?*

I'd been tricked into serving them again, but I had to search deep within myself and decide whether or not I'd have done their bidding had I been in full receipt of the facts from the beginning. No, never. But nothing would have changed concerning my own reasons for taking down Carswell Hicks or Samuel Gant or any of the others threatening Don or his family. In part, I realised now, Arrowsake had placed them all in danger.

I thought about Vince's lies; the young agent had said he was tasked with finding Hicks, but that was bullshit. They knew where Hicks was all along, and Vince had gone along with Gant and his crew to push and prod them in the right direction. Their intention was that Don and his family were to be murdered, with the blame laid firmly at the feet of racists bent on revenge over the incarceration and subsequent death of their messiah.

I considered the shooting and the bombs at Adrian Reynolds' home, and how Gant had almost succeeded in killing Don at the logging camp. Don's survival was contradictory to Arrowsake's plan, and I now understood why Vince was really there. Vince had asserted that he'd tried a coup with the intention of stalling Gant's crew until help could arrive. That was a lie: Vince wanted to ensure that Arrowsake's plan was fulfilled. Seeing me as another possible stooge to be used in the plot was the only reason he'd released the garrotte before it throttled the life from me.

What did that mean now that I wasn't prepared to stay on their leash any longer? You're either with Arrowsake or you're against them, Walter had cautioned. I looked in the fragmented mirror, saw the burr on my flesh where Vince's wire had dug in. Well, on that occasion I'd been running and fighting for some time, I was fatigued, half frozen, bewildered by all that had gone on. Let Arrowsake come, if that was their plan.

A soft knock on the door, and Rink leaned inside.

'You ready yet, brother?'

Rink had also been thinking. He wore an expression that reminded me of a porcelain mask, calm and cold, expressionless. It was an inconsistent image in more ways than one: serenity concealing a tightly-wound fury just a hair's-breadth beneath the surface; a samurai warrior kneeling in Zen-like meditation but ready to erupt into action in a blink, to mow down enemies with the razor-edge of his katana sword.

I felt like a dishevelled tramp in comparison.

'Give me another minute or two, yeah?'

'OK,' said Rink, but he still came in.

I placed my hips against the sink so I could face him as he walked over.

'This is bull crap,' Rink said, 'but we have to make the best of it. We don't let those puppet masters jerk us around any more, but we still have to get this done.'

'Don's family are relying on us,' I said in agreement. I winced, not at the task ahead, but what that might still mean. 'What if they don't stop, Rink? What do we do then? Even if we stop Hicks and Gant and those others, Don is still a threat to Arrowsake.'

'Then we try to stop them too, like you promised.'

The phone call I'd made to Don Griffiths had been for more than to find out where Hicks was hiding or what he was planning next. Don's response was simple. 'I've no idea where Hicks would conceal himself, but he was always money motivated.'

He'd expounded and I had listened with the phone jammed to my ear. Don's studies had pointed out that Carswell Hicks wasn't just a white supremacist, he was also supremely greedy, someone who could never have enough cash. His attacks on the banks may have seemed racially motivated, but they also came with a rider: hand over a ransom or I keep on bombing. Don was certain that Hicks was planning something similar now, and that Arrowsake's failure to control him had given him the necessary tools to achieve his aim. 'Watch for huge demands coming soon,' Don had prophesied.

Then I had asked him, 'Why would Arrowsake want you dead?'

'Easy when you think about it,' Don had groaned. 'I was an analyst for one of their think-tanks. I was approached to look into a hypothetical scenario for them. They predicted that the War on Terror would mean an end to their existence. They posed the question: how would we engineer our rebirth?'

'You formulated this plan?'

'I offered a hypothetical solution. I told them that the only way the public would rise up and support the security services again was if they felt vulnerable in their own homes. Raising the potential for a rise in domestic terrorism was their most viable option for obtaining the backing they desired.'

'But instead of presenting a well-defined strategy for keeping the country safe they took things a step further . . .'

'It looks to me like they saw Carswell Hicks as a golden opportunity.'

'Jesus . . .'

'Don't be angry with me, Hunter. I was being used in the same way they've used us all.'

'I'm not angry,' I said, struggling to keep the bitterness out of my voice. 'I'm disappointed. Your make-believe scenario led to this, Don. But now it's very real, and it could lead to all our deaths. They're afraid you might talk, that their involvement will no longer be a secret. They might come for you again.'

'I'm an old man, I'm not afraid to die. But they can't hurt my family.'

'None of them are safe.'

'They don't know anything about this.'

'Arrowsake won't care. If they think there's even a chance you muttered about the plan in your sleep, they'll make sure that anyone who could've heard you will be silenced.'

'I'm not in the habit of sleeping in the same room as my daughters or grandchildren.'

'I'm speaking *hypothetically*.' I hadn't meant to sound sarcastic but it was there in my words nonetheless. 'You remember Vince went to your house, yeah? He convinced us that he was there to warn Millie, and he had to go through with the sham because Sonya Madden was watching. He was lying. I think he was ordered to kill your daughter, and maybe Arrowsake'll try again.'

'What about Brook? Do you think it was them who had her killed?'

I had no answer to that, but I did wonder for how long Vince had been on the case.

'Don't let it happen again, Hunter.'

'I'll try.'

'Please, I've already lost Brook. Don't let anything happen to Millie or the little ones.'

'I'm only one man,' I'd said.

Now, I looked up at Rink and saw that my final comment had been inaccurate. We were two. Rink would fight just as hard to protect the Griffiths family as I would.

'OK, I'm ready. Let's do this,' I said.

Rink clapped my shoulder, and we walked out of the restroom. The synapses had stopped projecting their crazy medley in my mind's eye, but one image was still ingrained, that of Millie and Brook squealing in glee as they splashed in a paddling pool. That idyll had turned into a nightmare of scorching flame for the older sister. I couldn't allow anything like that to happen to another innocent.

44

Samuel Gant stepped out on the deck of the yacht. His body was still in pain from the double shotgun blasts, but it was nothing to the agony piercing his heart. He was assailed with regret over what he'd just done. Carswell Hicks had been his mentor, more of a father to him than the drunkard who used to beat him senseless for any perceived slight. Demobbed from the US Army, he'd returned home to a country he no longer recognised, one where political correctness was making the white man seem like he was the second-class citizen. Women, blacks, Jews, Chinks, even the goddamn rag-heads he'd fought against in the deserts of Iraq and the mountains of Afghanistan, were suddenly better thought of than he was. Dissatisfied, he'd fallen in with a group of like-minded patriots led by a man who Gant believed followed the same vision as him. Carswell Hicks had taken him under his wing, treated him like family, and Gant had grasped at the attachment, and had adopted the older man as a worthy mentor. Hicks had introduced him to *The Turner Diaries*, and had spoken of his plan to take back the USA from the destructive forces led by the government. That vision had hooked Gant and until now his mind had never been swayed.

Together they'd conducted a bombing campaign against their enemies. Hicks had targeted mosques and temples, had even murdered a black minster and his small congregation when he'd torched their church while they were gathered in prayer. Hicks believed that fire was the cleansing agent required to set their nation free again. Then he'd turned his eyes on the banking system. There the intrinsic problem was that the Jews had taken control of the money, and he believed that they must take it back.

But then Hicks had been caught, sent to prison. In Gant's mind it didn't change anything. Gant had waited, kept their group together through the fallow years, promising that the plan would be borne out. He didn't have to argue too hard, because while Hicks was incarcerated, things had grown even worse.

Jesus Christ Almighty, while he was locked up, we even got ourselves a nigger president!

When he heard the news that Hicks was being transferred from prison to a less secure hospital, he had been overjoyed. With Hicks back in the fold, their dream could become a reality. He launched the attack on the hospital, whisked Hicks away in the commandeered helicopter, and then they'd ditched it into the sea and transferred to a getaway craft. They had blown the chopper up; the ever-present desire for flames offering cover for Hicks' missing body.

The only thing that had given Gant pause was why the authorities had bought his death so readily. Hicks had explained, though. It served the government if he was presumed dead. The name Carswell Hicks, he reminded Gant, was anathema to the race-mixing bastards taking control of their country.

'Do you think they'd be happy if they knew I was out here and preparing to destroy them all?' Hicks had asked.

Gant moved over to the rail, looked down at the turgid water of the Hudson. It was fully dark now, the lights of the nearby city swarming on the crests made by the eddy and flow of water. He spat into the river.

Carswell had told him that a man was dangerous to their mission. Don Griffiths, the pig who'd led to his capture the first time round, had figured out his plan. He was worried that he might do so again. Carswell asked that Gant go and bring Griffiths to him, so they could force from the man the location of any files or other information Griffiths had kept on him. Gant had done that, as uneasy as he felt at helming the mission, and that was where all his problems had started.

I should have just killed every one of them when I had the chance.

While he was over in Pennsylvania, freezing his butt off in the hills, Hicks had been here, formulating his get-rich-quick scheme. If Gant had been around then, Hicks wouldn't have got these idiotic notions in his head. Hold the fucking government to ransom; force the President to step down? Who was he kidding? He understood now that Hicks had never been the zealot he claimed. He was all about the money. He should have seen it first time round when Hicks launched his assault on the banking system – even then he'd wanted to be paid to stop the bombings. It wasn't about money for Gant, but he'd acquiesced to Hicks' argument: you can't fight a war with empty coffers.

That single phrase was what had snapped inside him earlier: for the first time the blindfold had been lifted from his eyes and he'd seen Hicks for the pathetic, greedy fool that he was. *We don't need their money, Carswell! We need them all dead*, he'd wanted to scream. Standing in the way of that was his mentor, his *pseudo*-father. Instead of screaming, Gant had shot him. And each time he'd fired his vision had grown clearer.

That he had actually murdered Hicks didn't come as a surprise to him; he'd boarded the boat expecting that might be the outcome. Yet now that he had Hicks' blood spattered down his shirtfront he couldn't help but wish it had ended differently. In a more agreeable scenario, they would have gone through with everything they'd plotted together. He felt no anger at Hicks, didn't blame him as he'd assured Darley, he was only sad that Hicks had been lured from their true path by the same greed that had infected this great country. The love of money, the Bible warned, was the root of all evil, and he couldn't agree more. You didn't need cash to succeed: just the will, the guts and the sheer determination to keep on fighting.

And it seemed there was only one man around here with those traits.

Out on the Hudson a motor growled. Gant straightened from the rail, scanning the water, but couldn't see another vessel there.

Disappointment struck him anew.

He limped across the deck, slip-sliding on the wet planks, and leaned out over the dark water again. The boat on which he'd arrived here was gone. He caught a sleek shape moving away at speed. Darley, the chickenshit son-of-a-bitch, making off the second his back was turned. He must have sneaked aboard the motorboat and let it drift away on the current until he was sure he was far enough away before firing up the motor.

He knew he shouldn't have trusted the little turkey-necked freak. Darley didn't like it that Hicks had targeted his old neighbourhood, or that Gant planned further destruction of Manhattan. If it wasn't for the fact that Darley had been the one to brain Vince Everett when he'd tried to usurp command, or that it was Darley who'd dragged him away from certain death in the logging camp, he'd have kerb-stamped the little punk to death when first he'd shown his doubt on the ride back to New York. He pictured it now, bundling the little man out of the van, forcing his open mouth on a raised kerbstone and then hammering down with the heel of his boot until his face was mush.

That wouldn't happen now, but it wasn't enough to stop Gant from trying to kill the little puke-ball. He snapped out his handgun, firing at the source of the engine sound. It was a waste of .22 shells. At this distance he wasn't close enough to kill the man, but Gant kept on firing and yelling in wordless fury as the engine sound receded into the distance.

Worn down by the betrayal of his two closest allies, Gant allowed the gun to drop to his side. He stood there blowing hard, trying to steady himself. The wound in his ear pulsed like a drum beat, keeping rhythm with his heart. He glanced around, saw the shore off on his left, then across the broad channel the lights of the Manhattan financial district. He watched for search lights flicking on, seeking out the source of the gunshots, but nothing stirred. Luckily he was too far out on the water for anyone to have heard, or if they did, they'd no idea where the noise originated.

There was a growl coming from somewhere and it took him a moment to locate where. The sound was in his throat; anger taking shape again in a building curse. He spat it out, turned quickly from the rail and went back into the large cabin. It was pointless dwelling on the failure of others.

The two men that Darley had killed were in the corner where the buckshot had thrown them. Carswell Hicks still sat propped up against the silver lock-box. The smell was overwhelming. Too soon to be putrefaction, the stench was a pungent mix of spilled blood, voided bowels and opened bodies. Gant was familiar with the stench. It had been a constant companion when he'd fought against the Iraqis and the Taliban. Still, he threw a forearm over his nose as he stooped down over Hicks' body. With the barrel of his gun, he flicked open Hicks' jacket. Darley had stripped the two minders of their weapons, and because he wouldn't risk leaving Gant anything larger than the .22 to shoot at him with, he would have taken them with him. Gant hoped that Darley had forgotten about the Ruger MP9 that Hicks carried concealed in a shoulder rig.

The gun was there and Gant reached for it. He trembled as he neared the body of his friend, expecting Hicks to snap out his hands and go for his throat, seeking vengeance from beyond the grave. It was a fanciful thought. He unsnapped the holding strap and withdrew the Ruger. It was a compact machine pistol that Hicks had adapted for concealment under his suit jacket. The folding stock had been removed, making it not much larger than any other handgun, but the firepower was awesome in comparison to Gant's weapon. Under Hicks' other armpit he found three extra magazines of nine mm hollow-point rounds.

Gant studied the gun and smiled for the first time in hours. With this he could take the war to his enemies. But there was something infinitely better.

He placed the weapon and ammunition on the desk and returned to Hicks. His aversion to touching the man had fled, and he grabbed Hicks and dragged him away from the lock-box. A broad smear of blood and urine stained the boards before he was finished, but the lubricant helped him slide the heavy box from concealment. He jostled it over to the centre of the cabin and threw back the lid. Inside were the two flasks that Hicks had shown him earlier. They had been packed into slots in the foam interior. He thought they'd be heavier, but when he lifted one of the flasks free it wasn't much weightier than a two-litre bottle of Coke. The flasks looked like elongated eggs, nine inches from rounded tip to rounded tip. One end was capped with a screw-down lid. He unscrewed it, peered inside. Some sort of viscous liquid was pooled at the bottom of a glass vial. He was no scientist, but judging by its heaviness the lock-box had to be lead-lined, which assured him these things were the real deal.

Radioactive isotope.

He screwed the lid back on and replaced the flask in its foam enclosure. Then with the lid shut he grasped one end of the box and hauled it off the floor a few inches. He could manage it, but it would be a struggle to cart the entire box off the boat with him. He could take the flasks themselves, but the lead was there for a good reason. Last thing he wanted was to damage the flasks and kill himself before he was through. He stood there a moment before the solution struck him. Why even remove the box from the boat when he could take the boat directly to his target?

45

'Pity we missed him, huh? I would've liked to kill Carswell Hicks. What about you, brother?'

Rink had to shout over the roar of the engine as he angled the speedboat out into the deep channel between Ellis and Governor's Islands. He was at the controls while I braced myself in the belly of the craft. Hanging on to the back of Rink's seat, I squinted through the darkness.

'We can't complain,' I said through clenched teeth. 'Sam Gant might be hard enough to kill for the both of us. I missed him last time, but at least we're going to get a second chance.'

'Going to have to do this quick, brother,' Rink said.

'Yeah, real quick.'

The news that Darley Adams had run to the police, throwing himself at their mercy with a plea bargain in exchange for leniency, caused a ripple of activity. He swore that he was an innocent dragged into this against his will, and that he'd have come forward much sooner if he hadn't been terrified for his life. Wide-eyed, with drool pooling in the corner of his mouth, he told his captors how he'd been forced to accompany Samuel Gant and Carswell Hicks. He even swore he'd tried to stop Hicks detonating the bomb in Lincoln Square, *his old neighbourhood.* He was adamant that he'd only gone to the boat with Gant in the hope that he could snatch the canisters of radioactive waste so he could hand them over safely to the police. He said that Gant had murdered everyone on board, going crazy with a shotgun and an automatic weapon. He tried his hardest to get away with the plutonium but had to abandon it when Gant came after him. He should be treated like a goddamn hero, not a piece of crap!

No one believed a word he said, other than his closing statement. 'Gant is crazy! He's going to blow up a target in the city and there's no way you'll stop him.'

Although we wanted to interrogate Darley further, we would be the last people allowed to enter a police station and have access to a prisoner. As a sub-division controller of black ops Walter Hayes Conrad's power was finite, so on this occasion even his influence was swatted aside. The FBI, the NYPD, Homeland Security, every other federal agency drafted in to contain the threat to New York City, had jurisdiction over him when it came to domestic problems like this. The CIA was forbidden from conducting clandestine operations on the mainland and by rights their involvement in the case was restricted to investigating Kwon's part in the plot to detonate a dirty bomb in Manhattan. Still, with that said, Walter wasn't the type to let jurisdictional hierarchy impede him. He didn't get us in to speak to Darley Adams, but he fed us the information bleeding from the interrogation room like a gushing wound. With so many agencies involved, the flow of information was easily tapped, and while orders and instructions were flying up and down the chain of command from the lowliest uniformed officer to Capitol Hill and back, we were already on the speedboat appropriated from a berth near to Battery Park and streaking out into New York Harbor.

Darley had explained about the big old boat that Samuel Gant was aboard. Navy blue, with all its lights extinguished it would be difficult to spot; it would be a dark slice of shadow against the night. It didn't help that the rain had returned with a vengeance making visibility little more than a few boat spans in any direction.

The likelihood was that a take-down team was being assembled at this very moment. The Coast Guard, the Port Authority, maybe even the US Navy would be on high alert, and launching a flotilla to surround and contain the boat that Samuel Hicks had commandeered. There was even the possibility that gunships were on their way with teams of Navy Seals on board. They'd be under strict orders to stop the boat at all costs. As far as any of them were aware the potential of a cataclysmic strike on the city was imminent. The cadre of nodding men must be rubbing their hands in glee at the effect that Darley's confession had caused.

Not that I believed we should downplay the threat. In his mental state, Samuel Gant could engineer massive destruction. Even if the effects of the contamination didn't cause a no-go area for decades afterwards, he had a vessel, fuel, and a means of detonating both. A bomb delivered to the right target could cause massive structural damage and numerous deaths, and that was what we couldn't allow.

Chances were if Arrowsake knew that we were heading out to intercept Gant, they would try to stop us. For Arrowsake to regain their seat of power they would prefer the madman to succeed. The thought of that was enough to motivate us to stop Gant or die trying.

I had to stop thinking of them as Arrowsake. This was something different; this was not what I was part of for fourteen years. This modern incarnation was an evil-minded offspring, a seething, roiling, muddy reflection of the past – the personification of everything that I'd stood against all my life.

'Heads up, buddy,' Rink shouted. 'Over there, you think that's him?'

Snapping out of my thoughts, I followed where Rink pointed. At first I couldn't make out anything against the oily depths. The lights of Jersey bled on to the water, refracted and twisted by the undulating surface, the streaking rain making it difficult to pinpoint anything. I caught an image of a turquoise figure rearing into the night sky. Concentrating on the pale glow of light on verdigrised copper I saw a bulky shape at its base. It looked out of place, an unfamiliar addition to a world-famous landmark.

'Man, I hope not.' I cast my gaze back across the water towards Manhattan. I was sure that Gant would've taken the boat that way, maybe at ramming speed towards the financial district where he thought he could cause the most disruption. What the hell had made him turn the other way? 'Jesus Christ! I think he intends attacking the Statue of Liberty.'

'You've gotta be kidding me!' Rink swung the speedboat towards Liberty Island regardless of the rhetoric he blurted.

'I wish I was.' Maybe Gant's plan wasn't as out there as it first appeared. The Statue of Liberty was a symbol of freedom from oppression; to a person who thought he was the victim, that he was one of the downtrodden, the statue would stand for something else. Maybe Gant saw Lady Liberty as the beacon that had attracted the many races of the earth to these shores, her beckoning torch waving at allcomers to enter the country and despoil his race. I could be wrong, maybe the island was just the nearest target he'd latched on to and there was no hidden meaning for the attack. But it was as plausible a reason as any. If he desired to strike against the US government, then what greater target was there out here on the water?

A hundred yards out from shore and I recognised the battered old yacht that Darley had described. The term 'yacht' didn't fit the boat very well: it was more like an industrial barge that had been converted to include living quarters. It was eighty feet long, almost half as wide, a blunt ugly-looking thing that wasn't helped by the poorly applied coat of paint.

Rink headed towards the yacht. It was moored at a crazy angle and we could see now that Gant had beached the boat on the pilings at the base of the island. The dock was never made to accommodate a vessel as large as this, usually being the domain of pleasure boats and the small water taxis that transported day-trippers back and forth. Gant's boat had rammed the pier, partly demolishing it, then slewed round and into the concrete wharf. It had then ridden up on to it before settling down a few feet as concrete and hull crumbled under the impact. Over it all, the statue reared her head in lofty disdain.

I looked down at the SIG in my fist. Somewhere along the way I'd withdrawn it and manipulated the slide. Instinct was overtaking my capacity to keep up and I experienced a slowing of reality as adrenalin shrieked through my system. I only gave it a second's thought, trying to recall the last time I'd felt like this. Nothing since the near-fatal battle with Luke Rickard had got my blood pumping so fiercely. Even the stirrings I'd felt while hunting Gant's crew back in the Alleghenies hadn't approached this sense of impending action. I'd felt alive then, but now I felt supercharged.

'Take us in on the far side of the yacht,' I said.

'Looks like he's ditched it. Maybe he's already on the island.'

'We have to check. I don't want him up on that deck shooting at us as we cross the open ground.'

'Good point.'

Rink swung the boat round the stern of the yacht, cut the engine and allowed it to drift in for the last few yards. He stood up, pulling out his Glock. 'You going up here? I'll take the front, OK?'

'Yeah, but take it real easy.' The cautionary words were for us both. Supercharged was one thing, but it didn't make you superhuman. Charging in full of spit and venom would only get the two of us killed.

I jammed the barrel of the SIG between my teeth, reached up to the gunwales of the yacht and hoisted myself up. Rink steadied the speedboat, then jammed his palms against the hull, used a walking motion powered by his thick arms to manoeuvre the speedboat towards the shoreline. By the time I'd slipped over the rail and on to the deck, Rink had clambered on to the prow of the speedboat and leapt the final few feet to shore. I swung round and brought up my gun, sweeping the deck for a target.

It was too quiet. Rain still pattered down, and the river lapped at the boards and the pilings, sloshing and chuckling, but I could hear neither footsteps nor any other movement from inside the boat. Didn't mean that Gant wasn't on board, just that he could have heard us coming and was preparing an ambush.

From the vantage on the deck, I scanned the approach to the statue. The eleven-pointed plinth that Lady Liberty stood upon was lit with spotlights, but the angles offered plenty of shadows to hide in. I couldn't pick out any movement and searched to the right. The trees that swathed the northern end of the island were bare of foliage, but their trunks could easily conceal a man. Distractedly I wondered what security precautions were taken on the island. Was there a police or Port Authority presence here? I didn't know, and it was too late to worry about the consequences of law officers mistaking me for the crazy man who'd beached his craft. I looked for Rink, couldn't see him, but knew that he'd be there watching my back.

First thing first. Find the plutonium. I'd a good idea that Gant would have it and then I could finish what we started back in the Pennsylvanian logging camp. The old yacht boasted a large cabin-cum-galley structure in the centre of the deck. Perched on top of it was a bridge that was open to the elements at the back. I reared up on tiptoe to get a clear view but there was no one at the wheel. Headed for the galley. At some point someone had been creative with a brush here as well, and everything including the circular windows had been painted over in the same navy colour. Maybe whoever had once owned this vessel was severely agoraphobic.

The only way to check inside was to go in through the double doors. If Gant was waiting then I'd be shot the second I poked my head inside, and I didn't relish the idea. Could have done with Rink joining me up there; together we could launch a one-two assault on the cabin and at least one of us would get an opportunity to kill the tattooed man. Still no sign of Rink, though, and the clock was ticking. Not the best choice of words, true, but fitting nonetheless. Gant could be preparing an explosion now and I didn't want to be caught on the boat when it went supernova.

Taking a deep breath, I lunged at the double doors, booted them open and went directly inside. I swept the area with the barrel of my SIG, the finger caressing the trigger missing only the fraction of pressure necessary to discharge the weapon. There was a dead man at the far end of the long room. Twisting to the left I found two more bodies heaped in the corner. The smell was enough to suggest they were dead, but I had to make sure. The two corpses piled here were both big men, rough-faced, built like brawlers. Hicks' bodyguards. Both men were missing a significant portion of their torsos and their shocked expressions hadn't been lessened by the laxity of death. I looked again at the man at the far end. It occurred to me that I'd never known the face of my enemy, and being honest, this professorial-looking man wasn't what I'd expected. Taking Gant as a template, I was expecting tattoos, shaved skull, earrings and steel toe-capped boots. The slim silver-haired man with matching goatee looked more like someone who'd cross the street rather than associate with neo-Nazis. Looks are deceiving, though. Take the genial-looking old men who headed Arrowsake; who'd ever guess they were capable of the madness they planned?

Carswell Hicks was lying on the floor in front of a desk, the only furniture in the room. Beyond the desk was an open door, but the closet behind it was empty. I approached the only hiding place where Gant could be, going round the desk quickly, gun poised to shoot.

Gant wasn't there, but I found a metal lock-box with the lid thrown wide. Indentations in the foam interior were empty. The spaces in the foam were large enough to contain a couple of thermos flasks and it didn't take a genius to deduce that there had lain the plutonium receptacles. They were gone, and so was Gant. Searching around, I found scuffed footprints formed of blood and at this angle saw that they led back out the way I'd come. I followed them to the doors and outside on to the deck. The beating rain obscured the tracks here, but there was only one place where Gant could have headed. I craned up, looking at the elegantly robed woman towering three hundred feet above, her torch held high as if to ward off the rain.

Just as I feared, Gant was going to despoil the symbol of freedom. It was ironic; I had always fought against tyranny, and now it looked like I was going to have to be the champion of Lady Liberty herself. I strode along the deck, eyes still on the proud face high overhead, hoping that she would approve of me if she was given voice.

The rattle of a machine pistol rang out, followed by a shriek of pain, and all whimsical thought fled.

It was time to get deadly serious.

46

Public access to the statue halted at six p.m. sharp but the National Park Rangers and support staff responsible for the upkeep and maintenance of the site stayed on hand later into the evening. Luckily for Gant, by the time he'd decided on his target and had steered the yacht to its cumbersome arrival at the island, only a skeleton crew was left behind. He killed one stetson-wearing Ranger down on the dock, and a black woman lugging a cart full of cleaning materials at the entrance to the foyer to Old Fort Wood, the eleven-pointed star that Lady Liberty loomed over. Luckier still, the cleaning woman had been on her way out of the door, because passing through the portal he found it to be at least four inches thick and even his machine pistol wouldn't have been enough firepower to gain entrance.

He had visited here once, back when he was a gooey-eyed kid, blinded by the lies told to him by his schoolteachers, the government and even his parents. The original torch had been relocated to the lobby at some point in the past and he'd joined the throng of school brats oohing and aahing at it. Following stairs to the second floor, he'd found an exhibition hall where he recalled marvelling at full-sized replicas of Lady Liberty's face and one of her feet. Now, as an adult, with the blinkers lifted, none of this mattered to him, and he went up the stairs at a run, heading for the tenth-floor observation platform where he could get a good view of Liberty Island all the way back down to the abandoned yacht.

He exited through of a door fitted with push bars. There he pulled off the cumbersome rucksack he'd brought from the boat and wedged it against one of the doors so it wouldn't close on him. It was good to drop the heavy weight for a while, and he worked the kinks out of his muscles, then crept out on to the balcony and scanned the area below him. He thought he heard a motor, but it idled and then went silent. He tried to peer through the rain and was sure he saw someone clamber over the gunwale of the yacht. He blinked raindrops from his lashes, stared but couldn't see movement now. Deciding it was more than likely just a play of the shadows caused by the shifting of the rain, he shifted his gaze across the harbour towards Manhattan. The downtown financial district dominated the skyline, but since the Twin Towers had come down it just wasn't as impressive any more. He wished he'd been responsible for 9/11 instead of goddamn bin Laden, but then thought, to hell with it. Ground Zero still attracted thousands of visitors; in contrast no one would be coming to Liberty Island for a long time.

He smiled, holding it until it slipped into a grimace. He'd never planned on being a suicide bomber like one of them Islamic zealots, but it could come to that now. Fuck it. It'll be worth it. His name would be revered in the white supremacist movement: he'd be bigger than McVeigh, Matthews, Dr Pierce and even James Earl Ray.

He took one last look, searching the heavens for helicopters swooping his way, or boats racing across New York Harbor, but it looked like he had a few minutes' grace yet. He didn't doubt that Darley had run squealing like a pig to the cops, but the advantage was still his: they didn't know where he was.

'Excuse me, sir. The attractions are closed for the day. Uh . . . can I ask you what you are doing here?'

Gant heard the voice and his grimace became a rictus smile. Slowly he turned and looked at the tall black man standing with one hand on the open door. Rent-a-cop or domestic staff, Gant couldn't immediately tell. The man was in a beige shirt and trousers, a broad leather belt holding nothing more dangerous than a walkie-talkie.

As the man got his first good look at Gant's face he was at first offering up a genial enough smile. Christ, he'd just caught a terrorist and he was still being polite. Ain't that just the state of things these days? In the next second the man took in the tattooed visage, the shaved head, the gun in Gant's hand and the smile flickered and disappeared.

'What I'm doing, nigger,' Gant said, 'is what every good white man should've done a long time ago. I'm making a stand against the likes of *you*.'

The man knew he was going to die, and all he could do was throw up his hands. Little good they did against the nine mm hollow-points that tore through his body. The man was thrown back into the interior of the building, a shrill scream following him inside.

Gant went quickly after him, scooping up the rucksack and its weighty contents with a grunt. He swung it on to one shoulder, as he covered the man with his Ruger MP9. The man's scream of agony petered out, sputtered and went silent.

Below him other voices were raised in question, more of the night crew responding to the shocking sound of death inside such a sanctified place. Give them their due, they were no cowards. He heard footsteps from below. Gant loped to the head of the stairs, looked down and thought he saw movement. He aimed and fired a short burst downwards. He was rewarded by shouts of alarm, followed by running footsteps as the once brave hearts made a dash for freedom. He heard squawks of alarm bleating from the radio on the dead man's belt.

'Oh, well, the cops will be on their way now.' His voice reverberated back to him from the hollow shell of Lady

Liberty above. He went up a short flight of stairs, looked up into the dimness. The lights that adorned the steel structure inside the statue had been turned off hours ago. Only an occasional security light offered a dim glow on each landing of the stairs that wound up inside the body to the observation platform in the crowned head. He took one last look down, before turning his attention to the spiral stair. It was going to be difficult lugging the cumbersome rucksack, but as a soldier he'd carried heavier packs and for much further.

He recalled this climb from his youth, charging in noisy abandon up the steel staircase alongside a crowd of his school mates. Back then they'd been forbidden from using the elevators, but as kids they didn't mind. Going all the way to the top was a challenge that young Sammy had relished. He was only pissed when on reaching where the arm stretched into the sky he was halted. Only maintenance personnel were allowed up into the torch these days, he'd been told by a member of staff. Well, there was no one around to stop him this time.

He found the entrance to the arm, looked up the undulating tunnel. What if he lit a real flame up there inside Liberty's torch? He could imagine the after-effects posted on the internet for the entire world to see. It would be iconic, like the Berlin Wall coming down, the Twin Towers collapsing. But he decided, no. He wanted to poison the entire monument, and if he blew the torch most of the fallout would drift away on the wind and rain. He continued towards the next landing and the observation deck in Liberty's crown.

From one of the twenty-five windows in the crown, he peered out towards Manhattan as he caught his breath. Lights darted high over the tall buildings, there one second, gone the next as they streaked through the tattered low-lying clouds. Either he was witness to an alien invasion, or these UFOs were police helicopters responding to the calls for assistance from the maintenance crew who'd fled earlier. For a second he glanced down, saw the tablet held in Lady Liberty's left hand. Roman numerals depicted the date July 4th, 1776. Independence Day, my ass! More like the beginning of the end. He spat at his feet, saying out loud, 'The white man built this nation. We allowed others to come in. That was our mistake, and now it's our duty to put things right.'

He looked for the lights again, and others had joined them, this time on the water. They were coming. Time to get this done.

He crouched down and pulled the contents from the rucksack he'd lugged here. The two flasks of plutonium he placed carefully on the floor, but then yanked out the makings of an IED he'd scrounged from the engine room and galley of the yacht. There was nothing fancy about it, nothing as glamorous as plastic explosive or Semtex, just gasoline in a large tin container, rags, gaffer tape and a lighter. Exploded here inside the head of Lady Liberty the highly inflammable fuel would erupt everywhere, spill down the stairs and over the copper sheets and steel structure, spreading and poisoning the entire statue with the radioactive particles.

He laid out his materials and reached for the first flask. He unscrewed the cap and teased out the glass vial inside, placed it down gently. He repeated the process with the second one, then gaffer-taped the two vials to the outer surface of the gas can. He started wondering: can I do this without killing myself?

He looked down at his high-top boots and the red laces he wore with pride. Quickly he crouched down, unfastening each lace until he had enough. He cut them away with a knife he carried, leaving just enough to tie over his insteps to keep his boots on. He knotted the strands together, dipped them into the neck of the gasoline can. He was careful not to get too much fuel on them, just enough to ensure a constant flame, and ended up with almost two yards of fuse. That should do it.

He wadded rags and fed them into the neck of the can, letting another trail out so it gave him another few seconds of leeway, then tucked one end of the impregnated lace under the rag. He positioned himself at the head of the stairs, fed the fuse down the first four steps and left it hanging there, because flame always travelled upward.

All he had to do now was light it before running like hell.

47

A flash of movement through the billowing rain caught my attention, and I recognised the panther-like figure of Rink as he rushed over the grassy approach to Fort Wood. There was nothing to be done for the dead Park Ranger over whom I'd stooped, checking for nonexistent vital signs. I set off after Rink. My friend had obviously responded to the rattle of gunfire, rushing to give aid.

Pounding up the shallow incline to the eleven-pointed plinth, I searched upward but got no sign of where Gant could be. Rink had already sprinted to the right and out of view. There were voices shouting in alarm, and the dulled *pock-pock-pock* of machine-gun fire from somewhere inside the building. I put my head down and raced hard to cover the distance. I reached the fort's thick wall; placed it between me and a sniper's aim from above. I followed the wall to the northern end where visitors to the landmark could file inside.

Rounding the final corner, I found Rink standing at the front of a small group of people. They were all extremely agitated, some of them wanting to flee while Rink tried to direct them around the side of the building and out of any possible line of fire.

I ran up to them, aware of but ignoring the pulling in my thigh. A couple of people flinched and were about to run, taking me for one of the mysterious gunmen assaulting the statue. Dipping my hand in my pocket, I dragged out the identification badge I'd lifted from Vince earlier. 'Hunter, FBI,' I called out, sounding officious. 'Everyone listen to me. We have a situation here, people, and I need every one of you to leave the vicinity immediately. Do as my colleague says, and head around the back there. Keep close to the wall and you should be fine.'

One of the group, an older woman wearing a beige uniform, pointed at a woman lying close to the entrance door, her cleaning cart overturned next to her. She blinked raindrops or tears from her eyes. 'What about Mrs Lopez?'

'We have back-up coming,' Rink reassured her with a hopeful squint towards me. 'Mrs Lopez will be taken care of. For now, y'all are our priority and we need to get you out of here.'

'Bill Jefferson is still inside,' the woman said.

Recalling the machine-gun fire and the scream that followed, it wasn't likely that Mr Jefferson would be coming out on his own two feet. I spared the woman that insight, though, saying, 'We'll find him. Now . . . have any of you any idea where the gunman is?'

A younger male who looked like he might have spent time on a football field pointed up. 'I heard him upstairs. But he fired at me and I had to get away. Jeez, I didn't want to run, but what could I do?'

'You did the right thing, son.'

The youth wasn't fully satisfied, but he went on, maybe in an effort at reconciling himself to his perceived cowardice. 'But I didn't keep on running. I stopped a couple flights down and I'm sure I heard him going up the metal stairs into the statue. Then I—'

He was about to launch into some tale of heroics and I cut him off. To preserve his sense of honour I gave the boy a way out. 'What's your name, son?'

'Liam Walsh, sir.'

'Well, Liam, I'm looking for a good man to help us out here. Can I rely on you?'

'Uh, sure, sir,' he said, while blinking at the faces of the terrified group who were now focused him.

'This is what I need you to do, Liam: I need you to get these people safely away from here while we go and stop this maniac. They need someone they trust to lead them. Now . . . do as I said, OK? Keep close to the walls of the fort, then when you know you can't be seen from any of the viewing platforms make a run for it to the far shore. From there you can backtrack down to the head of the island. The police are coming and they'll take over from there.'

'Won't one of you come with us?' asked a third member of the group, another woman, this one thin and dark-skinned. Some of the others nodded in agreement, their faces full of concern.

Rink opened his mouth, but Liam saved him the trouble. 'Come on, you heard what they said. We're just holding these good men back from doing their job. Follow me; I'll get us all outa here.'

The boy couldn't know how right he was. I nodded at him, respect. He gave me a lopsided grin, pushed his hand through his hair, then led the group away, round the nearest point and out of sight. Not a one of them challenged his leadership, though someone was yelling frantically into a radio and I caught an incredulous squawk in responsc.

'Maybe we shoulda took their radios,' Rink said. 'They're shouting for help and that only lessens our chances of getting to Gant first.'

I was in agreement, but I looked up at the statue looming overhead. 'This isn't about revenge, or even Don and his family any more. This is about stopping an attack on the USA itself.'

'So we gonna get on with it?'

'Ready when you are.'

'Let's go, then.'

Going first, I jogged through a short passage and into a foyer of the large building. A barrier used for controlling the flow of visitors had been knocked over, but that was the only sign that something out of the ordinary had occurred here. I scanned the room, ignoring the exhibits, searching for movement. Using hand-speak I motioned Rink forward, and then went on into the room. Rink came in behind me, moving off at an angle, covering while I searched for a way up into the bowels of the building.

In a brick vault-work passage on the right, there was a way up. We were taking much on faith when we assumed that Gant had indeed continued upwards as the youth said, because there was no way we could follow normal procedure and clear each level as we went. I started up the stairs and heard the scuff of feet as Rink followed. Taking it in turn to advance then cover for the other, we worked our way up through the original fort to the statue's pedestal and found another chamber where doors led out on to the promenade that once held gun platforms. We ignored them and went again for the next set of stairs. There was an elevator up to the top of the pedestal but neither of us wanted to confine ourselves in an enclosed space that could be hosed down by bullets at any of the stops.

We went up in absolute silence but for one time, when Rink was passing to take the lead. He whispered, 'If we get out of this alive, I'm definitely renewing my gym membership. I suggest you do too.'

I didn't reply; I was too busy sucking in oxygen. As Rink reached the next point, I headed up once more, legs feeling like I was wearing lead-soled boots. I came to a standstill when we found Jefferson, and saw that the man was beyond help. There was a new spring in my heels when I set off again.

Finally we came out into an area that took me by surprise. I'd never been in the statue before. Like a lot of people I expected that it was solid but found it to be a large empty space, sheets of copper over a steel frame. It was like standing under the vaulted ceiling of a cathedral, that same hushed sense of awe thick in the atmosphere. From somewhere overhead there came a dull clink, followed moments later by a shuffle of movement that was multiplied by the echoing effect of the massive bell-shaped construction. We searched above us for the source of the sounds, but the reverberation made that impossible.

Speaking was unworkable now. Even at a whisper our voices would carry to Gant. Our saving grace was the rain pattering against the outer shell of the statue, a drum roll to hide our advance up the stairs. Each step needed to be measured, and we kept our elbows clear of the rails of the spiral staircase. Its design, like those found in medieval castles, made it difficult for more than one of us to advance at a time, so I stayed in the lead. The way I saw it, I'd led Rink here, so if anyone should be shot first it wasn't going to be my friend.

We'd made it almost to the top when the sounds emanating from the observation point in the statue's diadem grew louder. There were a couple of clunks, some metal being dragged, a few more indistinguishable sounds, followed by a thunder of feet pounding downwards. The stairs beneath our feet shook under the tread and we prepared ourselves.

Rink, being the taller of us, could angle his arm over my shoulder without impeding my aim. I also levelled my SIG at the stairwell above.

It would have been different if the staircase had come with walls, we'd have easily ambushed Gant as he ran into our line of sight, but the stairs were open for the purposes of visitors marvelling at the construction from within. Above us Gant skidded to a halt. He swore savagely, leaned out over the railing and fired his machine pistol.

We had nowhere to go, so we stood our ground. We returned fire as bullets spanged off the railings and steps. The angle saved us, but ricochets were a dire threat. A couple of bullets bounced off the steps and punctured the copper sheeting like moths had holed Lady Liberty's robes.

'Get the fuck out of here. There's a bomb up there and it's gonna blow any second!'

Gant's voice came to us as a shriek of panic, all thoughts of glorious martyrdom gone now that he'd been thwarted of a free run for safety.

'Stop it, then!' I yelled back. 'You don't have to let it explode.'

'I can't, goddamnit, I can't!' Gant let loose a further hail of bullets, then followed them part way down the next flight.

Angling my gun I fired at the steps overhead. The rounds flattened against the steel supports, but the loud bangs that accompanied them caused Gant to come to a halt.

'You're not coming down, you prick,' I shouted. 'If that bomb goes off, you're going with it.'

'That's you, isn't it, the bastard who shot me back in Pennsylvania?'

'Yes, the name's Joe Hunter.' I pressed an elbow in Rink's ribs, nodded down the stairs. Rink shook his head vehemently; he wasn't going anywhere. *Go*, I mouthed. Then I motioned that I was planning to draw Gant down after me. We could get him when he came down. Either that or we'd pen him in and leave him for his bomb to kill. Rink slipped away, while I covered his retreat by shouting, 'You hear me, Gant? You defuse that fucking bomb or I'll be the man who kills you.'

'Motherfucker, you won't be killing anyone. Don't you get it? If we don't get out of here in the next few seconds we're both going to die. I. Can't. Stop. It.'

'Then we're both going to die.' My voice was firmer than I expected. I didn't relish being caught in the blast, but I wasn't moving until the sounds of Rink's descent faded.

Gant didn't like the idea of being scorched to the bones; he came, shooting as he pounded down the stairs. The angle offered no protection now and I was woefully outgunned. I was forced to retreat, but that was OK, I had no intention of being immolated either. To slow Gant down, I fired, picking the shots so that they were just enough to make the man above slow in his descent.

Gant was roaring in frustration, his anger rising in pitch with every second, but he had good reason.

Several flights above Gant I saw the inner curves of the statue change hue, going from a muted green to blossoming orange. Then there was a pop and the world held its breath.

The explosion that followed was deafening, and the flash of light that followed caused Gant to scream and me to jam a crooked elbow over my eyes to avoid being blinded. But that wasn't the end of it. There was much worse to come.

48

The rain had been such a feature of the last few days that I had grown familiar with it. But this rain was like nothing I'd experienced before. It was fire and brimstone flung from heaven to wipe out life. It came in droplets first, then in a molten curtain that spilled between the rails from above. Where it struck the steel structure, or the copper sheeting, it adhered to it and continued to burn, black smoke coiling everywhere. My coat, wet from the rain, wasn't spared. Spatters of flaming petroleum set me on fire, and I ripped at my clothing to get out of it. I back-pedalled, slapping at another patch on my jeans, feeling the heat transfer to my palm as residue stuck there. I wiped my palm rapidly up and down a leg to put out the fire.

A klaxon sounded, the alarm like the shriek of an animal, and fire sprinklers jetted into life. It only made matters worse, spreading the flaming rain even further. Underlying the rise and fall of the fire alarm and the hiss of water, the dying roar of the explosion was a dull reverberation throughout the structure. Something clattered and bounced, fell past and I recognised it as a misshapen hunk of blackened metal – probably whatever receptacle the petrol had been in – and wished it was Gant's gun. Better still, Gant's head.

The man was somewhere above me and by the thrashing and howling he was having a devil of a time smothering the flames that had ignited his clothing. There was another noise, Rink yelling from down below. Some of the flaming petrol had spilled all the way down through the structure on to the lowest level. I hoped that Rink had made it to safety before the splash hit the floor and it wasn't my friend shrieking in agony. Over Gant's roars of anger and pain, I searched for Rink's voice again. My friend's words came back, measured, controlled, but tinged with anxiety. 'Hunter, Hunter, you OK up there?'

All thought of keeping Rink's presence a secret was pointless now that the dynamics of the exploding bomb had changed everything.

'I'm OK, Rink. What about you?'

'I'm fine, but there's a goddamn wall of flame between us, and all this water ain't helping. Don't know how you're gonna get down.'

'I've still got something to do up here first.'

'What about the radiation?'

Rink had a point. There was no way of knowing if I'd been drenched in the poisonous stuff, but it was highly likely in this confined space.

My silence said it all. If the plutonium had got me, coming down wouldn't help. Fatalism struck. If it wasn't going to kill me immediately, I might as well make good use of the time left.

If Gant was in full charge of his senses he would expect me to flee downwards. So I went up. And I went at speed, dodging pools of flaming fuel, leaping over others. I clanged up the last few steps and on to a platform. Off to the left was the hollow tube forming the upraised arm of Lady Liberty. Burning petrol spilled from above, a mini-cascade that made the tube an unreachable escape route. I spun to the right, feeling heat scorch my features. If I hadn't already been wet then my hair would have spontaneously combusted. The heat forced me to move back a pace. Just as I did a writhing shape burst out of the smoke in front of me.

His clothing smoking, Gant came at me like a maniac, teeth bared in a rictus snarl. He fired the machine pistol, and I had to lunge away, almost going over the railing. I fired from the hip, and the bullets struck Gant in the body. The man staggered at the impact, but it didn't stop him. I rebounded from the railing and launched myself at the skinhead's gun hand. Gant tried to swing it on me, but I knocked it aside with a forearm, smacked Gant under the chin with the butt of the SIG. We went chest to chest, grappling each other's gun hand. We were so close I could see the eight-eight pattern on the other man's face: one of them as a bullseye for my forehead.

The blow stunned Gant, and I used the moment to turn him. I arched him over the rail, my knee jamming between his thighs. Gant exhaled sour breath in my face.

'You fucker!' I snarled at him.

'Traitor,' Gant snapped back.

'I'm a traitor? You've just blown a bomb in the fucking Statue of Liberty!'

'Liberty? This is a symbol of everything that's gone wrong with this country.'

There wasn't time for argument, this was all about fighting. We wrestled and jostled and Gant managed to knee my injured thigh. I ignored the pain and rammed my own knee into Gant's groin. We both fell to the platform, and ended up perilously close to the edge. Gant kicked with both legs, and I had to snatch at his feet to avoid going over.

Gant brought round his gun. It was do or die, and I wasn't ready to breathe my last. I fired the SIG, uncaring where the target was, only that it deflected Gant's aim. The bullet struck the man's left shoulder. Gant yelled in agony and tried to scramble away. I got a hold on one of his boots, but it was loose and slipped off, and almost spilled me off the platform to a sure death. I clutched at one of the supports, but my legs went over the edge. A drip of molten heat seared the back of my neck.

Gant came up to his feet. 'I got a look at your friend down there. The Nip. You're consorting with the fucking enemy, you asshole.'

'Rink's an American,' I grunted as I swung my legs back on to the platform. 'He's a hero who has fought all his life for his country. You? You're just a piece of white trash who wants to sit on your lazy arse and have everything handed to you.'

Gant flicked the lever on his gun to fully automatic. He laughed, jerked his head upwards. 'Does that look the work of a lazy man?'

'It looks like the work of a crazy man.'

'No. No. No. I'm not crazy. I know exactly what I'm doing.'

'Do you?' I laughed. I'd wondered what Kwon had meant when he'd said, 'You don't understand.' Well, now I'd an idea why the Korean had been so sure of himself. He'd demanded to talk with the CIA . . . was that because he knew there was nothing tangible they could hold against him? 'Your bomb up there? If you'd cared to check you'd have found that the flasks didn't contain plutonium-isotope. It was just heavy water. Enough radiation to set off a Geiger counter, but anyone who knows about these things would have realised it was a very low yield. Your fire will have vaporised it in the initial explosion.'

'Bullshit.'

'Carswell Hicks bought nothing more dangerous than dishwater.'

'You're lying.'

'Why would I?'

'Because you're an agent of a lying government.'

'No.' I stared up at the man's gun, challenging him. 'I'm not.'

Gant's face shadowed as my hastily formulated theory struck. Everything he'd done was for nothing? The flames, though intense for now, had no fuel, and the splash of petroleum would do little more than singe the inside of the statue. A quick clean up and the Statue of Liberty would be open for business as usual.

'Ain't life a bitch?' he asked sarcastically. Then he swung his gun at my face. 'But don't worry; you don't have to suffer it any longer.'

Engaging Gant in conversation wasn't an effort to explain the skinhead's failings, it was to give me an opportunity to fight back. Hanging precariously over the edge of the platform I had no hope, so I'd taken the opportunity to squirm up on to the deck, keeping my gun out of view. Gant thought I was at his mercy, but I didn't expect mercy. From a prone position I fired along the deck, and the bullet struck Gant's unguarded ankle. Gant shrieked, his gun exploding into life, but his arms had also reacted to the agony in his shattered foot and his bullets spanged along the platform in front of me. Ricochets whizzed everywhere, as hot as the falling rain. Something scorched my scalp, whether it was dripping petrol or a fragment of a bullet I didn't know or care.

Gant couldn't take his own weight on his shattered ankle. He began to buckle.

Swarming up, I caught the tattooed man's gut with a shoulder. Like a prop on a rugby field, I drove with my feet, then at the last second thrust out with both hands and propelled Gant back and into the opening to Lady Liberty's upraised arm. The skinhead disappeared into the darkness on the far side of the molten fluid that still sheeted down the wall.

Gant's shrieks were horrendous. It was no clean death for him, but the intense agony of immolation. I stepped away from the sickening sounds of thrashing limbs and crackling flame.

I was still standing in the same place a few seconds later when something erupted back through the flames. *Something*: that was the only way my mind could describe Gant now because very little of him was left that was recognisable.

When trained in Point Shooting, you've achieved mastery when your gun becomes an extension of the hand. No conscious effort is necessary to target and discharge your weapon. I lifted, squeezed and fired three rounds directly into the central mass of the *thing* approaching.

Maybe Gant was wearing a bulletproof vest like he had been back in the Alleghenies, because like before the rounds didn't stop him. He came on, and he still had the machine-pistol in his hand. I almost fired again. But I allowed the gun barrel to drop.

Gant was sheathed in flames, his clothing burning, disintegrating and adhering to his body, his skin blistering, his gun fused to the flesh of his right hand. He had to be insane with agony. He came to a stumbling halt, opened his mouth in a silent scream. I fancied that there were even flames in his throat. Then Gant dropped to his knees, flopping back so he sat propped on his heels. He continued to burn. His entire face was turning the same blue, black and scarlet as the tattoo that decorated him. One eye was swollen shut, a blister filled with fluid threatening to pop, but the other was wide open and staring at me. The eye gleamed with hatred.

I lifted my gun and shot him through the skull.

Not out of anger or even a sense of justice, but in an act of mercy I'd never have offered the man before now.

He flopped down, arms twisting up towards his chest. I thought of Brook; if this bastard was the one responsible for burning her then he'd got everything he deserved. I turned away, unable to look at him any longer.

Gant was dead, and if I didn't get out quick I would probably join him. I thundered down the stairs with the fire alarm whooping, as though urging me on. Molten drops still pattered around me, and a few times I slapped at my skin where they struck. It was as if I ran through a descent into hell, but every step I took was in the right direction. Above the flames still crackled and hissed and poisonous fumes collected in the head of the statue.

Coming to the lowest level, I found where the spilled fuel had gathered on the surface of pools of rusty water. Some of it had burned down now to a thick, oily smudge on the floor, but in the main it was still alight. I leaped the flames without stopping, experienced a split-second of intense heat, but then was through it and felt Rink dragging me down on to blessedly cold tiles. Rink rolled me, patted with his open hands and I was only then aware that my hair was smouldering and that patches of my shirt had ignited.

'Holy Christ, brother,' Rink panted. 'If I knew there was gonna be a bonfire I'd've brought marshmallows.'

I pulled up on to my feet, smarting at the raw spots on my arms and face. There was a particularly raw spot on the back of my neck too. 'Through here, quick.'

We pushed through a door and down into the observation gallery of the pedestal, the klaxon shriek lessened now that we were out of the reverberating statue. Apparently the fire-fighting system worked on separate units depending upon the individual floors. We thought about going out into the rain, but the deluge had chosen now to lessen. Something else was needed. I scanned the ceiling, saw what I was looking for and took aim with the SIG. There was more to this shot than those I'd put into Gant upstairs: this one was designed to save lives. I'd convinced Gant with my theory that Kwon had double-crossed Hicks, but I couldn't be sure.

The bullet struck the sprinkler-head in the ceiling and water gushed out. An automatic override flicked into action and all along the hall and throughout the remainder of the building the fire-fighting system kicked into play and water blasted down on us. Klaxons here now joined the wail from above. I pulled off my clothing, stood there in the altogether and allowed the showering water to cleanse me of any of the plutonium particles that might have found a way on to my flesh. When I looked around, Rink was scrubbing his naked body similarly.

The beating water didn't go on for ever. Soon it turned to a trickle and we forged a way down a staircase flowing with rusty-coloured streams. I wondered what kind of spectacle we'd make when we staggered outside, both as naked as newborn babies, our only possessions the guns in our hands.

There were too many other worries on my mind than if we'd raise a chuckle or two from the cops descending on the place, but I felt that stripped naked like this we were vulnerable to more than embarrassment. On the ground floor of the fort, I led Rink round the plinth displaying the original torch and towards rooms at the back. We went through one door marked PRIVATE and found a locker room. Inside we took some of the beige uniforms the staff had been wearing. We searched through various items, and pulled on trousers and shirts. I was easily kitted out, but Rink had broader shoulders and thicker arms than most and the shirt he pulled on was stretched across the chest and back. He had to leave the buttons undone, but he didn't mind. He just grinned, puffed out his pectorals, and said, 'What do you think? Poster boy for the National Park Service?'

I laughed along with him as we made our way back through the foyer. We were still laughing when we were greeted by gun-toting FBI troopers who disarmed us and led us off, giving way to the fire crews that had arrived. Others had arrived too, mysterious figures wearing hazmat suits, ready to clean up the fallout.

As we were marched across the sward, I looked back up at Lady Liberty. I'd like to say that she winked in approval, but it was probably just the play of flames and smoke behind her eyes.

49

I made the drive to Bedford Well in a rental car paid for by the bogus Danny Fisher credit card. I felt I'd earned the right, seeing as it had been supplied as expenses to help bring down Carswell Hicks' outfit. I enjoyed the drive this time. The rain was a memory, and now the hills were backed by a clear sky and hazy sunshine. I drove with the windows open, taking pleasure in the breeze ruffling my hair and snapping at my jacket collar. It was good to be outside again.

It was a full week since the events at the Statue of Liberty, but it felt more like months. Both Rink and I had spent time in cells, then in interview rooms where we were interrogated about our part in the horror that had struck Manhattan. We told our tale over and over again, but neither of us mentioned Arrowsake or its inclusion. Not through loyalty, but through necessity. In a cell we were sitting ducks for an assassin. We would deal with that problem ourselves. Another time, I promised. Special Agent Vincent was conspicuous by his absence. I wondered if Arrowsake had already deemed the young hothead a liability and had him terminated. There was always that possibility, but I doubted it: Vince had the instincts and the ability to disappear if he wished. I thought the young man might just make a reappearance somewhere down the line. A quote came to mind. A seventeenth-century author called François de la Rochefoucauld once wrote: 'Absence diminishes little passions and increases great ones, as wind extinguishes candles and fans a fire.' The author's words could be true of Vince's disappearing act, meaning when he showed again it would reignite a firestorm. Let him come, I decided, just not while we're penned in a jail cell.

Deals were struck on Capitol Hill, favours cashed in, warnings levied: whatever occurred, we were kicked loose from jail and into the waiting hands of the CIA. Walter Conrad met us, suggested we take a vacation for a while until he could straighten everything out. He wasn't referring to the screaming and accusation coming his way from the senators and congressmen who made up the Judiciary Committee, but to the lack of contact from his overseers at Arrowsake.

'What's their problem? Makes me wonder if they secretly wanted Gant to succeed,' I said. 'That would have proved their point that domestic terrorism *is* a dire threat.'

Walter didn't answer. Perhaps he was thinking the same thing.

'I've a business to run,' Rink said. 'I don't have time for another vacation. I've already had a few days break on taxpayers' money, thank you very much.'

'Seriously, boys, I think it's best that you lay low for a while.'

'We aren't hiding from them, Walter,' I said. 'It's those old men who have to cover their heads in shame.'

Rink grunted. 'They *need* to cover their asses. I see their wrinkly butts again, I'll pop a cap in 'em.'

'Stay away from them, boys. They're very dangerous people.'

'So are we,' I said. 'When I last spoke to Don Griffiths, I suggested he put everything he knew about this plot in a file someplace, with instructions that it should be opened if anything suspicious happened to him, his family or any of us three. Maybe you should whisper that in one of those old bastards' ears.'

'You think that's enough to keep us safe?'

'It will be for now. Maybe somewhere down the line they'll try something but not now. Our silence keeps them safe, so they have to keep us all happy.'

Walter's face settled into a semblance of resignation. 'Leave it to me, son.'

I hugged my mentor, a show of full forgiveness for the old man's indiscretions. 'You should watch yourself, Walt. Maybe it's you who should take a vacation.'

'I'm too busy overseeing damage control for that.' He dug in his pocket and brought out his ubiquitous cigar. He looked at it fondly. 'But maybe I should give up on my old ways, huh? Once I've passed Arrowsake your message I'm going to sever all ties with them.' He flipped the cigar into a waste basket.

We left him then. I wondered if Walter would delve in the basket after we were gone, because bad habits weren't as easily dropped as that. As he was to the cigar, I felt the old man was too much of a slave to Arrowsake to let it go so easily, or it him.

Together we took a ride out on the Staten Island ferry. There were a couple of hundred passengers, all jostling for places on one side of the boat, cameras poised, as the ferry chugged past Liberty Island. Everyone had come to see the Lady in all her glory. She'd stood here as a symbol of freedom from persecution for a century and a quarter and she'd stand here for many more years to come.

Gant's attempt at destroying her had failed miserably. My theory had proven unfounded: Kwon hadn't double-crossed Hicks; he'd delivered to him the real deal: plutonium 238. Only Samuel Gant's ham-handed attempt at jerry-rigging a bomb had failed. The petrol container had blown as he'd planned, but it wasn't enough to damage the plutonium flasks. They'd been fabricated to withstand blunt force in case they were ever mishandled or involved in a collision. The containers had come without the capacity for fission or fusion, and with no spillage the plutonium retained its atomic structure – although it had degraded substantially from its original weapons grade capacity. Thank God. The containers had been found undamaged, and already maintenance teams had scrubbed the scorch marks and soot residue away and Lady Liberty was once more open for business. She had thwarted the attack with stoic will, her torch still bright.

Later, Rink took a flight out of Newark, and once he'd passed through security, I had detoured to a rental booth and picked up the car. I'd set off through New Jersey, a rhythm and blues collection playing through the CD system. Maybe it was sheer coincidence that the first track was John Lee Hooker's 'Boom, Boom.'

I only stopped once on the drive over. Eating at a diner, I downed more mugs of coffee than were good for my health, then looked for a telephone booth. I called Imogen Ballard and apologised for missing spending St Valentine's Day with her. I meant every word, as well as the promise that I'd come over to Maine as soon as I was finished up. She told me to bring flowers and maybe she'd forgive me. Flowers *and* chocolates, I promised. After hanging up, I returned to the rental car and I was smiling. I only wished that I'd had the nerve to tell her I loved her.

The road past Hertford wound up into the hills. It went over the crossroads and I followed it with barely a glance to the north. Up along there was the shell of the house where Adrian Reynolds had died. I didn't want to think about that now. Most of the journey here from New York City had been filled with those thoughts already. For now I felt at peace. It wouldn't last, I knew, so I relished the simple comfort. I passed where I'd concealed the first two men I'd killed. I didn't think of their deaths as murder any more, not when it had been proven that Rooster and Cabe had both been part of Hicks' gang. I passed the Seven-Eleven where all of this started, and on into town to the green and its wishing well. I thought of the coins I'd dropped into it and how it had proven a waste of money after all.

I parked on the drive outside Don Griffiths' imposing house. As I sat in the car, I took a steadying breath, not quite sure how I should play this.

Nice and easy, I told myself.

Finally I got out and walked up the path to the door. There were new vehicles on the drive. Before I could ring the bell the door opened and it was déjà vu as I was greeted by Millie. Her smile didn't extend to her eyes, perhaps because she understood why I'd come.

50

Millie let me in and we walked to the kitchen. There I found an old friend waiting for me. Not Don, but Fluffy the tomcat. It stared at me from the top of a counter. The cat had been cleaned up, the matted fur brushed, and it looked like it had gained a few pounds in weight. At least its name suited it better now. I scratched it between its ears and the cat purred. 'Looks like you're being well looked after, boy.' Millie was watching me from across the kitchen, trying to decide why I had come. 'My lifestyle makes keeping a pet a little awkward these days. Fluffy can stay here, can't he?'

'Beth and Ryan have fallen in love with him. It's good that they have something to keep their minds off what happened.'

'Where are they?'

'In the sitting room, watching TV. You want to say hello?'

'No, it's best if they don't know I'm here.'

She nodded. The children had lost their parents in terrible circumstances and they didn't need reminding of that by my reappearance.

'How are the little ones?' I asked.

'It isn't easy on them. They're both traumatised, as anyone would imagine, but my dad has brought in the best counsellors that money can buy. Time's a healer, they say, but I'm not sure they'll ever fully recover from this.'

Children should be insulated against the horrors that Beth and Ryan had had to endure, but that was not the way of the world. My hope was that they weren't victims of such terror ever again: my real reason for being there.

'What about Don?'

'Dad's upstairs in bed. You can go up, if you like. I'll wake him.'

'Later, Millie. It's you I've come to see. Come take a walk with me.'

'Where to?'

'Somewhere else. I don't want the kids hearing any of this.'

Millie followed me through the house. At the front door she paused and looked back along the hall to a closed room from where canned laughter filtered. No children's voices joined in with the merriment.

'C'mon,' I said softly. 'They'll be OK alone for a few minutes.'

She trailed me down the path, across the road and on to the green. I led her to the wishing well where I rested a hip against the brickwork. Millie stood beside me, her arms folded under her breasts, her dark hair hanging past her eyes. I looked all around. A few townspeople were out and about, but none of them in earshot. I patted the wall next to me, invited her to sit.

Millie squeezed herself tightly, reluctant to leave the children unchaperoned for long. She held that pose for a beat, then it was as if she deflated and her hands swung listlessly by her sides. She sat on the well alongside me, head down. 'You've come to tell me that this isn't over with, haven't you?'

'Hicks and Gant are finished with,' I reassured her. 'The final few members of their organisation have been rounded up and are in jail. All the others are dead.'

'Good!' She snapped her head up and her eyes were no longer full of sadness. They were hard chips of ice, full of resolution. 'They deserved to die.'

'Perhaps.'

'Perhaps? There's no perhaps about it? They burned my sister to death, Joe.'

I wasn't so sure about that any more.

'Why would they?' I asked.

'To torment my father . . . What else?'

'Hicks wanted your dad dead. Why would he have Brook murdered then wait so long before attacking your family at Adrian's house? It doesn't fit . . .'

Millie stared at me, realisation hitting her like she'd run full-pelt into a brick wall. 'It was Vince Everett? Is that what you're telling me?'

A couple of things Vince had said to me had got me thinking: '*What I sometimes have to do isn't FBI procedure either*,' and even more damning; '*I had to get into his mind, become Vince Everett in every way. I had to think like him, act like him, do what he would do. It wasn't nice being in his head like that, but I had to show those assholes that I was a worthy ally*.'

To gain acceptance into Hicks' hate-filled organisation, it wasn't a stretch to think that they had demanded an act of loyalty from him. Had Vince's test extended to murdering Don Griffiths' daughter?

'I can't be sure, but it's beginning to look that way,' I said.

'But he's supposed to be one of the good guys . . .'

'Sometimes the boundaries aren't so easily defined.' Considering even myself a good man wasn't easy when my track record of violence screamed back at me in argument. 'Vince works for the government. He does what they tell him. Maybe they ordered him to do whatever was necessary to infiltrate Gant's crew.'

'You're saying that the government advocated it, that *they* are responsible for Brook's murder?'

'Not *the* government, just certain self-serving factions within it.'

'What can we do about that?'

'Right now? Nothing.'

'I won't accept that. My sister was murdered . . .'

I held up a hand. 'No. Actually, there is something. You can keep on living.'

Millie snorted and made to walk away. I grabbed her wrist and held on to her, pulled her close and gathered her in my arms. Whispering, I said, 'As much as it hurts, you must keep quiet about this. Your dad could still be seen as a threat to them. If you speak to anyone about Vince or his bosses, then I'm afraid I won't be able to save you.'

'Brook was my *sister*,' she said. She looked up, her eyes filled with tears. 'She didn't deserve to die like that. The people responsible should be made to pay!'

'I agree.' I released her and she took a step backwards. I could see the devastation in her face. Her features had folded in on themselves. She was reliving the horror, seeing her sister burning to death in the wreckage all over again.

'You're going after them?'

The garrotte mark on my neck was a distant memory now, but it still burned.

'I think that Vince will show up somewhere down the line.'

'But you don't think it will be here?' She cast a fearful glance across at her home, thinking about the children.

'That won't happen,' I reassured her. 'Not unless you talk.'

Her eyes became slits again. 'What if I shout it to the rafters?'

I stood up. 'Come on, Millie.'

'We could draw him here, couldn't we? You could be waiting. You could get the bastard.'

Part of me considered the proposition, but only for a nanosecond.

I shook my head. 'Forget him, Millie. Forget your hatred of him. Just get on with your life again.'

She looked disbelieving. 'You're going to let that bastard get away with this?'

'I've no option,' I said. 'There's always the chance I could fail and I'm not prepared to let that happen. Beth and Ryan still need someone around to love them.'

Millie's head finally went down, and the relaxing of her shoulders made her look small and frail. It seemed my words had pushed through her anger and offered her something else to concentrate upon. She reached out tenderly and touched my chest. Then her fingers dropped away and she walked slowly across the green towards her house.

I didn't follow.

My time here was over.

At least, I hoped so.

Maybe it was just the sun through the clouds, casting shadows in the alleyway across the green. For the briefest of moments, I was sure I'd caught sight of a face peering from within the darkness. But when I focused on the place, the face was gone. And so were the killer eyes I could have sworn were staring back at me.

THANKS

As any author will tell you, there are far more people who help in shaping a book than you can ever remember or credit. So, to all those who go unmentioned, thank you anyway.

My special thanks as ever go to my agent Luigi Bonomi and to Alison Bonomi, two people who have built and shaped Joe Hunter in ways I'd have once thought unimaginable, and to Ajda who works behind the scenes at LBA but is a valuable member of the team. Your guidance and support is very much appreciated.

Also, a huge thank-you to Sue Fletcher at Hodder and Stoughton, editor par excellence, and someone else who should take equal credit for the creation of Joe Hunter. To Eleni, Swati, and Alice, thanks to you all for the support. There's a whole bunch of friends who I owe my thanks to, so in no particular order, thank you to: Col Bury, Richard Gnosill, Lee Hughes, Sheila Quigley, Adrian Magson, Pete Nicholson, Paul D. Brazill, Val and George Steventon, Pat Reid, and Gina Metz. Thanks also to Mandy, Geoff, Jacky, Val and Bunny. And to the real Mike Dillman, Sonya Madden and Liam Walsh, thanks for the use of your names.

And the biggest thanks of all to my wife, Denise.

Want to find out what Joe Hunter does next?

Here is a taster from Matt Hilton's

Dead Men's Harvest

PROLOGUE

Conchar is an ancient Gaelic term for those who admire the king of all hunters: the wolf.

To some, the wolf is a magnificent beast, the pinnacle of predatory evolution. To others, the wolf is a thing of nightmare.

Castle of the wolf: it was a good name for an Army Confinement Facility. Imprisoned within its walls were men and women who were ultimate predators and, often, also things of nightmare.

Criminals housed at Fort Conchar generally fell into four categories: prisoners of war, enemy combatants, persons whose freedom was deemed a risk to national security and, lastly, military personnel found guilty of a serious crime.

Occasionally it housed criminals that did not meet any of these criteria, but that was an extreme circumstance. Only once had it opened its arms to a man who checked all four boxes and then some. Designated Top Secret, his name was withheld even from those who guarded him night and day. Known only by a number – Prisoner 1854 – he was a cipher in more ways than one.

Mostly he refused to speak to his jailers. Some even thought him incapable of speech. But his mystery went much deeper than that.

He was a living dead man. According to official records he had died, not once, but twice. And yet he still breathed.

If all went to plan, like Lazarus, the dead man would rise again. And people would know him. And they would scream his name in fear.

I

A breeze stirred and the susurration of foliage was like the whispering of lost souls. Frogs croaked. Water lapped. All sounds indigenous to the Everglades pine lands. Jared 'Rink' Rington ignored the natural rhythms of the Florida night, listening instead for the soft footfalls of the men hunting him.

There were at least four of them: men with guns.

From the cover of a stream bed, Rink spied back to where he'd left his car. The Porsche was a mess. Bullet holes pocked it from front to back and had taken out the front windshield. He'd wrecked the sump when he'd crashed over the median and into the coontie trees. There was a wide swath of oil glistening in the moonlight, as though the Boxster had been mortally wounded and had crawled into the bushes to die. Rink cursed under his breath, more for the death of his wheels than for his own predicament, but it wasn't the first time he'd had to consign a car to the grave.

Neither was it the first time he'd been hunted by armed men.

It kinda came with the territory.

The stream was shallow, stagnant almost. He used its steep bank as cover as he headed left. Above him someone stepped on a twig and it was like the crack of a gunshot. The insects grew still. There was a hush on the forest now. Rink crouched low, pressing himself against baked mud.

A few yards further on, another twig creaked beneath a boot.

Rink wormed himself out of the stream bed. A man was moving along the embankment above him, periodically glancing down towards the water, but more often towards the road.

Through the bushes Rink saw another man moving along the blacktop. This one held a Glock machine pistol, the elongated barrel telling him that it was fitted with a sound suppressor.

Frog-giggers want to do me in silence, he thought. Well, all right. Two of us can play at that game.

From his boot he pulled a military-issue KA-BAR knife, a black epoxy-coated blade that didn't reflect the light.

His options were few. He had to take out the men hunting him or die. Put that way he'd no qualms about sticking the man in front of him.

His rush was silent. His free hand went over the man's mouth even as he jammed the KA-BAR down between the juncture of his throat and clavicle. The blade was long enough to pierce the left aorta of the man's heart, killing him instantly. Rink dragged the corpse down to the ground.

The man on the road was unaware that his companion was gone.

From the dead man's fingers, Rink plucked free the Heckler and Koch Combat .45 and shoved it into the waistband of his jeans. There was no suppressor on this gun, so the knife would remain his weapon of choice for now, because the man with the Glock had to be done as silently as the first. There were two other assassins out there – possibly more – and he wanted to even the odds in his favour before exchanging rounds.

Rink was tall and muscular, built like a pro-wrestler. The man at his feet wasn't. But by exchanging jackets and with the man's baseball cap jammed over his black hair, he'd fool the other hunter for a second or so. Everything weighed and bagged, that would be all he'd need.

In the corpse's clothing, Rink moved through the bushes. For effect he pulled out the .45 so the disguise was complete. He held it in a two-handed grip, or that would be how it looked in silhouette.

The man to his right gestured, soldier speak that Rink recognised. These men weren't your run-of-the-mill killers; they too must have had military training. Rink hand-talked, urging the man towards a stand of trees. As he moved off, Rink angled towards him. Ten paces was all that separated them. The moon was bright on the road, but its light helped make the shadows beneath the trees denser. If Rink moved closer he could forget the charade.

The man halted. Something stirred in the foliage ahead. He dropped into a shooter's crouch, his Glock sweeping the area. Then a bird, disturbed from its roost, broke through the trees in a clatter of plumage on leaves. The man sighed, turned to grin sheepishly at his compadre.

Rink grinned back at him and he saw the man's face elongate in recognition. Charade over, he whipped his KA-BAR out from alongside the .45 and over-handed it at the man. Like a sliver of night, the blade swished through the air and plunged through tissue and cartilage.

The man staggered at the impact, one hand going to the hilt jutting from beneath his jaw, the other bringing round the Glock and tugging on the trigger. Rink dropped below the line of fire, the bullets searing the air around him, making tatters of the bushes and coontie trees. It was a subdued drum roll of silenced rounds, but no less deadly than if the gun had roared the sound of thunder. The man was mortally wounded, though not yet dead, but the Glock was empty and no threat. Gun in hand, Rink moved towards him.

Weakened by the shock of steel through his throat, drowning in his own blood, he couldn't halt Rink's charge. He was knocked off his feet and went down under the bigger man.

Then Rink had a hand on the hilt of the KA-BAR. A sudden jerk sideways opened one half of the man's neck and that was that.

Dragging the corpse off the road, Rink concealed it amongst a stand of palmetto.

Two down, two to go.

Rink was beginning to fancy his chances.

Armed now with two reliable guns and his KA-BAR, he decided it was time to show these frog-giggin' sons of bitches who they were dealing with.

'My turn now, boys,' he whispered.

A faint click.

'No, Rington,' said a voice from behind him. 'Now it's *my* turn.'

Rink swung round, his knife coming up in reflex, but it was too late.

Something was rammed against his chest and he became a juddering, spittle-frothing wreck as fifty thousand volts were blasted through his entire being.

2

The headstone was the only feature that held any colour. Everything else was the grey of a Maine winter, with sleet falling like shards of smoked glass across the monochrome background. Even the trees that ringed the small cemetery were dull, lifeless things, their bare branches smudged by the shifting sky. The sleet was building on the ground, not the pure white of virgin snow, but slushy, invasive muck that filled my boots with a creeping chill that bit bone deep.

I hunkered over the grave and wiped the accumulation of icy slush off the headstone. The granite marker stood four feet tall, pinkish-grey, with a spray of flowers carved down one side and painted in vivid splashes of red and green. The name had been inlaid with gold leaf, as had the date of her premature death: almost a year ago.

I'm not a religious man, not in the accepted sense, but I still mumbled a prayer for her. Religion, or more correctly the effects of others twisting it, had been a factor of my professional life. I'd seen people murder one another for having a different faith; I'd seen people tortured and mutilated. I couldn't believe that if there was a god, then such a benevolent, loving figure would allow such outrages in His name – whatever that might turn out to be. For fourteen years I'd fought men whose minds had been poisoned by fanatical teachings; they all swore that they were doing His bidding. Made me wonder who was guiding me when I put the bastards down. I hoped that Kate Piers was in more caring hands than those of the god of war that must have propelled me.

I rose to my feet and folded my hands across my middle, looking down at the grave. The sleet stung my face, but it was small penance for failing to save the woman I'd fallen in love with.

'Are you ready, Joe?'

Lost in the past, I'd momentarily forgotten that Kate's sister was standing beside me. I looked at her, and her eyes shone with tears. Her sister had died protecting her life and Imogen had never got over that. She felt guilty that it was her little sister lying cold in the grave and not her. But, more than that, I knew her tears were because she feared the man she loved was thinking the same.

I took one of her gloved hands in mine, pulled her in close so that I shielded her under my arm and placed a kiss on her cheek. 'Ready,' I told her. 'Come on. Let's get out of this cold.'

Imogen leaned down and placed a single rose against the headstone, then together we walked across the cemetery towards the gates. The cemetery wasn't large, just a half-acre ringed by a stone wall, and now almost overgrown by trees. The Piers family plot held five generations, including the body of my old army friend, Jake. This was where Imogen would come when her time on earth was over. Made me wonder where I'd end up. Nowhere as sanctified as this, I supposed; more likely an unmarked hole in the ground. Perhaps that would be fitting, because I'd sent plenty of others to such an ignominious resting place.

Imogen's house was perched on a rocky bluff overlooking Little Kennebec Bay, a short drive from Machiasport. The cemetery was situated on the Piers land, but even the five-minute walk was unpleasant in this weather. We clambered into the warmth of my Audi A6. I'd had the foresight to leave the engine running and the car was snug. I felt the blood rushing to my cheeks. Imogen struggled out of her gloves while I headed the car up the incline towards the house. In this half-light Imogen's home looked like something out of a Poe story, its pitched roof and steepled corners rearing against the slate sky. We didn't speak much in the car, nothing beyond complaints about the weather anyway, and the transition from vehicle to house was done in a hurry.

There was a fire burning in the hearth and I stoked it, piling on logs, while Imogen brought us both a drink. Hot, dark coffee for me, cocoa laced with something stronger for her. I never did get that drink. In the next few seconds we were in each other's arms as we navigated the stairs to her bedroom. Survivors' Guilt Syndrome is a powerful thing, but I couldn't blame that for the surge of passion that rose up in the two of us. She just looked so damn ravishing, her cheeks pink with a flush of warmth, her hair slightly in disarray from having pulled off her hat. She looked fragile and vulnerable and in need of reassurances. I hoped that actions were more profound than words. All I did was put down my coffee, take her cocoa from her hand and place it next to mine. Then I pulled her into a kiss, one that I meant dearly. That was all it took for us to wrestle our way through the house, undressing each other as we went.

Imogen's original bedroom had been violated when she'd been attacked by a misogynistic killer named Luke Rickard. Rickard had wanted to kill me and had targeted me through Imogen. She steered me past that room and into the one she had now commandeered. It was a big house for a single person, and the master bedroom only accentuated that. The bed would be best described as super king-sized, but we made use of every square inch.

Afterwards we lay side-by-side, our bodies glistening with perspiration, Imogen's hair in even more disarray. She lay with one hand on my stomach, tracing lazy circles with her fingertips, enjoying for the moment the companionable silence. Perhaps there was more than that to the silence; there were things yet unspoken, but now was not the time or place. Beyond the windows night had fallen, and the sleet had turned to snow. It was like a shroud that blocked out the rest of the world. We were cocooned in our own little bubble and I wished that things could stay that way forever. But I knew they couldn't.

Some sixth sense in me had been anticipating the thrum of an engine and the squeak of tyres on the new snow. I sat up and looked through the window. The vantage didn't allow a view down to the parking area outside. Naked, I stood, and then stooped for my abandoned clothes. First thing first, I lifted my Sig Sauer P226 and racked the slide. After that I dragged on my jeans and then padded back to the window.

'Who is it?'

Without turning, I said, 'Don't know yet. You'd best get dressed.'

We weren't expecting visitors. On a night like this, with the blizzard driving in off the Atlantic, only someone very determined would be out and about. In my world that meant law enforcement officers or enemies. Experience told me neither would be good news.

A vehicle crept into view. It was a dark coloured SUV, the windows tinted so I couldn't make out who was inside, or how many. The snow didn't help because it was swirling on the breeze, dancing a dervish jig between me and the vehicle. I watched until it pulled up alongside my Audi. No one got out. Maybe they were running the tags on my car.

I quickly pulled on my T-shirt and a hooded sweatshirt. I shrugged into my leather jacket, still damp from earlier, even as I stepped into my boots. The clothes went on almost as frenetically as they had so recently come off. Behind me, Imogen had pulled on a robe and cinched it round the waist. She joined me as I took another peek out the window.

'Joe,' she said in a whisper. 'Who could they be?'

'I don't know, but I don't like it. I want you to stay up here until I find out. OK?'

This was Imogen's home. She shouldn't have to live in fear within its walls, but she did. Once already it had been invaded by a killer, and a cop had died on the threshold, trying to help her. Luke Rickard wasn't the one she feared now. I'd killed that piece of shit. But there were others who might still want to harm her. I met Kate after Imogen had gone missing, running for her life to avoid the wrath of a Texan mobster and his sadistic enforcers, the Bolan twins. I had found Imogen and then took the war back to its source, but that was when Kate had died. Imogen didn't have to worry about Robert Huffman or the twins: I'd killed them too. But the mob was far-ranging and had a long memory and she waited for the day they'd seek retribution. She didn't argue with my request for her to stay hidden.

I went down the stairs and threw on the spotlights I'd fitted round the eaves. The light would momentarily blind those in the SUV. While they were blinking, I stepped out of the front door, the SIG hidden alongside my thigh. Enemies would do one of two things: reverse the car out of there, or come out with their guns blazing. I readied myself for either eventuality. Instead, the passenger door opened and a single figure stepped out. He held his hands over his head, showing me that they were empty.

'Step away from the car.' I allowed the SIG to be seen, so he knew I wasn't taking no for an answer.

He nodded and took two exaggerated steps to the side. I left him standing there in the snow, his hands reaching for the heavens, while I angled for a look into the SUV. There was a driver, but no one I could see in the back. 'You as well, pal. Out of the car and show me your hands.'

These weren't men lost on the road and seeking directions, neither were they enemies. Their approach told me that quite eloquently. They showed they meant no harm by lifting their hands, without raising a fuss about their treatment. I waved the driver round the front of the car, ushering them both together. It was easier to keep an eye on them like that.

Both were alike the way men of military bearing are; strong and lithe, with short haircuts and hard eyes. They were dressed similarly in thick windcheaters, dark jeans and rubber-soled boots. Bulges under their left armpits told me they were packing, both of them right hand draws. The only thing that differentiated them was that one was missing a chunk of eyebrow, and the other, slightly heavier, had ten years on his friend.

'You're not cops,' I said. 'So I'm guessing you're with the government.'

The older man was the designated driver, which made me guess that the first man to get out the car was the one who'd come to speak. I wasn't wrong.

'We should get out of the storm.' He nodded towards the house. 'Better if we talk inside, Mister Hunter.'

He used my name as a tool, couching his words so that they were more than a suggestion. He wanted me to know who was really in charge. It didn't work that way with me. 'My girlfriend is inside.' I left things at that. Let them think what they wanted.

'She knows all about you?' The man was wily, and he left the hint about my past unsaid.

'She knows that I'm not the type to let strangers inside without checking them out first. So . . . who are you, and what brings you here?'

The men lowered their hands. The younger of the two reached towards his armpit. Left hand, so I didn't flinch. He pulled out a leather wallet and flicked it open. He showed me an FBI ID badge. I smiled cynically at him. 'I've got one just like that. I bought it off eBay for five bucks. Who supplied yours, Charles W. Brigham? The CIA, I bet.'

Brigham chuckled. His mouth twisted, and the skin on his face puckered all the way up to his damaged eyebrow. Once he'd been very lucky that a knife blade hadn't taken off his entire face. 'As you know, CIA agents aren't in the habit of carrying badges. It's too much of a giveaway. But that's my real name. You have the ability to check it out.'

I did, but I wasn't going to bother. There was no reason for Brigham to lie. 'And who are you?' I directed at the older man. 'Your name will do, forget the Mickey Mouse badge.'

'Ray Hartlaub.'

'Brigham and Hartlaub? It sounds like an accountancy firm to me.' I smiled to show I was only fooling, but also that they held no fear for me.

'That would be Hartlaub and Brigham,' the older agent said. 'Seeing as I'm in charge.'

I'd thought as much. The one in charge never gets out of the car first. Not when there's an armed man waiting for him. 'So why are you here?'

'We were asked to come fetch you.'

I shook my head, more an act of derision than to dislodge the snow off my hair. There was only one person who could be behind this round-up. My old CIA contact from when I was hunting terrorists. 'Walter Hayes Conrad. What has that old goat got up his sleeve this time?'

'Nothing,' Hartlaub said. 'In fact, you can forget about SDC Conrad upsetting your life ever again.'

'So old Walt's finally retired then?'

'No, Hunter, Walter Conrad is dead. He was murdered a few hours ago.'

JOE HUNTER

BRITAIN'S BEST VIGILANTE V AMERICA'S WORST CRIMINALS

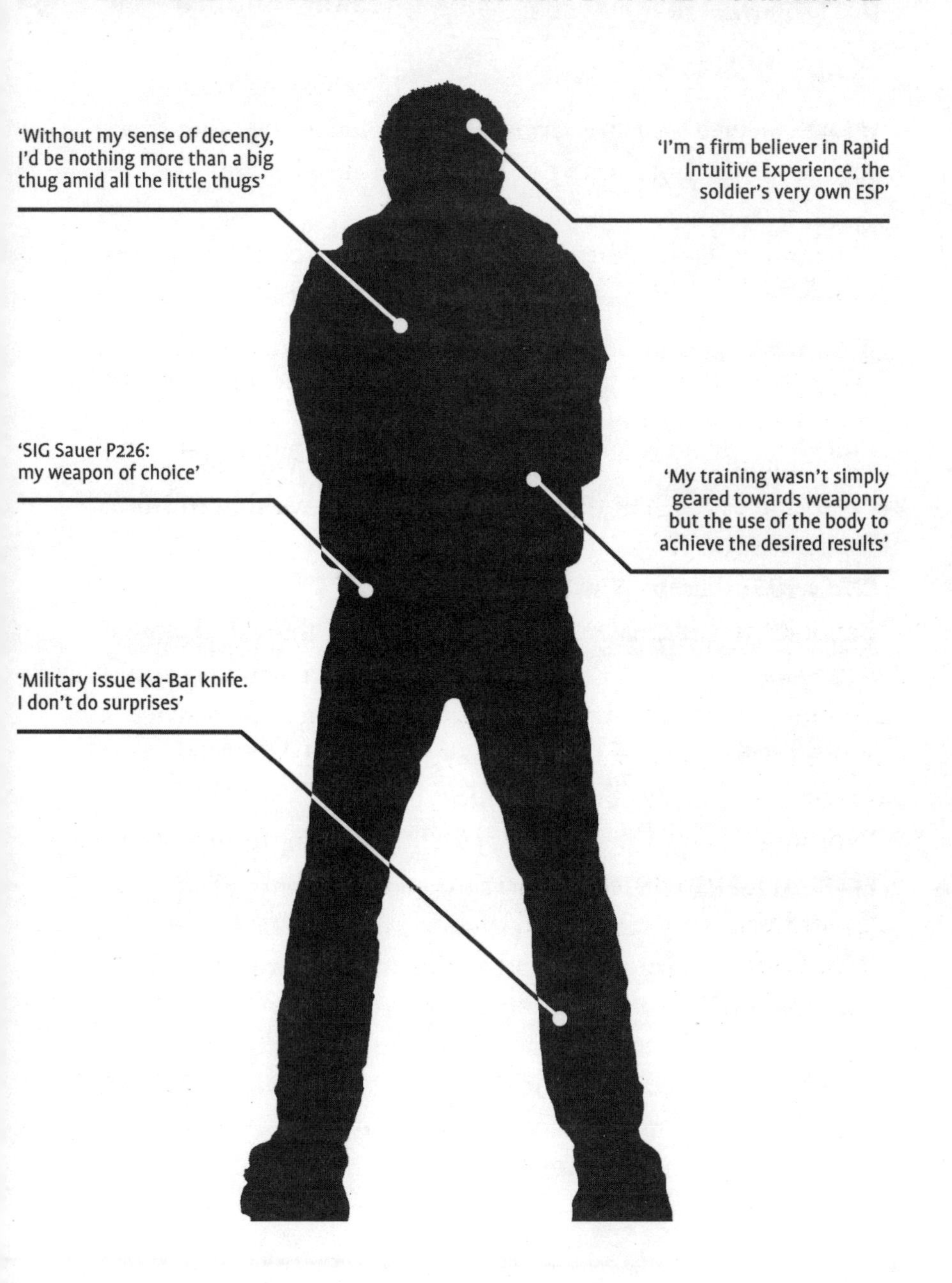

CURRICULUM VITAE – JOE HUNTER

NAME: Joe Hunter.

DATE OF BIRTH: 8th August.

PLACE OF BIRTH: Manchester, England.

HOME: Mexico Beach, Florida, USA.

MARITAL STATUS: Divorced from Diane, who has now remarried.

CHILDREN: None.

OTHER DEPENDENTS: Two German shepherd dogs, Hector and Paris (currently residing with Diane).

PARENTS: Joe's father died when he was a child and his mother remarried. Both his mother and stepfather reside in Manchester.

SIBLINGS: Half-brother, John Telfer.

KNOWN ASSOCIATES: Jared 'Rink' Rington, Walter Hayes Conrad, Harvey Lucas.

EDUCATION: Secondary school education to 'O' level standard. Joe received further education and underwent self-teaching while in the British Army and Special Forces.

EMPLOYMENT HISTORY: Joined British Army at age 16. Transferred to the Parachute Regiment at age 19 and was drafted into an experimental coalition counterterrorism team code named 'ARROWSAKE' at age 20. As a sergeant, Joe headed his own unit comprising members from various Special Forces teams. Joe retired from 'ARROWSAKE' in 2004 when the unit was disbanded and has since then supported himself by working as a freelance security consultant.

HEIGHT: 5' 11".

WEIGHT: 13 stone.

BUILD: Athletic.

HAIR COLOUR/STYLE: Short brown hair with slight greying.

EYE COLOUR: Blue/brown.

APPEARANCE: Muscular but more lean than bulky, he has the appearance of a competitive athlete. His demeanour is generally calm and unhurried. Due to his background, Joe has the ability to blend with the general public when necessary, but when relaxed he tends to dress casually. He doesn't consider himself handsome, but women find him attractive. His eyes are his most striking feature and the colour appears to change dependent on his mood.

BLOOD TYPE: AB

MEDICAL HISTORY: Childhood complaints include measles and chicken pox. As an adult Joe has had no major medical conditions, but has been wounded on several occasions. Joe carries numerous scars including a bullet wound in his chest and various scars from knife and shrapnel wounds on his arms and legs. He has had various bone breakages, but none that have proven a continued disability.

RELIGION: Joe was raised in a Church of England environment, but is currently non-practising.

POLITICS: Joe has no political preferences and prefers morals and ethics.

CHARACTER: Joe can come over as a little aloof at times. He is a deep thinker who prefers only to speak when he has something important to say. He is very loyal to his family and friends. He dislikes injustice, hates bullies and will stand up to defend others in need of help.

MUSIC: Wide choice of music, but particularly enjoys vintage rhythm and blues.

MOVIES: Joe's favourite movie is 'It's a Wonderful Life'. It is a morality tale that resonates with his belief that a person's actions – good or bad – continually affect those around them.

BOOKS: When he was younger he enjoyed classic fiction by HP Lovecraft, RE Howard and Edgar Allan Poe, but currently reads a wide range of crime and suspense novels.

CIGARETTES: Smoked various brands but gave up.

ALCOHOL: Drinks only moderately and infrequently. Prefers beer to liquor.

DRUGS: Has been subjected to drugs during his military career, but has never personally taken any illegal drugs. Joe hates the influence that drugs have on the world and stands against those producing and supplying them.

HOBBIES: Fitness. Joe works out whenever he can with a combination of running, circuit training and martial arts.

SPECIAL SKILLS: As a soldier Joe gained many skills pertinent to his job, but also specialised in CQB (Close Quarter Battle), Point Shooting, Defensive Driving and in Urban Warfare Tactics. He is particularly adept with the handgun (usually a SIG Sauer P226) and with the knife (usually a military issue Ka-Bar).

CURRENT OCCUPATION: Joe describes himself as a security consultant and sometimes PI, but some people call him a vigilante.

CURRENT WHEREABOUTS: USA.